THE ENGLISH BOOKSTORE IN BOLOGNA

ALSO BY
BOO WALKER

Red Mountain Chronicles

Before We Say Goodbye
Red Mountain
Red Mountain Rising
Red Mountain Burning
A Marriage Well Done

Other Novels

The Secrets of Good People (with Peggy Shainberg)
An Echo in Time
The Stars Don't Lie
A Spanish Sunrise
The Singing Trees
An Unfinished Story

Writing as Benjamin Blackmore

Lowcountry Punch
Once a Soldier
Off You Go

PRAISE FOR *THE ENGLISH BOOKSTORE IN BOLOGNA*

"Boo Walker delivers a sparkling, bighearted novel about reinvention, regret, and the risky magic of connection. Set against the irresistible charm of Bologna's porticoed streets, his story features a band of misfit toys who embody the wit, longing, and beautiful flaws that mark their humanity. With humor and tenderness, Walker reminds us that it's never too late to begin again—and that love, like a good book, can find you when you least expect it. A delight from first page to last."

—Susan Wiggs, *New York Times* bestselling author of *Wayward Girls*

PRAISE FOR BOO WALKER

"Bring tissues because there will be tears, but the good kind—the kind that let you know you are alive."

—Emily Bleeker, *Wall Street Journal* and Amazon Charts bestselling author

"Walker dazzles . . . The characters all earn the reader's emotional investment, and the pacing is perfect. Readers will fall in love."

—*Publishers Weekly* (starred review)

"Walker's attention-grabbing and surprising plot highlights the engaging characters in this tale of second chances. For fans of women's fiction such as Nicholas Sparks's and Kristin Hannah's work."

—*Library Journal*

"A heartwarming read."

—Historical Novel Society

"Boo Walker is a true talent, and his latest novel is a captivating tale of one man's journey to reconcile who he used to be with the person he's becoming. *The Stars Don't Lie* is a beautiful reminder that sometimes returning to the past is the best way to find your way forward."

—Camille Pagán, bestselling author of *Good for You*

"Boo Walker has written a book with a tender heart . . . a great story of redemption that carted me away."

—Barbara O'Neal, bestselling author of *When We Believed in Mermaids*

"The perfect mix of character-driven, heartstring-pulling drama and sharp-witted humor. Clearly Boo Walker is an author whose time has come."

—Julianne MacLean, *USA Today* bestselling author

"I love books with breathing characters you can root for, a narrative of human life to which you can relate, a conclusion that can stop the heart, and an author who can bind them all together with passion and soul. Boo Walker proves he's that kind of writer."

—Leila Meacham, bestselling author of *Roses* and *Titans*

"If Nicholas Sparks and Maeve Binchy had a baby, he might sound a lot like Boo Walker."

—Jodi Daynard, bestselling author of *The Midwife's Revolt*

"I was swept away by Boo Walker's deft storytelling and incredibly complex characters. Soulful but also full of sharp dialogue and humor, [this] is exactly the sort of book you get lost in, then mourn when it is over."

—Suzanne Redfearn, #1 Amazon bestselling author of *In an Instant*

"Boo Walker is that rare writer who is both a master storyteller and a wordsmith all at once. This is a book to bring you to tears but leave you with a light in your heart."

—Eoin Dempsey, bestselling author of *White Rose, Black Forest*

"In this beautifully written story of an old crime, a secret has shaped a family for generations, until one woman goes in search of the truth that will allow her to reconcile the inherited traumas in her life. Celebrated author Boo Walker deftly explores the curious power of genetic memory in a modern American family . . . *An Echo in Time* vibrates at the sweetest frequency and pulls gently at just the right heartstrings."

—Kimberly Brock, bestselling author of *The Lost Book of Eleanor Dare*

"*An Echo in Time* is a beautifully written, emotionally powerful story of a young woman's journey to break the cycle of generational trauma . . . I found myself cheering for Charli at every turn and smiling at the deeply satisfying and nuanced ending."

—Yvette Manessis Corporon, international bestselling author of *When the Cypress Whispers*

"*An Echo in Time* is a captivating novel about the generational legacy of secrets and shame and one woman's journey to love herself by righting the wrongs of the past. Walker has crafted a beautiful and moving tale of loss and healing that is part love story, part mystery, and all green lights."

—Melissa Payne, bestselling author of *A Light in the Forest*

THE ENGLISH BOOKSTORE IN BOLOGNA

a novel

BOO WALKER

LAKE UNION
PUBLISHING

This is a work of fiction. Names, characters, organizations, places, events, and incidents are either products of the author's imagination or are used fictitiously. Otherwise, any resemblance to actual persons, living or dead, is purely coincidental.

Published by Lake Union Publishing, Seattle

www.apub.com

EU product safety contact:
Amazon Media EU S. à r.l.
38, avenue John F. Kennedy, L-1855 Luxembourg
amazonpublishing-gpsr@amazon.com

ISBN-13: 9781662523786 (hardcover)
ISBN-13: 9781662523793 (paperback)
ISBN-13: 9781662523779 (digital)

Cover design by Faceout Studio, Addie Lutzo
Cover image: © Elly Schuurman, © fotograzia, © Kathrin Ziegler / Getty Images; © Cool-Hunter, © SeanPavonePhoto / Adobe Stock

Printed in the United States of America
First edition

For Linda and Nico, our ride-or-die expat amigos

The very essence of romance is uncertainty.

—*Oscar Wilde,* The Importance of Being Earnest, act I

After the fighting, the wars, the pointless battles, with yourself and others; after the storm passes, when the clouds break, when the birds resume their song, you'll still be standing, because that's what we do. We find a way to push through and begin again.

—*Bianca Briggs,* From Meh to Megawatt:
Supercharge Your Life

YOUR "DAZZLING" CAST OF CHARACTERS:

Sandy, the belle of the Bolognese ball, our true hero, a feisty expat who loathes love and keeps the romance section in her English-only bookstore in Bologna purposefully minuscule. Some may call her The Porcupine behind her back. Definitely not to her face or she'll cut you.

George, an uneasy go-getter wrestling with the agony of retirement. Regrets, he's had a few; also, father of Bianca.

Harold, an anxious and awkward, arguably unlikable young "entrepreneur" who has taken his first jump into the seductive pool of love—from the high dive.

Bianca, a psychotherapist with control issues who's currently waking from the trance of racing through life. One-third-life crisis much? Self-actualize much? Also, daughter of George.

Oh, and Moira, the worst bookseller in the universe, a twentysomething, British expat who so desperately wants the world to shine bright, despite having glimpsed the ugliest bits of it. She's everyone's favorite.

Chapter 1

The Porcupine

Wearing stilettos that could kill, Sandy twisted the accelerator of her Vespa and sped through the mass of tourists who apparently couldn't tell where the sidewalk ended and the street began. No matter, she'd make it clear, the Moses of Bologna, parting crowds like the Red Sea!

"Guarda dove stai andando!" she yelled. Watch where you're going!

She'd once dated a test driver at Ducati, and aside from leaving her with a few memorable orgasms, he'd also taught her to drive. She charged forward, and with near biblical beauty, the sea of bird-brains parted.

She might have considered removing a heel and jabbing one of the tourists in the eye, but they were fantastic shoes that she'd only picked up yesterday. Would have been a shame to damage them. Besides, she'd made the risky choice to wear *white* satin cropped pants along with one of her go-to tanks, this one in lavender; all the blood would be a disaster.

It was barely March, for God's sake; why were the tourists even here? Spring hadn't kicked in, the weather was wretched. Now that Bologna had been discovered, she'd accepted that summers would be epic misery—the sweltering heat, the long lines, the need for reservations, the onslaught of morons and *cretini*—but couldn't she and the others who lived here have a few months to themselves?

The sales at the bookstore didn't climb during the summer, that was for sure. None of these fleshbags read books; they were too addicted to watching Siberian huskies sing tracks from *Frozen* on TikTok.

Sandy passed close enough to a woman to have slipped the pleather tote off her shoulder. She let loose a rant in Italian about pulling their eyes from their phones for one damn second. These cretins should stay where they belonged: lining up to see Michelangelo's *David* in Florence or pouring into the Colosseum in Rome. She'd moved to Bologna twelve-plus years ago, before *Fodor's* and a thousand bloggers had sunk their teeth into it, an Italian city drenched in culture and authenticity, not yet poisoned by the masses.

Yet here they were, coming for the magic that Sandy didn't feel like sharing.

Reaching the Piazza Maggiore, Sandy made a hard right, two more fast turns and down a tight, crooked alley, then she was back to Via Giulia, the cobblestone street where she both lived and worked, a proximity decision that had once seemed like a good idea, only to come undone by her poor choice of how to pay the bills: opening an English bookstore in Italy.

Sandy parked amid a cluster of other scooters. Careful not to damage her heel—in case she might need to use it as a weapon later—she deployed the kickstand with a bit of sass, then climbed off the machine and removed her helmet.

After attempting to tame her lengthy golden-bronze hair, which was a shade or two lighter than her natural color of a decade ago (never would she be seen in public with even a strand of gray), she grabbed her leather shoulder bag from under the seat and started toward the scaffolding that blocked nearly all evidence that her bookstore even existed.

She tried not to growl at the three handsome construction workers in neon-green vests, who were doing absolutely nothing but eating panini and pretending like they weren't checking out her figure (as if they could be so lucky!), certainly not making any progress toward repairing the hundred feet of portico, or sidewalk covering, that had started to crumble over the winter.

For three months now, the scaffolding and other equipment had hidden the splendor of the bookstore's tiled portico with its sun-bleached stone columns. The mess also blocked potential customers from seeing the books and author pictures in the window displays or even noticing the sign above the entrance that read, in Baskerville font, THE ONLY ENGLISH BOOKSTORE IN BOLOGNA.

She'd done her best to combat the blockade by hanging signs on the scaffolding that stated, in both Italian and English, DON'T MIND THE CONSTRUCTION; WE'RE STILL OPEN!, but even the most die-hard reader would have to muster incredible courage to get close to this shit show construction nightmare without a hard hat and a death wish.

Coming into the shade of the portico, she maneuvered through the scaffolding, ignoring the men who muttered *"ciao"* and *"buongiorno"* to her, then pulled back the door to what had once been the greatest love of her life.

When she'd opened this place ten years earlier, at the ripe age of . . . Nope, not saying. At that particular age, it had seemed like a grand idea. An English-only bookstore, modeled after Shakespeare and Company in Paris, a place where expats and travelers could find exactly what they needed. Being a hungry reader, Sandy had nearly lost her mind trying to find books when she'd moved here to start a new life, until it dawned on her that her literary need had created a potential occupation.

What a marvelous idea that had been, in the most sarcastic sense. Never had it occurred to her that most people rarely bought books after wandering into a bookstore. Instead, most of them would stroll the aisles, bend the spines, then respond to an offer of help with, "I'm just perusing." Even worse when she caught them checking the prices online.

Peruse! The worst word in the English language. Apparently, she'd opened a charity. "Hey, I've got an idea," the perusers must say. "Let's buy a coffee and then go walk around a bookstore, bend and dirty the pages with oily fingers, while also bending the store owner's ear sideways about the last book they read, then walk out without spending a dime." There you go. The wonder of the English-reading collective.

Nevertheless, the business might have worked had a few other obstacles not stood in the way. She'd liked—no, adored—the location at the time. Via Giulia was a standout street in a city full of charming streets, a Renaissance painting with more grit and modern soul. Dazzling arched porticoes propped up by either stone or wooden columns covered the sidewalks on both sides. If you looked up to their ceilings, you could enjoy impressive frescoes with floral and religious motifs that had quietly endured the centuries. But at eye level, bright and tasteful street art, pulsing with anarchic energy, added a touch of modern rebellion to this otherwise ancient part of town.

Somehow, though, the store could go an hour without any foot traffic. Little had she known that tourists were afraid of wandering down tight streets that weren't featured in *Lonely Planet*. How awful it would be to discover something that wasn't in their Rick Steves guidebook. On slow days, Sandy liked to play a game with Moira, her sole employee. They'd watch the window and wait for someone to pass, then they'd cheer like survivors in the Alaskan wilderness who'd spotted a plane.

Foot traffic wouldn't help much, though, because of the construction project. It wasn't only the scaffolding; it was the equipment: ladders, ropes, filthy buckets of stucco and concrete, massive machines on wheels. As Sandy had learned, a supposed short-term construction project in Bologna could easily take two or three years, as if they were building a second cathedral. Construction work in her home state of Florida was finished faster, and that was saying something! The Italians did *nothing* quickly. Sure, that was nice when it came to enjoying their long meals and relaxing, not a care in the world, indulging in *la dolce vita*. And she had no complaints with the way the young Italian lovers she'd conquered took their time pleasing her in bed, but when it came to getting things done, it would be nice to have a little more American *oomph*.

During the holidays, Moira would make a Christmas tree out of books and dangle lights from the ceiling. If Sandy would let her, she'd decorate for every special day on the calendar, including National Fried Chicken Day or Eat Ice Cream for Breakfast Day, both of which existed according to Moira, who stayed knowledgeable in such things.

If Hallmark had a poster girl, it would be Moira Sacks.

The top sellers, some bookish tchotchkes, a stand of postcards, and the checkout counter filled the front room. With its stuccoed walls and low ceiling crossed with wooden beams, the place felt more like a cozy tavern than a bookstore. It was mind boggling to imagine the centuries of conversation that must have been had here since the building's initial construction in medieval times.

In the far corner, a narrow and steep, winding staircase, not unlike one that might lead to a church bell, led up to Sandy's small office, where she hid when she got tired of people. Needless to say, she spent a lot of time up there, huddled over her computer answering emails, rejecting salespeople, and ordering more books that people wouldn't buy.

But it was the main room that had captured her heart ten years ago. Through a stone arch, the store opened to a much larger space crowned by a stunning vaulted ceiling—an elaborate masterwork that must have taken years to bring to life, its plaster alive with frescoes depicting Bolognese men and women from centuries ago trading their wares beneath the porticoes. What a place to honor the world of books.

In this airy space, a series of shelves on rollers were organized by category. The mobility allowed Sandy and Moira to move them out of the way for the occasional event. Along the back wall were the staff favorites. Sandy and Moira each had a section and had written on a blue index card what they liked about each book.

Sandy had written one or two lines on her cards, whereas Moira filled every possible space with the results of her exhausting contemplation, elaborating with turgid prose on how the book had changed her life or opened her eyes. And where Sandy's choices were of a more serious ilk, realist works such as *A Little Life*, *Hamnet*, and *All My Rage*, Moira's were uplifting, harmless, and unrealistic, like the newest Emily Henry, *Eat, Pray, Love*, or *The Five People You Meet in Heaven*.

The Only English Bookstore in Bologna was one of the most beautiful bookstores that had ever come to life, but Sandy had a hard time appreciating it when the headaches involved brought her to blindness.

She wasn't surprised to find the store empty today, other than Moira. Oh, that poor girl. Sandy knew she herself wasn't the best bookseller in the world—let's just say she'd lost her mojo about eight years ago—but she also knew she wasn't the worst. Because Moira held that crown, unquestionably the worst bookseller on planet Earth. Maybe the worst salesperson of any product in the multiverse.

She had a squeaky, British-accented voice, and often Sandy had to tell her to speak up. "No one can hear you, Moira!"

Why didn't Sandy fire her? She didn't know. Maybe it was because she wasn't as mean as she let on. Perhaps it was her way of seeking forgiveness for being so awful half the time. Keeping Moira around proved that Sandy had a heart.

Moira poked her head up from behind the counter. She dressed and applied makeup like she'd learned at a morgue. She kept her hair in a short boy's cut and wore purple glasses with lenses so thick it was like looking into a fishbowl. And don't even get Sandy started on the big floppy, black hat she donned when she left the building.

Moira was a mouse and, as touched on earlier, a terrible bookseller, but she loved books and read more than anyone Sandy knew, including Sandy. In theory, she *should* have been good, but she was terrified to speak up. In fact, she interacted with people as if they were about to lunge at her.

Moira was Sandy's only friend, though, and vice versa, if only because of forced proximity. If push came to shove, Sandy might admit that she liked talking with Moira, but it would take a hard shove off a steep cliff into boiling water.

As far as what brought Moira to Bologna from Bristol, Sandy wasn't sure. The couple of times Sandy had asked her, Moira had flushed red and mumbled something about inheriting money from her aunt and starting over. Sandy guessed she was either in the witness protection program or the black sheep of a wealthy British family.

"I've been thinking . . ." Moira said, half hiding behind the computer screen.

"Please don't do that," Sandy replied, straightening several postcards that some numbskull had messed up. "You're going to hurt yourself."

Moira ducked lower behind the screen.

"Oh, toughen up. You won't make it another year if you let me start hurting your feelings now. Go on with it. What have you been *thinking*?"

Even Sandy hated how she treated people sometimes, but her tongue often had a mind of its own, spewing out the muck of what this world had done to her.

Like an astronaut jabbing her flag into the moon, Moira stood taller and finally revealed what had been stewing in that mind of hers. "I think we should start a book club."

"A book club? For all seven of our clients."

"I think it would be fun."

"Oh, sure. A bundle of joy." Sandy reached into her pocket and felt for the piece of fossilized coral that always brought her comfort. "Moira, the glory days of this bookstore are long gone. I'm not trying to create more work."

The mouse twirled what little hair she had. "May I say something?"

"You are saying something."

"I know you don't see it anymore, but this bookstore is magic, and I believe we owe her more than what we're giving her."

"Her?"

"Yes, her. To me, she's a living, breathing entity. And I don't want her to be just *meh*. I want to supercharge her."

The makings of a headache started. "Does this have anything to do with the advance copy of that self-help book you're reading?" Sandy already knew the answer, of course.

Moira came alive like someone had tased her. "Yes, it's so good! *From Meh to Megawatt!* Bianca Briggs is an international treasure!"

Already tired of hearing about this stupid book, Sandy crossed herself. "Dear God in heaven, please spare me from even ten more seconds of living on this hell ball." She let go of the coral and came around the counter to stow her purse.

Moira backed away as if Sandy were a leper.

"If this bookstore is living and breathing," Sandy said over her shoulder, "she's on a respirator. No one wants a book club in this town. No one even wants to buy books! Don't burden yourself by trying to build something out of nothing. I tried the whole community thing, creating a place to gather, to share thoughts, to meet people. It was fun while it lasted."

It *was* fun. Those first two years had been wonderful. Perusers bought books. Humans actually *read* books. That time felt so distant that it was hard to believe, but opening the bookstore had given her such renewed hope and joy in life. She'd given her all, creating a profitable bookstore that had not only emulated Shakespeare and Company but also rivaled it.

Gone were those days, though. *Finito!*

Sandy straightened up around the computer. "All I want is to come into work, sell enough books to keep the lights on, and then get on with my life without any other interference. *Capisci?*"

Standing at a safe distance on the other side of the postcard stand, Moira said, "You might fire me for saying so, but I disagree, with all of it. There are a ton of expats in this city. We might all be running from something, but we crave connection too. People might find that here if you let them. Though you may not know it, even you might be craving connection."

Sandy put her hands on her waist. "Moira, I'd fire you but then I'd have to get used to putting up with someone else's shit. So you're stuck with me and this godforsaken place till you smarten up and realize you'd be better off scooping gelato. The good news is you don't have to overthink all these things. There will be no supercharging my bookstore. Come in, sell your six books a day, turn off the lights, and lock the door. That's the perfect life. Got me?"

The mouse shook her little mousy head.

Self-loathing Sandy started feeling bad for her. There was nothing more miserable than feeling pity for someone. Especially when you're the cause of their misery. She almost—*almost*—asked whether Moira wanted to go get a glass of wine, but she'd managed to avoid fraternizing with her employees for ten years. She sure as hell wouldn't start today. The girl would have to pull up her big-girl panties and get over it.

It's a good thing you could hide your internet history, because even after he was gone, George Briggs didn't want people to know how meticulous he'd been in researching the best way to extinguish his life. The last thing he wanted was to survive a failed attempt. He couldn't shake the picture he'd seen of a man who'd blown his jaw off, only to have to face the world after waking up in the hospital. The guy couldn't even kill himself properly.

George would not make that mistake.

What had shocked him was how easy it would be to buy a gun in Arizona. No waiting period, no permit. A background check that would only take a few minutes. According to ChatGPT, a Glock 19 would be the wisest choice, as it was both dependable and easy to operate. He'd driven by the gun stores right off the Black Canyon Freeway several times but hadn't found the courage (if that was the right word?) to go through with it.

A gun felt so damned violent. Well, of course it did, especially for a guy who'd grown up in a gunless household in South Phoenix. Hold on, *household* was a strong word. An exaggeration. He'd grown up in a single-wide trailer in poverty. His mother had died when he was nine, leaving his father, Mason, to go it alone. If they gave grades for overcoming grief, let's just say Mason would not have made honor roll. He likely would have had to repeat a grade.

George kept thinking of Bianca, his only child. She lived in Austin, so it wasn't that she would discover the body. It's that the image would haunt her. The gore from a gunshot seemed far more terrible than something like . . .

. . . what he'd settled on now.

It was a Tuesday in March, and George sat in the living room of his apartment in Midtown Phoenix, the place he'd lived since the divorce. He held a bottle containing twenty-five pills of Percocet, which the internet had confirmed were well beyond a lethal dose. A much less dramatic way to go. All he had to do was knock them back like Tylenol, a few at a time, washing them down with the glass of ice water that he'd set on a coaster because even though he wouldn't live to see it, he still couldn't imagine leaving a ring on the coffee table. Maybe Bianca would want the table for her place in Texas.

Twisting off the cap, he poured the first few in his hand, white pills that would take him away from this living nightmare. Most of his things were in boxes all over the apartment, packed exceptionally well and labeled appropriately. In a burst of naive inspiration shortly after his dismissal from Intel, he'd decided he'd try to embrace his forced retirement by cashing in his stock and buying a house in Red Hawk, a gated golf community in Scottsdale. The movers were coming in three days.

It was a move that he couldn't face, though.

A lot of people didn't understand the pain of retirement. In fact, most people couldn't stop dreaming of the day they retired. But for the unlucky few, work was what kept them going. Without it, they had no purpose, and without a purpose, there was no point.

He jiggled the pills in his hand, like candy, then tossed them into his mouth. As badly as he wanted to go, the fear of making it happen riddled his insides. But the depression was so deep. Hopeless. Though George knew being jobless was the problem, he was in such a dark place that this awareness didn't cast even a glimmer of light on finding a remedy.

Well, there was a remedy. And it was right before him.

Thoughts of what had brought him here filled his head.

"Thanks for making the time, George," the kid had said in late January, waving him into a corner office.

Clueless, even after decades at Intel, George had thought he was being called in to be offered a raise. It was strange that this new kid who'd somehow become his boss was the one giving him a pay bump; he'd accepted that he'd hit his ceiling there.

Once George had taken a seat and the kid had started talking, he'd understood why he'd been called in. "You know we're having to tighten things right now," the kid had said. "Lots of competition. As you know, we're having to make some strategic shifts."

Strategic shifts. Soon as you heard that, you were done.

The most painful part was that George hadn't been allowed to return to his desk. Almost thirty years with the company, and he was suddenly an outsider. They'd had his belongings delivered to him a day later. He hadn't even been able to say goodbye to his colleagues because security walked him out of the building and watched him drive off the property.

He'd given his fucking life to that company. He'd skipped meaningful moments with his wife and daughter because he'd believed in Intel's mission. Riding the microprocessor wave through the boom of the eighties, nineties, and early aughts had been a thrill—albeit a demanding one—and he'd let himself get too consumed. Honestly, he'd sacrificed his marriage and perhaps being a good father for that company.

Almost for naught.

George gathered the second handful of pills in his hand but paused, setting his eyes on his goodbye message. He'd already shredded fifteen typed letters and hand-scribbled notes in the last three days. The first had been so formal, the date up top, then "To whom it may concern," the location of his will, a broad apology, and on and on. Followed by his signature in ink.

Subsequent drafts grew more informal from there.

He'd written a few directly to Bianca and his ex-wife, Faith, telling them he was sorry, that he wished he could go back in time. Hoped they'd understand. As a psychotherapist, Bianca would likely get it. Some people were beyond hope.

He'd finally settled on a simple handwritten letter because who was he kidding? He didn't need to explain himself. Though Intel had been polite about it, giving him the chance to take his retirement, everyone, including Bianca and Faith and his friends, knew that he'd been put out to pasture.

All he'd said in the final copy was that he was sorry for the mess.

Sorry for the mess.

Because when you're about to kill yourself, you wonder who will find you and what shape your body will be in and how the experience might affect them. He'd studied and found that he'd likely empty his bladder and bowels. Rigor mortis would set in within two to six hours.

He'd decided the best course of action would be to preemptively call 911 and spare his housekeeper, who had a seven-year-old daughter, from finding him. That's why he had his phone resting next to the coaster. One more handful, once he was past the point of no return, he'd make the call.

Sorry for the mess.

His eyes watered as he lifted the second handful to his mouth. He pushed the pills in, whispering apologies. His hands shook as he chased them with water. Killing yourself was awful business. Though it was dead quiet, he was screaming inside.

Ping.

His phone lit up with a text.

He was tempted not to look, not to get sidetracked.

But out of the corner of his eye, as the pills reached his belly, he saw that it was Bianca. He managed to find a way to feel even worse, dumping more guilt onto the depression that had filled his days after getting axed.

He reached for the phone and opened the message.

Hey Dad, letting you know I'm sticking an ARC (advance reader copy) of my book in the mail today. Don't feel like you have to read it, but I wanted to share. Thirty-two years old, and I still want my dad to be proud of me.

A sigh escaped him as he set the phone back down. Perhaps it was psychosomatic, but he felt the rumble of the pills as they began to break up in his stomach.

Proud of her? Yeah, he was proud of her. How could he not be? She'd conquered the world! Grad school, starting her own business, building it up so successfully, *and* writing a book. In a world that was black and ugly, she was its one redeeming feature, the one light that never faded.

Guilt and shame poured over him, the gravity of what he was doing hitting even harder. He'd break her heart and brand her the daughter of a man who took his own life. Sure, she might understand, but she damn well might wrestle with it the rest of her life.

He shook his head, hearing his stomach gurgle. "What have I done?" he whispered, sadness sinking into his belly, caving in his chest. "What have I done?"

Chapter 2

The Scenic Road to Sanity

Slouched over, heart puttering like a car running on empty, Bianca Briggs let the newest one-star Amazon review of her first and definitely *last* book run through her, hacking away at her self-confidence, filling her with regret.

It was mid-April, and she was in the office of her psychotherapy practice in Austin. She corralled her thick, dark hair into a bun to get it out of the way; she'd let it back down before her next client.

Her agent had told her not to read reviews, so why was she doing this to herself? Because it was a *grrrrreat* way to start her workday. Because it was a degree more painful than self-flagellation.

Mostly, because she couldn't help it, like watching the aftermath of her own head-on collision. Couldn't readers keep their stupid opinions to themselves? Having put *everything* into what she now knew was her failed attempt at a contribution to the self-development genre, she was in a perpetual state of shock from the angry reception and lackluster sales.

She should have stayed in her lane and been satisfied with the successful psychotherapy practice that she'd created in the last seven years here in Austin. Why on earth had she thought that she needed more, that she needed to be the next Mel Robbins or Dr. Nicole LePera?

How could people be so mean, so evil? If she could speak to each person who'd torn her apart in the two weeks since release, she'd say, "If you only knew how much love and thought and care I put into what feels like a baby to me; if you only knew how much self-doubt I waded through, you wouldn't write such hateful things. I was just trying to help people."

As if taking another step on hot coals, she read the one-star review again.

By the time I gave up on From Meh to Megawatt: Supercharge Your Life, *I'd found myself in such a panic that I had to crush up and snort a Xanax. There is such a thing as over-self-actualizing. Who has the time to do everything the author prescribes? She definitely doesn't have children. I'm exhausted even typing this. Don't even get me started on the cheesiness of the Peggy Meh character. What am I? Four?*

Each review came with its own accented voice; this one was the rant of a witchy British schoolteacher with a hairy wart on her nose. And obviously a girthy broom rammed up her saggy tush.

Bianca thought she would have gotten used to it by now, but each bad review cut deeper than the last. Why? Oh, she knew why.

Because the motherfucking witch was right.

So many of the one- and two-star reviews were right. Using an uber-flawed, anonymized client named Peggy Meh as the device for sharing Bianca's methods had been a *terrible* idea. And there probably was too much information, *an overprescription of holistic garbage*, as another had put it. Not everyone could keep up with Bianca's pace. Three days ago, she'd said to her mother, "If you want to tear open your wounds and expose your flaws, there is no better way than to write a book."

Only in the last few days—with the help of an army of insensitive, albeit accurate, psychopaths—er, reviewers—had she woken from this ten-year trance to realize the truth. She'd become exactly the person she didn't want to be: a rabid go-getter like her father, always attempting to do more. She never should have let herself think she had what it took to become an author.

Bianca set her phone down and picked up the framed photograph she'd asked her mom to send from Palm Springs. It had come in yesterday's mail and had kept Bianca up all night. As she looked at it for the hundredth time, she thought, *I dare you, Bianca.*

The picture showed a lively crew sitting at a rickety wooden table inside the Osteria del Sole in the old town of Bologna. It was taken at a time when the world was oh so different.

Bianca let her gaze settle on the couple in the booth against the wall, the younger, skinnier her, a high-spirited brunette with one leg crossed over the other, a cigarette poking out of her mouth, and a handsome, mustachioed Italian who had been caught midsentence, surely talking about the origins of the bubbly red wine in their glasses. It had been no surprise that Corrado would soon chase his chef dreams in Paris.

"What do you have to say?" Bianca asked the couple. "You have a problem?"

She'd taken a gap year in Italy when she was twenty-two to find and save herself, because attaining two undergrad degrees at Pomona College had drained her and she'd wanted to recharge before grad school. She'd succeeded, rediscovering herself, recapturing her youth. In fact, she'd almost bailed on grad school and stayed put in Bologna. She now wished she had.

That night the photo was taken, her last night before returning to the US, she'd promised herself and Corrado that she wouldn't get sucked back into her old ways: the overworking, the worrying about the future, the desperate need for control.

How naive could she have been?

Back in her office in the now, her frustration with herself rose up into a burst of fury.

She spun the frame across the room, a sharp "fuck" shooting from her mouth. The edge jabbed into the wall, then shattered on the hardwood floor.

Her eyes widened, shocked by her own rage. But this was it, her midlife—no, *third-life* crisis, reaching the exact moment of eruption.

Crossing the room, Bianca dropped to her knees, retrieved the bent picture frame, and shook loose the broken glass that hadn't already scattered across the floor. Tears slipped down her cheeks.

A soft alarm chimed, and Bianca whipped her head around toward the clock on the wall. "How is it already eleven?" A client had canceled, so she'd had the last hour to wade through her self-despair and investigate the origins of her demise.

Pushing up, Bianca went to the phone on her desk and buzzed her receptionist. "Buy me five minutes."

"No problem," came a lively voice. "Is everything okay in there? I thought I heard something fall?"

"I . . . I knocked over something. Sweeping it up now." Bianca cleaned up the mess, spruced up in the mirror, then sashayed down the hall with false bravado to the waiting room, where her lightly damaged clients thumbed through their phones until it was their turn to be picked apart by a woman who wasn't afraid to tell it like it was.

Bianca's smile could have scared the sunshine. "Lacy, so good to see you." She could do vivacious when she had to, even when the inner Bianca wanted to burn everything to the ground.

"I pushed him into the pool," Lacy said fifteen minutes later, while stretched out on the angular gray couch in Bianca's counseling room. "At the Four Seasons. He was in a tux. And it was cold. For Austin, super cold. Steam rising off the water."

Lacy was Bianca's age, early thirties, and wore all white with espadrilles and a beaded turquoise necklace. She sat with her ankles crossed and held a gold pillow with tassels over her stomach. Above her hung a large canvas painting of an elephant with feather earrings that Bianca had bought at an auction last year.

"How many people were there?" Bianca asked, a smile splitting her lips, as unprofessional as that might be. She'd been trying hard to pay attention. At least Lacy's story was getting interesting.

"Maybe sixty? All in formal dress, all influencers. Every one of them twisting their heads to gawk. Next thing you know, they have their phones out, filming the show like paparazzi. Now all of Austin knows our marriage is coming apart, and I can't go anywhere without hearing whispers. Thank God for Whole Foods delivery. I come see you, and I go to the nail salon. Other than that, I'm imprisoned at home."

Lacy paused. "Why did you stop taking notes?"

Sitting in her Swedish chair, Bianca pretended to glance at her "notes," but actually looked down at the comic strip she'd started to draw, a series of panels, the first starting with a rough sketch of a plane taking off. In barely legible text, it read BIANCA AIRLINES across the side. The second panel showed the same plane but included large-caliber gunfire chasing after it.

"I'm listening," Bianca said casually, wondering how fast the state licensing board would pull her license if they got a load of today.

Lacy kept going. "He tried to play it off. You know how men are. A big smirk as he rubbed the water from his eyes. Then he pronounced with an *awful* grin that still makes me want to fill his mouth with broken glass, 'It's nice in here. Anyone else want to join?' Men are such fucking idiots sometimes."

Bianca did not comment. What she did do was continue drawing the third panel. Gunfire had struck the plane, and a part of the wing was falling from the sky. A cloud of smoke indicated lethal danger. In the distance, a missile gained ground.

Lacy kept rambling. "I need you to fix it, Bianca. I'm a mess. I can't stand being around him, and I feel like I should introduce him with a disclaimer." She dialed up the drama in her voice to say, "'I'm Lacy, this is my husband, Gregg. For the record, we did love each other at one time, and he was interesting back then, but something happened, and now I'm drowning in regret.'"

This was what, Lacy's third session? The woman could squeeze more words into an hour than any other client in history. Maybe Bianca should charge by the word.

While Lacy kept spewing her emotional vomit, Bianca drew the second and third missile strikes, showing the plane starting an emergency descent. The second-to-last panel showed the Bianca Airlines jet nose-diving toward its doom.

If only Bianca could recast the spell she'd been under, jump back into the bottle, keep sleeping through this life, but she now couldn't unsee who she'd become. All because of the book!

From the outside, it looked like she had it all, didn't it? A fancy apartment, a practice with an enviable waiting list, women around Austin raving about her. "That Bianca Briggs," she imagined a client proclaiming to a friend after tennis over a lightly dressed Caesar salad and glass of pinot grigio at Austin Country Club, "She's a woman whisperer. You *must* get on her list."

Her online brand was growing too. Her Substack blog had reached almost fifty thousand subscribers, and she had even more followers on Instagram, where she offered weekly live sessions that expanded on many of the practices in her book.

But no one knew the truth. They didn't know that Bianca was worn down to a nub. She was, or had been, on a trajectory—yes, that was the word, *trajectory*—but whether it was the colossal failure of her book or listening to clients drone on about their problems that weren't really problems or the inevitable fact that no matter how much she did it was never enough, this so-called *trajectory* had lost its momentum. It might even be pointed in the wrong direction.

Thinking of her book again, she winced. Though she hadn't seen numbers yet, she knew it hadn't gone gangbusters in these first two weeks. It was a freaking belly-busting flop with reviews that could lead someone to jump out a window.

"I know I'm talking a lot today," Lacy admitted, clasping her hands together. "I don't want the kids to go through a divorce and definitely don't want to split custody. I can't imagine waking up without them in the house. What do I do? Do I leave him?"

Bianca shook away her own troubles and leaned forward. "You know I can't answer that."

"Why not? That's why I'm here. I need you to tell me if I'm crazy for staying with him. I need you to figure out what went wrong."

After a long pause, Bianca locked eyes with Lacy, a bitter taste in her mouth. "What went wrong? You're kidding me right now, aren't you?"

"No," a shocked Lacy responded.

"You let life get the best of you," Bianca said, feeling fire rise in her core. "You burned your youth to the ground and started chasing some stupid fucking American Dream because you thought that if you achieved success, then maybe, maybe you'd matter."

Lacy covered her mouth.

Bianca wasn't done. "It's not about what went wrong. It *all* went wrong. We're not where we're supposed to be, but we're pretending like it all worked out. Posting the life we wanted on Instagram and TikTok, showing the world our shiniest, polished selves. What went wrong, you ask? Birth, or even before that. When your parents poked each other because they thought they were in love—but it was actually lust. You ask if you're crazy for staying with him? Yes, you are."

Bianca took a deep breath, enough time to see Lacy looking like she feared for her life, gripping the pillow like it might save her.

How much sympathy did this elicit from Bianca? Exactly zero point zero.

"Oh, c'mon," Bianca continued. "Don't be a baby. These are not problems; they're *inconveniences*. You were at the Four Seasons. I'm sorry his *tux* got wet at the charity ball. Or that he frustrated you. I'm sorry that he's *boring*. Go out there into the dating world. Download an app and see where that gets you. You think he's boring. They all are, Lacy."

Lacy probably should have stormed out the office, but she sat up, set aside the pillow, and asked with teary eyes, "Then what do I do?"

Bianca couldn't help herself. This release felt better than anything she could remember. A third-life-crisis orgasm. "You suck it up and deal with it. Maybe go get a prescription for an SSRI. Welcome to the American Dream."

Lacy wiped her eyes. "Is this why people love you? I . . . I've never had a therapist like this. And I must admit I've bought your book but haven't read it yet. I guess you tell it like it is?"

"Is that a question?" Bianca chuckled to herself. She wished she cared enough to reel in her rant, but she did exactly the opposite. "What else do you want me to say? I'd rather be honest. Stay with him, and things will be *okay*, in the dullest sense of the word. Despite not having lost any weight in months, go work out because you can at least talk about how you worked out while you feel the jiggle of your arms. Then have your blueberry kale smoothie—"

"I don't do smoothies."

"No one's asking, Lucy. I mean, Lacy." Bianca raised her hand. "And after your morning routine, race into work and go, go, go, maybe skip lunch so you can bang out a blog post, eat dinner while you hammer out emails, and then watch the depressing news until you crash."

Bianca clapped her hands together. "Do all that or . . . or . . . you can take a leap of faith. Doesn't that sound romantic? Do what your younger self might have done. Leave the comfort of this life, this first-world-problem life, and go find who you used to be."

"Who I used to be? I'm confused."

Bianca ignored her. "Or. *Or*, Lacy, you can take that leap and fall about fifteen stories into a giant pile of trash. You take that leap, leave what you have in the hope there's something better, and it doesn't work out, and you spend the rest of your life wondering why you couldn't have found happiness in a life that was supremely fine on all levels. You can spend the rest of your life apologizing to yourself for yet another wrong turn."

Lacy curled her thick hair behind her ears and took a long time to respond. "Isn't it condescending to say *first-world problems* now?"

"I need a drink," Bianca said. "Do you need a drink?"

"It's . . . like eleven in the morning. And . . . really? We're going to drink together? Do you have drinks here?"

Bianca let the pitch of her voice rise. "I wish. No, I'm saying let's go walk down the street and find a spritz. No, fuck it, a Negroni. Because the end of the world is here, and I'd rather not do it in this office where dreams go to die."

Lacy looked around, as if someone might save her. "You know what? Maybe we're not the right fit. I probably should have read your book first. I don't know that this is what I—"

"Of course it's not what you *want* or *need*. Look at me right now." She gestured toward herself. "What about *this* makes you think I can help you?"

"But everyone said . . . Um, I've never experienced therapy like this before. Is this the leave-a-burn-mark mindset?" She was referring to a piece of Bianca's wisdom that superfans, otherwise known as Megawatters, had latched on to. Despite the book torpedoing toward hell, she'd sold hundreds of LEAVE BURN MARKS shirts and coffee mugs leading up to the release. It was a wonder that people weren't returning them.

Bianca held out her notebook with the unfinished comic strip and dropped it with a *smack*. (Life imitating art!) Then she removed her glasses and chewed on the frame while staring at her client.

A good minute went by, then Lacy finally asked, "Do you really think I'm overweight?"

Bianca let her head fall back. "Let me get this straight. We're talking about the paramount issues that plague womankind right now, our desperate clawing to find meaning, and the one thing that stuck out to you is that you might be overweight?"

"I try hard, protein-focused, calorie counting, and I—"

"No, you're not overweight. You're a stick."

"Then why'd you—"

"I don't know. Because maybe I was expressing some of my own frustrations. You wanna know something else? These glasses, they aren't even prescription. Transparent glass. I wear them because it makes me look less like a ditz." Bianca chucked them across the room.

Lacy watched them hit the wall, then timidly looked back at her world-class therapist. "I don't know whether this is part of your normal spiel or if I need to get up and give you a hug. Do you need a hug?"

Bianca softened. Tears were trying to break out. She fought them away but eventually caved.

"Wait, are those real tears?" Lacy asked. "God, you're good. Are you faking?" In a shocking turn of events, Lacy crossed the room, knelt, and took Bianca's hand. "Oh, you poor thing. Here I am, going off about my issues."

Bianca quickly swept away the tears. "No, that's . . . I'm here for you."

Lacy ignored her. "You're overworked. You've helped half of us in Austin, but who's taking care of you?"

"You know what." Bianca pulled her hand away, wanting it all to stop, and she instantly walled off her emotions. "Let's end this session for now. I won't charge you, obviously. You're right; I need to step back for a minute."

Lacy frowned. "Do you want to talk about it? Go get that drink?"

Bianca chuckled. Her client, the one on the couch a moment ago, was now trying to help her. After a thank-you and a barrage of apologies, she ushered Lacy out of the office before things got any worse. When the door shut and her client was safely on her way back to her less-than-perfect life—where she'd probably phone whomever had recommended Bianca to her and ask, "What in the ever-living FUCK was that?"—Bianca walked down the hall to her young receptionist and said, "I need you to cancel everything today. Please."

"You okay? You don't look—"

"Never been better, thank you. You know what, once you're done, take yourself out to lunch on me. We'll talk tomorrow."

Chapter 3

Strawberry Love

Often, here in Bologna, when Harold Gibler looked across the table at Alice, her freckles scattered across her cheeks like glitter, her sparkling statement of hair the same red as an Aperol spritz, his mind would slip back to his life in Denver before she'd strutted into the coffee shop with her headphones on, shaking it like she was listening to the Black Pumas. He couldn't believe it had only been a couple of months since he'd first had the pleasure of witnessing her take over a room simply by appearing.

It was dangerous territory, going back to that day, that bad place where guilt waited. In his twenty-three years on earth, he'd never pretended to be someone he wasn't before, and though effective, it had become increasingly difficult to keep up the ruse.

Stay here in the present, he would tell himself. The relationship might eventually go down in a burst of flames, but he was *not* ready to let what they had slip from his grasp.

Despite having created a souped-up version of himself, Harold still wasn't exactly sure why Alice was so into him, but she was, and therefore miracles do happen. She'd made him believe in himself for the first time in his life.

He was a scrawny geek who'd been picked on and bullied throughout his youth. How many times had he begged his mother to move to a different state, even a nearby town, anywhere in a different school district? Harold didn't tell anyone what growing up was like—how his father had left one day and hadn't come back, how his mother had to figure out a way to make a living, often working three jobs at a time, which meant Harold had come home from school every day to an empty house. Perhaps his struggles were unexceptional, but that didn't dull the hurt he still carried with him.

Nevertheless, Alice saw something in him no one else could. She appreciated his intellect, his quick wit (as subjective as such a trait might be), his deep trivia knowledge, and his ability to do complicated math in his head. If only he'd had Italian lessons growing up, he'd likely be getting along fine here in Bologna, as he never forgot a thing. She'd be extra dazzled. Due to his linguistic deficit, though, he'd become a prisoner to Duolingo, the language learning app that stalked him with notifications on all his devices. Even his new watch!

A spritz at the wine bar was their routine after she'd finished her classes and studying for the day. They'd join the army of tourists and locals alike who filled every table in the city to linger over late-afternoon spritzes and bowls of free *aperitivi* like potato chips, peanuts, and olives. She'd come up to the apartment, drop her backpack, and then they'd storm out into the city, two lovers ready to rise as the sun fell.

This place was one of their favorite haunts, an ancient wine bar called Sorso Sospetto that was two blocks down on the same street as her (their?) apartment on Via Giulia. The eight outdoor tables were almost always occupied—no matter the season or weather. Cigarette smoke and perfume wafted through the air, mixing with the aroma of warm chocolate from the *pasticceria* across the street. Chatter in multiple languages buzzed through the air. The late-afternoon sun cast long shadows across the cobblestones. Around the corner, someone—likely a busker—played a violin, the slow and easy bowing matching the hum of city life and creating a perfect soundtrack to their love.

"Question," he said, all smiles and fully relaxed, never wanting to go back to the person he used to be. "Would you call your hair an Afro? I would assume it's either politically and/or factually incorrect." He didn't stammer with her, which was beyond unbelievable. He'd been stammering all his life.

"What do you call it, this . . . this sort of Bob Ross thing?" He gestured toward her hair. Maybe she even liked the way he talked, how his words ran over each other sometimes.

"Who's Bob Ross?"

Harold grabbed a fistful of his own hair in a dramatic display of surprise. "*Who is Bob Ross?* Happy little trees? Did you not watch PBS growing up?" He and his mother certainly had while eating their microwave dinners on TV trays. Those were sweet memories.

Alice let loose the creamiest of giggles. "We didn't have a television in our house, so no, I don't know who Bob Ross is, and no, I don't call this an Afro. It's just a perm."

"Just a perm?" Harold said with great animation, his voice nearly chirping. "It's exquisite, the best hair I've ever seen. I'd like to put whipped cream on top and eat you like a strawberry shortcake."

A standard eye-roll response followed, but one that came with a smirk, making her look even more tempting. Perhaps he'd top her off with a gumdrop and sprinkles.

"I will be forever curious about your childhood," he said. "What does a family do without a television? My mom and I, that's how we bonded. Dinner in front of the television. And she grew up watching Bob Ross and would always track down reruns. He's a painter guy, had this big, I don't know, bloom of hair and had the worst clothes and was always holding his palette of paints. It's a nice memory. Anyway, take me once again back to your strange household in backwoods Colorado? Tour me through the early life of Alice Richter."

She pulled her spritz toward her, still a smirk on her face. "How many times do we have to do this?"

"Until I see it. Till I see my girlfriend when she was younger, finding her way toward the exceptional woman she's become."

She reached for a cigarette, and he was there with his Zippo, a recent purchase. "We did chores," she said with the first exhalation of smoke. "We read the Bible. Prayed. Went on walks. We shared what we learned that day at the dinner table."

He closed his eyes and imagined this younger Alice among her six siblings. "Okay, okay. I'm seeing you. It's very cultish. Was there any part of you that wondered if your life was normal?"

She shrugged. "I don't know. It seemed normal at the time."

He lit a cigarette himself, trying hard not to cough, then snapped the lighter closed. "Was there any fun to be had? Not that my childhood staring at a computer was any better, just trying to understand here."

"We played lots of games."

"Ah, there we go. Four Square? Monopoly? Cards Against Humanity—Religious Edition?"

Her smile sprouted again, a flower stretching for the sky after a rain shower. "Parcheesi."

"*Parcheesi?* I should have known." He took another drag, a lighter one this time. "My mother and I played our fair share."

"And we read," she continued. "A lot. Not only the Bible. Reading is how I came to know the world, how I realized I wanted to travel." He was well aware of her love of reading. She'd dragged him into the bookstore below her apartment multiple times. The comic selection was abysmal.

For the first time, he looked around at the other tables, a blend of students, businesspeople, and travelers, five or six languages among them, all easing into their evenings through the same Aperol spritz doorway. "They'd let you read whatever you wanted?"

She smiled as she blew out an oval of smoke. "For the most part. They were strict in some ways, but they gave us a thirst for knowledge and understanding. Let me study in Italy my senior year, you know. After some coercing, of course."

He might be the smartest person in the room, but she was no slouch. He adored talking to her, the way they could go on forever, forgetting even where they were. Though he was not a smoker, he was learning, because it seemed to enhance this person he'd become and these wondrous Italian moments they were inhabiting.

Alice was near the top of her freshman class at the University of Bologna and had lived here for almost a year now. Having studied in Bologna when she was in high school, she spoke impeccable Italian, and there wasn't anything sexier than when she rattled off their order like a native.

Only because fate does exist—as Harold could now attest—had she happened to be in Denver visiting her best friend when the two came upon each other.

Their meeting in fast-forward: her grand entrance in the coffee shop in Denver, a surge of energy as they spoke for the first time, a few lies spilled, followed by a fancy lunch together, then an even more expensive dinner, then a weekend of museums and art galleries, Harold falling harder with every passing hour, followed by Alice saying as she kissed his lips, "I'm going to miss you, Harold."

There had been only one possible response to that: "What if I came with you?"

Sometimes he couldn't even hear what she was saying, as he was too taken with her presence. Her sunglasses were pulled up and nearly lost in her Bob Ross, strawberry hair. Her leprechaun eyes (a *cute* leprechaun, naturally) sparkled like emeralds in the setting Italian sun. Somehow, he had the sweet fortune of being in current possession of those lips, molded by the Stradivarius of lip makers. Her petite body was a masterpiece of wonder, and she was currently offering a glorious, braless side-boob shot due to the nature of her loose top. If he were a poet, he could write endless verse on the wonders of her small but mighty breasts.

Alice was the perfect balance of sexy, brilliant, and adorable. For God's sake, she was Gen Z, but she loved The Cure and her favorite movie was *Say Anything*, about as eighties as you could get. In other words, she was into the oldies.

She had a silly, bubbly nature that made up for his own shortcomings. He could embrace his geekdom, staying quiet, while she played the role of the spokesperson, the press secretary of the Harold Gibler White House, if you would.

"Are you listening to me?" she asked, pulling the president from his musings.

"What?" Harold asked, stubbing out his only half-finished cigarette into the marble ashtray. "Oh, yeah, of course."

"What was I saying?"

"Well," he started, reaching for the hand sanitizer in his pocket, smoke still rising from the ashtray. He squeezed out a dime of gel and smoothed it into his hands. "You were saying a lot of things."

"That's the third time you've gone for the sanitizer since we've been sitting here."

He shrugged and took an olive from the bowl. "You can never be too careful."

Her face grew serious. "Anyway, you're *not* listening to me."

The only problem with dating such a smart girl was that she could see right through him.

With the olive now traveling south down his throat, he said, "I'm distracted by work stuff, that's all. I have a new account in Beijing that wants me to build their backend for a new line of watches, and they're proving to be difficult to work with. Kept me up all night."

Cooling her offense, she poured a handful of peanuts into her palm, then tossed a few into her mouth.

"And another guy in Copenhagen who's driving me crazy," he added. "Doesn't want to pay his bills. I might have to go up and see him."

She finished chewing, then: "Are you going to go beat him up?"

"That's right."

"Maybe one day you'll explain to me what you do. Because I have no idea."

Harold washed the olive down with a long sip of his spritz and signaled the server for another round. How could they make money selling six-euro drinks, especially when so many of these restaurants served them with free snacks? If only it were this way back in Denver, but an Aperol spritz would cost closer to twenty bucks. No wonder Americans didn't sit around for long; they couldn't afford it!

"Computer stuff, my dear. Nothing worth talking about. A way to pay the bills so I can chase you across the world. Anyway, what were you saying? Forgive me."

"I was talking about walking. We're not hitting our ten thousand steps. That's what you're supposed to do in Europe. Walk. I feel like you always have an excuse."

Looking at the Apple Watch he'd bought at her encouragement, and ignoring yet another Duolingo notification, he said, "Why walk? Tha . . . tha . . . that's what taxis are for? Walking is for horses and—"

"Walking is the way you experience the world."

The Giblerator knew when he'd been beat. "Fine, then, let's walk more tomorrow. Ten thousand steps it is. In the meantime, I got you something." He reached into the leather man bag, or murse, she'd bought him and drew out a small brown box wrapped with an ivory bow.

"What are you doing?" she asked, her frustration fading at the sight of a potential gift.

"To show you that even when I'm not paying attention, you're on my mind."

She reached for it with a skeptical smile.

"C'mon, open it." He couldn't believe how much joy he found in giving her gifts.

Alice untied the bow and lifted the top of the box; her mouth fell open. "They're gorgeous," she said, beaming at the sight of the overpriced gold earrings he'd bought her from the Quadrilatero market. If he was being honest, he'd bought them with his mother's money, but he'd pay back every cent he'd been borrowing.

"Thank you," she whispered. "I love you."

He blew her a kiss across the table, then did his best to spit out, *"Anch'io ti voglio bene."* And there you go, Duolingo. One step at a time.

While basking in the glow of their union, his mind returned to what had happened in Denver, the land of overpriced everything. It was almost hard to believe that only a short time ago, he'd been a barista at a somewhat hip coffee shop, barely making a living wage and staying with his mom. His story had changed in an instant, the moment Alice had waltzed in. Never had he approached a strange girl before, but love can give you courage where there is none. Taking off his apron, he'd slid up next to her and started a lie that had grown every day since.

Wincing at the truth, he pinched himself in the thigh to keep his focus here, where time slowed and fairy tales came true.

Harold's phone alarm woke him at two in the morning, which is when he got online to "start his day." He snuck out of bed, dressed, and crossed the apartment to the living room, then slipped out onto the Juliet balcony where Alice kept a pot of sun-loving herbs. If she weren't perfect already, she also happened to have a green thumb and was a wonderful cook.

Aside from the construction underway, Via Giulia, their narrow cobblestone street, was as alluring as any in the city. The stucco buildings were various warm shades of terra-cotta. Standard doorways had been cut into centuries-old wooden doors that were large enough to ride horses through. Tasteful works of graffiti revealed themselves when the shop owners pulled down the metal doors for the night. Plants in pots of various primary colors flanked many of the entrances. English ivy cascaded down the walls.

Like most of Bologna, the sidewalks were covered by porticoes that had been built in the Middle Ages as a way to extend living space. According to Alice, Bologna had forty kilometers of porticoes, some of which rose several stories high, each featuring unique, elaborate arches that kept tourists walking with their heads angled upward in awe. They created a wonderful series of tunnels, these porticoed sidewalks. You could walk throughout the city under the cover of these works of art and avoid the harsh summer sun and the winter rains.

Their balcony protruded from one of the porticoes. Directly below them was an English bookstore. To the right was a *fiorista*, a *pasticceria*, and Sorso Sospetto, the *enoteca*. The other direction led to an art gallery, a couple of clothing boutiques, and a cobbler. Only scooters and the smallest of cars could get through, so it was mostly foot traffic that passed by, especially this time of night. The last of the late-night warriors were strolling by in happy clusters, many of them singing late-night songs.

He began early mornings with a few minutes out here, as something about a quiet city captivated him. In a few hours, the trashmen would wake everyone with their racket, then a line would form at the *pasticceria* for the coveted *torta di riso* or *certosino* cake. Not long after, the workmen would gather and start hammering and drilling, forcing Harold to do his daytime sleeping using Alice's noise-canceling headphones.

He wasn't the only one who loathed the construction. The owner of the bookstore below never missed a chance to snap at the workers for either making too much noise or sitting around and causing delays. At least, that's how Harold interpreted her Italian rants with his A-1 level, Duolingo-accredited language skills.

Returning inside, he grabbed a bag of potato chips and a can of Coke and plopped down on the couch next to his laptop. He responded to a few WhatsApp messages and emails, including one from his mother in Denver asking for pictures and scolding him for not calling her yesterday. Her closing words: I WANT MORE PICTURES. Also, don't forget to be yourself. Love ya! Your mama.

She could never stop mommying, which was awesome most of the time.

He proceeded to grab a game controller and join his gamer friends back in the States for several hours of their latest obsession. Lately, they'd been playing *Project Zomboid.* Though he'd never met them in person, these guys were his best friends.

Harold and Alice's days had fallen into an easy rhythm. He would wrap things up in time to visit Le Briciole di Via Giulia (the Crumbs of Via Giulia) for fresh pastries, oftentimes stopping by the *fiorista* as well—*if* the owner was in early. Alice loved the breakfasts Harold prepared for her, and he took great pride in them. By the time she appeared from her daily shower, he'd have the table set with a flower in a ceramic vase, a selection of pastries, freshly squeezed orange juice, and her favorite: hard-boiled eggs. Without fail, he always wrote a quick thought on a sticky note to place on the place mat. Cheesy stuff in Italian: *Mia cara; Mia Alice, mio amore; Fiore mio; mia gran bellezza.* Upon her entrance in one of his T-shirts, he'd give her a kiss and then rush into the kitchen to make her a cappuccino, a skill he'd acquired back in the old days.

Once she left for class, Harold would crash till well after lunch. Then he'd wander down the street to find a mortadella panini and spend the afternoon being punished by Duolingo, watching television with English subtitles, and catching up with more "work" before she returned home. Truthfully, work always equaled gaming.

She'd suggest they'd go on a walk, and he'd do his best to talk her out of it, only occasionally conceding. How had people become so duped by the random ten-thousand-steps number? There was *no* science to back it up, yet the users of these wearable devices desperately clung to the goal of reaching this number each day. He'd tell her he'd already walked several miles, dealing with conference calls. "So much of my life is conference calls," he'd say. "All I do is walk and talk while you're gone."

The constant nagging about the walking aside, their routine was perfectly wonderful, and he hoped things would never change. But one day in early May she came home in an atypical mood.

He quickly cleared the history on his browser and closed his laptop. "You don't look very happy? *Tutto bene?*"

Her extremely short tan shorts showed off her long legs. She collapsed onto the couch next to him, her shorts inching up even more, revealing the porcelain white of her thighs. "I have to tell you something."

An ache instantly presented itself in his chest. Before Alice, he'd never been in a true relationship, but he'd noticed a few signs recently: the lack of eye contact, disinterest in sex, less glee when she sat down for his breakfasts.

It took her a moment, but she eventually said, "I've met someone."

The world went black and bitter.

"What do you mean you've met someone? We all meet people."

"No, I met a guy at the café, and things have taken a turn."

He felt like he was suddenly passing through an asteroid field, being struck in every part. "What kind of turn?"

"I'm in love, Harold. His name's Renzo; he's a little older. I'm sorry. I don't know what to say. You can stay here and take over the rent. I'm moving in with him."

"A little older?" Her words echoed in his brain. He looked at the stunning girl that he planned to marry, the beauty radiating from her green eyes even when she was cutting out his heart. He tried to speak but he'd taken too many hits. His spaceship was going down.

"Want me to give you a minute?" she asked. "Harold?"

They sat there a long time. She spoke, though he could barely hear her, mentioning a few details about Renzo as if Harold might cheer them on, then added that she and this imbecile would find a good time to collect her things, that Harold could have the kitchen stuff. Eventually she stood and said goodbye.

"Alice," he finally said as she reached the door.

"Yeah?" Her hand touched the knob.

"Wh . . . wh . . . what about love?" he asked. "What about our evening spritz?"

"It was fun."

Fun? he thought, as he watched her disappear.

Chapter 4

A Fling to Remember

In early May, one month after Bianca's breakdown, she flew to Bologna, Italy, to begin again. She'd called each of her clients, explained her situation, and offered them alternative psychotherapist recommendations. She'd put some things in storage and rented out her apartment. Now she was armed with a purse, a backpack, two suitcases packed to the maximum, and her Italian passport courtesy of her Bolognese grandmother. Bianca's mother, Faith, didn't have the most Italian first name, but she came from a long line of Malatestas, a family who'd inhabited Emilia-Romagna for centuries.

Even from the moment the wheels touched down, she felt a surge of life. Through the window of the taxi that took her to her Airbnb, she could see her twenty-two-year-old self wandering these same streets, connecting for the first time with her heritage and shaking off the aggro-American ways she'd picked up from her father and four years of grinding at Pomona College. She'd gotten accepted by the University of Texas to pursue a master's in clinical psychology but had been granted a deferment for her Bologna adventure. In so many ways, the break had saved Bianca's life.

Faith had always encouraged a gap year. In fact, years earlier, she'd started a "gap year fund" for Bianca, squirreling away savings from her part-time work at a clothing boutique in Phoenix.

Bianca's father, George, on the other hand, had stood strongly against the idea, saying that the world wasn't a safe place and that she'd lose her academic momentum. He was the one who'd burned corporate words like *trajectory* and *momentum* into her psyche. Fortunately, he'd lost the battle then, and he'd lost it again this time. He'd desperately protested when Bianca had called him weeks back to inform him she was returning to Italy for an undetermined amount of time. His arguments echoed those of years ago. "B, the world isn't the same as it was. What if we end up at war? Italy is unstable at best. And what about your work? You might not be able to build up your client list again. Don't take your life for granted, honey. Play this one safe." That mindset was exactly why she'd found the courage to return. She didn't want to reach her deathbed realizing fear and "playing it safe" had dictated her life.

Coupled with her first taste of independence, she'd also enjoyed her first taste of love when she'd lived here, with Corrado, the chef. Perhaps the brevity of it had been perfect, as it would forever stay in her mind as her greatest romance. She could see herself now, her arm slipped around his, two young lovers weaving through the city streets.

Per his social media, which was covered in food porn, Corrado was in Paris now, cooking at the famous L'Ambroisie. Even ten years ago, as a sous chef in Bologna, he'd set his sights on Paris. They'd had fun together, the day trips to Verona and Venice, the countless late nights with friends, the meals he'd cooked for her in his apartment. Tastes and scents of him and his food caused goose bumps to rise on her flesh.

What had happened to that Bianca? She'd been so free and full of joy, unworried about the future. Maybe her gap year had saved her, but she'd reverted right back to who she'd been before, a reflection of her father, a soldier of life, fighting an enemy within.

Had she and Corrado still kept in touch, he out of anyone would be the most disappointed in her. "Promise me, Bianca," he'd said at the table on her last night in Bologna, the night the picture was taken that led her back here. "Don't get pulled back into that American thing, pretending to be living, all the rushing around. You're Italian deep down. Don't forget it."

Oops.

The first few days of her return to Italy went by in a blur. She worked with a woman she'd found in an online expats' group who helped people find apartments. Bianca's Italian had deteriorated, so it was nice to have a guide. They saw two or three places a day, but nothing had resonated yet.

In her free time, she strolled the streets, searching for the ghost of her past self as she paused to enjoy the graffiti that gave Bologna its wonderfully youthful vibrance, or as she dipped into the countless museums and churches, studying art and architecture that had once mesmerized her. Though she was tempted to fill her Instagram feed with photos of all things Bologna, she held back, feeling like this recalibration was not for public consumption.

She could feel the other part of her—the rigid, achievement-focused American self—kicking and screaming. No matter; she'd keep filling herself with this life, waiting for Bologna to cast its spell.

To her followers who asked if she was working on a new book, she'd offer vague responses, like "Who knows?" But no, she wasn't working on a new book. Let's try that again: *absolutely fucking not!* Been there, failed at that. No more rejection, thank you. Besides, she was trying not to think about the future too much. She had enough savings to safely get her through a year, which was plenty of time to recalibrate and figure out her next steps.

Outside the building where she'd lived as a youngster, she touched the ancient wooden door and attempted to recall that feeling of satisfaction she'd found then, the sense of being in a state of peace. This was a land where it was okay not to rush. The Bolognese and even the city's adopted children, the expats of foreign lands, lingered, talked, savored, and flirted with life, perhaps more aware than most that life was not defined by what was etched on your gravestone; it was defined by how you lived in the moment.

She sat on the steps in the Piazza Maggiore to watch a man juggle fire, then she dipped into the Basilica di San Petronio for mass. A short walk away, climbing the Asinelli tower, one of the remaining two towers in a city that was once dominated by hundreds of them, she soaked in the view of the city and the surrounding Apennine Mountains, imagining life during the evolution of this land from an Etruscan settlement to a Roman colony to what it was now.

Was this where she belonged, the ultimate return to her roots? Intentionally slowing herself down, she strolled under the elaborate porticoes that covered nearly every sidewalk, popping into boutiques, open-air markets, and art galleries. And she ate far more pasta Bolognese and *tortellini in brodo* than she'd ever care to admit as she sat alone at small candlelit tables in quaint restaurants, reading a book or scribbling in her journal.

It was hard not to get mad at herself when her Americanness flared. She'd once enjoyed countless three-hour meals, but now she often found herself antsy after thirty minutes of sitting alone. It was so hard to be fully and wholly in the present. But it would come back with practice, she knew it. It's just that she'd trained herself to be comfortable in a baseline state of movement. What could be trained could be untrained, though.

Five days after landing, she met an old friend at Osteria del Sole, the exact wine bar where the photograph Bianca had thrown across her office had been taken. In fact, they sat at the same table where they'd last seen each other in person.

The Osteria del Sole was one of the oldest taverns in all of Italy, and what it lacked in modern appeal, it made up for with the palpable energy of a place that had been a watering hole for nearly five hundred years.

They were sharing a bottle of Lambrusco, a sparkling red wine favored by the Bolognese for its ability to cut through the rich dishes of the local cuisine. Bianca had drunk entirely too much of it way back when. "I can't believe you're back. You just up and moved?"

Carol was from Seattle and had been studying Italian in Bologna when Bianca had lived here, and they'd become fast friends. Since they followed each other on Instagram, it had been easy to reconnect. She was the same age as Bianca but looked like she was still holding on to her twenties, so light and free—and skinny, despite having two children. A streak of orange ran through her indigo hair. Her silk blouse was tucked into fashionable baggy pants.

"How long are you here?" Carol asked. "What are you going to do? What brought this on? All the things."

Bianca beamed because there were so many unanswered questions, and what could be better than that? "I'm embracing my inner Italian. Learning how to cook, finding an Italian teacher who can remind me of all my verb tenses, catching up on my reading. I don't know, just enjoying *la dolce vita*. But slowly, all slowly. I've been running a hundred miles an hour since grad school. My nervous system is a wreck."

Bianca shared a copy of the old photo on her phone.

"Weren't we a crew," Carol said, memories of her own clearly shimmering through.

"You wouldn't remember this," Bianca said, taking her phone back, "but Corrado told me something I'll never forget. He made me promise not to get pulled back in. Remember how he was always making fun of us Americans for chasing our tails, never able to slow down? 'You Americans,' he'd say, 'you're like the movies. Go, go, go. Don't get sucked back into that, Bianca.'"

"Hey, that was a good Corrado accent," Carol said. Both of them eyed the derrière of the handsome bartender who reached up high for a bottle of vermouth. Some things never changed.

"I still hear him, like it was yesterday," Bianca replied, blushing when she heard the longing in her voice. "No, not because I still miss him . . . but because I broke that promise." Bianca couldn't believe how nice it was to talk to someone. She didn't have too many close friends in Austin, as she'd sadly not made the time to cultivate them.

"You're adorable," Carol said after hearing Bianca's tale. "Sounds like you're exhausted. Who wouldn't be?"

Bianca set her elbows on the table and interlocked her fingers. "I look at you and see what I could have been. I'm all wound up, chasing all this . . . this external achievement. For what? We're all destined for the same place, and I'm living like we get to take our trophy case with us."

Carol gave a nod. "The US will do that to you."

"No kidding."

"What kind of visa did you get, the nomad one?"

"No, I'm Italian on my mother's side. The Malatestas. My grandmother was born in Modena before immigrating to the States."

"Maybe I did know that. You'll have to join my yoga studio. I still teach a morning class almost every day."

"I'd love to."

A collective song of church bells rang and echoed around them, signifying 8:00 p.m. "Listen to those bells. That's why I'm here. The magic of Europe. Honestly, I'm jealous of you. Full on, want-to-kill-you-in-your-sleep jealous."

"Oh, c'mon."

"I'm serious. You never left. You found your Italian soulmate and have built this amazing life."

Carol batted her eyelashes. "It's not terrible."

Bianca paused to drink her wine, the bubbles tingling on her tongue. "Tell me about it. Rub in my face all the things I'm missing. When can I meet this husband of yours?"

"Silvie is charming. A doctor, an orthopedic surgeon. We have a home up in the hills and our pied-à-terre here."

"Of course you have a pied-à-terre. God, I hate you so much."

As Carol painted the picture of her life, Bianca couldn't stop shaking her head. "You even have a slight Italian accent when you speak English. That's how long you've been here. Would it be awkward if I took your life? We could trade. Would your husband notice?"

Carol laughed. "I remember how funny you used to be."

A deep longing came over Bianca, a voice harkening back to the good old days. "Yeah, well, I hope I can find that person again. I remember how much we used to crack each other up. Youth fades away, doesn't it? I feel like a frog in boiling water; adulthood snuck up on me."

Carol raised her wine. "To frogs that better jump out of the pot before it's too late."

Bianca clinked her glass, feeling desperation in her chest. *"Cin, cin."*

"Are there really cracks in the veneer of Bianca Briggs?" Carol asked. "I don't believe you. You look so happy in the pics I see of you. You're famous back home. And the book. I'm jealous of you!"

"Oh, there are cracks all right. I did a good job of hiding them, even from myself. Italy definitely has her hands full with me." At Carol's prodding, Bianca elaborated on what she'd been doing the last ten years and how it had started to come apart at the seams.

"Still, you wrote a book. That's a big deal. Were the reviews that bad?"

"Oh, yeah, they were bad. Want to hear a few?" Bianca found them quickly, as she'd become Christopher Columbus when it came to finding the awful shit people said about her book.

"My favorite from last week, from Self-Help Junkie02: *This could have been an email.*" She looked up. "My life's work could have been an email? Or this one: *Clearly written by someone who doesn't understand real human beings.* Or this: *Meatless, not even a bone. Three hundred pages of overconfident, tone-deaf cartilage.* Or: *I would give it negative one star if I could. I'm actually worse off after digesting this drivel.*" Bianca moved to the next page. *"And she calls herself a therapist? The only reason I'm not returning it is I don't have the energy to drive to UPS."*

The last one caused a chuckle. "You probably shouldn't be reading those. Besides, I'm sure some people loved it."

Bianca set down her phone. "Firstly, every author reads their reviews. If they say they don't, they're lying. And that first review on Amazon, the five-star, that's my mom."

Carol brushed her hand through the air. "You're hitting a nerve with these people. They're not ready for what you're throwing down."

"Yeah, maybe." Bianca let herself relax. "You want the truth since I'm letting it all out? I got too ambitious. I let my insecurities get the best of me and got caught up in thinking that if I became a big deal, then I'd matter. So I've been relentless, clamoring for things to achieve, whatever it took to get to the top."

"Spoken like a true psychotherapist."

"At least I'm self-aware."

Carol twisted her glass between her fingers. "So that's it? You're giving yourself over to Italy, letting her resurrect your spirit? And maybe or maybe not returning home afterward?"

"*Esattamente.* I'm leaping headfirst into the proverbial bowl of pasta. See if there's some meaning to be found by the time I *scarpetta* the last of the sauce with my bread."

Carol patted her hand. "I like your plan. You'll be good as new before too long."

"Let's hope so. It worked last time." Moving on, Bianca asked, "You remember the fortune teller Donna Bologna, right?"

"Naturally. I went for a reading last year."

Bianca's mouth fell agape. "She's still around? I'll have to go by and thank her for ruining my life."

"How'd she do that?"

"She told me I'd write a book. There I was, innocent Bianca getting ready to go to grad school, work my way to building a practice. And she had to drop that bomb on me. Writing wasn't even on my radar, but once she said it, it was like I couldn't put the idea back in the box."

"I believe it. First time I went to see her, she said I'd never leave Italy. And here I am."

Later, Carol said, "Speaking of Corrado . . . I'm sure he'd love to see you."

Each time Bianca heard his name, her heart kicked. "He's in Paris now, isn't he? I see his food porn on Insta." She knew damn well he was working at L'Ambroisie, but she wasn't about to admit it.

"No. He's *here*. In Bologna."

"What?" Her chest seized. The violin music he used to play while she studied ran through her head.

"He's about to open up a new restaurant in the Hotel Minerva, going for a Michelin star. He was in the paper last week. One of Bologna's own, coming home."

"A Michelin star? Good for him." She could taste one of the spectacular frittatas he used to make when she'd stay over at his place.

"Is he married and all that?" Bianca asked, loathing the overly curious tone in her voice.

Carol bit back another smile. She was having too much fun. "You really don't keep up with him? He's single, a bad breakup in Paris last year. Probably half of why he's back. You should call him."

"No. I couldn't. I . . ."

Carol exhaled dramatically, then said something in rapid-fire Italian having to do with love.

"Slow down," Bianca said.

"Have you forgotten your Italian?"

"A lot of it."

Carol continued to speak Italian but dumbed it down. Bianca did her best to keep up.

"You haven't lost everything," Carol said. "I know a good tutor. He's cute too. You'll be back to normal in no time. So, Corrado. Are you going to call him? I have his cell."

Bianca reddened. "*No.* I have to focus on me for a while."

Carol waved her hand through the air. "Oh, please. Famous last words."

Bianca almost didn't say it but did anyway. The wine had removed her filter. "I don't even want him to see me right now. I feel so ugly."

"What? You look better than ever."

"Right. All this carbo-loading since I've been here, on top of what the last ten years has done to me. Ugh." Bianca couldn't imagine seeing him this way.

"You need to stop," Carol said. "You look fantastic. I'd kill for your curves."

Hating the way she seemed to be searching for pity or compliments, Bianca swiftly thanked her, then: "More importantly, I still need to find a place to live. I only have the Airbnb another week."

Carol crinkled her eyebrows. "You changed the subject on me."

"Maybe. But seriously, I'm not relationship material right now."

The seconds passed by like pounding heartbeats. Yes, Bianca was going to leap back into everything Italy—except for him.

"Fine, fine," Carol said. "I might have a place for you, on Via Giulia, one of my favorite streets in the city. Do you know it?"

Bianca couldn't recall.

"A friend of mine is moving out. Cobblestones, sconces. There's the most adorable English bookstore, a wine bar, *pasticceria*, wonderful clothing boutique, and get this . . . a man who sings opera from his balcony."

As the image came alive in her mind, Bianca sat up straight. "Please call your friend right now."

Harold hadn't left his apartment in a week. The Deliveroo delivery guy knew him by name. He'd been carbo-loading pizza and pasta like he was prepping for the apocalypse. His trash cans were full. A stack of pizza boxes on the dining room table reminiscent of the Leaning Tower of Pisa threatened to tip over at any moment.

These details mattered little to Harold as he moved from bed to kitchen to couch, the repetitive life of a young man who'd been stripped of love, a man who'd ignored the data and allowed the idea of fate and love and the cosmos to play a part in his plan.

It hadn't helped that he'd watched Alice's favorite movie, *Say Anything*, with John Cusack and Ione Skye, about ten times since she'd left. Toward the end, when John holds up the boom box and plays Peter Gabriel's "In Your Eyes" outside of Ione's house, Harold would cry till he was out of tears, wishing he could find his way back to Alice.

Harold's stomach twisted when he imagined someone else touching his girl. He tried so hard to avoid thinking about what this guy must look like, but in his mind, he saw a wealthy heir to Lamborghini or Ferrari, a man several inches taller than Harold, who wore his starched white shirts halfway unbuttoned, revealing a perfectly shaved chest and perhaps a Saint Christopher medal dangling on a gold chain, an exquisite Bulgari watch on the man's wrist. He probably wore designer glasses, thick frames to further enhance his style, because he was certainly a fashion model, or used to be before taking over the family business. Naturally, he was a skier, as everyone with money in Bologna was, so he probably planned on taking Alice up to his chalet in Cortina on the weekends, where he would teach her how to navigate the slopes before he took her home to explore the slopes of her body.

Harold had finally broken through, though. After a long seven days—and they were excruciatingly long beyond description, pain ticked off by the second hand on the clock, black holes of emptiness, soul torn by loneliness—he'd found the answer he'd been looking for.

His whole life, he'd proved to be his father's son, running away at the first sign of adversity. No more would he let that happen. He'd come so close to booking a flight back to Denver, forgetting this whole thing happened, picking up where he'd left his life. It hadn't been that bad, right?

Yeah, it actually had. He *couldn't* go back to that old life. At least, not without a fight.

Alice was having a fling, that was all. What gorgeous youngster who studied in Italy didn't meet an Italian man or two? It seemed almost a requirement. She'd come back to him eventually, Harold knew it.

The idea caused his lips to curl into something that might be considered a smile. Hope danced in his heart, helping it to properly beat for the first time that week. He sat up and reached for the lone T-shirt she'd accidentally left when she and the demigod had come by to pick up her things. Harold had promised to leave for a few hours, and he'd done just that. What he should have done was lingered in the shadows to get a glimpse of this Renzo, but he'd been too afraid.

Not anymore, though. As he sniffed the scent of the woman he still believed to be his soulmate, he decided to go find her and inspect her new life, look for the weaknesses, look for any indication that their false love affair was ending. Maybe Harold could find a way to give a final push to bring things to a close quicker.

After one last sniff, he popped up like a man possessed. He'd been lost but now he was found, and he marched into the bathroom, shucked the clothes he'd been wearing for two days, leaned against the counter, and stared at himself in the mirror.

He had work to do. He needed to shower and shave and clean up the place. At some point, he'd have to call his mom and explain that he wasn't ready to come home, but it was better to put that conversation off for now.

An hour later, Harold hauled out two big bags of his trash. He weaved through the construction that all but blocked the entrance before escaping onto the street. He noticed the open sign on the English bookstore he lived above and wondered whether they had any books that might aid in his rebirth, perhaps the *Kama Sutra* or maybe a *Sex for Dummies*–type manual. But the thought of approaching the counter with something like that in hand made him feel queasy.

After he dropped the trash in the dumpster (he'd have to make a separate recycling run with all the pizza boxes), Harold began to wander along the cobblestones. Today was simply about getting out, his first adventure in a week. Alice would have been terribly disappointed with him if she saw his step count since she'd dumped him. It was time to change. He needed sunshine and fresh air, something to bring him back to life. Because never had he hurt like this before.

Not even when Brandon Paine and two other guys beat the shit out of him at the mall when they were twelve, writing *sissy* on his forehead and leaving him with a cracked rib and a black eye.

Not even when his dad disappeared.

Chapter 5

Romance Is Dead

Aside from Moira the Mouse, the only other person in the bookstore was a woman likely in her early thirties, a curvy brunette with thick eyebrows and lips. Judging by the fact that she'd found the place, she had to be a direct descendant of Sherlock Holmes.

"Are you looking for the mystery section?" Sandy jokingly asked the young woman, who ran her finger along the spines in the barely existent romance section.

As a survivor of two devastating marriages, Sandy loathed romance books of all types and would have preferred to keep her store romance-free, but if she did, she'd likely have gone under by now. Besides, she enjoyed it when these pitiful seekers of love asked, "Is this all you have for romance?"

Sandy wanted to respond, "Is this all I have? Yes, it is. Go read something with some substance. Good God." But her typical reply was, "Yes, it's such a tiny store, and I prefer realism."

In true clichéd fashion, the younger woman turned to Sandy. "Do you have that new Bridgerton book?"

Oh, God, Sandy thought. *Another delusional Bridgerton disciple who actually thinks there are men out there like that.* She wanted to grab the woman and whisper in her ear, "Wake the fuck up. Love died with Romeo."

But she didn't because she didn't want to eclipse Moira for worst bookseller.

"I don't," Sandy replied with only a sprinkle of snide. "Keep meaning to. I'm sorry."

"Are you the owner?"

Sandy had started to walk away but pivoted. "I am." *If she asks for a Lucy Score book, I will hit her in the head with a hardback of* Lolita.

"I'm so glad you're here," the impressionable, and obviously Italian-American, woman said. "I live almost across the street, moved here from Austin, and I was so worried I'd have a hard time finding books. And not that I'm a big deal at all, like *at all*, but I noticed you have a few copies of my book. Thanks for that."

Sandy looked at her deadpan. *Oh, great, an author. If this one is anything like the last one, she'll ask me why I'm not selling more copies.* But Sandy played it cordial. "You're an author? How wonderful." Her sarcasm dripped off her words like honey.

"Well, *author* is a strong word. I've written one self-help book." The not-really-an-author-because-she-only-wrote-one-book held up a copy of *From Meh to Megawatt: Supercharge Your Life.*

"Oh, that's you?" Sandy turned toward the cash register and called out, "Moira."

No response.

"Moira! Are you playing solitaire again? Can't you hear I'm speaking the two syllables of your dumb name?"

After what felt like an hour and a half, Moira appeared from the back and crept up like she was negotiating a sheet of melting ice.

"You won't believe who this is," Sandy said.

"Who?" Mousy Moira looked through the telescopes she called glasses. It took her a minute to process who she was looking at, but then light bulbs appeared over her head, and she sprang to attention like someone had shocked her with jumper cables. "No way. Bianca Briggs?"

Surprise hit Bianca's face like wind from a commercial fan. "That's me." It sounded more like a question than statement.

"You have no idea how much I love your book! I'm a total Megawatter."

Here we go, Sandy thought, recalling the time Moira had chased the famously introverted Fredrik Backman all the way down the street like he was Robert Redford.

"Look what I got last week!" Moira rolled up her sleeve and aimed it at Bianca, then Sandy. A tattoo on her forearm read, LEAVE BURN MARKS.

"And?" Sandy said, clueless as to what it meant. Also beyond shocked that Moira had this secret Megawatter life—and a tattoo?

"Leave burn marks," Moira said. "That's the battle cry of the Megawatters. Live life in such a way that you leave burn marks. I was telling the tattoo artist it's like the crater after an asteroid crash. Live loudly, you know? *Boom.*"

Boom? Sandy questioned silently.

Bianca looked to be in her own state of shock. When Moira finally gave her a moment to speak, she said genuinely, "I'm beyond flattered."

Moira rolled her sleeve back down and whisper-screamed in her English accent, "I've been pushing it like crazy. It's on my shelf of favorites in the back too. What brings you here?"

Sandy thought she better go find some cheese and lure Moira away before she scared their visiting author.

"I just moved here from Texas."

Moira opened her mouth so wide in surprise that you could have crammed all 849 pages of Stephen King's *11/22/63* in there. "To Bologna?"

"Here, to Via Giulia," Bianca said.

The mouth of the mouse opened even wider, making room for the entire *Outlander* series. "We're neighbors?" She performed a double fist pump. "Yes! Megawatters unite!"

Sandy looked for a wall to ram her head into.

Bianca explained that she'd done a gap year in Bologna ten years prior. Moira pointed out that Sandy had opened the bookstore around the same time. What a coincidence! Then she took over with a barrage of squeaky literary praise, how Moira had been following the steps in the book, how her life was different, blah, blah, blah.

Sandy worried Bianca would run out the door like Backman had, but she held her ground and listened with what could be construed as grace, though Sandy hated to give anyone *that* much credit.

When Moira finally took a breath, Bianca touched her chest and batted her eyelashes. "I don't know what to say."

Sandy wanted to shout, "You just said it. By saying 'I don't know what to say,' you said something." Bianca and Moira were two peas in a stupid pod.

Starting toward the counter, she decided she better get some work done because Moira would be distracted all day after this celebrity encounter.

"I'm serious," Moira continued. "Peggy Meh is my favorite. The whole idea is so funny! And the way you talked about lighting the fire . . . the Let Go days . . . and . . . and then your analogy of jumping into a cold lake and how you're terrified, but the moment you've done it, then you're free. You won't believe it, but I took the train up to Lake Garda and jumped into the lake myself." Of course, Moira was whisper-screaming all this. Then she added, "Naked. I was naked!"

Bianca lit up and let slip a cackle.

It was the first time Sandy had heard this story, and she wondered whether it was true. Maybe Moira wasn't as boring as Sandy thought.

Nevertheless, the worst bookseller in history looked like she was about to start humping Bianca's leg. "I'm trying to follow all the steps, but it's a lot."

"Yeah, I've received similar feedback. Maybe a bit much to cram into each day."

"I'm picking and choosing, a choose-your-own-adventure kind of thing. Hey, what if you did a book signing?" Moira whipped her head to Sandy. "What do you think, Sandy? To welcome her to the neighborhood?"

Sandy pretended like she wasn't listening, but then gave in. In a tone devoid of enthusiasm, she said, "Yeah, that could be good."

Book signings were hit-and-miss and required a tremendous amount of work, what with the promotion and having to rearrange the store to accommodate an audience, but Sandy couldn't imagine losing what she and her son, Jack, had started together, and that meant she somehow needed to find a way to start getting people in the door again.

"What do you say?" Moira asked the author.

Bianca took a giant breath. "I . . . the thing is. My book didn't do that well back home. Part of me is here to escape. I'm still processing that you liked it."

"What's not to like?" Moira asked, staring at the book cover like it was a Picasso. "Peggy Meh, so brilliant—and hysterical. How did you even think of that?" Moira turned to Sandy. "Bianca's a therapist, but instead of using different real-life clients as her case studies, she created this made-up, Frankenstein-monster of a client with all the problems. And her name's Peggy Meh. By working with Bianca over the course of two years, she turns into Peggy Megawatt." Back to Bianca, she said, "A couple of weeks ago, while I was looking in the mirror, I called myself Moira Megawatt. That's when I knew I had to get the tattoo."

Moira stopped there, exhilaration written all over her.

Bianca was shaking her head, smiling sincerely. "I'm so full of gratitude right now. You have no idea."

Two peas in a pod, for sure.

"You've been quiet on your socials lately," Moira said. "Now I know why."

"That's right—busy moving and all that. I'm going to get back to it soon."

Sandy hadn't heard Moira talk so much in one day since Ann Patchett's visit. She felt mortified all over again.

Moira finally gathered her breath and spoke in a more controlled manner. "We haven't done many signings, but we're trying to do more. Right, Sandy? Maybe even a talk if you're up for it. I'd love to hear about your history, your process. What's next for Peggy Meh. Everything."

"Okay, Moira," Sandy said, stepping back toward this car wreck. "Let's let Bianca be."

Moira shrank. "Oh, okay. I'm sorry to bother you." Then she added, "But it would mean so much to me."

Bianca said with a sprinkle of defeat, "I'd love to do it. Why not?"

"Really?" Moira suddenly looked to be in the full throes of an orgasm. "When could we do it, Sandy?"

Sandy considered the question. They didn't have any scheduled events next week. Or the week after. Or the week after that. Or the week or month after that. Ugh, people were awful, especially a big group of them fawning all over an author.

Being put on the spot forced her to cave, though. "How about next Thursday, four to six? Would that work?"

Other than setting up her apartment, Bianca had no other plans. "If you guys want to."

"It would mean the world to us," Moira said. "Right, Sandy?"

"The world, that's right," Sandy replied gleefully. *Soooo* gleefully. She reached into her pocket and, with the pads of her fingers, caressed the rough coral that she never strayed far from, a pacifier that gave her strength.

Bianca couldn't quite process what had happened. It was nice to be recognized, but a tattoo? Wow. That was a first. Yes, she had her Megawatters, as she called them, die-hard followers who consistently responded to her social media posts and Substacks, and who'd claimed that they'd loved the book, but for someone to have branded themselves was next-level.

The bookstore clerk had likened "Leave burn marks" to an asteroid crash. Bianca wouldn't soon forget that analogy.

As much as she had wanted to refuse, Moira's plea had been hard to reject. It would be fine, a harmless hour or two chatting and signing books, a good way to ingratiate herself into her new neighborhood.

She hiked up the three flights of crooked stone steps to her new place, which had turned out to be everything she'd hoped. It was an adorable flat with abundant light and stark-white stucco walls. She'd rented the place furnished and loved the owner's taste: bright colors that popped against all the white. It had air-conditioning, a Nespresso machine, and some decent plates and stemware. Of course, she'd have to pick up a few things to make it homier, but it was a good start. Both bedrooms were cute and had decently comfortable queen-size beds. A balcony begging for potted plants looked down over the cobblestoned Via Giulia, which was just as Carol had described it: a Bolognese dream.

Last night, her first in the flat, she'd gone out onto the balcony to enjoy a glass of wine and people-watch, and her opera-singing neighbor two buildings down had appeared, setting his hands on the railing of his own balcony and breaking into a haunting aria that brought her to tears. By the time he finished, his music had filled her heart with hope. Maybe she hadn't messed up beyond repair.

Kicking off her shoes, she sat back on the couch to call her mom, who'd been blowing up her phone for two days. "Hey, Mom."

"You never don't call me. What's going on?" Faith was now Faith Morrison and lived with her new husband in his giant palace in Palm Springs. It was no secret that she'd married him for his money. Faith had a ton of endearing qualities, but she'd do whatever it took to never join the workforce.

After some chitchat, Faith broached the subject of Bianca's dad. She said he still hadn't found his way in retirement.

"How often are you talking to him, Mom?" Bianca asked with surprise, assuming they spoke every few months. They'd divorced twenty years prior.

"All the time."

Bianca wasn't sure what to make of that. "You're not, like, flirting with him, are you?"

"No, I'm not flirting with George. I'm married, Bianca. But he's struggling, and I feel bad for him. He's worked hard all his life, like really hard, and now he has nothing to do."

"It's good for him," Bianca said, imagining her father squirming in the quietude of joblessness. He was way worse than her. "Maybe he'll finally slow down."

"It's not that easy."

"I know, I know." And she did. She was experiencing it firsthand. "I'm supposed to talk to him tomorrow. I'll check in."

"That would be great. He loves you so much and always values your thoughts. I know you'll have some helpful advice for him, some daughter psychotherapy. I keep telling him he needs to get out, go take some classes at the community college. I don't think he's liking the golf thing."

Bianca had to laugh at the last one. He'd moved to a gated community on a golf course in Scottsdale shortly after he'd been let go. She'd known that was a bad idea from the beginning. He'd always hated golf.

"I'll check in on him tomorrow, see what I can do to help."

Bianca already knew he was struggling from their occasional chats. He'd worked so hard for the last however many years that he'd basically missed Bianca's childhood and had certainly destroyed his marriage with Faith.

After they hung up, Bianca fell back into her chair and closed her eyes. She'd crossed an ocean to get away from all these things, but already the book and her dad had found her.

Chapter 6

Candles in a Coffin

Deep within the belly of the Antler's Reach clubhouse in the gated community of Red Hawk in Scottsdale, Arizona, George washed his face at one of the ten sparkling-clean sinks. An abundant selection of shaving lotions, mouthwash, disposable toothbrushes, toothpicks, toothpaste, cologne, and Q-tips lined the back of each sink. To many, this was the glory of retirement. A counter with endless options, a clubhouse full of golfers cleaning themselves up after eighteen holes so that they could sit around a table and shovel out the winnings from the day while arguing current events and trading golfer gossip.

George was one of the club's younger members, and certainly the new guy. The whole thing was a travesty, this life he was living, but at least he was trying.

More than two months ago, on that day in March when he'd swallowed those pills, it was Bianca's text that had saved him. Well, her text and also cramming his index finger down his throat.

Maybe the only thing that was getting him out of bed now was the Zoloft that Faith had talked him into when she'd swept in on a rescue mission a few days after his near-death experience.

In a moment of weakness, George had confessed the truth about his sudden onset of depression and how he'd come close to ending things. Despite her husband complaining about it, Faith had immediately flown in from Palm Springs. Was there a better ex-wife on earth? The last thing he'd said when he'd taken her back to the airport, after he thanked her for the hundredth time, was, "Promise me you won't tell Bianca. I'll get through this. I swear to God I will."

Faith had gripped him tight and kissed his mouth. "I know you will."

George cupped warm water in his hands and splashed it on his face. Looking in the mirror, he could almost see the young man he used to be. He shaved every morning because he had so much damn time to kill, so his face glistened. His walnut-brown hair had turned silver but was still thick and wavy. His tanned skin showed how much he'd been golfing lately, despite not enjoying it.

A guy two sinks down asked no one in particular, "D'you know some of the members—an anonymous group—are trying to push through a rule to keep us from driving the cart close to the green?"

"If they want to do something good for this club," another replied as he slid a razor down his face, "they need to stop booking so many damn tee times. That's why the greens are looking shabby."

George thought of the bottle of pills he kept in the medicine cabinet. Not the Zoloft. The other ones. He was not meant for this life. But here he was, trying, and trying was his big win every day. It's what had kept him alive the last two months.

Joining his foursome at a table by the window that overlooked the driving range, he slipped into his seat and poured a handful of trail mix into his hand. A Michelob Light waited for him.

"Throw down twenty, Georgie boy," said one of them.

George polished off the nuts, drew out his wallet, and coughed up the cash. Not a word said.

"Maybe it's time you get some lessons," another offered. "Quit hacking at it, let the club follow through."

"I'll let you know if I need any advice," George replied, letting his leg bounce under the table. He'd be fine if he never swung another club. What in the ever-living hell had he been thinking, moving here?

Unable to take it another minute, he excused himself and scurried for the closest exit.

George had been emailing with the folks at Intel, mentioning that he'd be happy to keep contributing if there were any opportunities—perhaps consulting—but the microchip world had changed, and his expertise was now considered overpriced and dated. He'd fallen into management during the rise of AI chips and had lost his grip on the new technology. The young bucks understood tech in a way that made him constantly scratch his head. What could he even offer now?

Faith kept suggesting ideas to pass the time. Chess. Volunteering. "George, you're not the kind of person that can sit around."

If she only knew how much he agreed.

"Why don't you pick up a musical instrument?" she'd suggested last week. They made better friends than lovers, and they'd been speaking on the phone even more lately.

"What the heck am I going to do with an instrument?"

"Play music! You always liked the saxophone. Or the ukulele? There's an adorable group of retirees here who play at the farmers' market. Bet you could find—"

"Faith. Please stop." A horrid vision of himself playing the ukulele flashed before him. "You're going to give me nightmares."

"It's not golf," she kept on. "We both know that. I bet you could find a pretty woman in a baking class. Or build a boat!"

"In the desert?"

She wasn't the only one who made these kinds of suggestions. Bianca did the same thing when she called him from Bologna—the city that she'd moved to on a silly whim. They had a call set up for tomorrow, which would indeed be the highlight of his day.

George was happy that Faith was enjoying life, even if it hurt sometimes, a reminder of how he'd let her slip away. And he was glad that his daughter was successful and happy too—no thanks to him. Maybe the one thing he had passed on to her was his work ethic.

If only she hadn't screwed up and moved to Italy. He was still scratching his head over that one. Apparently, she went there to "find herself," whatever the hell that meant.

He drove his golf cart back home, a place on the sixteenth green. Not for the first time, he wondered what it would be like to close that garage door, stuff a rag into the muffler of the tailpipe, and go to sleep in the front seat.

The funny thing was that his HVAC person had found mold in his air vents, so he was slowly dying by simply breathing, but it wasn't fast enough to quell the pain of retirement.

Sixty-five was way too early to stop working. He would have kept going another fifteen years easy, had they let him, but Intel was scrambling to keep up in the industry, and the last thing they needed was an old codger like him. When it came to pleasing the board and shareholders, old men like him were easy pawns.

George poured himself a Scotch and sat down on the couch in front of the big television. He didn't know what to watch. The news made his head hurt, and he didn't have the patience for movies.

Noticing some movement out the window, he leaped from his chair with a curse. "Not today, you son of a bitch." He raced to the door, nearly tearing it off the hinges as he pulled it open and grabbed the rake he kept within reach. His archnemesis, an evil squirrel he'd named Mr. Nutz, sat perched on the feeder, munching on the birdseed that George had put out earlier that morning. The little devil had been taunting him for a week now.

"Get the hell out of here," he said through gritted teeth, scurrying toward his target with a focused determination.

The tree rat paused, looked over, possibly gave a wink, then went back to his meal.

As George drew near, he yelled and raised the rake like a baseball bat. Before he could get him, the squirrel leaped onto the grass. George swung at him, but the little bastard was too fast and moved a few feet away. The tines of the rake slashed into the earth.

The damn thing winked at him again, and George tightened. "You're messing with the wrong guy. I've got *nothing* but time."

The squirrel laughed, sounding like Rodney Dangerfield. At least, that's what George heard. He made a few more attempts to get the squirrel before it finally disappeared behind a row of cacti.

Back in his chair, George flipped through Netflix, unable to find anything interesting. Then he took a shower and ticked off some items on his to-do list, killing time till he made himself a chicken breast, baked potato, and steamed broccoli for dinner.

After more channel surfing, he decided he might as well go to sleep, so he could fast-forward to something that mattered in his life: Bianca. But he stared at the ceiling for a good two hours, concocting ways to design a better bird feeder. He'd draw up some blueprints tomorrow. When he finally drifted off, at God knows what time, Mr. Nutz visited him in his dreams, teasing him, laughing at him, popping seeds in his mouth with an evil eye.

But George woke with the eagerness of a child coming upon a toy store. Unfortunately, they'd made plans to talk at seven and it was only five. After coffee, he texted her to see if she was available earlier.

She FaceTimed him about twenty minutes later. It took him an unnerving couple of minutes to work through an audio issue, but she finally gave him a thumbs-up. One would think a man who'd been building microprocessors all his life could figure out the basics of online communication, but these simple tasks now eluded him.

"Hi, honey," he said, resting his forearms on the kitchen counter. It looked like she was sitting on her couch.

"You look handsome this morning," she said.

"I have a date with a squirrel."

"What?"

"Long story." Always, when these calls started, the first thing that hit him was how kind she was even after what he'd put her through, what with the constant work and then the divorce. *And* his tendency to offer up perhaps too much unsolicited advice.

"Tell me what's new? How's Boloney?"

Her playful annoyance with him showed through the screen; she looked like her mother. "Ba-lone-ya, not Boloney, Dad."

"You know, there was a time when you and your mother found my humor charming." He shrugged.

"And I still do."

"Yeah, yeah, yeah. So what's new?" He went after a smudge on the counter, rubbing it off with his finger.

When she'd texted him, mentioning that she'd found an apartment, it was hard not to hurt inside. His hope that she might return home after a couple of weeks died a painful death in his heart. She'd signed a one-year lease.

He buried his sadness when she told him how happy she was there, how she was finally able to find some quiet and reconnect with herself. Okay, he'd worked a bit too hard all his life, but she was now doing the opposite, not working at all. She needed to find that happy medium before it was too late. Of course he bit his tongue. Sometimes it felt like their relationship was on life support, and whenever he tried to drop a note in the suggestion box, it was like yanking the plug.

He forced even more enthusiasm when she told him about the book signing. Actually, that made him proud. "So are you writing another? Is that part of this taking-time-off thing?" He hoped for a yes . . . but . . .

"No," she said. "I told you. I'm not doing anything right now. Just seeing what the universe brings to me."

Dear heavens, all her talk about the universe. The universe this, the universe that. Accountability had died somewhere in the early aughts. Sparing her more advice, he reminded himself for the thousandth time that you can't teach kids everything; they have to learn some lessons the hard way.

"How about you?" his daughter asked him. "Mom says retirement's still hell."

"Nah, it's not that bad."

"Dad, it's me."

He tilted his head left and right, seeing a clear vision of his retirement party, all the people he'd worked with for so long cheering as he faced a cake with candles. But he no longer saw candles. He saw nails in a coffin.

"I suppose it's not all it's cracked up to be, honey. As you know, I'm not good at sitting around. Doesn't help that they've found mold in the air vents, so they have to tear up some walls. And I realized I hate golf more than life itself."

"And yet you bought a house on a golf course."

"What else was I supposed to do?" He held up his index finger. "But I am chasing down a squirrel that keeps eating all the birdseed."

She laughed, a genuine one. "There you go. You better not hurt him."

"I would if I could. He's a ninja, though. There's no catching him. Anyway, forget the squirrel. Tell me more about Boloney."

"No, no. I'm worried about you, Dad. Are there any charities you could—"

"B, I'll figure it out. Your mom's already given me enough 'talks.' No, I don't want to chase cougars in a baking class. Or join a chess club."

His daughter looked at him for a long time, pondering a solution. "Know that I'm here for you, okay? If you ever want to talk."

"I appreciate that." But no, it wasn't right for a daughter to help her father. Actually, he wished she'd invite him to come visit, give him a place to go while the mold was dealt with, but no way he would poison her Italian journey with his miserable self.

Two hours and two more cups of coffee later, he'd done thirty minutes on the elliptical machine, cleaned the house, folded his laundry, and scanned four newspapers on his iPad. What was he supposed to do now?

The same group of guys were about to tee off, but George couldn't bear another round.

Dammit, he missed Bianca. He hated that he hadn't soaked up every second of her childhood, every moment of their time together. All he wanted was a second chance . . . but he wouldn't dare ask to come see her. Besides, he hated to travel.

He pulled out his legal pad where he kept his to-do list. It was sadly short compared to what it used to be. He reviewed each item, scratching off what he'd already accomplished.

- *Fix window screen*
- *Call bank*
- *Buy BB Gun*
- *Make eye appointment*
- *Clean garage*
- *Bird feeder: equipment, wood, disc, cayenne pepper, Vaseline, guillotine blade, remote zapper, rotating baffles*
- *Grocery: yogurt, blueberries, burger stuff, chicken, green beans, red potatoes, lettuce, radishes, ice cream*
- *Bianca—7am tomorrow! (be early to prepare)*

Setting down the list, he shook his head, seeing those candles morphing to nails again. He had to get another job. He just had to. But who in the world hired hardware engineers in their midsixties? The world had passed him by. He couldn't even figure out FaceTime.

It was awful that dads couldn't talk to their daughters for real, that they couldn't ask for their help. Because Bianca had always proved to be so wise, and he loved what she had to say. He wanted to call her back and keep talking, maybe get some advice.

Maybe ask if he could come see her.

His eyes lifted to the sky as he pondered the idea, the tug of desperately wanting to but terrified that he'd screw it up.

That's when Mr. Nutz made his first appearance of the morning. The bastard. It was time to scramble the troops. One of them was going to die today.

George rushed through the door, nearly slipping on the mat. The tree rat was eating away, delighting in the birdseed as if it were caviar and champagne. The jealous and starving birds that were supposed to be enjoying their meal were nowhere to be found. The scoundrel did what he always did, casting a sideways glance and giving an insulting wink, before returning to his meal. Rake in hand, wishing he'd already bought the BB gun, he raced across the patio and into the rock garden.

Only at the very last minute did the squirrel dodge him. But he didn't go far, only inches farther up the feeder. George swung the rake and smacked it right into the feeder, knocking it off its post, the feed showering down. The squirrel narrowly escaped.

Landing on all fours on a rock, Mr. Nutz stared at George, waiting for his next move.

Up the hill, a group of men was teeing off on sixteen. Thankfully, they were looking the other way.

George approached slowly, raising the rake again. "I will bury you on this land," he warned. He came down hard with his weapon, missing the squirrel yet again. This happened several more times, until the squirrel sought refuge behind the grill on the patio.

When George pushed the grill away, the squirrel started toward the back door. George had left it open, and a potential future played in his head as he saw Mr. Nutz move in slow motion toward George's living room, scurrying under the couch and then getting lost somewhere in the house. No being would enter his domicile uninvited, so George squeezed tight on the rake and ran like no man in his midsixties had ever run before.

What was it, a hose, a crack in the sidewalk? A misstep?

George fell forward with tremendous speed as he raced to catch his archnemesis, and only a second before he smacked the ground, he saw the rake fall in front of him, the tines sticking up. His forearm crashed into it with incredible force, and the tines jabbed into his skin, instantly drawing blood as he yelped in pain.

Everything in his body hurt as he peeled himself off the ground to meet eyes with a giggling Mr. Nutz, who gave a belly laugh before disappearing into the house with a seed-eating grin.

"Hey, sorry to bother you again," George said to Bianca that afternoon after he'd returned from urgent care, where they'd given him a tetanus shot, disinfected the wounds, and bandaged him up. He kept his arm away from the camera so she wouldn't see it.

"I have something I want to ask you, and I wanted to . . . Could I . . . Do you have any room for your old man? I have to leave the house for about a month for this mold thing, and I was looking at extended stays, but maybe, I don't know . . ."

Silence. She didn't move an inch.

He hated that he'd asked her, especially how he'd fumbled it. He added even more clumsily, "And I'm missing you like crazy."

Dead. Silence.

"You there?"

"Absolutely, Dad. I'd love for you to come."

"Really?"

Another pause.

"Yes. You shouldn't be breathing that stuff for another minute."

"I don't want to be a bother."

She smiled. "You wouldn't be. I'd love it."

"You sure about that?"

She perked up, maybe faking it. "You've got nothing on my clients. Bring it on. And you know, I could use the company—and some fatherly sage advice, the wisdom wrought from your sixty-five years on this planet."

In his mind's eye, he saw hammers driving nails into coffins and rakes coming down on evil squirrels. And he saw flashes of Bianca when she was first born, her first word, her first steps. Then she was in middle school, exhibiting her mother's sassiness, then high school where he had to fight off suitors, and then she was crossing the graduation stage and moving her tassels from right to left, and then off to face the world.

"I know you're messing with me," he said.

"I'm not."

Tears pricked his eyes. She could never know how much he loved her. Forget the Zoloft. Bianca was the only thing keeping him alive.

After a long breath, he said, "You sure?"

He thought he detected something that looked like terror hiding behind a smile, but maybe that was his own fear mirroring back on him.

"One hundred percent," she finally said. "Italy will be good for you."

He didn't know about that, but seeing her, getting a chance to redeem himself, might be enough to keep him fighting another day.

Chapter 7

Without a Story to Tell

Harold stayed a safe distance behind, watching the couple stroll through serpentine alleys, dash across streets, hand in hand, sharing the occasional kiss under the shade of a portico. May had brought with it the first tastes of what he imagined to be a Bolognese summer: hot days, tourists in shorts bumping into each other, lines to churches and museums extending out into the streets.

He'd been following the couple for a week now—not as a stalker, but more as a concerned citizen, a man looking out for his former lover—and he saw no signs of decay yet, no cracks in the foundation of Alice's relationship with this man known as Renzo. It wasn't love, though. He knew that. The guy was way too old for her. She'd been deceived.

The couple stopped into Il Gelatauro, a busy gelato shop near the university, where scents of fresh waffle cones and vanilla and summer berries wafted out onto the street. Harold hid behind a column to watch them. They each tried a sample, giggling, sharing the same spoon. A pang burned in Harold's chest.

After Renzo paid, the couple stood outside the entrance to enjoy their dessert. Two spoons and one cup, exchanging saliva, Renzo stealing kisses, as they delighted in a scoop of *stracciatella*. Harold cringed when they took a moment in between bites to have a sword fight with their spoons.

Renzo was no doubt an ex-lover's worst nightmare, not too far off from the image Harold had painted in his head while he played the heartbroken vampire trapped in his castle post–Alice's departure.

After a week's worth of reconnaissance, Harold had determined that Alice's new lover was an architect. Likely about thirty years old. He dressed like he was off to a magazine shoot, a far cry from Harold's normal attire: tennis shoes, jeans, and one of his various polo shirts.

Compare that to Renzo up ahead, holding Alice's hand. He wore dark slacks paired with freshly polished leather shoes and a crisp lavender shirt. It was always a similar outfit, always exceptional. Harold's snooping (remember: concerned citizen) had also revealed that Renzo went to the gym five days a week before work, most often running on the treadmill, but sometimes he'd opt for the exercise bike.

Harold hadn't spoken to Alice once since The Great Abandonment. She'd left him a note with contact information for the landlord, who was happy to allow Harold to take over the lease. It was a surprising amount of money, and Harold considered finding a place that was less of a rip-off, but it would have been a blatant retreat from battle. He had to hold his ground, so the place was his now, no matter what it took. Thank God for Mom!

Had Harold been in better shape emotionally, he might have snuck up ahead and pretended to run into them. "Hey, what's up, guys? Yeah, was out for my afternoon run. Training for a marathon in Rome later in the summer. Did seventeen yesterday." He might have even said, "You two look so good together. I hope you're so happy, Alice."

If he'd been more together, Harold might have even realized he'd left the protection of the column and was now gawking at them from the middle of the street!

He wasn't aware of his exposed position until he heard Alice's voice. "Harold? What are you doing?"

Harold woke from his stupor like he'd been dunked into an ice bath. Scrambling to collect himself, he wondered if he had any chance of escape. Maybe she was saying his name but not actually sure it was him. He eased backward toward the column he'd been hiding behind earlier, as he considered his options. No, he had to face them. It was time to meet his enemy.

She called his name again.

Tapping into what little confidence he had left, he finally looked in their direction, finding the two lovers staring at him in bewilderment.

Even from thirty feet away, Harold could see their gelato mustaches. He wished he could have laughed at the absurdity of the situation, despite him being the butt of it, but *nothing* about it was fucking funny.

In fact, knowing he'd been busted and knowing he'd have to engage with both of them made him slip into tunnel vision, his body disconnected from his mind.

It took all he had to say, "Oh, h-h-hi, guys!" He trudged toward them, lifting his hand to wave, but he could barely feel his arm, as if it weren't his.

"How are you?" Alice asked, wrapping one arm around him and offering a cheek.

Harold hadn't figured out the European dual kiss and bumbled it mightily.

With her smell of strawberries and cream lingering in his nose, he said to himself: *This is your chance, Harold. Pull it together!*

Then out came words. "I'm quite nice, thank you. Out f-f-for a stroll. Well, running a marathon. Training for a . . ." He had to take a breath and only then realized he was speaking in an English accent. He could pass out at any moment.

"Meet Renzo, my . . ." She paused, not finishing her sentence. "Renzo, this is Harold."

Renzo moved the cup of gelato to his left hand, then offered his right. "*Piacere di conoscerti,* Aroldo. Good to meet you."

Had he just called him Aroldo? Also, never had Harold wanted to be fluent more than now. How wonderful might it have been to spit back some witty Italian.

Instead, as Harold accepted Enzo's shake with a clammy hand, he looked away. Weak eyes seeking an escape from having to engage with the enemy. (In the years that would follow, no moment would haunt him more.)

"How's . . . how's it going?" The stutter of his youth was killing him now. Harold wasn't a religious guy but whispered a prayer in his head anyway. *Please God, save me.*

He attempted to form a sentence but kept thinking that he'd lost her to this . . . to this Italian God in a lavender shirt that looked like its own flavor of gelato. And the way the dark skin of his handsome face glowed in the sunshine. His appeal was arresting. Never had Harold felt more inferior.

Alice's mouth was moving, but he couldn't make the words out. How long had they been standing there?

He wanted to run. Or he wanted to go down on his knees and start crying. This was awful. The panic attack took on a second wave, dizziness tugging him toward collapse.

The next thing he knew, Renzo was guiding him to a seat and offering him a bottle of water from his man bag. *"Prendi un po' d'acqua, ragazzo."* He had a gentle touch and a calming voice with a sort of maternal softness. Wanting to be held, Harold nearly pulled the man into a hug before catching himself.

More mouths moving. Harold took a long sip while Renzo patted his back. He was no stranger to panic attacks, as he'd been having them ever since he was a kid, his first one being when his father had shut him in the trunk of his car as an unfunny joke.

Harold drew in deep breaths, wishing that he could disappear. He'd trade death for this moment.

When he finally came back to reality, deep breath after *deep* breath, Harold looked around. Passersby had stopped to watch. Water dribbled down his chin. Alice and Renzo flanked him and were both rubbing his back and talking sweetly to him.

"You okay?" Alice asked.

He could finally understand her. "Yeah, I'm . . ." He almost said that he'd been training too hard for the marathon but bit his tongue. He had to get out of there.

"Here, have some more water," she said, dangling the bottle near his mouth.

"I'm sorry. I have to go." He pushed up, avoiding further eye contact, then mumbled something about having been ill and backed away, his feet wobbly under him. He nearly tripped on the curb as he started down the sidewalk.

A glance back.

Renzo and Alice watched with sympathetic eyes.

Rounding the corner and getting away was like plugging into an oxygen tank, and he was finally able to breathe normally again, to think normally again. He stumbled through the piazza and then picked up to a run, lefts and rights toward the apartment, one step after another, faster and faster, his chest heaving.

Unable to run any farther, he came to a halt, desperate for air. He now knew exactly what his custom-designed version of hell would be. Desperate to find some privacy, he snuck down a quiet alley and then cupped his hands to his face. With shame and heartache and disappointment oozing over him like toxic sludge, he began to cry.

Why did he have to be him? Why did he have to be born? Why couldn't he be better? Why had his stupid fucking weak body betrayed him? He cried and cried and cried, letting it all out, not caring if anyone was watching. That was it, his one chance to prove that he was worthy of her, that he could stand up against any man, including Renzo. He'd blown the ever-living shit out of the opportunity. Never would she want to return to such a weak example of a human, a faulty product on the production line that should have been thrown into the trash.

When he had no more tears to shed, he wiped his eyes and headed back toward the apartment. Back on Via Giulia, he was beelining it through the scaffolding to the entrance of the apartment when he heard a timid English accent say, "Excuse me?"

Harold turned. "Yes?" He had nothing left to give, no fight in him, no energy.

It was one of the women from the bookstore. She looked a couple of years older than him, short hair, crooked glasses.

"I'm . . . We've never actually met, but I'm Moira. I work here."

He touched his chest. "Harold." It was like he'd been about to parachute out of a plane into hostile territory, but someone had stopped him to chat about the Bologna football team.

She held a stack of flyers in her hand. "I wanted to make sure you knew about our book signing. We have a celebrity that moved onto the street, a self-help writer named Bianca Briggs," she elaborated. And then: "Do you know her book?"

"No, I don't think so." Did he look like he read self-help books? Could she not see that he was right in the middle of fighting the biggest war of his life?

"I'd love it if you and Alice came. She's always been such a great supporter of the store. For what it's worth, this book is life-changing."

He might have run away from her, but she had a sweet and timid voice and held herself in such a way that made him think she might be fragile. And he knew fragile.

"Life-changing, huh?" he said, wishing no one in the world had to ever know what it was like to be fragile.

She nodded, then seemed to retreat into herself. In a moment of lunacy, he said, "Yeah, I'll come." He figured he could always bow out later. Anything to escape right now without hurting her feelings.

Moira looked like Harold had handed her a hundred bucks. "Really? It's just . . . I don't want to let Bianca down. And my boss, Sandy, she hates doing these things, and I want to prove to her that it's worth it. I love having authors visit."

Harold locked eyes with her and said the thing he wanted to say least. "I'll definitely be there."

If everything that Bianca had missed out on while laboring away in Austin could be captured in a moment, it was now, as she sat at a long table on Carol's terrace, taking in one of the finest views in Europe, the ancient city lit up and shining, the two towers and the dome of San Petronio poking up from a sea of red terra-cotta roofs, the swollen earth of the Apennine hills surrounding them, the full moon lifting up over the horizon, dizzying in its grandeur.

And there at the table, twelve fascinating souls, people from all over the world—New Zealand, South Korea, Sweden, Canada, Germany, Egypt. The simple act of sitting there listening to the dynamic conversation, which was mostly held in English, was enough to make Bianca cry—for so many reasons, so many emotions. Longing to have lived their lives, recalling how she used to be one of them.

As the wine flowed and cigarettes burned, and as Carol's husband brought out dishes that were so simple but had taken generations to perfect, they talked about the nasty corruption in Montenegro, and about their favorite beaches in Corfu, the best *chiringuitos* in Estepona, their day trips to Naples to taste a pizza on Via dei Tribunali, ski trips to Chamonix, their cheap jaunts to Ireland or Iceland on Ryanair. They didn't talk about work—certainly didn't define themselves by it. They talked about their adventures, about the things they'd seen and heard and felt.

These expats were open-minded soul searchers who wanted—no, *needed*—to see and live in different parts of the world so that they might understand it. People who found joy in watching the sun set over new horizons, in meeting people so very different from themselves; wanderers who refused to be pulled into the trance of the unliving, refused to be shepherded into the flock of humans who were too afraid to take chances, too afraid to not fall into line.

Then there was Bianca, who'd missed a turn along the way and lost connection with her thirsty soul, and who had become exactly the person she'd promised herself—and Corrado—she wouldn't be.

As these interesting creatures shared tales of their escapades, Bianca recalled her own wanderlust, when she'd first landed in Bologna with nothing but a big backpack, when she'd taken trips by train or plane with Carol or other friends to Copenhagen, Munich, Dublin, Nice, Madrid, Valencia. Bunking up with strangers in youth hostels, making fast friends, messing around with boys from foreign lands, learning what it meant to have an open mind.

There wasn't anything wrong with work, of course. There were people at the table who led companies, either here in Bologna or abroad, but they hadn't let their occupations consume them like she had. To think she'd prided herself in Austin on being the hardest worker in the room, barely making time for vacations. It was a sad fact that in the ten years since she'd left Bologna, she'd barely traveled at all, and when she did, it was more of a brief escape to Mexico or Hawaii, a chance to sit by the pool and finally read a book. There was certainly no adventure to it, no craving of the unseen.

When these masters of life asked her about her own, she dismissed the question as best as she could, muttering how she'd left her practice in Austin and was trying to figure out her next step. Though Carol bragged that Bianca had written a book, she dismissed that, too, certainly not telling them about the signing.

And don't even get her started on Peggy Meh.

Dumb.

Dumb.

Dumb.

Upon leaving, amid the nearly debilitating voices in her head, she told herself that it wasn't too late, that she could still be one of them, that maybe she'd had to go the wrong way to finally make it here now.

Sandy slid the olive off the spear with her teeth as she took in the younger man sitting across from her. What she saw worried her. Salvatore was handsome in the way creatives were, attire slightly off center, hair that had a mind of its own, and soulful eyes. The problem was that those eyes could be too penetrating at times, like they were now.

They sat at a tall table in an old haunt of Bologna, a trattoria that had been around since Dante strolled these streets. She had a sense that ghosts lived within these walls, sharing the tables and dance floor with the current patrons, returning to the place they'd liked most. Besides the fact she loved coming here, it was an easy place to remain anonymous, a long walk from Via Giulia and the bookstore.

The couple's knees touched. Sandy's heels made her feet uncomfortable, but damn, they looked good. His foot bounced to the sound of the bebop dancing out of speakers perched on a shelf otherwise reserved for liquor bottles. Unmatching chandeliers cast down a golden light.

Sandy glanced at herself in one of the many antique mirrors. She wasn't old enough to be his mother, thank God. And being with a younger man somehow drew out her youth. He'd never asked, but she'd indicated that she was in her forties, not her true fifties, and sometimes she actually believed the lie.

Salvatore was a jazz guitarist that she'd met at Cantina Bentivoglio, the best spot to listen to live jazz in town. A few months ago, he'd slid a chair up to her table moments before his set and made easy conversation. He'd asked her to stick around till he was done, and then he'd strapped on his archtop guitar and torn a hole in the fabric of the night with his magnificent talent. She'd thought for a moment about playing hard to get, but he'd eyed her from the stage, and later, when he'd invited her back to his place, she'd taken his hand.

She'd started sleeping with younger men years ago. They seemed to gravitate toward her, while at the same time, anyone her age and older somehow knew to keep their distance. It was marvelous, as these younger fellows were far easier to deal with. They weren't looking for anything serious—at least, not most of them.

Salvatore had been living in Bologna a couple of years but performed across Europe in various jazz groups. It was a joy waking in his place in the morning (she kept her apartment off-limits) and hearing him practice a tune in the other room. He was especially perfect because he was on the road so much. They could enjoy a passionate night together, rattling the walls, then break apart for a few weeks. It worked well, because by the time he contacted her again, her fervorous craving for him had returned to boiling.

The only problem was that Sandy had detected a shift in his behavior. He was texting her more from the road and seeking her out the moment he got back into town. Now here they were, together for the first time in a couple of weeks, and he was looking at her differently, something past sexual craving. She'd been around the block long enough to know what was going on.

"What's on your mind?" she asked, wishing she hadn't accepted his invitation. She sipped on her G&T and waited.

"So . . ."

Here it comes, she thought, readying herself for battle. They could as easily speak in Italian, but he liked to practice his English with her.

She set down her glass. "No, don't do it."

"Don't do what?" Salvatore smirked, ignorant of the stop sign ahead.

"I don't like how you're looking at me," Sandy said, feeling her attraction for him die.

"How am I looking at you?"

"Like you want something."

"I do. Naturally. I haven't seen you in a while. I can barely sit here without wanting more."

Wanting more. There it was.

He reached for her hand, and all she felt was a cold dead thing. "I know we drew boundaries, but I like you, Sandy. I want more from us. I want to see your place, see your bookstore. I almost came by the other day."

She jerked her hand back. "Do not do that."

"*Perché no?* What are you afraid of?" Frustration wrinkled his brow.

Sandy peeled open her hands. "I'm not looking for anything serious. Simple as that. I told you that from the beginning."

"You can't deny we have a very special relationship."

Sandy shifted her feet. She hated when this happened. *"Mi dispiace. Non cerco altro."* I'm not looking for anything more.

"What is that about? Why do you have to be a mystery?"

Sandy reached for her purse and counted out twenty euros, set them on the table.

"That's pitiful, you know. Sad," he said.

She looked at him one last time, then: "Please don't come to the bookstore. I was honest with you from the beginning. *Arrivederci.*"

Sandy's apartment was across the street and fifty meters down from the bookstore. Not one person, aside from her son, Jack, and the electrician and plumber, had entered in the ten years she'd lived there. When she'd moved in, she'd thought it would be so nice to have such a short commute. Now, she wasn't so sure.

She flicked on the light, kicked off her heels, and slung her purse onto a chair. "Nicolo, *sono a casa.*"

Her mixed-breed cat, what the Brits called a moggy, came racing down the hallway, a flash of gray. He weaved around her legs, and she knelt down to run her hand through his fur. "You're my true love," she said in Italian. "There's no room for anyone else."

Nicolo's purr was the sweetest sound in the world, even better than the morning ballads Salvatore played.

"Are you hungry?" Sandy went into the kitchen to prepare his meal. As always, she mixed dry and wet, then shaved some cave-aged Parmigiano-Reggiano on top. Only the best for Nicolo.

While the prince enjoyed his meal, Sandy poured herself a glass of pignoletto and went out onto her terrace. A half-moon glistened in the night sky, and down here in her little part of the world, Via Giulia glowed under the warm streetlights. If she squinted and ignored the scaffolding blocking her bookstore across the street, she might even admit that life was okay. Nicolo and Sandy forever.

There had been such wonderful energy inhabiting the store at one time. She could see herself standing next to Jack, coming alive for the first time in forever. He'd been so encouraging, agreeing with her that the bookstore idea was a great one and that they'd found the perfect location.

It really had been wonderful for a while, the bookstore. Till it wasn't.

If Bianca's slogan was "Leave burn marks," then Sandy's was "Till it wasn't." Moira could tattoo that one to her other arm.

A copy of *An Echo in the Bone*, the seventh in the *Outlander* series, called out to her from the small table next to her. Maybe she'd jump back in, but her mind was a mess.

God, Moira would *love* to know that Sandy had broken down and cracked open the first book in the series about two months ago. Sandy had gotten tired of everyone raving about it and had been curious why such drivel had captured readers everywhere. Okay, it wasn't drivel. That Diana Gabaldon was a storyteller, plain and simple, and if Sandy had been forced by threat of waterboarding, she'd admit that she might have recently fallen back in love with reading because of these stupid books. And no, they weren't romance, Moira; they were so much more than that.

Either way, Sandy still didn't believe in romantic love—not the kind that lasted. Sure, it was nice to enjoy a fictional love story, to imagine that kind of thing might be possible. But Sandy had tried and failed too many times to ever give love another proper go. That was fine, though. Casual flings could be just as enjoyable, like eating the frosting off the top, then discarding the rest of the cupcake.

Why did Salvatore have to do that, want to take their relationship up a notch? He'd been a good one, a good lover.

Nicolo popped up on her lap. She petted him as she thought of all the lovers who wouldn't escape so cleanly tonight. They'd eventually learn. In truth, Salvatore owed her a thank-you. She'd just saved his little heart from one day shattering.

The endings weren't always as ugly as what she'd experienced with her two marriages, but what she knew with all of her heart was that endings always came, and they were never pretty.

She took a long sip, set down her glass next to the book, and nestled into the chair. Gazing up into a sky streaked with clouds, she accidentally let herself think back to the two men who'd turned her into the hard-edged, distrusting pessimist she'd become.

Husband #1, the world-class tight end for the Tampa Bay Buccaneers who'd impregnated her with Jack at age twenty-two, had about killed her. Thank God, Jack had been young and couldn't remember much of it. Once he was finally old enough to understand, she'd had to beg her son not to seek revenge.

Sandy had met Will at a nightclub in Ybor City, a lively Tampa neighborhood where one could dance late into the night. That's exactly what they did, this huge hunk of a man who could move with the grace of a ballerina wrapping his big arms around her. Will had been so sweet during their courtship, and he'd been beyond charming at their huge wedding at the Ringling in Sarasota. Such a romantic on their honeymoon in Saint Lucia, where they'd conceived Jack. She'd only just started her career as an English teacher, but Will had talked her into retiring so she could focus on raising Jack and follow Will around the country during the NFL season.

Then, out of nowhere, Will had started showing signs of a temper that she'd never seen before—well, at least not off the football field. She couldn't pinpoint the change (was it a particular hit during a game?), but it was around the time Jack took his first steps. He'd start screaming at her, often over the smallest of things. When he hit her the first time, it hadn't occurred to her that he'd crossed a line. The emotional abuse had been growing so steadily that the natural progression to violence hadn't even surprised her.

She should have left him a thousand times, but that's the moment that should have been the point of no return, when his club of a hand struck her face, knocking her to the floor. Instead, she let him do what he always did: beg for forgiveness. He picked her up and stroked her hair and told her he didn't know what had come over him and that it would never happen again. And it wouldn't for a while. He'd return to being as charming as when they'd first met. But eventually, the monster reemerged.

She'd eventually learned that he was likely suffering from chronic traumatic encephalopathy, a brain disease caused by getting hit too many times. The last time he struck her was in the hallway of a hotel in Atlanta, several hours before his game against the Falcons. There'd been several witnesses who went on to testify against him in an unbearably public trial.

How mortifying it had been to be gossiped about on the news, everyone knowing that she was nothing more than a woman who stuck around for domestic abuse. She'd stupidly signed an airtight prenup, and despite him going to jail, the only money she was awarded by the judge was monthly child support. Thankfully, it was enough to get by without working, because she barely had the energy to raise Jack, let alone find another teaching job.

Five years after the divorce, Husband #2, the real estate agent, had swept in and rescued her from a potentially loveless life. Howie was the gentlest soul in the world, always mindful of what she'd been through. He took his time getting to know her, learning how to love her. After six months of dating, she'd decided it was time for him to meet Jack. Howie embraced him as if he were his biological father, and that's when Sandy knew it was time to give marriage a second try.

It might have worked out if Howie hadn't fallen in lust with their housekeeper, a twenty-year-old Cuban girl named Alena who had dreams of one day winning *American Idol.* Nine years into their marriage, shortly after Jack had first been deployed, Howie came home with Alena's perfume clinging to him. The hardened Sandy didn't have an ounce of forgiveness left in her heart and filed for a divorce the next morning.

Not long after, Jack had taken leave and helped Sandy move to Bologna, the city she'd fallen in love with while studying here during her teenage years. Once again, she found herself begging her powerhouse marine son not to seek revenge against her poor choice of a husband, the man who'd raised him from age ten.

It was Jack who'd named the bookstore. They'd walked through the city, looking at different properties, and when they'd found her dream location, the one down below, she'd said, "It'll be the only English bookstore in Bologna, that's for sure."

Muscles pushed out from his tight T-shirt. His head was shaved. A dog tag hung from his neck. "That's what you should call it, Mom. What could be better?"

Till it wasn't.

Chapter 8

Well-Intentioned Cupids

Bianca couldn't believe Carol had done it, told Corrado she'd moved to town and given him her number. She'd seen Carol and company a couple of more times, taken her yoga class, met more of her expat friends from all over the world, joining them at big tables over exquisite food and wine for hours, a cluster of nomadic outcasts finding union together. And Bianca had meandered through museums and stared at world-class paintings, finding new elements in the art, finding pieces of herself placed like hidden messages somewhere on the canvases of the great masters.

Forcing herself to break away from achieving goals and playing games where only the ending mattered, Bianca chased the joy of being an explorer, a nomad, a wanderer; she found new streets, new museums and churches and parks, new paths that led out of the city, where she could breathe the fresh air of the Apennine hills and let nature soothe her soul.

Somewhere in all this, Carol must have decided that she needed to play Cupid.

Bianca and Corrado had only caught up for a minute on the phone when he'd invited her to coffee. She'd suggested Le Briciole di Via

Giulia, the *pasticceria* down the block. Now that he was back in town, there was no way to avoid an encounter.

So here she was, a few minutes early, standing awkwardly off to the side, unsure whether she should go ahead and get a table or wait for him. So many Italians liked to take their coffee standing up.

Le Briciole looked like it hadn't changed in fifty years, still stuck in black and white. Of course, that was the charm. The bar and a display case full of exquisite pastries and sandwiches lined the right side of the long and skinny space. A series of tables were tucked up against a wall plastered in dated floral wallpaper. An ash-haired *nonna* shuffled in and out of the kitchen, restocking her quickly depleting goods. Two men with tightly cropped, dark hair wore aprons over their pressed white shirts and moved with impressive precision from the espresso machine to the display case to the cash register, doing a decent job of whittling down the ever-present line.

Bianca had spent entirely too much time trying on outfits, finally settling on newly acquired leopard-print pointed flats and a flowy black dress that was as flattering as something could be right now.

Corrado was right on time, and he hadn't changed much at all, still the same strapping guy who'd cast a spell on her a decade ago. Standing a few inches over six feet, he wore dark jeans and a tight white T-shirt that could easily set a girl's mind to sizzle. He'd bulked up some, too, his biceps stretching his short sleeves. She also noticed a tattoo running down the length of one arm. A butcher's knife maybe.

"Queen Bee," he said in a thick Italian accent as he approached her. *"È passato tropo tempo."* It's been too long. His voice catapulted her back through the years.

Bianca held strong as he came in for two kisses, taking his time, possibly even sniffing her like a flower as their cheeks touched. An organic woody scent rose like a gift to her nose, and she had to take a moment to recalibrate and remind herself to be careful.

"You look angelic as always," he said, staying close enough to kiss her again.

"Angelic?" she said skeptically, refusing to fall prey to his games. His charm required a shield, or a can of pepper spray.

His shaggy hair was all over the place. A faint scar ran north of his left eyebrow. Sharp cheekbones brought attention to his arresting cobalt-blue eyes. His shadow of a beard enhanced his ruggedness, a quality that Bianca had always loved. He wasn't the kind of guy that shied away from a bar fight.

"I thought you were in Paris," she said, inching backward.

"Yeah, well, I was, but it was time to come home. And you? You're here for good?"

It was indeed a chef's knife running up his toned arm. She met those daring blue eyes that had once captured her heart. They were warm and kind and dangerous—the eyes of a protector.

"I have no idea. I'm testing the waters."

"I see." He extended his arm. "Shall we?"

They stood at the bar and caught up as they shared a croissant with raisins and crème and drank cappuccinos that came with a small shot of sparkling water. Bianca couldn't believe how easy it was to talk with him, as if those ten years of absence didn't exist. They made trivial conversation for a while till he bored into what she'd done since they'd last seen each other—college and grad school, then her practice. She didn't mention the book, and he didn't ask. Apparently, he hadn't been following her that closely.

"Are you seeing anyone?" he queried after a while, slipping the question in like a penknife into her belly.

"I'm not even done with my cappuccino yet, and you're getting personal."

He shrugged it off. "I'm sorry. Should we ease into it, as you Americans do? You know how the *Romagnoli* are; we cut to the chase."

She remembered loving when he used American slang. Like so many over here, he'd perfected his English watching American television and movies.

"No, it's okay. I like being real. And no, I'm not seeing anyone. Focusing on myself for a while."

"Always so cerebral. I loved that about you. Trying to find yourself." He pretended to look around, behind the counter, up on the ceiling, down to the floor. "Where is the lovely Queen Bee hiding? Has anyone seen her?"

Her laugh felt like first blood had been drawn. Damn him.

He stared and stared and stared, meanwhile she told herself, *Don't fucking do it, B. Hold strong. Don't let him see how much of a mess you are.*

"How about you? Married and kids and opening a restaurant?" Even as she asked it, she scolded herself for continuing the thread of personal entanglements.

His lips simmered into a smile. "Yes to the last. The restaurant is my child, you know. No girl. Not anymore. I'm . . ." He looked to the ceiling. "Still searching." He went back to exaggerated looking around, over Bianca's shoulder, out the window, to the display case of chocolates. "Where is this woman God has promised me? Hello, hello? Soulmate, where are you?"

Though she felt a flutter in her heart, she refused to laugh again, reminding herself of his extraordinary ability to make every girl feel that way. She used to fight them off back in the old days.

She broke a piece of the croissant off and stuck it in her mouth with a moan. "I missed this."

He chuckled.

"What?" she asked.

"You appear out of nowhere. I've thought about you a lot."

"Yeah?"

He studied her mouth and only spoke after she'd finished chewing. "Yes, I admit it. Even thought of reaching out a few times, but what would be the point? It took me a long time to get over you, Bianca Briggs."

She thought she better drop an ice cube into the sparkling water before it went to boiling. "Enough about me. I'm assuming you went to culinary school, then Paris. Carol says you're going after a Michelin star?"

He laughed, clearly because he knew she was avoiding his confession. And he allowed it. He caught her up on his past, including a bad breakup with a website developer, then added, "And that's right, a new restaurant opening in six weeks. A few blocks from here, a great space."

"I still remember your scrambled eggs," she said.

"I make them even better now," he said, the corners of his mouth flickering. "Butter and eggs in the pan before I even turn on the stove. Then low, low heat. You have to be so gentle."

"No," Bianca said, shaking her head at him. They were right back where they'd left off. "Don't even try."

"What? I didn't even say anything." His evident joy was maddening.

"Look, it's so good to see you, but I'm not looking for anything right now."

His eyebrows crinkled. "What are you doing tomorrow night?"

"What did I say? My God, you're confident. Seriously, I'm . . . the last thing I'm looking for is a relationship." On top of her father coming? Get out of here.

"Why put labels on it? I want to see you again. We could go to church if you like. Or a museum."

"Right. A harmless museum."

"Exactly. We could go see the Michelangelo eagle, the one you liked so much."

"How do you remember that?"

He tapped his head. "I remember a lot about you. You broke my heart."

What felt like an hour passed, neither of them blinking.

"No," Bianca finally said. "Don't try to charm me. Actually, my dad's coming in tomorrow morning from Arizona, so I need to give him my full attention. He's not doing very well."

"I'm sorry, is he sick?"

"No, worse. At least for him. He's retired, and it's crushing him."

"If I can be of service, let me know."

"Thanks. The issue is that he's always trying to fix things, so I can only imagine how much worse it's gotten. I suspect I'll be ripe for fixing, as far as he's concerned."

"At least he cares."

"Yeah, I guess so."

They danced around the topic for a bit, then Corrado said, "By the way, where can I find your book? I'd love to read it."

He *did* know she was a writer, which meant he'd been keeping tabs on her. A flush of delight ran through her.

But then he added, "Carol told me."

Guess not.

Bianca instantly blushed, mortified by what he was doing to her. "It's probably not your type of book; a female-focused self-help thing. You're not exactly the target audience. I mean, I could give you one if you really—"

"I would. I want to jump into the head of my old friend Bianca. See what she's done with her life. *From Meh to Megawatt*, right? Does this mean you are now supercharged?"

She gave him the eye. "Don't pick on me."

"I think it's wonderful, my supercharged American pal."

She blushed, hating the idea of being supercharged when it came from his mouth. "Now you're not allowed to read it."

He inclined his shoulders. "Fine, then. I'll have to find another way to supercharge myself. Are you working on another one?"

"No!" she said. "I don't know what I'm doing right now, but definitely not writing another book." Bianca wished Peggy Meh had never been born.

"Sounds like you and your father are in the same boat," Corrado said, moving closer to her. "Two people seeking new identities."

She shrugged. She hadn't exactly thought about it that way, but Corrado was right.

"Well," he said, glancing at their empty cups and plate, "you know where to find me. Let's get you out of here so you can go on with your searching." He placed a couple of euros on the bar and led her out for an awkward goodbye.

A block down, she texted Carol: I can't believe you.

"Deep breaths," George said as he walked through the airport gangway in Bologna four days after inviting himself. He'd barely slept and was running on caffeine from the bad coffee on the plane.

It had been more than a year since he'd seen Bianca. He'd flown into Austin for a weekend, visited the Continental Club with her and a boyfriend who'd only lasted a few months. Thank God. He was a finance guy that was far too into himself. George and Bianca had done a few touristy things, then he'd gotten out of there before he drove her mad.

He might not make it to baggage claim if he didn't pull it together. Wouldn't that be a way to go, a heart attack on the escalator. God, the hospital in Bologna was probably decades behind an American one.

Heart attack or not, he was hurting and worn down. He'd sat upright throughout the night, hoping the Benadryl would kick in while absorbing the awful smells of the other passengers and being jolted by turbulence and unruly food carts.

He wasn't much of a traveler and had only left the country a few times, all of the trips forced on him by Bianca and her mother. In this moment, he knew exactly why he preferred to stay at home.

Then he found her, her arms open wide. She wore a knee-length floral dress. A smile graced her face. It was a vision to behold, seeing his daughter so joyful, and all the shit that was wrong with his world fell away, if only momentarily.

"There she is," he said, offering a genuine smile. But it was a smile painted on top of a depressed skeleton of a man, and he hoped she wouldn't see how badly life had broken him down. What was he thinking, though? She was a therapist because she'd always been able to see inside people. She'd know it in minutes.

"Hi, Dad." They held each other for a while.

"You look like . . . the best I've ever seen you. Someone's happy."

"I am." She pulled away to inspect him. "What's going on with your arm?"

"Oh, this? War with that squirrel I told you about." He touched the bandage wrapped around his forearm, wishing he'd worn long sleeves. "Yeah, he won."

Her eyebrows curled, so he elaborated, ending with, ". . . and while trying to keep him from getting into the house, I fell on a rake. Mr. Nutz 7, George 0."

She'd covered her mouth while listening to the story. As she pulled her hand away, she shook her head. "I'm not even sure what to say, but I'm glad you escaped with your life."

If she only knew what she was saying.

"And look at those shiny white tennis shoes. You're a regular Larry David."

George looked down at himself, the golf shirt tucked into khakis, his brand-new New Balances with their cushy soles.

"I'm so glad you're here," she said.

He wondered if that were true. "Thanks for letting me barge in."

His first test on Italian soil came moments later, when the baggage carousel quit working midway through delivering bags. They were forced to wait twenty more minutes as one guy—no, not a crew—*one* guy brought out two bags at a time. C'mon, Italy, you can do better.

But. *But!* George did not lose his cool. He wondered whether Bianca even noticed how patient he was, despite his lack of sleep and how he'd never seen a baggage carousel break back home. Some might have even called him a hero for being so easygoing. Okay, maybe that was an exaggeration, but he at least deserved a pat on the back.

They took a taxi back to her place, and George delighted in the excitement that radiated from her. He remembered visiting her here ten years ago, and she'd been the same, playing tour guide, bragging about this city that she'd discovered.

"That's the bookstore where I have the signing," she said as they reached her street, Via Giulia. "And that's my local wine bar and then the *pasticceria* where Corrado and I had breakfast yesterday. You remember him, right?"

George hated when his daughter talked about the men in her life—they'd never be good enough for her. Before the finance guy, there was a golf pro (far too obsessed with sports), a psychologist (too many therapists in one room), and some sort of AI entrepreneur (he'd been okay but never stopped talking about money). All of them unworthy.

"The kid you liked way back when?" he asked.

"Yeah, we had coffee, no big deal. He's a chef now, opening a fancy restaurant in the Hotel Minerva."

George hadn't meant to say *kid*. In the country an hour, and he'd already screwed things up. Not that she'd gotten hung up by it.

"And I connected with Carol; you remember her. I've started her yoga classes and hang out with her crew some. Mostly expats." She told him how they'd sit for hours, doing nothing but chatting, this big group of them. *Nothing but chatting?* George tried not to judge.

"Here I am," she said, swinging open the apartment door.

She needed his enthusiasm now more than ever, so putting true effort in, he forced his spirits to lift as she gave him the tour. "Oh, how wonderful," he said when she showed him the kitchen, which was disjointed and dusty. "Lovely!" he exclaimed when she pushed open the door to her large bedroom, an all-white affair, her laptop on the desk by the window; and "I love it!" he chirped in an even higher-pitched voice when she showed him the guest room.

Light spilled in from the two windows that looked out over Via Giulia below. Several thick pillows lay across the top of the queen bed. A bouquet of flowers sprang from a vase next to a gift basket overflowing with what looked like chocolate and some other snacks, hand lotion, and a couple of fancy bottled waters.

"You're too good to me," he said, a lifetime of guilt going after him like a snake in a sleeping bag.

She faced him, took his hands, and said, "I'm glad you're here. Let's figure out a way to shake these retirement blues."

Though it was a lot—the intimacy—George held eye contact. "You know me. Gotta find a new way to direct my energy."

She squeezed his hands. "Let's see what Italy does to that."

A yawn escaped his lips, and he turned away. All at once, the heaviness of the travel came at him.

"You must be exhausted," Bianca said. "The best thing to fight jet lag is to stay up. Can you make it to seven tonight?"

He ran a hand through his hair, doing math with his foggy head. It was around 9:00 a.m. now. "Phew, I don't know. I might close my eyes for a while. An hour or so."

"You'll regret it."

He inclined his shoulders. “I’m not in my thirties anymore. Give me an hour and a shower, and I’ll be great.” He shook his head and gave her a peck on the cheek, thanked her again.

Once she’d closed the door to his room, he climbed onto the bed, noting the cheap pillows and the firmness of the mattress and the unbearable fact that his feet hung off the edge. He might as well sleep on the floor. It was a good thing he’d booked a one-way trip. No idea how long he’d last. Still, being here with Bianca sure beat sitting alone in some sort of extended-stay situation while they cleaned up his HVAC system. But he had to make sure he didn’t bring any of his darkness into her life.

A few minutes after closing his eyes, he popped up and unzipped his bag. He moved everything to its rightful place, socks and underwear in one drawer, T-shirts and shorts in another. He hung his pants and shirts, then took his toiletry kit to the bathroom and arranged everything neatly, the shaving cream and razor on the right side, toothbrush, floss, and paste on the left, the Neosporin and gauze for his arm on the small shelf above the toilet. He kept his bottle of Zoloft hidden, not wanting Bianca to know that he was on an antidepressant.

Then he stared at the bidet, just stared at it, wondering what in the world you’d do with such a thing. This wasn’t the first time he’d wondered it, as he recalled his question from last time he visited, but he couldn’t remember Bianca’s explanation.

He stretched out on the bed again, clicked together his magnetic readers, and thumbed through his phone. It was the middle of the night back in Arizona, not much happening. Mr. Nutz had probably weaseled his way into the house and was drawing a hot bath and using George’s robe. The bastard.

Another yawn came fast and fierce, stretching his whole face. Setting his phone down, he slipped under the covers and shut his eyes again, his neck at a ninety-degree angle. The pillow was thicker than a car seat cushion and even stiffer than the mattress. One night here, and he'd need a lifetime of chiropractic care.

He tossed the pillow aside. Took him another twenty minutes of tossing and turning, churning up thoughts and fears, worrying that he could at any minute slip back into that awful place he'd been in March, till finally he drifted off . . .

An hour later, George limped down the three stories to Via Giulia, every muscle in his body suffering from fatigue. He told himself to buck up. Bianca pulled open the building door, making way for a heap of sunshine splashing through. George slipped on his sunglasses and came onto the street. His cushiony new shoes were the best thing going, as she'd already warned him that they'd be walking everywhere. He could use the exercise; maybe it would get him out of his head.

They stopped for coffee and a tasty *pinza Bolognese*, which was a doughnut with jam in the middle, then kept going. George hid his yawns. All he wanted was to be easy, so that she wouldn't regret hosting him. No, he wanted to be more than easy; he wanted to be fun. If only fun were easy.

After walking through the University District, they left the city walls, crossed over a big road called Viale Giovanni Gozzadini, and entered Giardini Margherita, which she claimed was her favorite park in the city. Fountains in a large pond shot water into the air in wide arcs. The sun spilled through the trees, painting yellow lines in the green grass. There were worse places to be.

They took a seat on one of the benches that wrapped around the oak trees. George all but collapsed, and as he wiped the sweat from his brow, he said, "I don't know much about steps, but I'm sure we did our ten thousand."

"It's a good thing we got some exercise, because I'm taking you to my favorite pizza place for lunch. We have a while, though. Italians don't eat lunch till two or so."

"Two? That's dinnertime." He'd forgotten this tidbit about life here.

"We'll be there right when they open." She checked her phone, then sat back. "So . . . I know you're tired and never want to talk about things, and I should probably wait till I get a glass of wine in you, but how are you? I'd like to help."

Her abrupt question punched him in the gut. There was nothing worse on this earth than making your kids feel like they have to help you. It should always be the other way around. He'd better head this off right now. "Don't worry; I'm already coming out of it."

"Right."

"Seriously, I'm finding my way now."

"Don't bullshit me, Dad."

He laughed. She was always the one who could make him laugh.

"There has to be something good about retirement. Isn't it nice to not have to deal with all the Intel bureaucracy? Isn't it nice to finally have some free time?"

"I don't need a session, honey. I'm here for you."

"We're here for each other. C'mon, humor me. What are the good things?"

"The good things? Plural?" After they shared a smile, he patted her hand. "I don't need to be analyzed or fixed. Your mom's already done enough of that. I'm not taking cooking classes or knitting or whatever else it is. I'm going to find another job."

"Another job? Why? You have enough money, don't you?"

"Maybe I do. Who knows how long I'll live, how much money I'll need."

"If you make it to one hundred, I'll be there for you."

Please, please don't let me last that long, he thought to himself. "I have feelers out about some consulting work. Might move back into Phoenix, get away from the purgatory of the golf course."

A brown bird with a white head landed in front of them, and they both watched it peck at the ground.

"My sun is setting," George said after a while. "Let's figure you out; what you're going to do next." Even as the words left his lips, he knew he'd crossed into the demilitarized zone.

"Figure me out?" Bianca said, her tone confirming that he'd breached the boundary. "I'm doing great."

He sat back, chewed on possible responses. "You walked out on everything. Might be nice for a minute, but trust me, you need to get back to work."

"And you're the expert?"

How quickly their conversation had escalated. He did have over thirty years on her, but he forced himself to stop. On the plane ride over, he'd planned his angle of attack, even practicing what he'd say to her. Now that he was in the heat of it, he'd bungled it mightily.

Calmly this time, feeling his love for her, he said, "I get that I'm not exactly a role model, not someone you aspire to be like, but all a dad can do is hope he can save his daughter from learning *everything* the hard way. Sixty-five years is a lot of time out there hacking away at life."

Bianca stared off toward one of the fountains on the pond. Was she listening with an open heart or grinding her teeth and wondering why the hell she'd let him come?

Whatever it was, he had to get the rest out. "You're going to get bored fast doing nothing. If you wait too long, you'll realize the world back home has passed you by. It might not be as easy as you think to rebuild your client list. Your friends will move on."

She came back hot. "I didn't put my world on hold back in Austin. I have no plans to return. I might. Or I might not. I might stay here forever. Or move to Thailand . . . or try the East Coast. This whole thing I'm doing is not living in a paused world. I'm taking a step toward living a better life, breaking free from this trance that I got pulled into. And it's not that I don't aspire to be like you, Dad. That has nothing to do with it. But I don't aspire to work as hard as you. No offense, but I don't. There's so much more out there."

George resisted saying, "You'll see soon enough." He saw the candles of his retirement cake again, the way they had turned into nails in his mind. He said nothing, though, because he knew he'd already gone too far.

She plowed ahead. "All I've done since grad school is go, go, *go*. Where has it gotten me? I barely remember the last few years. I want what the people have here, soaking up each second, living like they might not wake up tomorrow. That's why I'm here. If I run out of money, I'll figure it out. But that's not right now."

George was incredulous. She didn't get it, the millions of people back home who didn't have degrees, who didn't have jobs, who floated around without contributing. He'd been *so proud* when she opened her practice and grew it into what it was. It sounded more like she needed two weeks of sitting by the pool in Honolulu, not a year of whatever this was.

He looked around, the people so not like them sitting in the grass or circling the pond, the city's skyline rising over the trees, so, so foreign from anything he knew, wondering what she saw in Bologna. Okay, the food was surely tasty, and despite it being a crumbly old city, it had its charm. But there was a reason the US was the leader of the free world. Wait till a labor strike kept the trash from being picked up for a month. Wait till the electricity went out for a week. Or until she realized how terrible the pay was here, the job market, the economy, the *government*. Sure, she and her mom had Italian blood, but they'd been born in America. They were American!

He leaned forward and rested his elbows on his thighs. "You know I support you. I just worry about you. Of course I want you back on

American soil. It's a crazy time right now. What if we end up at war? We're on the edge of World War III. You're not safe here. And not that this makes the argument, but selfishly, I can't keep coming back over here to visit. I'm too old."

To her credit, Bianca held back a rebuttal and soaked it all in. She smoothed her hands together, her eyes set on the fountains, her mind surely in motion.

She eventually turned to him. "Will you please stop trying to fix me, Dad? I'm not broken; I'm healing. And you're not too old. That's one of the many stories you're telling your subconscious. What's happening is that you're lacking in purpose since leaving Intel. And I get it. That's so tough. But the great news is that all you have to do is find a new purpose. That seems far more appealing than giving up."

She stood abruptly. "Now, let's stop before it gets ugly."

Great job, George, he told himself, as he watched her stalk away.

Chapter 9

Madmiral Briggs

Lying in bed the next morning, Bianca didn't want to open her eyes. She thought she could deal with her dad, but one day in and she was exhausted. It took about all she had to shift her mindset, but eventually she reframed the situation.

She was a warrior and today was a day for warriors. Her father's visit, on top of everything else, was the ultimate showdown, her opportunity to grow, to mend the broken parts of that little girl inside of her for good.

If she could survive this, then she might finally be set free.

In her book, Bianca had helped Peggy Meh change the stories she'd been telling herself, urging her to become Cap'n Megawatt, the director of her own thoughts. Bianca Briggs would take her own advice and become Peggy's direct superior, Admiral Gigawatt. How silly!

"Her royal wattness, Admiral Gigawatt," she said out loud, seeing a supercharged Bianca standing at the helm of her boat.

She chuckled and pulled a leg out from the sheets.

God, this was fun. New ideas for Insta posts and even a live Substack sprang to mind. Creativity shot up her spine. Maybe she did have another book in her.

Hold on. There were *far better* ways to suffer than to go to war with another blank page, only to be shat on by reviewers. She'd been trying not to read reviews, but she'd gone down the rabbit hole late last night and found a one-star that called *From Meh to Mega* a nothing burger. Ouch.

Recalling some of the other reviews, a wave of shame knocked the last of her smile off her face. Maybe it was fun thinking about becoming Admiral Gigawatt, but she wasn't a *funny* person. Aside from Moira and the other Megawatters, the self-help reading collective had either rolled their eyes at her attempt at humor or hadn't even picked up that she was being playful—and even silly—in the first place. So what was she doing laughing at herself?

Fighting to stay positive, she set her bare feet on the rug and stretched.

"What a blessing," she said, careful not to speak too loudly. "I am so fortunate for this opportunity to grow." Captain Peggy Megawatt had said exactly these words multiple times. Admiral Gigawatt—no, *Madmiral* Gigawatt from the helm of her ship—added, "I'm eager to spend more time with my dad. We have a lot of catching up to do."

Charged with determination, she dressed for the day and made a Nespresso shot, telling herself she'd figure out how to use the Moka pot in the cabinet soon.

She'd not planned it this way, this battle. Her time in Italy was a time to heal and recharge, but it had become more than that, a battle against—no, *a dance with*—her father issues too.

Today, she would focus on looking at George Briggs, the ultimate to-do-lister, through the lens of understanding, knowing that she had the same desperate need to check things off, to accomplish, and knowing that everyone had their faults and hers and George's were mostly to do with being insecure overachievers.

The floorboards on the other side of the apartment creaked. Her dad was up; it was go-time for the madmiral.

In the living room, George said, "I'm sorry about what I said yesterday. I was tired and let my mouth start running. You have your own path, and I need to be okay with it. It's not my business anyway."

Bianca slipped her arms around him. He still smelled like "Dad" after all these years, like a pine tree. "I can handle some advice from time to time, but I need you to understand that this is where my ancestors come from, at least half of them, and when I'm here, my soul glows. Don't hate on my journey."

"I'm not hating on it," he said. "Just micromanaging you, as I've been known to do. But I'll do my best not to meddle."

Bianca appreciated his honesty and self-awareness. "Thank you. Now let's get on to a great day. I thought we might leave in an hour or so and go do all the touristy things, see a few museums, that kind of thing. Then we'll have lunch, take a nap, and then I have my signing this afternoon at four. How does that sound?" She was trying not to think about the signing, how empty it would be.

"Yeah, sure, to all of it. And I thought I might help you get organized around here too. Just a bit of the old George touch, sweep off the balcony, get your closets and cabinets straight."

Bianca smiled, at first resisting but then remembering that George was George, and she had to let him do his thing. This was his way of expressing his love.

"I could definitely use the help, but no rush. Rome wasn't built in a day."

"Had I been there, I could have built Rome by noon on Monday." Then he winked.

Only once they had reached the Fountain of Neptune did George start to niggle at Bianca's sanity again. What had happened to her earlier pep talk?

They'd had a perfectly nice morning, enjoyed a pastry at Le Briciole and eaten it while talking about the latest news in Phoenix and Scottsdale, and shared some wonderful memories from back when her mom had still been in the picture. They'd even laughed, and Bianca felt so proud of both of them, escaping the headbutting of the previous day and facing forward.

But then something had changed in George, a shift in his easy demeanor, as if that last cup of coffee had done him in.

As Bianca passionately relayed what she knew about the Fountain of Neptune, an evocative work with nude mermaids staring up at the well-endowed Roman god of the sea, George's eyes kept drifting away.

Piazza del Nettuno formed an L shape with the adjacent and grander Piazza Maggiore, and together they were the heartbeat of Bologna. Each brick building that surrounded the piazzas was a work of art worthy of its own history book, but dominating them all was the exquisite Basilica di San Petronio, a giant church the Bolognese started building in 1390. 1390! They'd never finished the exterior due to political and financial reasons, but that was part of the charm. While the bottom half featured some of the most important marble work in human history, the top half consisted of merely exposed brick, creating a unique masterpiece.

As the Italian sun warmed the crisp May air, pigeons bathed in the water of the fountain. A guitarist sang pop songs. Scents of coffee beans swirled in the air. Groups gathered for their walking tours, the guides holding up signs. People sipped cappuccinos and planned their days at the many tables tucked under the colorful awnings of the lively cafés.

In short, Bologna was giving everything it had, singing its best song, reminding Bianca exactly why it had grabbed her heart. And yet her father was beyond detached and distracted.

"What is it?" Bianca asked calmly, stopping midsentence as she explained how the fountain had been built for the pope.

George wore another pair of khakis with a golf shirt and those bright-white tennis shoes. He couldn't have looked more American if he wrapped an American flag around his body and started singing Lee Greenwood.

"Sorry," he said, "I was looking at the line forming. That's the entrance to where we're going next, right?"

Bianca looked across the square to a line of maybe thirty people waiting to get inside the Palazzo d'Accursio, where one could enjoy the municipal art collection, climb the clock tower for a view of the city, and maybe even get a glimpse into the stunning Sala del Consiglio comunale, or city hall, where Bolognese leaders had been meeting for hundreds of years, debating politics as they sat in hand-carved chairs under a gorgeous frescoed ceiling that rivaled any in the Old World.

"Oh, the line's not that bad," she said. "We're still early."

"Yeah, but it's growing."

What was he in such a rush for? Last time she checked, he was a tepid art lover at best, but right now he had the energy of a bull about to be let into the ring. Taking another breath, pausing for four seconds before exhaling, she touched his arm. "We're not in a rush, Dad. Besides, I want to show you my favorite thing in all of Bologna." She took his hand. "Come here."

They walked twenty feet toward a daunting stone wall of the Palazzo d'Accursio. Just out of reach stood two eagles sculpted in stone. Bianca pointed to one. "Niccolò dell'Arca did that one; he was the reason Michelangelo came to Bologna and spent so much time here. And then Michelangelo did this one."

"*The* Michelangelo?" George said, suddenly interested.

"That's right."

George stared hard at the eagle. "Hold on; it's not even protected. You're telling me one of the most famous artists in the world did that, and I could pull up in a pickup truck with a chisel and drive away with it."

Bianca imagined the two of them executing a father-daughter heist. "It's not very well known, and not everyone agrees that it's a Michelangelo."

He pulled his eyes away. "Then how do you know?"

Bianca touched the stone under Michelangelo's eagle with her full palm and looked up at the sculpture, feeling the bird's wings as if they were her own. A rush of energy ran through her, generations of her ancestors standing there with her.

"I just know."

As they joined the line to get into the palace, you would have thought George was a little girl dressed in a princess outfit trying to get a picture with Minnie Mouse.

Bouncing in those white shoes with their cushioned soles, he kept peering past the people in front of them, trying to see when the doors would open. He'd likely trample small children if need be.

The moment the guard unlatched the gate, George said, "Okay, I'm thinking we go right."

Bianca shook her head. "You may be the most excited person in history to ever walk through this gate."

He shrugged it off. "I don't like waiting around."

Oh, she knew. She'd endured thirty-two years of her father's impatience. And he'd passed it along to her too.

As the line started to move, a young couple snuck in front of them. Bianca wasn't that bothered. These things happened, but George puffed up his chest and said loudly enough to hear in Venice, "No, sirree. The line starts *way* back there."

The couple, both with large matching Fuji cameras around their necks, ignored him.

Little did they know that George was all about right and wrong, and cutting lines was one of the Seven Deadly Sins in his world.

Bianca set a hand on his shoulder to prevent an altercation, but George stepped forward anyway. Mortifying her to no end, he knocked on an imaginary door only inches from the man's shoulder while making a knocking sound. "Excuse me."

The couple finally turned.

George aggressively gestured with his thumb. "Back of the line, please. We're not savages."

The couple attempted to play dumb.

George wasn't having it. "I don't care what language you speak, Italian, English, German. You can see where I'm pointing. Now go."

Bianca was pretty sure no one in the vicinity had taken a breath.

Thankfully, the couple finally moved away from the line with halos of shame glowing over them. George coached them along with, "There you go, keep going, keep going. All the way to the back." He didn't take his eyes off them till they reached their rightful place at the end of the line, and as he turned to Bianca, he had the proud look of a man who'd saved a drowning victim.

Bianca tightened and questioned whether she was truly ready to face this battle, this attempt to help a man who'd lost his life rudder. He might be her toughest client yet, and that was saying a lot. What was that saying? That guests smell like dead fish after three days?

"Can you believe the nerve?" George said, as if Bianca had been cheering him on. As if he'd saved the lives of everyone there.

She focused on her steps as they followed the slow-moving line.

"What?" George said. "I don't like people breaking the rules."

"We can see that," Bianca whispered.

He nearly flew through the museum, leaving dust in his wake. He'd attempted to read a few of the signs on the various exhibits but had clearly given up. In the Etruscan-Italic section, George got tired of waiting for Bianca and flipped through his phone while she took her time studying the pottery.

She found him twenty minutes later waiting under an Exit sign. "You blasted through there."

He scratched his head nervously. "Great museum; I enjoyed it."

"Yeah, looked like you were pulled in."

"You know me and museums. They're fine. Just getting hungry."

She didn't mention that he sure had been eager to get in. Also, she was loath to tell him, but lunch was hours away.

As they returned to the plaza, a text message from Corrado came through.

How's your visit with your father?

She started to tap out a response but then slipped her phone back into her purse. Not responding was the only way she could think of to establish boundaries. He was the last person on earth who should see her at rock bottom.

Back on Via Giulia, Harold was having familial troubles of his own.

"Mom," he said, video-chatting with her via WhatsApp, "I mean this with love. Please get off my back. I'm figuring it out."

It was half past three in the morning in Denver. She'd always had trouble sleeping, which is probably why Harold did too. She lay in bed with her head sideways on the pillow; her violet reading glasses rested on her nose.

"What do you mean, you're figuring it out. I'm worried about you."

When was she not worried about him? With all due respect—especially after sharing all the money she didn't have to support his adventure—she needed to get a life of her own.

"Mother, I'll be back soon enough, but I have unfinished business here. Believe me, she'll come around."

"I hate to break it to you, but she might not. You didn't know each other that long."

"I refuse to accept that."

A coughing fit seized her. He didn't bother giving her a hard time about starting to smoke again, namely because he'd picked it up too! She'd spent a lifetime stopping and starting again, and he'd sworn it off himself till Alice had come into his life.

When she'd finally gotten it together, she said with a craggy voice, "If only Alice could see the man that I see. And if she doesn't, then there's someone better out there."

"Thanks. I have to run, but I'll be around later, okay?" He didn't have to run. He had nothing to do today, but her mommying was making him squirm.

Hanging up the phone, he fell back onto the couch. He hadn't dressed yet for the day, and it was approaching noon. Actually, he still hadn't dressed for yesterday or even the day before. All he'd worn were his tighty-whities.

Tissues that he'd cried into lay wadded up on the glass table next to his Xbox controller and an army of pop cans. He'd been playing *Call of Duty* all morning, wishing that he could sleep, but his schedule was totally out of whack now. Sometimes, he couldn't even drag himself out of bed at the usual hour to join his gamer friends online.

Additionally, Duolingo was stalking him, and yet he refused to turn off the push notifications on his phone and watch. He'd given up on speaking Italian. Who was he kidding? What was the point without Alice? But it was something akin to self-flagellation to endure the constant Duolingo reminders.

Hi, it's Duo. Looks like you skipped another day of Italian lessons.

Hi, it's Duo. Are you traveling?

Hi, it's Duo. Even five minutes a day can help?

In a way, Duo was his only friend.

> Hi, it's Duo. Get off your lazy ass and take a lesson, Harold. It's not like you have anything better to do! By the way, great job showing Alice what you were made of the other day. I'm sure she was in a hot debate of who to choose between, you and Renzo.

The thing was . . . things weren't getting any better. How long had it even been since she'd left him? The days ran together. And who cared anyway? A day without Alice wasn't a day at all. He was sitting on hold, as if he had his phone to his ear listening to Muzak while waiting for the operator to return and say he could go back to living.

He hoped that Alice would surprise him and walk in the door any minute . . . No, that's not true. He'd prefer a heads-up so he could shower and shave, make the bed, reset his watch so she couldn't see his step count, and knock down the Leaning Tower of Pizza boxes while he was at it.

What if she didn't come back to him, though? What if what they'd had wasn't real at all?

Alice was out of his league in every way. If only she knew the truth, that he wasn't at all a successful entrepreneur. That he lived with his mom! That he was a loser! She was the kind of woman who could do anything, be with anyone. She might even truly love this man, this Renzo, and he might convince her to stay in Italy forever, perhaps raise his children.

Harold winced at the overly graphic image that passed through his skull, that of Renzo slipping the panties off Harold's Alice and . . . and . . . and penetrating her with his . . . Ugh.

He'd likely do a finer job than Harold, who didn't have much experience. Should she give him another chance, he'd devote his entire life to gifting her orgasms that would turn the night into day, flashes of lightning in the sky of her carnal desires.

He pressed his eyes closed, wishing he'd worked harder. That he'd listened better, that he'd walked ten thousand steps a day. Dammit, he'd walk fifty thousand a day if she'd come back to him. And why hadn't he learned Italian yet; why was he so damned ugly? Why did he have to be a *nerd*?

Hi, it's Duo. Why are you such a fucking dipshit?

Who was he kidding, thinking that she'd stick with him. He was lucky enough to have enjoyed the time he had with her. It would have all come crashing down anyway once he'd confessed to his lies.

It was all lies, lies, *lies*!

A knock on the door stole him from his misery. His heart began to hammer.

Was that really a knock, though? How many times had he answered the door to realize he'd been hearing things?

Another knock, followed by a soft female voice.

Harold's head swiveled like someone had tied a string to his chin and jerked.

What to do. Alice couldn't see the place like *this*. Him like *this*. He hadn't even brushed his teeth in a couple of days.

He tiptoed to the door and lowered to the ground, peeking under the crack. Shadows of feet in flats darkened the floor, but he couldn't see if it was his strawberry love's perfectly cast toes.

"Alice?" His voice cracked.

"Harold?"

It was her! Who cared about what he was wearing or what he looked like or how he'd let the place fall apart. She was here, back to him. Maybe fate did exist.

Suck an egg, Duo!

He cleared his throat and spoke a notch deeper than usual. Confident, relaxed, assured. "Yes, it's Harold. What's happening?" He looked down at his own scrawny frame—*his tighty-whities!*—ashamed of anyone seeing him this way.

"Sorry to bother you, but I was checking to make sure you were coming today."

Wait, this person had a chirpy British accent. Was it the Moira girl from the bookstore? His heart fell from his chest and died a quick death on the floor. It turned into a congealed mess and slipped through the cracks like the monster in *Stranger Things*.

Heartless and broken, Harold cracked open the door a half inch. "Can I help you?"

With a black floppy hat drooping down over part of her face, Moira backed up and raised a hand. "I'm sorry. I didn't mean to bother you. Were you sleeping?"

She had a strong accent that required an extra layer of processing. "Uh, yeah. Just a nap. I work odd hours. Clients in Asia." His speech came out like bubbles from the mouth of a deep-sea diver.

"I wanted to remind you about the signing downstairs. I'm telling all the neighbors. Four p.m. on the nose. The author is going to read for us, then answer questions. Did you happen to get to her book?"

He stopped himself before saying, *Are you kidding me?* "No, I didn't get a chance."

"No problem. I suspect you'll still get something out of the signing. And invite Alice, too, if she's around."

He didn't bother mentioning that she was probably riding in the passenger seat of Renzo's Lambo at that exact moment. "Yeah, okay, thanks for coming by." With that, he clicked the door shut and let his head fall back. No way in hell he was going to a book signing.

Chapter 10

Encounters of the Fourth Kind

Someone please tell me why I let Moira talk me into hosting a book event. Anyone? Hello? Sandy's mind was ablaze with regret, and quite frankly, shock. Moira, the worst salesperson to ever have attempted to peddle anything in the history of earth, had somehow made this thing happen. Oh, Sandy knew why; Moira had begged and pleaded as though nothing mattered more. Even the most hardened eventually give in.

But as the four o'clock hour drew near, Sandy wished with all of her heart that she hadn't said yes. She'd have to race to move the shelves back and fold up the chairs in time to get to her tango class.

Moira had taken the liberty of using the store credit card for several large prints of the cover of Bianca's book, and Sandy was currently staring at one of the two that stood on stands on either side of the table where Bianca would soon be.

The title, *From Meh to Megawatt: Supercharge Your Life* was presented in an annoying font, like Comic Sans, over a background of a purple that would be better suited for a sex worker's nail polish. Below the title was an exhausting take on Rudolph Zallinger's *The March of Progress*, the drawing of the evolution of man that had been parodied into oblivion. In this version, it showed the evolution of a woman becoming "supercharged" by way of lightning bolts striking each version of Peggy Meh who, as Moira explained, by the end of the book evolved into Peggy Megawatt.

There weren't enough eye rolls in the entirety of Italy to respond to the cover or the concept. How did one say "Give me a break" in Italian? *Dammi una pausa* didn't translate well. Maybe *risparmiami.* Spare me.

Moira had hung blown-up copies of the cover throughout the store. Not that anyone would see them, because they had no customers, which meant printing them had been an utter waste of euros. Sandy was tempted to take the exorbitant expense out of Moira's paycheck, especially if no one bought any of the FIFTY books they'd ordered for the event.

"Did you get a chance to read it?" Moira asked, appearing out of nowhere with a box from Paolo Atti & Figli Panificio, which was likely chock-full of *torta di riso*, a soft rice cake that all the tourists clamored for.

Sandy made a note to take the cost of those out of her paycheck too. She wasn't sure why, but Moira's excitement always brought the worst out in herself, and she had a dark, ugly hope that no one would show up at all. She wasn't proud of thinking that way, but it was the truth.

The seating allowed for forty, though they only got that lucky with the big names. They'd once had William Kent Krueger come by, and the forty chairs had filled up an hour before the event. By the time he'd started speaking, they'd had to lock the front doors to prevent breaking the fire code. That was nine years ago, during the golden years of the bookstore, before everything fell apart.

While Sandy tested the microphone, Bianca pulled back the door and entered with an older gentleman whose awful taste in clothing vehemently detracted from his handsome face and well-maintained body. His brutally bright tennis shoes nearly forced Sandy to turn away, as if she were staring at the sun. A pair of readers with the snap magnetic bridge dangled from his neck and further emphasized his lack of style. A bandage wrapped around his arm.

Please say that this isn't Bianca's boyfriend. He was twice her age. Maybe he was her dad, but he certainly wasn't from the Italian side of the family. No doubt of Anglo-Celtic descent.

Moira flew like a bird to welcome them. "We're so excited to have you," Moira squeaked. "I'm hoping for a good crowd!"

Once her clueless employee had attacked Bianca like she was Beyoncé, Sandy walked under the arch into the front room to say hello. Bianca wore dark jeans with a blazer over a white shirt that did a decent job of keeping her ample chest in check.

"Hi, there," Sandy said, splaying out her arms in what had to be the most insincere gesture she'd ever performed. "So glad to have you." She wished she could be so warm, but she couldn't and that was that.

"It's my honor," Bianca replied with a shaky voice.

Sandy wanted to relieve her nerves by saying it was likely no one would show up, but they'd have to wait and see. The only thing worse than people not showing up would be for a crowd to arrive, proving that Moira had succeeded in her mission. How many useless social media posts had she made to their several hundred inactive followers, how many flyers had she printed, how many hours had she put in walking the city and inviting anyone and everyone who had ever taken an English class?

"I'm George; you must be the owner," the man said, offering a hand. Though it was silver, he had great hair, thick and wavy. How could a man waste a head of hair like that with such dated attire? If he pulled his khakis any higher, he'd strangle himself. If his shoes were any brighter, he'd knock Earth off its axis. She might even need those eclipse glasses to protect her vision.

When their eyes found each other, Sandy recognized his look—heat-seeking missiles locking in on a target. He was probably in his sixties but thought he had a chance.

"Yes, I'm Sandy." As he took her hand, she looked away. If he only knew that he'd been born twenty or thirty years too early to ever have a chance with her.

She was about to get back to work when George pressed on. "How long have you been here? You're American, obviously. Where are you from?"

Oh, God, Sandy thought. *Please don't embarrass yourself.* Rejection *is my middle name.*

She had to at least be polite, so she attempted to answer without letting her annoyance show. Squinting against the bright light of his shoes, she said, "Florida, originally. Moved here twelve years ago."

Trying to be sly about it, he took a glance at her bare ring finger. Why hadn't she worn her burner ring today?

"How do you do it?" he asked, looking up again. "I'm here two days and already miss home."

Finding the coral in her pocket, she rubbed its porous surface slowly, like trying to draw a genie from a bottle. "This is home to me."

As she started away, he tried again. "Can I ask you something?"

She made a reluctant pivot. "What's that?"

"What happens if someone opens a second English bookstore here?" A sly grin, slightly warm and not exactly annoying, took over his face as he ran a hand through his annoyingly perfect head of hair.

And she relented, allowing a smile herself. It wasn't the first time she'd been asked the question, considering the name of her bookstore was The Only English Bookstore in Bologna.

"They can't."

"What do you mean?" he asked, an eyebrow hiking up.

"Because I'm the only English bookstore."

"So there's a decree?"

"Exactly." Sandy was the first to look away. He had no business flirting with her.

"I do love the name. It's brave."

"Thank you," Sandy said, appreciating that maybe he understood.

She'd forgotten that Moira and Bianca were standing there till Moira interrupted. "It's so brave," she said. "And I always liked how long it is. Reminds me of titles like *Eleanor Oliphant Is Completely Fine*, *The Guernsey Literary and Potato Peel Pie Society*—"

"*Fried Green Tomatoes at the Whistle Stop Café*," Bianca said.

"Oh, that's a good one," Moira said.

Sandy had never seen her employee happier. If she wasn't careful, Moira might spring a gasket in that little head of hers.

Moira kept going, strangling yet another conversational thread to death, as she'd been known to do. "Tom Robbins had some too. *Even Cowgirls Get the Blues*. And Elizabeth Berg, *Earth's the Right Place for Love*."

George turned to Sandy and shrugged. She chuckled silently, as if they both shared in the thought that Moira was exhausting, then said, "I have things to do. Nice to meet you, George."

He asked if he could help, and she shook her head.

"Okay, well, I hope to see you around. And that no one else tries to open an English bookstore."

Though she didn't want to, she rewarded him by shaking her head with what might have been construed as another smile.

While Moira walked Bianca through the plan, Sandy climbed the winding stairs to her office. On the floor by her antique desk, a growing stack of books signed by various authors who'd visited over the years collected dust. Two framed pictures glowed in the light of the sole window, one of Nicolo perched on the highest accessible spot of her balcony, and the other of her son in his dress blues before he shipped off for his first deployment.

She sat in her swivel chair and fired up the computer, then proceeded to draw circles with her mouse for a good ten minutes, her gaze lost in space, wondering why she hated everyone so, why she had such vitriolic reactions. No, it wasn't that she hated everyone. She was just annoyed by everyone. Even people she'd barely met bothered her. Hell, people she'd *never* met were out there annoying her, fleshbags on other continents nagging at her by simply breathing.

Hand to the fire, she'd admit she hated this about herself. Of course, it would be nice to be a bubbly welcome basket of hugs and kisses and laughter, but not everyone was like that, and Sandy had come to accept and even enjoy the cloud of pessimism that had settled over her head. One thing was for sure: She rarely became disappointed because she kept the bar incredibly low.

Sandy was well aware of how spiky she could be, but people kept intruding into her life. She hadn't even been looking for an employee when Moira had timidly crept in the door and begged for work, gushing about her love of books and her need for a job that enriched her soul. Why did jobs have to enrich souls anyway? They were just a way to pay the bills, for God's sake.

Even George down there was encroaching on Sandy's space by attempting to be flirty. And yes, that's exactly what he'd been doing. How dare he.

Why couldn't everyone stay in their lane?

She reached for the coral in her pocket and held it in her palm, staring at it, petting it, letting it do its work.

As Sandy had told Moira, she wanted *nothing* to do with the signing. She'd handle the cash register in the front room while Moira led the discussion in what was sure to be train-wreck fashion. How many self-help books did the world need anyway? As if someone barely thirty years old had figured it out. Please.

No one that young knew anything about life. At that age, Sandy fell for the dazzling Tampa real estate agent with a yacht he probably still owed money on and a prick he couldn't keep in his pants. As they stood before their family and friends, her second marriage, his fourth, she thought she'd finally found it, the love she'd been so desperate for.

Dropping the coral back in her pocket, she descended the steps and winced when she saw only four people sitting in the cluster of chairs that faced Bianca, who couldn't have looked more uncomfortable if she'd had an accident in her pants.

Her dad sat about halfway back, stabbing at his phone. Two elderly women who frequented the store sat up front with Bianca's book on their laps. Oh, goody, they surely had a lot to glean from a book of wisdom written by a toddler. The fourth attendee was another regular, an effeminate man who'd flipped through every page of every coffee-table book in the store with his greasy fingers, but he'd never so much as bought a bookmark.

The unbearable silence was broken by the bell that chimed when the front door opened. Moira pushed through, followed by the kid Alice had brought back from Denver. Was it Harold? Sandy had only met him once in passing but had seen him around with Alice.

The building had turned into a hostel, the landlord converting most of the apartments into short-term rentals. That would be fine if the occupants bought books, but no one did. They were all broke kids in their twenties who barely had the attention span to get through a three-minute news article about their latest pop-star idol, let alone a book.

"Trust me, you'll love it," Moira said, all but dragging the kid in.

"How long do you think this will be? I wasn't planning on going, just headed out to grab a—"

Moira turned and whispered, "Less than an hour. I'm so grateful."

Sandy had to give her credit; Moira's determination deserved admiration.

As Moira ushered her latest victim into the main room, Sandy pinched the bridge of her nose. *And now there were five.* A whole city of expats and only five of them—one coerced and another the father of the author—had made the time. Was it any wonder why she didn't host more events? Still, she had the pleasure of being right. And it was sweeter than the *torta di riso.*

Had she any sense, Moira might have waited a few minutes to see if anyone else might show up, but God bless her, she started right on time, timidly holding the microphone like it was an electric eel. Her nerves were written all over her. What did she think this was, a State of the Union address?

"Thank you all so . . . so . . . much for coming." The mouse wore a long black skirt with a white top. The only color on her was her purple fishbowl glasses. She looked more like a guppy than a mouse!

Bianca sat at the table next to Moira, facing the minuscule audience, and she looked like she was working hard to hide the embarrassment of the poor attendance.

"I wish there were more of you," the guppy said, "but it doesn't matter. What I know is that each of you who have read or will read this book will be forever changed. You are Megawatters in the making."

Like a bad Vanna White from *Wheel of Fortune*, Moira held up the book but didn't realize it was upside down.

"I can't take this," Sandy muttered to herself.

"*From Meh to Megawatt* is the kind of book . . ." Moira suddenly stopped. She'd forgotten what she was going to say. She extracted a card from inside of the book—still not noticing she was holding it upside down—and tried again, this time with the eloquence of a four-year-old reading *Hamlet*. "*From Meh to Megawatt* is the kind of book that stays with you, that rings all the bells, that resonates with your soul. It's my great pleasure to introduce you to a woman who has done it all. She's a therapist, a blogger, a podcaster, an author—with a *wonderful* sense of humor—and now, to our great fortune, an inhabitant of this great city. She's packed up her life in Austin, Texas, and now lives right across the street. Please welcome Bianca Briggs."

What was the opposite of thunderous applause? A drizzle of hand taps. George clapped the loudest, the proud dad with the fabulous hair and the shoes that redefined *hideous*. Perhaps Sandy should google how to make those eclipse glasses. The two women in the front looked like they were dealing with too much arthritis to draw sound from their hands. The coffee-table booklover had his face buried in his phone, not having noticed the signing had even started.

Sandy dropped her elbows to the counter in front of the cash register to bury her head in her hands. Despite her earlier signs of nerves, Bianca seemed rather comfortable in the spotlight as she thanked everyone for coming, then turned it over to Moira for the first question.

"Firstly, since it's our battle cry, could you talk about what 'Leave burn marks' means? As you know, I have the tattoo and adore it. But I'd love to hear it from you."

"That's a great question," Bianca said. "And I like what you said the other day, Moira. It's like the crater an asteroid leaves when it crashes into Earth. You know, we have choices in our life. And I think we need to do things that matter. We need to live like we're already writing our eulogy." And on and on, Bianca went. The blind passion of youth.

Then Moira asked Bianca to read a passage, and as the author did so, Sandy went about online shopping for purses on the computer, trying to drown out the supposed life-changing wisdom. If the book was so wonderful, why was Moira, who'd supposedly read it twice, still a moron?

The tiny audience clapped after Bianca finished reading. Having tried as best as she could to tune Bianca out, Sandy had still heard clips, something about the power of self-reflection, of stepping into the confessional of your heart and speaking to your higher self; how self-assessment was the key to releasing guilt and shame.

Moira turned her microphone back on, causing ten seconds of ear-piercing feedback that forced everyone to cover their ears. Why she was using a microphone for this tiny group was anyone's guess.

After an apology, Moira finally got out, "I think about that passage all the time, the idea of there being two of us, the higher self and then this hurt inner child who doesn't even know to ask for help. Or is she too ashamed to? I love how Peggy Meh reaches this point of enlightenment where she not only creates this space for dialogue in her heart, but she even confesses her deepest secrets to her friends, because she'd shed her need to keep pretending. Her higher self has nothing to hide."

"Exactly," Bianca said into the microphone, showing a bit too much enthusiasm. "All these lies we tell ourselves, the secrets we so desperately try to hide from ourselves—and others, to your point—they must be released if we're ever to set free our inner child."

Moira gave her version of a confident smile coupled with a poorly executed wink that made her look like her face had been overcome by Bell's palsy. "And we all have our secrets, don't we?"

Sandy smacked her head against her palm. What secrets did Moira have? That she washes her whites and colors together? That was no secret. Or that she secretly loves mortadella, despite saying she's a vegetarian. All these kids and their secrets and their life wisdom. At what age would they realize there is no special recipe?

"Bianca," Moira the Guppy started, still timid as a deer facing a cheetah, "can you tell us about yourself, about your journey to becoming a healer. I can only imagine the work you've done as a therapist in Austin, the people you've helped. It's amazing that you're sharing this life-changing recipe that you developed, all these ingredients that were previously only available to your clients."

There it is again, Sandy thought. *Life-changing.* Despite any evidence. In no way was Moira exhibiting any such characteristics. Still the same Moira who crept into work like a mouse with her heinous black hat, then scurried away at the end of the day to go lose herself in her silly romance novels and God knows what else. Microwave dinners? Dollhouses?

The bell above the door chimed. A potential customer dipped her head in, noticed the signing, whispered "Oops," and disappeared. Sandy could barely wait to point out to Moira that her event had actually hurt sales!

Never again!

Never. Again.

Ten minutes after Bianca had left, Sandy and Moira were folding chairs and moving the shelves back. Alice's boyfriend, Harold, lingered, hunkered down in a cushioned chair in the corner with his head in a Japanese manga book. A classic peruser. He'd never bought a thing, despite having lived above the shop for *weeks*. Not that she was surprised. Kids didn't even read these days. Sandy made a mental note to get rid of every chair in the place. Meanwhile, Moira would keep beating her build-the-community drum, saying they needed to offer free Wi-Fi, a coffee bar, more events. More chairs!

"That went well," Sandy said, mildly hating herself for her schadenfreude.

Moira didn't look up. "I know. You were right. I guess it was a waste of time."

Experiencing a rare moment of compassion, Sandy felt bad for her. It was like she'd been pulled out of her own hell and stepped inside Moira's skin, no, her mousy pelage, and felt her pain.

"This meant a lot to you, didn't it?"

Moira finally looked up, trapped behind her thick lenses, as if she were living in an aquarium. "Yeah."

The swarm of sadness that came over Sandy was nearly too much. She had to force herself not to cry. This was exactly why she couldn't start caring for everyone around her.

"I've tried these things before," Sandy said, shocked by the warmth of her voice. "They don't work anymore."

Aware that she wasn't *exactly* speaking the truth, she said, "The people around here, they're not looking for community. They're expats because they're running from their community. Wait, are you crying?"

Moira shook her head and turned away. Sandy finished folding the chair and set it against the others. Then she approached Moira, who kept trying to turn away and hide her tears. Sandy set her hand on Moira's bony shoulder. "All that matters is that you tried. I appreciate that you care about this store." She added under her breath, "More than me sometimes."

Moira sniffled. "I have this vision of what our store could be. And I wanted Bianca to know how much her book means to me and . . ."

"Will you please stop it? I can't handle tears." Sandy hated when her own tear ducts started getting all antsy.

"Sorry." Moira tried to shake it off.

"No, it's okay." Surprising herself even more, Sandy pulled off Moira's glasses and wiped the warm tears herself. "I think you need a hug."

"Really?" Moira had appealing eyes; it was a shame she hid them behind bulletproof glass.

"Come here. Before I change my mind." Sandy pulled her in. She recalled holding her son this way, and it hurt. She felt Moira's pain and the pain of her son all in one. It was almost too much.

"Why don't we close early and go get a drink somewhere?" Sandy asked. "We can talk about how awful humans are?"

"You don't have to do that. I know you don't like fraternizing with employees."

Sandy had told her exactly that, and they'd never once gotten a drink after work. Sandy didn't like fraternizing with anyone. But she was having a moment of weakness. "I don't feel like I have to," Sandy said, shocked by her own words. "I'd like to." Then she added in a tremendous lie, "I could use a friend too."

What had she just said? She couldn't use a friend. By God, why was she feeling such pain for the girl? Then she remembered her dance class in the evening. She'd have to make it quick.

"Excuse me," Harold interrupted, sounding nearly as meek and meager as Moira.

Sandy stepped back from the hug like Moira had turned to fire. "Yes."

The young man looked slightly terrified. Sandy could do that to people like him. Taking in his appearance, she wondered what anyone could see in this male version of Moira.

"I'm . . . looking for a book," Harold said.

Sandy was back to her old self. "We don't have those here. We're a toy store."

His forehead flattened. "Um."

"What book?" Moira asked, saving him. "Don't mind her. Sandy, this is Harold, by the way."

"Yes, we've met before." Sandy shook his hand.

Moira thanked him for coming. She was still sniffling but pretending to be chipper. "Where's Alice been? I haven't seen her in a while."

Sandy crossed her arms, slightly curious herself.

Harold swallowed something, maybe sadness—or an egg. He had one hell of an Adam's apple. Looked like a snake that had swallowed an egg. "We broke up, actually."

Concern painted Moira's face. "Oh, no. I'm sorry. And here I am bringing her up."

"No, it's fine. It's . . . Well, I almost said, 'It is what it is,' but I hate when people say that. I'm pretty sad about it."

Moira extended a hand to the guy, petting his shoulder. Was he a dog? A guppy and a puppy walked into a bar.

"My heart breaks for you," Moira said. "There's nothing worse. Is there, Sandy?"

Why was Moira bringing Sandy into it? She looked at one moron, then the other. "Of course not." With that, she returned to her work, reaching for the next chair.

Then Moira opened her big fat mouth again. "We were about to grab a drink. Wanna join?"

Sandy nearly had an out-of-body experience. She'd already regretted inviting Moira out, and now the mouse had opened the invitation to the whole world.

Racing to put out the fire, Sandy said, "I'm sure he has other things going on." *Please, Harold, take the hint.*

He stared into the eyes of Moira, seeking a lifeline. "Actually, I guess. Maybe. If that's okay."

George sat in the living room across from Bianca, both scrolling through their iPads. They'd had to pull one side of the blinds to keep the last of the sunlight at bay. An unopened bottle of wine stared at him from the counter; he was ready to go, tapping his foot to bluegrass music that she'd gotten into since moving to Austin, a Billy Strings guy.

Keeping it light, he said, "What's the story with the bookstore owner? Sandy?"

It took a moment for her to respond. "She's cute, isn't she? You should ask her out."

Though he'd considered exactly that, he faked a chuckle. "I'm too old for that, honey."

Bianca barely acknowledged his answer, keeping her eyes on whatever she was reading, moving her mouth to make it clear she was busy. He went back to his own chore: cleaning out his inbox. An empty inbox wasn't sex, but it was as close as he got lately.

Ten minutes later, the quiet was getting to him. "Don't beat yourself up for the turnout."

In a display of exhaustion, at either him or life in general, she closed her iPad and rested it on her lap. "It's embarrassing, you know. I should have said no from the get-go."

"You're in a different country," he said slowly, searching for the right words. "Nobody knows you. It's an honor your book is selling in other countries."

"Dad, we sold two copies."

George sighed. He wanted to lob over an I-told-you-so. What did she expect?

In the open kitchen, she jabbed the screw of a wine opener into the cork. Thank God! "I'm done with writing books," she said.

"There you go, then. It's good you figured that out."

"I knew that before coming here."

"Then what are you doing? What else are you trying to figure out?"

Red wine flowed from the bottle into two glasses. "I don't know yet."

Here was his chance. He cleared his throat. "If I may . . ."

"Do I want to hear this?" She rounded the counter and handed him his glass.

"I don't know. Just trying to help."

She sat and took a long sip. "Okay, get it out."

Go easy, but say your peace, George. She needs you.

"B, you can't wait for something to fall in your lap. It's not like I woke up dying to go into hardware engineering. I had a sense that I had that gift, and then I went for it. You've already found your gift as a therapist. But you're running from it."

Her jaws moved like she was chewing nails.

Tread carefully, George.

"All I'm saying is . . . don't fall out of the habit of working. Don't lose your groove."

"There's nothing wrong with a recalibration. People change paths."

"Sure, they do. But walking away, I don't know. I don't want you to get caught running out of money and regretting this whole thing. You know I'll always bail you out, but . . ."

He could recall his younger years in South Phoenix so clearly, his blue-collar father trying to get past losing his mother to Hodgkin's disease, barely able to get out of bed some days to make it to the steel mill. Skipped meals. Spoonfuls of peanut butter for dinner. Sometimes George would give his sister his portion because her ribs were showing. Besides, he was lucky enough to have a kind baseball coach who'd often take him for fast food after practice. Soup kitchens. Food stamps. The generous people at their church always stopping by to lend a hand, delivering casseroles and hand-me-down clothing. The electricity and water had been shut off so many times in their trailer that they kept flashlights and jugs of water at the ready.

Bianca brought him back to the present. "It's noted that you want me to come back home. It's noted that you disagree with my move." She had her eyes on the wall opposite her, where some sort of Dalí-esque painting hung. She was chewing even harder.

He let his head fall. How could someone possibly know what it was like to be broke unless you'd lived it? He'd never told her much about his upbringing. Didn't want her knowing too much about her origins. It might have held her back.

"You know this is all coming from me loving you."

She set her glass down on the coffee table—a little too hard. "You have to let me live my life. Tomorrow morning, I'm going to see a fortune teller, and I can only imagine how stupid that sounds to you. But it's not to me. I'm trying to find some sense of meaning. I have no idea if I'm staying here. It's only been a month. But I can tell you that I'm happier than I've been in a long time, and it's not because I'm getting closer to figuring out my next move. It's because I'm finally living, enjoying the space in between moves. I want to keep doing that."

A fortune teller? He'd heard nothing past that.

Chapter 11

The Misfits

What had led Sandy to be sitting with Moira and Harold at a table in one of the back rooms of Sorso Sospetto? Stupidity?

The name of the centuries-old wine bar translated to Suspicious Sip, quite a fitting name. It occupied a spot near her apartment and the bookstore, but she didn't frequent it often. She preferred to keep pleasure far from business and spent her free time a long way from Via Giulia.

Sorso Sospetto was one of the most elegant spots in the city. Day or night, no matter the weather, if they were open, people filled the outside tables. The equally busy inside made Sandy think of a Victorian house with multiple small rooms often divided by a few steps. Each was overdecorated to the point of being deliciously gawdy, abundant velvet and gold against uneven brick walls. The chairs were super comfortable, and the sturdy tables had loads of character, having collected carved initials and other etchings for God knows how long. They always kept the lights low, relying mostly on candles. It smelled of hundreds of years of cigars and cigarettes and spilled wine, and they never strayed from playing esoteric Euro-jazz.

When the *cameriere* appeared, Sandy fired off a request in Italian for a bottle of Lambrusco and a charcuterie board, then returned to prying words out of these mutes who were behaving like this was an eighth-grade dance.

"Okay," Sandy said, unable to take it. She pointed at Moira. "You first. You thought you'd get a good turnout, put some effort into it, only to find that I was right all along."

Moira shrank into herself. Any more and her head would collapse into her neck like a turtle. "It can't happen overnight, building something. We have to keep trying."

"I thought you were great," Harold said. "Asked solid questions. Bianca's super smart. I got a lot out of it." His voice had a softness to it. Not feminine but slightly nasal. Both of her table companions desperately needed confidence, to start living with some spirit.

"Did you read her book?" Sandy asked him.

"I'm . . . I haven't read much since Alice left." He scratched his face. The poor boy was broken.

"Then maybe we should start with you," Sandy said. "How old are you, by the way?"

"Twenty-three."

Though her son, Jack, couldn't have been more different when he was Harold's age, she recognized the struggles of coming into adulthood, attempting to figure out the world. Jack had always had a chip on his shoulder after his father went to prison for hurting Sandy, and as a single mother, she'd struggled mightily to help him find his way. Then he discovered the marines and there was no turning back.

The *cameriere* brought the wine, poured three glasses, and then left them alone. Sandy held up her effervescent red, the bubbles dancing in her glass, and said, "To heartache, kids. I wish I could say it doesn't cut as deep when you get older, but it's hard to dodge. *Cin, cin.*"

"Cin, cin," the other two echoed.

Sandy pushed Harold to talk about himself and what brought him here. It took him a minute, but once he started, he couldn't stop. He told the two women he had a fancy job building back-end software for various companies around the world, and how he'd been in a coffee shop in Denver when Alice had walked in, and the fireworks had been so explosive that they'd wound up in Bologna together.

"Let me get this straight," Sandy said, having a hard time imagining any part of Harold's love life being classified as explosive. "You followed a teenager back to Bologna and thought it would last?"

He raised his scrawny shoulders. "When you put it like that, it sounds absurd, but we love each other. Or did, I don't know." He leaned against the table and fell into thought.

Sandy could see that he was a bright guy. Love dumbed down everyone.

They let him stew in his thoughts till more words came tumbling out of him. "She was way out of my league, so I should have seen it coming. It just felt . . . I don't know. Real. I've never been in love before."

Something like empathy wedged itself into Sandy's chest. A girl named Lisa had been the first to break Jack's heart, leaving him in eleventh grade. His father was in prison, so he was already struggling, and she dumped him by having a friend tell him. He'd fallen into an ugly despair, and Sandy had more than once imagined tearing the limbs off a Lisa voodoo doll and teaching the girl a lesson. Jack had refused to talk about any of it, instead locking the door to his room and listening to Metallica till she called him down for dinner, where he'd barely utter a word.

"Why are you still here?" Sandy asked.

He looked up for a split second. "I'm hoping she might see the error of her ways."

"Oh, dear God. You're waiting for her?"

He stared into his wine.

Moira reached across the table and patted his hand.

"I've never felt like this before," he said, defeat dripping from each syllable. "It hurts. And I keep thinking that she'll realize what we had." He finally met Sandy's eyes, and it felt like a son looking at his mother. "I swear she was in love too. It wasn't only me."

Sandy sat up straight and crossed her arms. "Do you know how flighty a nineteen-year-old girl can be? I don't mean to be a *cagna*, but you're a gelato flavor, and she won't know which one she likes till she tastes them all. Dear God, please, please, *please* don't sit around and wait for her."

He couldn't stop fidgeting, scratching his face, shifting the table mat, sliding his glass left and right. "What else am I supposed to do? Go back home? Give up? If you love someone, you can't go out without a fight."

Sandy looked him up and down, a ticking time bomb setting himself up for even more pain. "For one, you're not dressed to fight. Look at you. You're a sad sack." She repeated the same in Italian. "You have this weird stubbly stuff that's not a beard. Please get rid of that. Get a haircut. Trim the hairs from your ears. Change the way you're dressing. No offense, but she's a pretty girl. The moment we met, I wondered what in the world she saw in you. Now that I've met you, you're a nice guy. But guess what, everyone's nice. You need to stand out. Become the man she wants."

Instead of being hurt by her words, Harold seemed to sift through them for a solution. His resilience impressed her. This kid had promise.

Only after she thought through what she'd said did her radar go off. She'd been slightly harsh. She added, "I tell you this *with* the understanding that you're a sharp and kind guy. Alice would be lucky to get you back. It's just . . . You have to try. You're a digital nomad who's apparently doing okay for himself, living in one of the greatest cities in the world. Free to do whatever you want." She tapped his glass with hers. A ping rang out. "You need to act like it."

"If it was only that easy."

"You have a lot going for you," Moira chimed in.

And the mouse doth speak. "Either give up and go home," Sandy said, "or put up a fight starting today. At this moment, you're caught in the middle, and that's no place to be."

After a quick nod, he twisted to Moira. "I'm sorry about your book signing. Now you know why I didn't want to come. But I'm glad I did."

"I think you're great," Moira said. "Sandy's right. Alice is lucky to be loved like that. A lot of girls would be envious."

Was it Sandy, or was Moira staring too deeply into Harold's eyes? Pity for both of them piled up like sand gathered behind a closed door.

The *cameriere* set down an impressive charcuterie board: fine cuts of Mortadella Bologna and Salame Felino, house-made pickled vegetables, squacquerone cheese, and the staple of Bologna: Parmigiano-Reggiano, offered in various ages.

They went to work on it in silence.

Once Sandy had enjoyed a few bites of the mortadella—a Bolognese delight she'd never tire of—she said to Moira, "So you . . . What are we going to do with you?"

Moira covered her mouth and finished chewing a piece of cheese, then shrugged.

The only person in Bologna more lost than Harold was Moira, and dammit if that pile of pity wasn't starting to seep through the cracks. Sandy wasn't about to say it, but she really did care for Moira. Maybe more so than any other human in Bologna. What she always wanted to say and hoped that Moira knew was that Sandy was the bitterest to the people she liked the most.

"Look," Sandy said, "I appreciate what you're trying to do with the shop—supercharge it and all. I tried that long before you were here, and I failed too. It's not a community kind of place. We've discussed this ad nauseam."

Okay, maybe that wasn't exactly true. She'd tried and succeeded for two years, the golden years. Then she lost faith, and the bookstore and Sandy had given up on each other. She reached for the coral in the pocket of her pants.

"But it could be," Moira replied, running a knife through the Parmigiano-Reggiano, a mouse going after her dinner.

Stop it, Sandy. Quit being such a bitch! She's not a mouse. What would your son say if he knew who you'd become?

All of Moira's desperation, the pure frustration. Sandy recognized it because she'd been a victim of it too. Things didn't work out how you hoped. Ever. And the sooner you came to acceptance, the better.

Sandy couldn't believe she was about to say it, but Moira's hopelessness made her want to leap off her balcony. "If your skin is thick enough to take it, you can try again. Start the book club you keep going on about. Build a community. Resurrect my bookstore."

Moira sprang to life. "Really?"

Sandy slowed the mouse's roll by wagging a finger. "But let's not forget how long it took for you to get over what happened with Emily St. John Mandel. You better thicken up that pale British skin of yours."

"Who?" Harold asked, with his mouth full. He'd been going after the mortadella like he might never eat again.

"You want to tell him?" Sandy asked.

Moira set the cheese down on her plate. "She's one of the most exciting working writers right now, almost genre-less really. She started out writing crime, but she's more into postapoc, spec, and time travel now. All quite literary, though. Breaks all the rules. Expertly plays with time. Everybody needs to read—"

"Okay," Sandy said, "let's move along, or we'll be here all night, listening to you go on about *Station Eleven*."

"That's not even my favorite. *Sea of Tranquility* was a masterpiece."

Sandy dramatically slapped her forehead. Someone should pay her to keep these kids on track.

"Sorry, okay." Moira collected herself. "Emily came in one day, randomly popped in while on holiday. I knew *exactly* who she was and perhaps overpraised her."

"Understatement of the millennium," Sandy couldn't keep from saying.

"Anyway, I asked her to sign her books, so we went over to the shelf. I'd filed them under St. John and not Mandel. Apparently, this is her pet peeve. She was nice about it, and I moved them that second, but it was a dark moment for me, considering how much of a fan I am. A few days later, I jumped onto Instagram to send her an apology, and her bio read: *File under Mandel. St. John is my middle name.* I think I'm the reason she did that."

Sandy cracked a smile. Moira brought this stuff on herself. A clueless romantic floating through life.

"That doesn't seem like that big of a deal," Harold said.

Sandy reached for her wine. "To Moira, the end of the world. She barely spoke for a week. Didn't eat. Couldn't look me in the eyes."

"Oh, gosh," Harold said. "You care that much, don't you? You must be the best employee."

Sandy wasn't sure whose eyebrows shot up higher, hers or Moira's. Holding back the snarky response that first loaded into the chamber, she said, "She's by far the best I've ever had."

Moira perked up like God had appeared to share with her the secrets of the universe. "You don't mean that. I know you. You're messing with me."

Sandy laughed, an honest-to-God laugh. "Though I do enjoy the occasional prank on your behalf, I'm serious. You're pretty amazing, Moira." Sandy's own words made her squirm some, but a sensation of warmth rose up her spine.

Moira had already launched into planning. "What would the book club look like? What would we call it? What books?"

"No, no, no. I want *nothing* to do with it. I'm giving you permission to run it. And I bet Harold here would be your first member. Right, Harold?"

His pupils dilated. "Uh, yeah, okay."

Sandy polished off her wine. "Okay, I'm going to leave you two to get to know each other. I have a dance class and a hungry cat waiting for me."

"Wait, but . . ." Moira had frozen in place.

"You'll be fine," Sandy said and then leaned toward Harold. "Be nice to her. She's a good one."

Harold picked at his fingernails under the table but kept trying to stop himself, hearing his father's voice. *"Stop picking at your goddamn fingernails, Harry."*

"I don't like being called Harry."

"And I don't like washing windows for a living. Tough shit!"

What Sandy had said had hurt, but maybe she was right. No, not maybe. She *was* right. He wasn't exactly living up to the person Alice had met in the coffee shop. Not anymore. He certainly wasn't leaving burn marks, per the book discussion earlier. No craters left by the Harold asteroid. He'd let himself get lazy, morphing back into someone less exciting.

"She really is lucky, you know." Moira's voice brought him back. "Alice, I mean. To be loved like that."

"I guess so." He scrambled for something else to say. "Have you ever been in love?"

Moira audibly exhaled. "I thought so, once, but things went sideways. I was apparently the only one living the fairy tale. Don't mind Sandy, by the way. She's like a bear cub wrapped up in cobra skin. Once you get to know her, she's appealing in a strange way. You'll never wonder what's on her mind. No filter with that one."

A genuine grin bent his lips. "I can see that. How long have you been working for her?"

"A year now."

"And before that? I'm assuming you were born in England. What brought you here?"

"Bristol, yeah. Arrived in Bologna two years ago, started with Sandy last year." Almost like she was reciting her history from a memorized script, she explained that she'd gotten tired of England and wanted a change. Came to Bologna because she'd visited with her parents once.

"And you snuck in before Brexit, I guess."

"Barely. I'm an EU resident now."

She was one of the good ones, Harold decided. A kind soul. "Thanks for inviting me. To the book thing and this. I don't know anyone, and it's been pretty lonely without Alice."

"And you've proved my point about expats. We're a strange bunch a long way from our homes, but we don't like being lonely."

They'd barely put a dent into the charcuterie board, and he went about deciding what to have next. He'd had five mortadella slices and three salamis, so he took two more salami to even it out.

"Do you want my advice?" Moira asked.

"Sure."

"Move on. If she realizes how lucky she is, she'll come back. But I believe, especially after reading Bianca's book, that we have to take control. That whole warrior mindset thing. We can't be victims. We have to look at our problems as challenges. You're faced with a decision right now. Get beaten up with heartache or see it as an opportunity to plug yourself in and go full megawatt. In other words, level up."

His head swiveled like a pinball lever. "Level up? You play video games?"

"Um, naturally."

"I just . . . really? I thought you were a bookworm."

"They go hand in hand, don't they? I love stories, what they teach us, how they pull us in. What's your console of choice, your desert-island game?"

"No, don't do that to me." He scrolled through some of the games he played most, hating the idea of being forced to choose. "No way I'm putting myself through such trauma. I'm taking all the *Witcher*s, *Fallout*s, the *Mass Effect*s, probably *Fortnite* for old school's sake."

"You're only allowed one."

Harold slapped the table, suddenly feeling claustrophobic. "Then I'm not going."

"The world is ending, pure chaos, nuclear winter, zombies eating humans, and you're not going?"

"Let the zombies come and get me. It's not happening. I don't want to play just one game. What a nightmare." He was half serious. He also realized that, for once, he wasn't thinking about Alice, so that was nice. He realized Moira was laughing at him.

"Are you enjoying torturing me?"

"I think this is adorable."

"There's nothing adorable about it." The momentum of their conversation was picking up speed in a slightly pleasurable way. "Okay, fine, you choose. You're about to hop on a plane as the nukes are dropping. A swarm of zombies is pulling at the chain-link fence, close to ripping it open, and yet you're given one minute to choose a console and game with which you will spend the rest of your life. Hopefully with margaritas and a hammock and all those Jimmy Buffett things."

Funnily enough, Moira squirmed more than he had. She sucked in air through her teeth as her gaze bounced around the room. A smile appeared and expanded by the second, till finally she said, "Nope. Not doing it."

"Aha. I knew it."

Basking in the afterglow of a fun moment, smiles lingering, they both took long sips of wine.

They stayed another hour, chatting about video games and their childhoods and anything else that came up in what proved to be a nice escape—albeit briefly—from thinking about Renzo undressing and finessing his Alice, with each kiss taking her further away from what was supposed to be.

In the morning, Bianca pulled on a robe and found her dad in the kitchen removing everything from the cabinets. "What in the . . ."

He stopped and turned with a Tupperware in his hand. He'd already dressed for the day, wearing his bright-white tennis shoes and another pair of khakis. "You know me. Couldn't sleep. I don't think anyone's pulled out everything and dusted since the Renaissance."

"How long have you been up?"

"A couple of hours. No big deal. I'm enjoying myself."

"Yeah, it looks like a ton of fun."

She found a Nespresso capsule, popped it into the machine, and made a cup. Once the noise had died down, she said, "Can I make you one?"

"Please. I didn't want to wake you."

Finding another pod, she said, "I've got to get going to meet the fortune—this woman. Can I do anything for you?"

"I'm fine, thanks. This'll take all morning, I suspect, then I thought I might go down to the bookstore, see if I can find anything."

"I'm sure it has nothing to do with Sandy."

Dead quiet.

"Dad?"

He took a random Tupperware lid and attempted to fit it onto a container. The size wasn't even close.

Bianca set her cup down and poked him in the back. "Hello in there? Does somebody have a crush?"

He turned back only long enough to show a face sans expression. It was adorable.

"You dog," she said.

"What? Your old man's too old to flirt with someone?"

"Of all the ways to fill your retirement, chasing women wasn't what I'd expected. But I like it. When's the last time you dated? Decades? Do you know what you're doing? Do you need help? She's a live wire, that one."

Setting down the Tupperware, he turned and leaned against the counter, still trying to keep a straight face, but Bianca could see a young boy inside trying to get out.

This was getting interesting. All the while keeping one eye on him, she reached for her espresso and polished it off. "What are you going to wear? Please tell me you have another pair of shoes?"

"Honey, I'll be fine, okay?" He couldn't have hidden his terror behind a stage curtain.

Deciding she wouldn't embarrass him further, she gave him a kiss on the cheek. *"In bocca al lupo, Papá."*

"What's that mean?"

"In the mouth of the wolf. The way they say 'break a leg' here. Know what you say in return? *Crepi il lupo.* May the wolf die."

George raised his arms to show off his muscles. *"Crepi il lupo."*

"Maybe there's hope for you yet."

What a turn it would be if they both were saved by Bologna.

The navigation on her phone led her on a few lefts and rights through winding corridors and ancient streets that she only vaguely remembered. Down an alley on the other side of the walled part of the city, she finally found it, a small storefront beside a food market, where oranges and lemons with their leaves still attached spilled out of wicker baskets and bouquets of happy flowers stretched out of metal bins.

The sight of the door with a crystal ball carved into it took her breath away. Ten years since her knuckles had rapped on this door, and she could sense her younger self standing there, maybe feeling the same skepticism that niggled at her now.

She was a believer in things unseen, in the world beyond the world, the magic of what was possible. At least 77 percent of her was, but there was still a part of her father in her that wondered whether she was an absolute idiot for thinking there were secret ways to navigate the world, energetic entanglements that science hadn't yet explained.

Still, when she was strong, when life slowed down and she could follow some of the advice she offered to her clients and readers, she had borne witness to small miracles.

There was no denying that she had, in fact, gone on to write a book a few years after the woman behind this door had prophesied it. That might even be described as bigger than a small miracle. Of course, Bianca would now call writing a book something more akin to a prison sentence. Maybe what Donna Bologna had done was put a hex on her.

Rumblings of movement came behind the door, the latch lifted, and there she stood, the *indovina*, or fortune teller, Donna Bologna, short and plump and radiant, in equal measure. A soft white dress fell over her body. A beaded necklace rested between the mountains of her ample breasts. Ribbons wove through her gray hair. She smelled like a greenhouse, that tang of fresh soil and the vibrancy of flowers and plants coming alive.

A nose ring sparkled when she greeted Bianca, offering a smile typical of someone tasting their first bite of *tagliatelle al ragù*.

"*Benvenuta,* Bianca." Donna Bologna invited her into her sanctuary, a large brick-walled room that smelled of incense and sawdust. A pair of birds chirped loudly from a cage. Light spilled in from windows in the back that looked over a minuscule yard. A table covered with a purple cloth waited for them in the corner. A crystal ball rested in the middle.

Once they were seated, Bianca asked, "Do you remember me?"

She knew from last time that Donna Bologna spoke English well, though her accent was strong. "You've been here before?"

"Yes. When I was twenty-two? Ten years ago."

"I'm afraid I don't; forgive me."

It was odd that someone who could see souls couldn't remember them. One vote went into the box of doubt.

"I see you, though," Donna Bologna said in a whisper. She drew in a long breath and ran her hands along the crystal ball. "Oh, yes."

"What is it?"

Donna Bologna pulled away from the crystal ball and took Bianca's hands, holding them palm up. Hers were warm to the touch, anchors of peace.

Eyes shut, she swayed to a rhythm, as if she were hearing Bianca's song. "Your chakras are like your smile muscles. Atrophied."

Bianca lit up, feeling like her bell had been rung. "Yes, exactly." And one vote goes to the believer box!

"Your ancestors know you're here in Bologna. They're happy . . . that you're here. And they know why you came."

"And can I know?"

"I think you do. To set free your spirit, no?" She spoke in Italian awhile, and Bianca did her best to follow. Something about holding on too hard, trying to stay in control.

"Can we stay in English, please?" Bianca finally asked, frustrated by how much Italian she'd forgotten. "Yes, to the freeing of my spirit. To figuring out what's next. Last time I was here, you told me I'd one day write a book."

"And?"

"I did."

A chuckle of satisfaction, like a Buddha laughing.

A minute passed. Only the sound of the caged birds chirping.

Donna Bologna finally looked up, and with wide eyes said, "That was not the book you were supposed to write."

"Hold on, what? You didn't tell me what kind of book I was supposed to write. You said that I was meant to write one."

"Apparently, more than one. You missed something."

"Well, I didn't cover everything in my book."

"No, that's not it." She rubbed her hands together as she again peered at the reflection in the crystal ball. "How was the book received?"

"Not well. Not well at all. A disaster really. A lot of the reviews are terrible, and I, frankly, would be happy to never see a copy of it again." She added, "That's not why I'm here. I'm not writing another one. Please don't even say that out loud or to my ancestors or anyone." Bianca had an urge to tear a blanket off the couch and throw it over the crystal ball.

The mystic hummed a few out-of-tune notes. "Often, that which we resist is the direction we should go."

"Yeah, I've said the same thing to my clients. That doesn't always apply. I resist swimming in chummed water with sharks. Don't need to do that."

"Chummed?"

"When you throw chopped-up bloody fish in the water to attract sharks."

"Sounds like dating these days." She gave a wink.

Bianca wasn't in the mood to stray from the topic at hand. "How about the idea of me living here, staying here, I mean? Forever. Is this my new home? What happens when my lease runs out? And what am I supposed to do with my life? Keep practicing or start all over? And how about my father?"

Donna Bologna sat back and looked around, lost in the middle space. "I think it might be best for you to quit trying to outsmart life."

Bianca was about to pull her hair out. The doubter box got another vote. "I need something concrete here. What do you see?"

"I'm telling you what I see."

"Am I in Italy or back in Austin or somewhere else? What am I doing?"

"That depends on you."

"That's a revelation."

Donna Bologna inclined her shoulders.

Bianca pressed her eyes closed and blew air through her nose. Of course there were no answers to be found here.

"Wasn't there a man in your life?" Donna Bologna asked.

"You mean way back when?"

The *indovina* dipped her chin.

"Corrado. Yeah, we lost touch." Bianca wasn't sure whether she wanted to mention the recent run-in. If the lady was a fortune teller, she should already know!

"And since. How has your love life been?"

As she thought back through the years, Bianca gathered her long hair, then let it fall. "I guess the guys I've dated haven't been much more than accessories. Yes, my clock's ticking, and I do want to be a mom, but I haven't accomplished what I need to yet. I've had a few boyfriends, some serious enough to last awhile, a few months. But honestly, they were in the way more than anything else." She sighed. "I'm just not girlfriend material. Not now, at least."

Bianca looked up as Donna Bologna focused on the ball again. She chuckled to herself.

"What is it? What do you see?"

She licked her lips. "If you let dough rise too long, it collapses."

"Now we're using baking analogies? Is food all this country knows?"

The woman clearly enjoyed the comment.
"Seriously, what does that mean?"
"It's time to stick yourself in the oven of life."
"You've lost me."
"Think it over. It'll eventually come."

Chapter 12

Taking in Strays

George hadn't asked a woman out in a few years. He'd dated some since his divorce, but nothing had stuck, and in the end, he'd decided that he'd lost his chance for more romantic love in this life.

Yet, here he was, standing across the street from the bookstore, looking beyond the scaffolding to the entrance.

He hadn't thought so much about a woman since Faith. Funny how they did that to a man, the right one, something like magnetism, giving courage where there was none. A guy smitten by a girl will do about anything to get a chance with her—even a fellow in his sixties.

They'd barely spoken, but there was something so utterly divine about Sandy, and he'd enjoyed their brief banter. A thousand voices told him to turn back; they'd been on him all morning, but he simply had to give it a shot. What was the worst that could happen, that she would reject him? Such a brick wall couldn't be nearly as bad as being dumped on his ass by his employer of almost thirty years. And a worse alternative would be returning to Arizona with the regret of not asking her out at all.

Deciding there was no more time to waste, he crossed the street, nodded at the workmen who flashed big grins with cigarettes poking out of their mouths, then ducked into the store. A bell dinged. Soft classical music played in the background.

A few customers wandered about, but he didn't see Sandy. Perhaps she was upstairs. As opposed to fixating on his mission, he thought he might play it casually. Unable to remember when he'd last visited a bookstore, he glanced over at the featured bestsellers, didn't recognize a single one. Meandering under the arch and coming under the impressive vaulted ceiling of the main room, he studied the categories on the signs above the shelves. Fantasy and Sci-fi certainly weren't for him. He wasn't even sure fiction was his thing. Maybe something nonfiction made more sense. A display of Bianca's books stood at the end of one shelf.

He tried not to think about how he hadn't read her book. He'd tried, for the record. Exactly two chapters when she'd first sent the advance reader copy. And it had just about killed him, how he was a mirror of Peggy Meh's father. Not that it was the first time he'd considered it, but the words on the pages had confirmed that he, George, had failed as a father and left lasting effects that his daughter was still working through.

"Mr. Briggs?" said a voice from behind.

He turned to find the young English woman who'd interviewed Bianca at the signing. Her glasses were so thick it made it hard to see her eyes.

"Hi, there," he said. "I'm sorry, what was your name again?"

"Moira."

"Moira, that's right. Good to see you." The purpose of his visit returned to him and gave him a fresh wave of nerves, a tingle in hands and heart.

"May I help you find something?"

All at once, his heart pounded, one big solid thud that made him feel dizzy. "Oh, no, just poking around. I . . ." It was now or never. He waited a moment to let his body settle. "I was hoping to find Sandy. Is she around?"

"She is indeed. I think she's upstairs. Let me go retrieve her."

George pretended to look at books, but he peered inward, talking to himself. *Play it cool, George. Be interesting. Most of all, be confident.*

"I wouldn't have pegged you for a Young Adult reader," Sandy said, appearing to his left moments later. *The Fault in Our Stars* faced him. He noticed the YA sign that hung above the shelf. *Busted.*

"Not that I'm judging," Sandy continued. "I enjoy YA from time to time. Just didn't see that one coming."

He turned fully in her direction. "I tend to surprise people."

"Is there a particular title you're looking for?"

He couldn't pretend another second. "I better come clean before it's too late. No, I don't read YA, was just off into space, thinking."

"Ah, another peruser without any intention of buying anything. Can I get you a latte and a *zuppa Inglese*?"

"A what?"

She allowed a hint of a smile, which he took as a gift. And boy was she pretty. The whole package, really. It was all he could do not to stare. She had the finest legs he'd ever seen, perched in heels as long as pencils.

"I'm kidding," she said. "We don't do food or coffee here. I'm venting some of my frustrations regarding the people who darken my door without spending a dime. Anyway, what can I help you with?" Her smile went away as fast as it had come, like a shooting star.

"I hate to have *darkened* your door, but I was looking for you."

"For me?"

What followed was a nightmare of stops and starts, coupled with scolding internal dialogue. *Get your words out, George! Quit acting like a teenager!*

He finally did. "I keep thinking that I'd like to ask you out, so here I am. Would you care to go to dinner with me?" He could have shaken a martini with the tremor in his voice.

She clasped her hands together and cast a glance over his shoulder before finding his eyes. "I'm not sure that would be the best idea, but I'm honored."

Her words filled the room, the rejection freezing everything, including George's body. How mortifying. Had he known how badly it would hurt, he wouldn't have dared an attempt.

He had to chip away at the ice of himself before he could respond. "Okay. Well, I tried." He almost added, "Let me know if you change your mind," but thankfully caught himself.

A man must admit when he'd been defeated, and the best way to respond was politely, before disappearing. At least, this was George's logic. He smiled with respect and started toward the stucco arch that led to the exit. "See you around."

It was all he could do to move his legs, but he did so with his chest up. Once outside, he sucked in air and started quickly back across the street. He fumbled for his keys and had to focus to open the door leading to Bianca's apartment. Once he'd made it into the courtyard—the courtyard that hadn't been swept in a decade—he leaned against the wall and stared down at the gravel.

What the hell had he been thinking?

Later, Sandy and Moira were shelving a new shipment of books when Sandy finally said, "What is it? Out with it."

"Out with what?" replied Moira.

Sandy slipped a copy of Stephen King's latest into its rightful place. The American travelers loved King. "Don't pretend with me. Let's get it over with. Just . . . please don't ask for a raise because we're making no money as it is. We're right on the precipice of either going out of business or filing as a charity organization." That last bit was funny, but Moira was too far gone into her own stream of thought to laugh.

"That's what I want to talk to you about. I don't mean to overstep, but I have a few ideas to go along with starting the book club—if that is something you're still okay with?"

Here we go, Sandy thought, pulling out a stack of the new Elin Hilderbrand, another one who killed it with the tourists. She could pick out a Hilderbrand reader right as they entered. They'd rush in like they only had a moment because hubby was watching the kids, then say, "I'm so glad you're here. I haven't been able to find any English books, and I can't stand reading on a Kindle. Do you, by chance, have the new Elin Hilderbrand?" Sandy could potentially mouth the words with them, it was so predictable. Then she'd correct the pronunciation of Hilderbrand's first name ("sounds like *ELLEN*, not *EE*-lin") and point to her bestsellers.

If Sandy had a dollar for every one of those—wait, she did. One dollar was about all she made selling these books, once you took out rent and bills and all. Which meant she needed to sell about three hundred times what she was selling now if she were to return this to a viable business. Okay, maybe a little more than a dollar, but not much more. The downward sales trend hadn't been such a big deal for a while, as the settlement on her divorce from the dumb-shit real estate agent had been substantial, but she was starting to worry. What if she accidentally lived till she was ninety? If God truly existed, that's exactly what he'd do to her, sentence her to a long life.

"What do you think?" Moira asked.

"About what? I was doing my best to tune you out." Sandy immediately felt remorse for her inexcusable behavior. God, Moira needed to toughen up. They *both* did! "Okay," Sandy said, "let's try again. What were you saying in your infinite wisdom from the entirety of your short bookselling career?"

What Sandy liked most about Moira was that she, for the most part, completely ignored Sandy's attacks. Moira had accepted that Sandy needed to express her frustrations, and someone had to be her punching bag. But Sandy didn't mean a lot of it. She didn't dislike Moira. As far as humans went, Moira was fine.

"About this community idea, a book club. A newsletter. All the things that could help us grow. You mentioned last night that you might let me?"

"Is that a question?" Sandy could hear how mean she was being as she gradually gave in. She'd thought about it, too, the book club idea and how Moira was such a soldier and loved her job so much and how she wanted to help. Maybe Sandy should let her. If only to give her some sort of purpose. Some people needed that.

Moira adjusted the windshields that hung over her face. "I'd like to at least try to build a community."

But people are awful, Sandy thought to herself. *Why would I want to bring them together?* Nevertheless, she might have to let Moira learn this one the hard way.

"Let's take it one thing at a time. A book club. What are you thinking?"

"We'd meet once a month, have the first one in a couple of weeks, which would allow me time to get the word out. We'll choose the books as a collective, a proper democracy. Maybe I could bring in some nibbles."

"Some nibbles? Is that what you call them?" Sandy put the last of the Hilderbrands in its place, then grabbed the next in the box.

"We could have themes. A few decorations. You won't have to lift a finger."

Sandy had a million ways she wanted to respond, but she was weak today and only found one. "Okay, why not."

"Really?"

"Yes, really. I'm feeling very much like I'll drown in regret in a few months when the whole thing blows up. Or maybe you can prove me wrong. I'd say the odds are in my favor."

What a testament to Moira's determination and naivete that Sandy's absurd negativity didn't even put a dent in the glee on Moira's face.

"I asked her out two days ago," George said.

"You did what? Why didn't you tell me?"

Bianca and George were walking under the porticoes of Via Rizzoli to the first day of a weeklong cooking course. It was a Tuesday morning, stunning weather, a gentle breeze blowing through the city like a long whisper. Flowers were in full bloom. Mannequins in stunning dresses stood behind the polished glass of the wonderful boutiques where Bianca had already spent entirely too much money. People on electric scooters swerved by tourists pausing for a bite in between visits to the countless sites.

"I don't know. It's embarrassing," George replied.

"I'm your daughter."

"Exactly."

Bianca looked over at him. Somewhere in the last twenty-four hours, she'd started to understand her father more.

She kept reminding herself how much he loved her. Him cleaning the cabinets was an extraordinary act of love, his way of giving. Him purchasing her a *pink* toolbox complete with *pink-handled* tools, as if she were still his seven-year-old princess, was love. Him biting his tongue last night during dinner when she could tell he had advice he desperately wanted to share. Love. Seeing through this lens, she felt how hard he was trying, how important it was for him to redeem himself as a father, and now she also saw how much he'd been let down by Sandy.

She took his hand, the first time in forever. "I'm sorry, Dad. That probably didn't feel too good."

Though he shrugged it off, she could see his pain.

Today, she told herself, she'd give her all to their relationship. He might have screwed up when they were both younger, but he was trying now, and he needed her, and she had to be strong.

Up a long set of stairs, they came into a sun-filled commercial kitchen with footprints showing in the layer of flour on the floor. Four older women of various sizes wearing hairnets welcomed them with cheery smiles and invited them to join the other students who'd already arrived, including a German couple and an American journalist.

They spent the first hour making tortellini, and if Bianca would remember any one thing from that morning, it would be how present she and her father were, standing next to each other, working as a team to mix and roll out the dough, laughing as they held up pasta that looked like it had been run over by a Fiat.

Once they finished, the ladies removed their hairnets and guided the class to the Mercato delle Erbe, an open-air market around the corner, to secure vegetables and meat for the rest of their lunch, which they'd enjoy back at the kitchen.

Bianca had strolled through the market a few times since she'd arrived, but seeing it with the help of a guide made all the difference. They started at a *formaggeria*, where the class stood in a circle while the cheesemonger told them about his shop and cut them mouthwatering offerings from all over the Emilia-Romagna region. It was amazing how many times Bianca caught George's eye and they both smiled. This was living, pure living, and exactly why she'd come to Italy. She hoped he saw it, too, what had brought her back to this city.

At the vegetable stand, their guide collected *broccoletti* and *spinaci* and a few vegetables Bianca had never tasted before. The purveyor cut slices of a blood orange that had more flavor than anything she could remember. When she went in for a second bite, and as the juice dripped down her chin, she looked up to see a pair of alluring eyes staring at her.

The owner of those eyes was none other than Corrado, who'd sent her a text a few days ago to which she'd yet to respond.

"Uh-oh," she said, locking eyes with him.

It would not be okay for George to see Corrado, so she said to her father, "Let me say hello to a friend; be right back."

Before he could respond, Bianca broke away from the group and led Corrado to a display of olives. He carried two canvas bags spilling over with vibrant vegetables.

"And here we are," he said, kissing each of her cheeks. His breath blew against her ear, causing her skin to tingle.

"I'm sorry I didn't text you back," she said. "I've been so busy."

"*Non c'è problema,* Queen Bee. I recognize your father. How is he?"

"Fine, but please don't say you want to go over there. It's already a lot right now. I don't want him getting any thoughts in his head." Not only would George likely embarrass her, but he might also worry a rekindled relationship with her former lover would keep her from returning stateside.

Corrado said that her dad had aged well in ten years, then thankfully, moved on. "Is my Bianca learning to cook?"

"Something like that." She both loved and hated how he often called her his Bianca. "How are you? How's the restaurant?"

Corrado held up the bags. "I'm testing recipes now."

He'd read her stop signs well, and a part of her wanted to apologize for being so cold to him. "Remind me when it's opening," she said, thinking of how disappointed Corrado would be if she let anything happen between them. Maybe if they ran into each other a year from now, she might be in a better place.

"The third of July. I'd be happy to reserve you a table."

"That's nice of you." She refused to commit.

"How is the search for Bianca coming? Have you found her?"

She gave him a playful look. "So far, I've found the bottom of a lot of pasta bowls, and that's about it."

"I see. Just not my pasta bowl."

She refused to match his devious smile. "That's right, Corrado. Now behave."

Noticing her group leaving, she said, *"Devo andare."* I have to go. She almost suggested they meet for coffee again, but there was no "friend zone" with Corrado. Whether it was coffee or tea or an afternoon mass, all things would lead to the bedroom, which wouldn't be so bad if sex didn't always come with baggage.

Backing away, she said, *"Arrivederci, Corrado."*

"Ciao, amici."

Someone had shoved Energizer batteries into Moira. She was scampering around at twice her normal pace, doing her daily chores while brainstorming this so-called "community" she wanted to bring to life. She'd not simply *mentioned* the book club to every visitor, buyer and peruser alike, but she'd also aggressively pushed it on them as she pressed flyers into their hands. She'd even spent her lunch break composing a newsletter to their small list of email subscribers. Afterward, she'd positioned a sign-up sheet by the register so that they could further grow their list.

The poor girl would likely learn her lesson soon, that it just wasn't meant to be. She'd put in all that hard work, and whether or not anyone showed up, they wouldn't sell enough books to pay for the effort. Oh, well; Sandy couldn't bring herself to let her down, so she let the Energizer Mouse run rampant with her new ideas.

They were closing shop when Harold walked in. Or more like crept in.

"Moira's in the back, turning off lights," Sandy said, standing behind the counter.

He inched forward. "Actually, I was hoping to talk to you, if you have a few minutes."

"Me? Don't ask for a job. I already can't afford Moira."

"No, not a job." He looked around to make sure no one was within earshot. "I've been thinking a lot about what you said, how I need to up my game if I ever want to get Alice back."

Oh, God, what have I done? This is what happens when I open my mouth and engage with others. And this is what I deserve, having invited Moira out for drinks. Note to self: stay wicked.

"Do you think you could help me?" Harold asked.

"Help you what?" Sandy peered through the arch to the main room as the lights switched off. She could see Moira's head bobbing over the shelves as she moved their way.

"Help me dress better, I don't know. Whatever it takes to make Alice want me."

What could possibly make anyone think Sandy was interested in becoming a life coach?

She was about to respond when Moira appeared. Though he did his best to make small talk, the kid shut down, clearly embarrassed about why he'd come.

Sandy jumped in, sparing them from the awkward quiet. "I was chatting with Harold about books. You're free to go, Moira."

"Oh, okay. You guys have a nice night."

A collective "You too" followed her out the door.

Once she was gone, Sandy said, "I don't know what to tell you, Harold. Go down the street to see Giovanni; he can help you dress. And look at your hair. Get a haircut. Shave your face. That's a start."

Harold nodded, somehow eliciting even more sympathy from Sandy, who asked, "What's the guy's name she's with?"

"Renzo."

"Be a better Renzo, Harold. Do you read poetry?"

He shook his head.

"Speak Italian?"

Another headshake.

"Know how to cook? To dance, to sing? Know how to make love?"

If he shook his head any more, it would break off. His blushing was enough to light up the now dark bookstore.

She lifted her hands. "There you go. The recipe to upping your game."

He slumped. "That's a lot of work."

"I wish I could say it'll be worth it, but I have two divorces and a few other failed relationships in my graveyard." *Cynical much, Sandy?*

she thought after hearing what she'd said. What else should she be, though? Turning into the wicked witch is the only thing that had saved her.

Still, Harold was young, sensitive. Hopeful. Maybe he had a chance. One in a hundred relationships stand the test of time. Either way, it wasn't her place to crush him by telling him the likely truth: Even if he got Alice back, something would go wrong down the line.

"Tell you what," she said. "Do what I mentioned, then come see me every once in a while. I'll help. But first, throw everything you're wearing away. Got it?"

A sad nod.

"Don't worry," Sandy said. "You're not a lost cause. I've met worse. You just need direction."

A hopeful pixel in his eye twinkled. "You'll help?"

"I don't know that I have a choice. For some reason, I take in strays."

Chapter 13

Killing Peggy Meh

"I know you hate lists," George said to Bianca as he faced his legal pad, pen at the ready, the greatest list maker to ever grace the land, "but it pays to be organized." He'd been there a week and had finally caught up with the jet lag.

Bianca was lost in her own world, tapping away at her computer in the other comfy chair in the living room. "One second. I'm finishing up a newsletter."

"That's your first since moving, huh? I bet you have a lot to say."

A nod.

Though he hadn't read her book, he'd never missed a newsletter and had always made it a point to respond to them.

"By the way," she said without looking up, "I can't believe you brought more than one legal pad to Italy."

"And I can't believe you brought more than one pair of shoes." Her mother had always given him a hard time about his legal pads and to-do lists too. In turn, he'd attacked her shoes or aprons or whatever else.

Bianca granted him a smile but kept tapping. Faith had ignored him a lot too. Especially when he was trying to get things done. They could never understand that his days began when he completed his list. All the other moments leading up to it were a mad scramble of anxiety, feeling like the world was on fire. That's what happened when you spent your first eighteen years living in a world that was literally on fire.

He sipped his coffee, the fourth Nespresso capsule of the morning, then revisited his list, which was exceptionally organized, by the way. Whether he supported her move, he wanted to help, and that meant doing the chores that no one else wanted to do. If only the recent daytime activities—the museums and cooking classes and all the walking—hadn't delayed him. Today was the day, though, when he could finally reclaim his sanity.

- *Labels for Tupperware*
- *Clean up courtyard*
- *Paint closet*
- *Contact landlord: additional lock on door, fix drip in sink*
- *Vacuum under and behind furniture*
- *Windex windows and art*
- *Reach out re. consulting work*
- *Update LinkedIn profile and photo*
- *Shopping list: Ziplocs, celery, ranch dressing, Cokes, Windex*

He added a couple of more items, including reading her latest newsletter. His leg shook, as he was itching to get started but wanted to review and make sure he'd thought of everything.

After she announced that she'd completed her task, he set his blue pen against the first item on the list. "I thought we'd prioritize, see if we could add anything. If you can help, great. If you're busy, I got it. You know I need something to do."

She stood and approached the refrigerator. "What about going to Verona or Venice for the day, Dad? Or having coffee at an outdoor café and people-watching. Try again with Sandy. Go find a good book and at least say hi. The Maserati and Lamborghini factories are only a bus ride away. Surely, you have better things to do than work on my place."

Just like her mother. The constant war against his getting things done. She knew damn well how badly he needed to tackle his list, how awful he felt when the list grew too long, how purely satisfied he felt when he scratched off the last item. It was silly to some, sure, but it wasn't silly to him.

Eyeing the Nespresso maker, wondering if a fifth pod might be too much, he said, "I can't stand buses, and . . . I'm not much of a car guy."

"But you're an engineer. You might like the factory tours."

They'd gone down this road yesterday and the day before. "I want to knock these things off the list."

She drew in a breath that sounded like a vacuum cleaner that had sucked up something big from under the couch.

He hated being the cause of her frustration. And yet that's all he'd ever been. Same with her mother.

He wanted to say: *Don't you realize I didn't come for day trips and factory tours and pasta? I'm here to make sure you're happy and safe and set up to thrive, even if it's in a country that's so far away my heart shatters when I think about it. It's the only way I know how to love, and I wish it was enough. And I know it's not.*

When George raced out the door to attack his shopping list, Bianca breathed a sigh of relief. Sitting back in the chair, she attempted to read through the newsletter she was about to send out to her fifty thousand followers, her official announcement that she'd paused her practice to recharge and was on a journey of rediscovery in the land of her ancestors, a leap into *la dolce vita* to recapture her youth.

It was not lost on her that she hadn't said what she'd wanted to say in the newsletter. If she'd had the courage, she would have drilled down into the specifics, written about the awful reviews of her book, her breakdown with Lacy, the photograph of a younger Bianca with Corrado and Carol that had been the death shot. That would have been an enthralling newsletter, but it would have been too much, too embarrassing. And her father would likely tell her, as he had plenty over the years, that you can't let people see you sweat. Of course, he'd grown up in that kind of world, where you keep your problems to yourself.

And that's what he'd done all his life. She wanted to shake him and scream, *Let's talk about you! Why can't you sit still? Why can't you trust me to live my life? Why can't we have a conversation without you trying to cram your beliefs into me?*

Bianca wanted to take all the legal pads and burn them on the balcony, for so many reasons, but perhaps most of all because she was just as bad as him. Did he know that? Maybe. He never asked.

She had several different lists, each broken down into priorities. One for her socials, one for her practice, one for the next book she swore she'd never write, another for her spiritual journey, another for cooking. And on and on. If she ever showed him how organized she truly was, he'd illuminate with joy.

After reading what she'd written again, a sense of pride washed over her. She wasn't that bad of a writer, even if only a few found her actually funny. More importantly, she had to admit, she enjoyed wrangling words. If writing another book and then releasing it into the world wouldn't be so painful, maybe she would consider it again.

Still, she had no idea what Donna Bologna had meant by the rising-bread comment or saying she hadn't written the book she was supposed to write. What *exactly* was she supposed to write? No matter what it was, what publisher out there would be crazy enough to give her another chance?

Bianca swung an arm through the air. "*Peggy Meh Strikes Again!* Urged on by a fortune teller, Bianca Briggs has written yet another non-bestseller, destined for the bottom of the charts. A *tour de force* of a disaster that will certainly leave burn marks."

How about *The Death of Peggy Meh* as the next title? Bianca imagined a cover with Peggy's head poking out of a guillotine, her stupid golf-ball eyes popping out of her unfunny face. Or maybe the cover would show her halfway through a skydiving jump and attempting to yank a poorly packed parachute. That's what the bitch deserved for having poisoned Bianca's creativity, a proper splat onto the ground while descending at a hundred miles an hour.

Bianca opened a blank Word document and typed the new title, then let her fingers dance for a while, exploring various scenarios of torturing and killing Peggy Meh. A car crash. A murderous husband. A leap off a cruise ship. Every gory detail.

She could hardly control her fingers, barely realizing that she was doing anything at all, especially the thing that she *least* wanted to do. She and her muse were simply satisfying her deepest urges, releasing the angst of having failed so miserably at this writing thing that she had once so adored.

Bull sharks were tearing off Peggy's limbs when George appeared out of nowhere, scaring the shit out of Bianca. "What the . . . ! Dad!"

"Sorry, didn't mean to scare you."

She slammed shut her laptop. It felt like she'd been snatched out of a dream. Her fingers shook. Finding her bearings, she briefly considered that she'd not fallen into a writing spell like that in a long time. She felt like she'd been mauling a *cannolo* in the closet when someone had pulled back the door to expose her.

Bianca took a walk to clear her head, working her way through streets surrounded by the red-hued architecture that defined this city.

The writing thing had shaken her. For someone intent on never writing again, she sure had spent her entire morning writing, knocking out more than four thousand words. In a way, she felt violated.

Finally shaking the experience from her mind, she dipped into a shoe store, tested a few different sandals but didn't buy anything. Then while peeking through the window of a purse shop, a familiar smell grabbed her like a hand reaching through time. Something sweet and salty all at once.

And then it hit her.

She was twenty-two again, walking this same street. Corrado had led her here, only a few days after they'd first kissed. There was so much magic in the air then. She'd figured out the entire world. Twenty-two years old and the queen of it, ready at any moment to take flight.

Bianca twisted her head to see the *pasticceria* where she'd first tasted *Ravioli di San Giuseppe*, a to-die-for, buttery cookie coated in powdered sugar and filled with a fruity jam. It was as if she'd lost control of her legs. In no time, she was walking in that direction, a hound following a scent. Time continued to pull at her, and there she was, her younger self, facing the impossibly handsome Corrado in the center of the store, barely noticing the other people around them. He held a square of *Ravioli di San Giuseppe* in front of her mouth, saying, "Don't touch; close your eyes and try it."

Younger Bianca had closed her eyes and waited a few long seconds, totally vulnerable in his presence, and then the sweetness of *mostarda Bolognese*, a preserve of pears, quinces, and apples, hit her tongue. Her heart whistled with delight at the seductive flavors that were unlike anything she'd ever tasted.

Her eyes had eventually peeled open when he placed an unabashed kiss on her powdered-sugar lips, which left traces on his own lips as he pulled away.

"Attento! Attento!" a voice cried.

Bianca came out of her stupor to realize she was standing in the middle of the busy street. *"Mi dispiace,"* she said, dashing out of the way of a group of tourists moving in a flock toward her.

Collecting herself, she set eyes on the *pasticceria*.

No.

She couldn't.

She had to stop eating. Like, completely stop and go on a soup diet. All she'd done was eat since she'd gotten here, her attitude being, "I'm going to shove Italy into my face till I'm healed."

A rush of passion swept through her, carting her away. "When in Bologna," she muttered to herself, accidentally wondering how this surrender to the sweet might fit into a new book. *Surrender to the Sweet Life. Arrendersi alla Dolce Vita.*

Moments later, standing exactly where she had in her memory, she closed her eyes and took a bite of Italy that nearly lifted her off the ground.

Harold didn't change in the next couple of days. He thought about change. He pondered going shopping for clothes, getting a haircut, cleaning himself up. He considered working on his Italian.

The only thing Harold had actually done, other than blow more of his mom's money and rack up more credit card debt, was up his social media game. Every time he put a post out there, he hoped that Alice might see it.

He'd begun posting his step count at the end of the day. Not his actual steps, because he wasn't walking that much. He'd spent too much time trying to hack the step count on the Apple watch. He'd even tried waving his arm in the air while playing video games. Okay, he might have even strapped it to his ankle to see if the app would count his nervous habit of shaking his leg.

It ended up being easier to simply lie. *Eighteen thousand steps today. Nearly walked to Modena!*

He also stole images from the internet, plates of food, shots of the city, a peek down a shadowed alley, a sunrise over the Apennines, and he'd posted them in between his fake step counts. Busy, so busy. Barely time to even register that Alice had left him. She wasn't even on his mind anymore. Alice who?

That's what he hoped she'd think.

Meanwhile, he fell deeper into the void of heartache, racing to the door at even the faintest whisper of a knock, holding his phone and staring at it as if he could manifest a text message or call. He scrolled her Insta and TikTok feeds, hoping to see a kink in the armor of this new life with Renzo. Strangely, she'd been silent. Perhaps she didn't want her parents to discover that she'd parked herself with an older boyfriend.

There was an idea. Maybe Harold should call her teetotaling parents. He'd never spoken to them, but with effort, he could find them in Colorado. They lived in Durango on a commune. Did they even have phones?

He also pondered looking into Renzo, maybe paying someone to do it, to find out if the man was hiding anything. No way he could be that good looking, that successful, *that* well dressed, that perfect, without harboring a few weaknesses . . . or secrets. But Harold didn't want to beg his mom for more money to hire an Italian private investigator, and he definitely didn't want to get busted spying on them again. That's why he hadn't followed them since that shameful day that was burned into his memory, Renzo calling him Aroldo and patting his back and offering water, Harold wishing himself away from this earth, wishing he'd never been born.

Ultimately, he'd decided that waiting was the right call. And in all this waiting, while games loaded, when he went to drain the lizard, when he decided to change up his pizza routine and make some mac and cheese, what Sandy had said began to chip away at him, an axe going after a tree trunk.

What would it even look like to up his game? Was he even capable? A haircut and a change of clothes, really? Alice had fallen in love with him the way he was. She'd never commented on his lazy approach to shaving or his sort of computer-programmer attire. Just as she was perfect for him with her youth and beauty and bubbly persona, he was what she'd been looking for: the introspective, quiet, and brainy older man who was far too busy tackling things that mattered to worry about trivial things like wardrobe or sharpening his culinary game.

It hadn't been enough, though, had it? He wasn't enough. As Sandy had so astutely pointed out, he'd been a gelato flavor, a *vaniglia*, only to be surpassed by Renzo, the *cioccolato e rhum*. Chocolate with rum would always beat vanilla.

He was dumping powdered cheese into a half cup of milk when Sandy's gelato analogy finally landed. He would become a new flavor. How absurd and also deviously wonderful at the same time.

What could beat cioccolato e rhum?

Flashes of a new Harold came to life in his mind, as he scrolled through the flavors he'd tried thus far in Bologna. *Crema Libanese*, *Caffe Bianco*, Pomegranate, *Ricotta Reale*. Come to think of it, he'd learned more Italian in the gelato shops than all the hours he'd suffered through Duolingo.

Later, as he shook himself off in the bathroom, he realized that he could no longer be Harold. As Wade Watts did in *Ready Player One*, Harold had to become his avatar, a higher version of himself. In a flash, he saw a much taller Harold, one with thicker hair, bigger muscles.

While washing his hands, Harold dressed his avatar in his imagination, wrapping one of those Euro scarves around his neck. Take that, Renzo.

He had to come up with a new name. Not one that he would share with others, but one that he could assume when addressing himself, a gamer tag that further enforced the illusion.

In the spirit of defeating Renzo, how about the name the stealer of girlfriends had bestowed upon him?

Aroldo.

Was that even Italian? It didn't matter. It felt right.

He happened to be in his tighty-whities and nothing else, which was par for the course with him lately. He stood in front of the mirror and examined himself. The peach fuzz that Sandy had called a miserable beard. His scrawny frame with a slight belly from carbo-loading since the breakup. Hairy, skinny legs with knobby knees. Thick hair that he didn't ever brush. And an imperfect face, slightly wonky with an off-center nose. Chest hair that Alice had once run her fingers through. He zoomed out with expanded pupils, taking in all of himself.

"Aroldo," he said, testing it, blurring his vision, dulling it from seeing the body that he'd always loathed, trying to see it morph into something spectacular.

He lowered his voice. *"Io sono* Aroldo. *Piacere di conoscerti."*

Flexing his biceps that barely rose at his best effort to squeeze them to life, he spoke even lower, this time with an international accent. "I am Aroldo Gibler, digital nomad expat, world traveler, and lady-killer."

Music played in his head, gamer music with piano and synth, a heavy drumbeat exciting him at the idea of coming alive as a new person, a new flavor. *Vaniglia* no more.

He couldn't keep sitting around and growing his belly and living like his life was on hold. He was now Aroldo, a flavor of which Alice would never tire.

Pointing his index finger at himself in the mirror, he said in this new accent, "You are *Aroldo*, and you are irresistible."

Charged with newfound hope, he scrambled into the bedroom and pulled on his shorts and tennis shoes and a T-shirt and ran down the steps like the building was on fire. He slowed down as he hit the street, adopted an Aroldo swagger, and walked under the scaffolding to the bookstore.

Aroldo is not afraid of Sandy, he told himself, as he took a breath and pushed through the door, sounding the bell. It was a busy day, a group of teenagers hanging around the comic section, a handful of solo shoppers weaving through the aisles.

Moira stood at the cash register and waved. "Hi, Harold."

"Buongiorno." Aroldo is not afraid. He rested a hand on the counter. "How are you today, Moira?" What eased from his lips surprised him. There was a note of confidence he wasn't used to. *There you go, Harold . . . er . . . Aroldo.*

"I hadn't gotten a chance to tell you," Moira said. "Sandy's letting me start the book club; it's the Only English Book Club in Bologna." Aroldo chuckled with her at that one. "First one's June 5," she continued. "I'd love for you to join."

Harold thought it would be a terrible idea. He had no time to read a book right now. But *Aroldo* stepped in and thought, *A man must grow his mind, and a man must be a part of his community.*

"You know what," he said, his deep, worldly voice feeling more comfortable. "I don't believe I have any big meetings that day. I'll make it work."

Moira lit up as if she were about to launch into space. "I'm delighted. Thank you, Harold. We'll decide on our first book at the meeting. I'm secretly hoping I can convince Bianca to join, and we can do her book first. Have you gotten a chance to read it yet?"

"I . . . I . . ." Harold started. But then Aroldo took over. "Started it today. Wonderful writing. A fascinating angle." His accent had a British edge to it now, perhaps soaking up some of Moira's, and that was fine. Aroldo would have studied in London, perhaps at Oxford.

Moira blushed, her cheeks swelling. "You've made my day."

Aroldo winked. Harold started to match Moira's blush, but then Aroldo stepped back in, asking with absolute confidence, "Is Sandy around? I wanted to follow up on a previous discussion."

"She's in there, helping a customer."

"Perfect, thank you, my dear." *My dear? Wow, Aroldo.* He knocked once on the counter, found Moira's eyes again, noting how supremely happy she looked, then strolled with a discerning sensibility under the archway and into the main room with the cathedral ceiling.

He waited patiently until Sandy's customer found what she was looking for, then stepped up to her. Aroldo had to work hard to hold eye contact, as Harold kept emerging. Duo was also in the mix: *Hey, it's Duo. You have serious problems.*

But Aroldo stuffed the timid Harold and persistent Duo back inside like a jack-in-the-box, and said, "Pardon me, might I have a minute?"

Harold was gobsmacked by how easily he'd mutated into Aroldo. He could hear the alien voice and noticed how he carried his body differently, and though it felt strange, the pleasure outweighed it all. He'd basically fallen into a video game he'd been playing.

"I have exactly one minute," Sandy said. "And you're ten seconds into it already."

Aroldo snickered. To him, her sassiness was a virtue.

"I thought I might go see your tailor, Giovanni, per your mention, but I've no idea how to contact him."

Sandy loosened. Was it his new voice, his posture? His confidence? Aroldo stood taller.

"He's three doors down, the only clothing store on the block. But he doesn't speak English. How's your Italian?"

"Simmering but not quite boiling." *How clever, Aroldo.*

"Right," Sandy said. "I'll call and let him know you're coming. And for God's sake, let me set up a hair appointment too."

"That would be lovely, *bella*!" Had he just called her beautiful? Why yes, yes he had. *Take that, Duo.*

She seemed as surprised as he did, and all he could do was toss a shrug. Aroldo was about to reclaim what was rightfully his.

Chapter 14

Let's Try This Again

On the first of June, almost two weeks into George's visit, he found himself hiding in his room, wondering how he'd made the decision to stay so long in this strange land. Italy wasn't his bag; a room at a Motel 6 in Scottsdale had more appeal.

Furthermore, why drive more nails into the coffin of his relationship with his daughter? He might as well quit while he was behind. Every day, they found a way to crash into each other. Sometimes, it was subtle, but he could feel the tension between them grow.

God, she was trying hard, so hard. He could hear it in every breath she took, every moment she paused to find the right thing to say, every time she bit back a response when he bumbled a conversation.

The last bright flickers in his life were his time with her, even if she was going mad being around him, so he was putting up with Italy a little longer. He hoped that she could see that he was trying, because his trying took a lot right now. Getting out of bed took a lot right now. Turning up his lips took all of him.

Ever-present in his mind was how close he'd come to taking his life in March. The Zoloft was still helping—and certainly the tasks keeping him busy here—but he was in the same boat he'd been in since being escorted out of Intel. Soon as he got back, he'd have nothing. What would happen then? How easily he could slip back to that darkness that had consumed him. Not that he wasn't wallowing in the dark now, but those days in March had been far worse. What he most remembered was how hopeless he'd felt. Not having any experience with depression in the past, not even a taste of it, what he'd learned was that there was no talking your way out of it, no plugging the hole by taking trumpet lessons or jumping into a baking class. When you're on the edge of suicide, there is no light.

Come to think of it, an extended stay at a Motel 6 might have been the end of him.

Detaching his readers, he sat back in the chair. There was still more that he needed to say to Bianca. She was making mistakes, and it was impossible to stand on the sidelines without at least attempting to save her. He might not be a great father, but he'd never stop loving her, never stop wanting the most for her.

He eventually crept down the hall to the living room, finding Bianca immersed in her work, perhaps another newsletter or some journaling.

Holding her fingers over the keys, she said in a tone rich with annoyance, "Just working, Dad." She said "Dad" like it was a bad word. It hurt worse than a blade shoved through his rib cage.

He didn't want her to see that, though. Trying to appear fearless and forgiving, he sat down. "We don't have to do lunch."

She went back to typing something.

"I know you're slammed," he said at the end of a long silence.

She stopped again, fingers hovering. "Sorry, just focused."

He could see she was fighting to stay calm. He did the same, saying in the most loving way he could, "I know I'm out of quarters, but I . . . May I offer something? I have to get everything out before I go."

She took a long time to respond, eventually offering a curt nod.

Feeling like he was dipping his toes into piranha-filled water, he said, "Look, I'm searching for a flight back. I know I'm a lot. But can I do a little parenting in the meantime?"

He paused, wishing she'd beg him to stay, but of course she didn't. She didn't say a word, so he continued. "I took the liberty of reaching out to a guy I used to work with, great guy actually. Grew up the son of a logger in Canada, got into Pepperdine, and eventually made something of himself. A higher-up in HR at Intel, then started his own headhunting firm. He helps people find their path. You pay some money, which I'd be happy to do, then he coaches you through figuring out next steps."

Her fingers still hovered over the keys. "That's nice of you, but I don't need any help right now."

"Oh, c'mon. You have to work."

She retracted her hands. "How many times do we have to do this? You've been working sixty hours a week since you were a teenager, and for good reason. You climbed out of a tough childhood. But I don't find the same satisfaction you do in working. The people here, they don't let their work define them."

"And that's why Europe is a shit show. That's why we've blown by them."

"Blown by them? In what way? Because of our economy?"

"Because of *everything*. Jobs, opportunities, tech. Yes, economy. We're the center of the world. Do you know how many people here would kill to be American, to have the lives that we have?" He'd said it before, but she still wasn't getting it.

"Not as many as you think. Do you see how healthy people are here? How happy?"

"I see the lines, the red tape. The bureaucracy."

"Are we doing this again, George?"

Ugh, there was nothing worse than when she called him by his name.

He raised a hand like a white flag. "As someone who's been around the block, I'm simply sharing some of what I've learned. Sure, enjoy this year, but then come home and get to work. Sitting around is what kills people."

She closed her laptop with a *snap*. "That's so your generation. And so American. I want to become a sponge for knowledge. I want to get my Italian back. I want to study art and history and read. To stop doing and start being." The decibel level of her voice rose by the word. "Sometimes, I want to do absolutely nothing but face my demons and get to know myself. I want to repair that damage I did to myself by working my ass off since the moment I started college. It may not make sense to you, but what I'm doing right now is *everything* to me."

If only she knew what she was saying. In a way, it was good that he'd been raised poor because he knew what happened when you stopped working. Nevertheless, the window of opportunity here had closed. He'd have to try again later.

He stood, held his hands in prayer position, and spoke calmly. "This is me loving on you, honey. And worrying about you."

"I'm the best I've ever been, getting back to the real me."

The real me? George thought. She wanted a time machine and to be eighteen again. That's not the way the world worked. Before he uttered anything else to anger her, though, he said, "I'm going out for a walk. Sorry for butting in."

She said a lot by not saying anything at all.

On the other side of the door, he pressed his eyes closed. Why did he think that would go well? He'd have to call his buddy, the career coach, and tell him Bianca wasn't interested.

Out in the fresh air, he looked left and right down Via Giulia. Maybe he'd go grab some lunch, take a long walk. As he'd done every five minutes, considering the pickpockets, he patted his pants to make sure he had his keys and wallet.

Keys, check, but he'd left his wallet back inside.

He climbed the stairs again and walked through the door. As he was about to say, "I forgot my . . ." he heard Bianca ranting into the phone. He realized she was talking about him. He didn't want to listen, but he couldn't help it.

". . . trying to help him, Mom, but I don't think he can be helped. Not even Italy can save him. He hates everything but work. Work, work, work. And the to-do lists. He has to-do lists for his to-do lists, and now that he's retired, he's grabbing into thin air for chores. He cleaned the freaking community courtyard yesterday. Like swept and—

". . . I know it's nice, and I know this is his way of showing me—

". . . What I want to say is that I'm here because I don't want to turn out like him. He screwed up his marriage to you, was barely there for me, and now that he has nothing to do, he's trying to swoop in and fix everything. Honestly, he's making it worse."

The air left George's lungs. Forgetting about retrieving his wallet, he slipped out, hoping she wouldn't hear the door click.

Back on the street, he started wandering. The only reason he'd come here, putting up with the plane travel and all the headaches of this fucking city, was to help her. To show her that he did love her. Sorry that he had worked all his life. His dad had barely worked a day, and George had sworn to break the cycle, to never let his family starve.

Any light that he'd found since March dissipated. What was the point in even taking the Zoloft? To keep masking the truth that his life had run its course and there wasn't much point anymore?

"Hi, George."

He looked up to see Sandy brushing past him.

Sandy wanted to keep going, but George was trudging along like there was something wrong, like he might drop. When he looked at her, his eyes were red, on the edge of crying.

"You okay?" she asked, truly concerned.

He faked a smile. Or perhaps tried and failed. "Do you have kids?"

Feeling that one in her chest, she gave a nod. "A son."

He rolled his tongue against his lips, his eyes searching the sidewalk, his head shaking. "I've never been good at this parent thing. Can't figure it out." He ran a hand through his impossibly perfect hair. "I'm driving Bianca crazy."

She stepped toward him. "Isn't that what all parents do?"

"Yeah, I guess so."

He said no more. Sandy could sense the pain bleeding out of him.

Another step toward him, one parent to another. "Don't beat yourself up. It's not easy."

When he looked up, she realized he was still handsome when he was sad. A sad handsome. "Got any books on how to repair relationships with your kids?"

This was his form of humor, perhaps. "We could order you one. I should have a whole shelf."

"How old's your son?"

"Almost thirty."

"Where is he?"

She took a long time to answer. "I don't know. He went into the marines, fighting classified wars in foreign lands."

"I can't imagine. When's the last time you saw him?"

She reached into her purse and ran her finger along the coral. "It's been a while."

A nod, a reverent moment of silence. "You're probably rushing into work, but I was going to take a walk. Wanna join?"

Her first instinct was to politely decline, but her pathetic heart betrayed her. "No one rushes to work around here. Why not."

They found an easy rhythm, wandering west under the porticoes out of the old town. The streets grew wider; modern architecture appeared. He needed no prodding as he opened up about his issues with retirement, then circled back to Bianca.

"What is it you did to upset her?" Sandy asked.

"Isn't that the question. Now or when she was growing up? You could say I'm a workaholic, which is obviously why retirement isn't working out. I wasn't around as much as I should have been, especially as she got into her teens. And it hurt my ex *and* Bianca. She's still blaming me for the divorce."

Sandy let him keep going.

"There's more to it than that, though. I can't help but slip in some fatherly advice every once in a while, and it never lands well. No matter what I do, I screw up. She can't stand that I'm the kind of guy who can't sit around. I've been cleaning up her place, getting her organized, touching up some paint, that kind of thing. Stuff that needs to be done. As much as I don't like her being so far away, I want her to be happy. And doing all that stuff is the best way I know to show her I love her."

What a kind man. Back when Sandy's love radar was on, she should have been looking for kindness. Husbands #1 and #2 seemed to only excel at it during their apologies.

"If you need to expend some of that energy," she said, "we can always use you at the bookstore. My handyman is currently ignoring my texts."

"Happy to help any time."

"She'll see it, George. I don't even know you, but I can feel how much you care about her. Maybe watch your mouth, hold back some of that 'fatherly advice,' but don't stop loving her. It'll break through."

It was almost refreshing to speak with someone so candidly. She even shared some of her own battered past when he prodded. She didn't get into specifics, but she spoke some truths, a cathartic release.

As they wandered down Via del Pratello, Sandy said, "This is my favorite place to walk. The best street art in the city. A bunch of hole-in-the-wall food joints. Prices are climbing, but it's still one of the less expensive areas. Lots of students. And I guess it's that youth that brings it alive. A lot of Bologna feels like you're seeing it from behind velvet ropes. Here, you're right in the madness of it, the truth of the Bolognese spirit."

George didn't respond but let his eyes wander, and she could tell that he was trying to see it.

The street was less polished than those of the old town, the shades of yellow, pink, and red buildings showing their age. Paint peeled off the shutters. Some of the wooden beams that held up the porticoes looked like they might be getting close to the end of their life. But between the off-the-beaten-path haunts, the to-die-for takeaway pasta places, the graffiti that rivaled any art in the museums, and the lively nightlife, there was a tangible and vibrant energy here that could make anyone feel like they'd stumbled upon heaven.

Even Sandy.

Twelve or so years in, this town still took her breath away. It would be hard to leave, but a new start had been on her mind lately. She'd been teasing a move to Lisbon, where she could escape some of her ghosts.

She pointed at a restaurant she and the jazz musician used to frequent. "Il Rovescio makes some of the most exciting bio food in the city."

"Bio?"

"Organic. Their food will make you cry, it's so good."

"I've never had a food make me cry before."

"Hang around Bologna long enough, it'll happen."

She watched him take in the graffiti that covered doorways and climbed up the columns of the porticoes—bright colors that bounced off the stucco. She could sense his wheels spinning, one foot here in the present, the other stuck in the quicksand of his relationship with Bianca. Though she hated that he was suffering, it was nice to see a man care so deeply.

Back on Via Giulia, George turned to face her. "Thanks for listening. I did most of the talking. Sorry about that."

Sandy felt a twinge of something dangerous. An attraction. "Sometimes we need an ear. Hang in there. She knows you love her. No more advice, though."

"Unless she asks for it," he said.

"She won't."

They both laughed.

Sandy turned and headed into work. She could feel him watching her go. Maybe in another life they could have had something.

Inside, Harold stood at the counter with a stack of books. Moira was ringing him up. "Well, look at this," she said with genuine surprise, eyeing Harold up and down.

His hair was cut high and tight, combed back with a product that had a slight glisten to it. His designer sunglasses were pushed up above his forehead. He wore skinny white trousers with a matching blazer and shiny loafers without socks. A blue shirt with a pronounced collar fit tightly on his skinny frame.

"Giovanni took care of you, didn't he?" Sandy said.

"Took all my money, and yes, took care of me. Thank you." He'd allowed a British accent to slip into his words. She'd noticed it last time. How puzzling. But maybe it was working.

"That Alice won't know what to do," she said. "What are you buying there?"

She looked past him to the stack. Moira set her hand on it. "I'm sending him home with some art history, an Alda Merini poetry book, *Italian for Dummies*, and then a few novels: R. F. Kuang, Elena Ferrante, Kazuo Ishiguro."

Sandy patted his shoulder. "You have your work cut out for you."

"I'm eager to get started."

She saw so much of Jack in this young man, more so every time she set eyes on him. "She better be worth it, Harold."

"What's anything without love?"

"Oh, God." She frowned. He might be a lost cause.

He looked like she'd pushed him off a cliff.

Oh, what the hell. The poor boy needed help. "Firstly," she started, "right now, you need to start acting as if you've moved on, because no girl worth her salt will come back to you if you're sitting around moping. You understand?"

A timid nod.

"How's your dancing?" she asked.

"My dancing?"

"Yes, Harold. Do you dance?"

Harold looked over at Moira, then back. "Not much of a dancer."

"I have my tango lesson tomorrow. Meet me down here at six forty-five."

"Really? I'm terrible, I can't even hold a—"

"Even you can learn to dance. You've remedied your style issue. Let's focus on your body, how you move."

After he'd left, Sandy caught up with Moira for a few minutes, then climbed the steps to her office. She switched on the small lamp and sat in her chair, then dialed a number. When Jack's voicemail message ended, she said, "It's me again. Calling from the bookstore that's going out of business. Unless maybe summer saves us. What's new in your world? Oh, wait, you can't tell me."

She found the coral in her purse and held it as she continued.

"Who me? I'm just trying to live my life amid a sea of helpless people. There's a guy, Harold, who lives above the store. He's a mess; you've never seen a mess like him. And he had this pretty girl who dumped him, and so I'm trying to help him clean himself up. I somehow feel like his mother. Then there's a guy named George who's after me. I keep deflecting him, but he's nice and kind of needs me too. You know, for a gal who tries to keep to herself, people keep coming at me. And Moira, don't even get me started. Anyway, that's it for now."

She set the phone down and stared out the small window, seeing rain clouds approaching.

Chapter 15

A Relentless Hunter

Bianca sat at a small table outside of a bar Lucio Dalla, a cherished Bolognese musician who first broke into the scene in the seventies, used to frequent. She'd stopped by the bookstore and bought the new Isabel Allende, which was doing a poor job of pulling her away from thoughts of her father.

Thoughts of Her Father. Sounded like a chapter in the next book that she now had to write unless she wanted to spit into the eyes of destiny. Not that Bianca was opposed to proving Donna Bologna wrong. It was either that or willingly leap back into the pot of boiling water.

How was it possible that she could be in Bologna, living this new life, a long way from the world that had pulled her down, book in hand in a bar in the old town of Bologna, and yet still be unhappy, unable to read even a paragraph without her mind going astray?

What Bianca kept trying to do, *trying* being the operative word here, was find empathy for her father. She could relate to the little boy inside him, the kid raised in poverty by a grieving father. George rarely talked about his childhood, even when urged, so most of what Bianca knew were bits and pieces she'd pried out of him.

She supposed it was understandable that he was this way and was likely never going to change. He didn't even recognize his constant movement as a problem. For him, it was a badge of honor. *I work the hardest of anyone in this room.* If he could say that, then he was doing well, a notion with which she could certainly empathize.

Further complicating the matter, Bianca's Megawatters had been delighted to read about her latest adventure. So many warm messages of encouragement. And at least a few hundred asking about another book. Were they crazy? Were they serious?

One message in particular, from Beth Anne in Wichita, had said: I'm so happy (and jealous) for your Italy adventure. Just tell me one thing. Is this research for *Peggy Goes to Italy*? Please say yes. Your book helped me so much, but I have a long way to go.

Realizing she wasn't in the right mindset to read, Bianca set the book down and people-watched for a while: a businessman in a hurry, a mom tugging on her child, saying, *"Andiamo, Andiamo."*

Then a familiar voice from the crowd. "Hey, you're the famous American writer, yeah?"

Slightly excited to be recognized, she searched for a Megawatter in the crowd. Of course, she'd been recognized in Texas and by Moira at the bookstore, but this was a first in . . .

Wait, it was Corrado smirking as he stood over her. He wore a chef's shirt with his name and the name of his restaurant woven into the pocket.

"Well, look at this. My stalker."

"Stalker? You're stalking me. It's my city, remember?"

"Your city? You're supposed to be in Paris."

He shook his head. "Paris didn't suit me."

A long quiet followed with some sort of stalled momentum in it, as if they were two tigers in the wild hiding behind tall grass and hunting the same prey. Who would go first?

"I won't bother you," he finally said. "Just returning from a meeting. Enjoy your—"

"Would you like to join me?" Bianca interrupted, not wanting him to go.

"*Grazie, ma no.* You keep reading your . . . Isabel Allende. It's nice to see you, *ciao.*" He didn't wait for her response, but eased back into the crowd.

What? she thought. Her jaw smacked the sidewalk, causing a slight tremor that might have registered on a seismometer. *He's going to walk away?*

Desperately she called, "Corrado! Sit your ass down." Her voice cut through the city noise, causing more than a few heads to turn. She set her book aside and watched him turn back and sit across from her. If he wasn't careful, she was going to smack that smile off him.

Ready for battle, she said, "Don't you need to be in a kitchen or something?"

"I was interviewing a sous chef down the street, now headed to the restaurant."

"To do what? Chop vegetables?"

"No, my Bianca. We're a month away. I have preparations. Deliveries to take, more interviews, marketing meetings."

"You sound so grown up now."

"I suppose so. Happens to the best of us, right?" He held up a finger, then ordered an espresso from the *cameriere*. Back to her, he asked, "How's Bologna treating you?"

"That's a loaded question." She now remembered his ability to give every bit of his attention to her. "It's great to be here, but my dad's complicated the mission."

"The mission?"

"You know, just my . . ." She considered how to answer. "My journey to reclaim who I once was."

A warm smile played on his face. "Life gets complicated, doesn't it?"

A breeze blew by, and she took a moment to enjoy it, then: "You probably won't, but do you remember the promise I made to you the night before I left? We were at Osteria del Sole."

"The one where you said you'd come find me, that you'd be back? Before you ravished me in my bed, a goodbye like I'll never know again."

A hurricane spun up her legs. "Stop it."

He bit his lower lip.

"Okay, I guess I broke two promises. The other was that I wouldn't get pulled back into the whole American thing, working all the time, not taking moments to breathe, not connecting with friends, not really living."

His face straightened. "Yes, I remember."

"I let go of everything I learned living here. It was like I drank a big Starbucks drink that swept me back up. If I'm being honest, I felt like the only way was to go kick ass out there in the world, make something of myself. Become an accomplisher. Isn't that silly? Wouldn't that be an interesting word on my gravestone. *Bianca Briggs died of a heart attack from working too hard; she will always be known as an accomplisher.* Then there would be a parenthetical at the bottom. *And though it turned out to be a dud, she even wrote a book.*"

She pulled back before saying more. He was the last person to whom she should be confessing.

His espresso came, and he took a sip, moaning with pleasure. She remembered that about him too. They could be talking, hanging out, doing whatever, but if he got near something worth tasting, he always paid deep attention to the flavor.

Once he'd set his cup down, he said, "The book didn't do well?"

"Fine, I guess. Definitely didn't shake up the world. Let's just say I was hoping for something that might outsell *The Secret.*"

A headshake. "I don't know that one. The accomplishment is enough in and of itself. I have a friend who's a writer, back in Paris, called Jacques. We worked together. Writes these mysteries solved by a crazy alcoholic blind detective. One time he told me that he became a much better writer when he stopped trying to write a bestseller, stopped trying to become this famous writer. Instead, he wrote for himself, what he wanted to read, and didn't care whatever the others said. Ironically, that's also when he started selling enough books to leave his restaurant job."

What had been her mindset while writing her book? She scrolled through the life of it, from the seed of an idea to print: Donna Bologna telling her she'd write one, the idea fading as she pursued her therapy degree at UT, only to resurface around the time she opened her practice. But she hadn't put pen to paper till a year after she'd finally established herself, proving that she had what it took to build up a client list. That time in between had been a blur of hard work. If anything, her book was just another product of her obsessive climb to the top of a mountain that actually had no top.

"I do like Peggy Meh," Corrado said, sticking a crowbar into the spokes of her mind chatter.

"Wait, what? You read it?" All at once, she was flattered and horrified.

"I'm reading it. Found it at that bookstore where you had your signing."

"I told you not to."

"Why not? I always loved diving into you, exploring your mind."

Diving into her. Birds flapped wings behind her rib cage while he sat there so innocently, his gentle (naive?) pursuit of her a glint in his eyes.

"I'm proud of you; you're a great writer. Not that my English is perfect, but I like your style."

"You and my mom."

"My friend Jacques said it took him a few books before anyone discovered him. I'm sure that's the case here. What's next?"

"That's the question." She smiled to herself. "If there is a next; I'm not sure."

"I like the name Peggy. You should keep her around."

"Peggy was a placeholder name," Bianca said. "I had the idea, a blend of all the clients I'd worked with or read about, but I couldn't think of a good name, so I called her Peggy Meh and planned on changing it later. But my agent loved it, and she convinced my publisher to love it. Then the idea of Meh to Megawatt took root. That's partially why it failed. People think it's cheesy. Some of the reviews tear the concept apart."

"People don't know anything," he said. "And who cares anyway? The act of finishing it must have been so rewarding. I imagine it would be similar to how I might feel on opening night of the restaurant. To realize the impossible dream, you know."

Why was he so easy to talk to? So honest.

"Would you say it's autobiographical?" he asked. The way he fumbled through the last word was adorable. "Did Bianca Meh become Bianca Megawatt?"

There he was again, picking on her. Not meanly, but it still cut deep.

"No, it's not autobiographical, but of course, I'm trying to better myself. Push myself. Like everybody else who wants to realize their potential. That's the point of my book." She hated how defensive she felt. "Don't tell me you're not supercharged, doing whatever it took to get a job at L'Ambroisie, then coming back to chase your own Michelin star. Talk about megawatts."

He touched his heart. "Fair enough. It's true, I've worked far too hard sometimes. That's partially why I left Paris. I didn't like that culture. So much ego, so much anger. I make slow food. And the only way to do that is to move slowly, live slowly. And though some might argue with me, I'm not in it for the awards. I don't particularly care about the acclaim or even getting the star. Cooking is what I'm here for, and my joy comes from serving people, seeing the delight on their faces when they're given an experience they won't soon forget, giving them an escape from the troubles of their world—if only for a while. What I like is the experience given by a Michelin-starred restaurant. I'll never forget my first time . . . but anyway . . ."

"No, please tell me." In the back of her mind, she acknowledged that maybe he was a lot like George, the way he wanted to help others.

As Corrado recounted his memory, she was struck by the way he saw the world. He wasn't megawatted, not in the slightest.

When he finished, they held eye contact for far too long. She could have knocked the table away and jumped him right then. Those ten years disappeared in a flash, like they were kids again, exploring each other as virgins.

He leaned in closer. “I missed you, my Bianca.”

She looked down. “No. Don’t do that.”

“Do what? Why so hesitant?”

“Do you have a few hours?” She felt herself redden. “I have to figure myself out right now.”

He didn’t blink. “We have unfinished business. I’m only halfway through, but does Peggy Meh find love? I’m imagining her male counterpart. Perhaps Billy Boring.”

“Billy Boring? You’re ridiculous.”

“Or maybe Anthony Awful.”

“Talk about awful. And no, Peggy doesn’t find love. It’s not a love story.”

“Ah, then there’s book two, right? Peggy Missing to Peggy Mesmerized, dazzled by her Italian lover.”

“Will you stop it?” She covered her cheeks.

He reached across the table and pulled her hands away. “Look at you. You’re even more beautiful when you blush.”

She shook him off. “I’m warning you. I’m about to go get on a plane and go back to Texas.”

He sat back in retreat. “What if your book failed, just to get you here? Ever consider that?”

Maybe she hadn’t considered it, which was weird. Had the universe conspired against her, making it impossible for her book to succeed? No, the book had failed because she’d clearly written the wrong book. Or given the wrong message. Thought she was funny when she was anything but.

“Or what if you came here to write this second book? Your love story.”

Bianca set her elbows on the table, stared down at her empty cappuccino, and began to massage her temples.

"What's going on in there? Looking for yourself in the cup? Bianca, where are you?"

She slowly looked up at him. His silliness deserved a kick in the shin.

"Would you like to come see my restaurant?" he asked.

She started shaking her head and didn't stop, staring at him, wondering if there was any possible way to escape this madness. No, there wasn't. Whatever this was, it was happening. Who was she kidding? Never had she been more attracted to a man. Ten years, and she could still taste him.

"Here we are," Corrado said twenty minutes later, stopping to admire the exterior of the Hotel Minerva, where his restaurant was located. The ten-story, stark-white building was constructed with modern taste: tall windows, a sharp and boxy design. Balconies on each floor. A doorman pushed open the door and greeted them.

As they walked through the lobby, Bianca asked, "Is he going to open the door for you every time you go to work?"

"He has so far. He'll get tired of me soon."

In the back left corner, a small, elegant sign above two white doors read Il Minerva. He twisted a key in a lock and then guided them to a small host area with a coat check. A second set of double doors led into the dining room.

She gasped as her eyes darted about, soaking it in. Crystal chandeliers hung from a thirty-foot-tall ceiling painted royal blue. In the corner stood an impressive glassed-in wine room with hundreds of bottles perched in tall racks. Potted white orchids rested on tall and skinny metal tables. Massive racy paintings hung from the cream walls. One featured two nude men dancing together under the moon, their hands on each other's backsides. Another depicted a woman's legs with a flock of birds forming a V shape at her thighs. A month away from the opening, but the tables were already set.

"I'm speechless."

"Not what you expected."

"You amaze me, you know that, right?"

He flashed a humble smile, so human, so gentle, so committed to creating something special. She shook her head as she searched his eyes, still seeing the young man who'd captured her years ago, but now seeing the man he'd become. Everything seemed to come so easy to him.

"I think you're incredible. This. This is incredible."

"Come see the rest." He was like a kid showing off his sandcastle, so proud and eager.

She followed him past a velvet curtain into an immaculate and impressive kitchen. Various vegetables and fruits were spread out on one of the long stainless-steel tables. All of the equipment, the ovens, stoves, fryers, the mixers, blenders sparkled.

He gave her a quick tour, explaining how he used each machine in the kitchen.

"I made an Italian take on an Andalucían gazpacho, you know, the tomato soup. Wanna try it?"

"Sure."

He washed his hands, then located a tray of plastic tubs in the refrigerator and set them on his workspace. He poured the soup into a bowl, a red color that could only come from Italy, explaining that he used Sicilian tomatoes that had been on a vine only two days prior.

As he began to dress the soup, he said, "Gazpacho is typically made with tomatoes, cucumber, bell pepper, bread crust, red onion, garlic, olive oil, sherry, and cumin, salt, and pepper. I add a dash of *colatura di alici*, an Italian fish sauce made with anchovies that are salt-aged in small chestnut barrels. Do you know it?"

She shook her head.

He professed his love for it in Italian, then returned to his work. "These are basil oil pearls, then a sprinkle of Burrata snow, made with liquid nitrogen."

She stepped closer to look over his shoulder as he transformed his soup into an art piece. Her mouth watered.

He took tweezers and set several tiny leaves in the center. "Microgreens I grow on the roof. And then I finish with a crisp of parmesan polenta." He set it sideways like a glacier poking up in the sea. "Finally, I top it with a compressed watermelon cube marinated in Campari." He set the small cube on the other side, creating a sort of landscape on top of the soup.

When he finished, he invited her to take a bite. How could anyone turn a bowl of soup into a masterpiece?

"It's too pretty to eat," she said.

He took the spoon and gathered a bite, including one of the pearls. He started to lift it to her mouth, then said, "Hold on. Don't move." It felt like he'd pulled away from a kiss.

Setting down the spoon, he raced back out into the dining room and returned with a candelabra. He set it on the steel table and lit all five candles, then switched off the fluorescent lights above.

As the candlelight flickered against his face, he pulled a bottle of wine from the fridge. "This is a white pinot nero, better known as pinot noir, that's pressed and removed of its skins so quickly that it barely retains any color. Grown by a family in Valle d'Aosta who've been making wine for eight generations."

He slid a glass her way. "Now, *buon appetito.*"

Her first sip gave her chills.

He watched her every move.

A tear welled up in her eye. Was it the wine or the entire experience, being around an artist of his caliber? And that's what this was: art. And he was a candle in a world where light bulbs had been guiding her way.

He picked the spoon back up and prepared once again her perfect bite, then guided it to her mouth. As he set it on her tongue, she let the flavors wash over her like a rising tide. It was almost too much, the taste, the texture.

"That's so good. Who are you, Corrado?"

Only inches from her face, he pulled the spoon away. "You like?"

She licked her lips and looked at his, then at his eyes and back again. She tasted the lingering flavors of this fresh, cool dish, the basil so lovely still on her tongue. She then grabbed the collar of his chef's shirt and pulled him toward her. An inch closer and she could smell the espresso from earlier on his breath.

Then they kissed, and she nearly lost her balance. Their hearts beat in harmony.

"Dio, ti voglio cosi tanto," he gently whispered. I want you so badly.

The two of them clamored for each other, grasping for curves, swallowing each other whole.

But as he tore open her shirt, the buttons splashing onto the floor, his hands on her, the shame of who she'd become washed over her. Any further and he'd see that she was nothing like the girl he once knew.

"Stop," she said. "I have to stop."

He pulled his head away, and she raced to cover herself. He'd known the better version of her, the happier her, the skinnier her, the younger her. As much as she wanted him, she couldn't let him see who she'd become.

"What is it?" His chest heaved.

She turned away from him, searching for a way out.

"Did I do something . . ."

"I have to go, I'm sorry."

Bianca couldn't even turn back to face him. Her heart flatlining, she left the kitchen and scurried through the dining room toward the lobby of the hotel.

After her walk of shame back to Via Giulia, she ran into a neighbor on the way into her apartment. "Sorry," Bianca said, almost bumping into the young woman. Half of her was still in Corrado's kitchen.

"No problem," her neighbor replied. She was in her midtwenties. A Scandinavian accent, maybe Swedish. Bianca had forgotten her name; they'd made chitchat a few times.

She held the door open, a foot on the sidewalk. "Hey, it's Bianca, right? I'm Hannah. I just wanted to ask, was that your father cleaning the courtyard?"

"Yes, it was. I hope he didn't get in your way. He's very project oriented. If he's here much longer, he'll probably try to come organize your closet."

Hannah shook her head. "How lucky you are. If my parents *ever* come see me, they don't lift a finger."

The idea was rather sobering. "Yeah, I guess I am lucky. He's painted walls. Reorganized three closets. Vacuumed behind the couches. Rearranged the Tupperware. Did the courtyard." The pride in her own tone surprised her. "Even pressed our 'lovely' landlord to do a few things."

"Now that's a feat in and of itself."

"Tell me about it."

"If you ever want to trade fathers, I'm on the second floor." Hannah offered a wave and then let go of the door.

Bianca watched it close. Perspective was everything, wasn't it?

Chapter 16

Lost Pieces of You

The vacillation between Harold and Aroldo happened at a more rapid frequency now. He—or *they*—found that it was simply a matter of pulling the proverbial switch. At 1:00 a.m., he woke as Harold, ready to race to the screen to hang with his gamer friends, but then he'd quickly decide that it would be Aroldo who rose out of the bed. And Aroldo did such a thing with a casual Italian verve. Slow. Methodical. Mindful. His friends had definitely noticed the change, many of them mentioning that he seemed different, a few asking if he'd fallen in love again.

His mother, who knew him best, kept asking whether he was okay, wondering what had changed. "Nothing, Mom. Feeling better about myself, having fun. I have to stay longer. I promise I'll pay you back every dime."

He grabbed a quick snooze once the sun broke over the city, but then he—Aroldo—popped up for a three-mile run, followed by a shower and then his new routine of dressing for the day. In the past, he'd had a Steve Jobs mindset regarding his wardrobe. He often wore the same thing every day—jeans and a polo or tee—so that he wouldn't have to waste energy making unnecessary decisions.

Aroldo was different. As Sandy had taught him, a person made a statement with his choice of attire. When you slipped into your clothing, you were choosing who you wanted to be. He stood in front of the mirror and inspected himself. Bits of Harold tried to tell him that he was still the scrawny punk from Denver, but he silenced that voice with, "Enough, Harold. You are Aroldo now." He pulled on one of his new white shirts, which Giovanni had tailored for him. He opted to leave three buttons unbuttoned to show off this new, polished chest of his. Then he pulled on a dark plaid vest and matching pants. Slipping into his light leather shoes, he checked himself again.

"There you are, Aroldo," he said. "There is no room for Harold here."

At precisely 8:31 a.m., he reached his desired location, an outdoor restaurant that faced Renzo's building, a place with impressive columns and arches that looked about as "high rent" as it got in this city. He'd not seen Alice or his archnemesis since the incident when he'd suffered a panic attack, but Aroldo had decided it was time to reassess the situation.

He took a table with a clear view to the entrance and started his surveillance. It had been almost a month since she'd dumped him, and the longing for her throbbed within him as he imagined this new life she was living.

She'd mentioned taking summer classes, but he had no idea when they'd begin. It could take days to figure out their routine, but Aroldo was in no rush. He would be patient and wait for his move.

After ordering an espresso, he sat back, crossed his legs, and opened Bianca's book. It wasn't exactly his first choice, but Moira had been so kind to him and kept asking whether he'd read it. With one eye on the door, he dove in.

In chapter 1, entitled "Assess and Confess," the anonymized Peggy comes into Bianca's office in Austin for her initial session. Peggy's a teller at a large bank in Cincinnati with a boss who has perfected skating the line of harassment. She eats a peanut butter and jelly sandwich with chubby carrots every day for lunch. She's in a tough marriage with a high-school principal named Matthew Meh, who forgot her last birthday. She's silently grateful for their infertility issues. Though they both work, he expects her to cook dinner every night, and as she does so, she always fantasizes about adding some arsenic to the mac and cheese. Her husband doesn't know that she's in major credit card debt. She has a crush on Mitch, her yoga teacher, and the best part of her week is when he presses down on her lower back when she's in downward dog. At night, she lies in bed and pretends her husband was kidnapped by aliens and she's now Yoga Mitch's wife.

After congratulating Peggy for being so open, Bianca tells her that it's her destiny to make the shift from Peggy Meh to Peggy Megawatt, and apparently, that would be the guts of the rest of the book.

Aroldo raised his head, thinking that he'd done just that in becoming Aroldo. He'd seen Harold's weaknesses and eliminated them, and it was working. He couldn't remember ever feeling so confident in his life.

Aroldo Megawatt, here to save the day!

Specific confessional exercises at the end of the chapter prompted the reader for a self-diagnosis, asking them to detail lies they were telling themselves and others, what they liked least and most about themselves, and so on.

Aroldo grinned. He told some lies, all right. But he had no intent of writing them down. In fact, he saw no need to even do the exercises. Who in history did the exercises in a book?

Aroldo was flipping the page to chapter 2 when he saw them, Alice and Renzo, leaving the apartment. The girlfriend thief was dressed for work, his face shiny from a shave. She wore a short skirt, showing off her freckled and shapely legs. A backpack hung over one shoulder. At the bottom of the steps, Renzo took her by the waist and kissed her, then whispered something in her ear that caused a giggle before heading in the opposite direction.

She watched him go with what Aroldo feared were heart-shaped eyes, then drew out her phone, typed a message, and started walking in Harold's—no, Aroldo's—direction. Harold might have cowered, but Aroldo reached for a pack of cigarettes that he'd bought yesterday and lit one up. He instantly coughed, but he smothered it and cleared his throat. He took a less aggressive puff and saw her passing him out of the corner of his eye. She hadn't even noticed him. He'd created that much of a change.

He left his table and, at a safe distance, followed her to the library at the university, where she sat on the steps with a group of friends and smoked a cigarette, then disappeared inside. It seemed her life hadn't changed much.

The wheels spun. How could he get her back? What was it going to take?

That evening, as Aroldo walked with Sandy across town to the tango lessons, he didn't dare mention that he'd followed Alice around all day. She might not understand. Instead, he listened to Sandy talk about how she'd been considering a move to Lisbon.

"What about the store?"

"Wanna buy it?"

"I don't think so."

Harold would have been mortified to enter the dance studio with its claustrophobia-inducing brick walls and tight cluster of strangers, many of whom looked as nervous as him, but Aroldo embraced new experiences.

Twenty-five people formed in a half circle around the teacher, a ripped young Italian man in baggy pants and polished black shoes. He introduced himself as Tommaso, then called for Sandy to join him and went over the initial steps of the tango in both English and Italian. Apparently, she'd been doing this a long time and was his go-to for demonstrations.

Harold tried to follow, counting in his head, tripping over himself. He couldn't recall ever dancing in his life. The only dances he'd ever attended were the ones his mother had forced him to attend in high school. Little had she known, he'd spent those nights hiding in the hallways or in an empty classroom.

Sandy had clearly been dancing for years, and her ability pretty much blew the doors off the box he'd put her in. He'd imagined she didn't have much of a life outside of her store, a lonely and often grumpy bookwoman who spent her free time curled on the couch reading.

Tommaso said, "We start with the simple steps, then we'll elaborate from there. Watch my hips, my hands. Listen to the music. This is an improvisation, that's what is so beautiful about the tango. Don't be rigid. Let yourself go."

With that, the familiar sounds of tango filled the room. He found Sandy's eyes, whispered a count, and then they were off, dancing so deeply and darkly that every other person looked awestruck. Sandy could have taught this class. It was simply incredible to watch her. She moved like a tigress tearing through the jungle.

When they stopped, the students applauded, then Tommaso said, "Now, find a partner. You'll dance together for several minutes, then switch, moving along the circle."

Harold tightened. It hadn't occurred to him that he'd be dancing with anyone other than Sandy. He looked around the room, feeling intimidation tear at him like a vulture on roadkill.

Then a tap on the shoulder. He turned to find a woman easily six inches taller looking down at him. The scent of her dizzying perfume drifted up his nose.

In an eastern European accent, she said, "Can we dance?"

His eyes widened. "I can . . . I'm not very . . ." He couldn't get the words out. Dammit, where was Aroldo when he needed him?

"You'll be fine. I'm not good either."

"Okay. Sorry, I'm already sorry."

Aroldo said into his ear: *Harold, go away. I am here now. I will show you how to dance.*

A man half Harold, half Aroldo stepped forward. He had to reach up to put his hand on the back of the woman's shoulder, which was the placement Tommaso had taught them earlier. They drew close, and he felt ashamed. This intimacy with a stranger was crushing him. But then they began to move and though he stumbled about, he couldn't help but laugh, and laughing wasn't something he'd experienced much since Alice had left him. Maybe with Moira once or twice.

The tall woman was laughing too. They tried again and again, getting modestly better each time.

"There you go," she said in her thick accent. "Listen to the music."

"I guess this isn't your first time," he said, hating how uncomfortable he sounded. *Dammit, Aroldo, take over!* Trying again, he said, "You're marvelous on your feet, darling. A natural." *There you go.*

He cycled through several partners, and all Harold could think about was how badly he needed hand sanitizer. He even danced with a man. Hands larger than his holding him, his hand up on the other man's shoulder, both of them attempting to move their feet with some sort of rhythm while avoiding looking at each other.

Thank God for Aroldo, who was comfortable in his own skin. He kept pushing Harold, whisper-screaming into his ear: *You don't need hand sanitizer. Who cares if you're dancing with a man? Lighten up. Loosen those hips. You are Aroldo. Harold is dead, dead, dead . . .*

Then he got to Sandy, whose forehead glistened with a sheen of sweat. She looked like she was having the time of her life, half the age of the woman he'd met earlier at the bookstore.

She set a hand on his waist. "Are you picking it up?"

"Not even close." He wasn't sure if that was Harold or Aroldo.

"Let's see what you got."

She counted out to the music, then they launched into the steps. He'd gotten good enough to get through it at least somewhat.

"Look at you," she said, a smile that he'd not seen before alighting on her face. "Who would have ever thought you could get those feet moving like that. Maybe there's hope for you yet."

As he'd discovered, Sandy wasn't one to offer much praise, so when she did deliver it, it hit home. So much so that he felt a determined Aroldo peel out of Harold's fragile skin. "Let's try again," he said.

"Stop thinking," she said, "stop counting, lose yourself in the music and go."

Aroldo did exactly that, focused on the rhythm of the music and on how her body followed his. It, of course, wasn't perfect, but there were moments in this attempt when he felt free.

Hey, it's Duo. Maybe you're not such a dipshit.

"Unleash it even more," she said. "Show me your passion, let it out here on the dance floor. Feel your love for Alice and what you'll do when she comes back to you. Feel the pain of having lost her. Put every damn bit of it into the music and the dance."

Aroldo was in complete control now, doing exactly as Sandy suggested, feeling his passion burning inside of him. He didn't even attempt to follow the steps. He immersed himself in the moment and led her into Aroldo's dance. A sexual urge pulsed through him when their bodies touched, and he finished by sharply raising her hand in the air and guiding her into a snappy twist that he pulled off with shocking precision.

As the instructor turned off the music, Sandy stepped back. "Where did that come from?"

While Aroldo might have stifled his glee, Harold flashed his teeth. "I have no idea."

"You made my heart flutter," she said.

His soul soared.

He didn't tell her that, though. All he could say was, "Thank you," but maybe that was enough, because he'd never seen her light up like she did then.

Accepting that his friends would give him a hard time, Aroldo skipped his gaming session and slept till six. Then he dressed in a new robe and sat on the balcony as the sun rose over the red city. He took his time reading the news, and once the caffeine kicked in, he turned on Duolingo and went to work. Though Harold might have an issue with the app, Aroldo loved it. He loved the punishment from Duo if he was weak, if he skipped a day. And he loved the challenge of wrangling this new language, the way the bouncy Italian phrases danced off the tongue.

When he took his morning run, flashes of being forced to play sports in PE back in Denver came to him. He'd never forget that horrifying day when a punk kid named Jamie Everhorn, who had been the first to lose his virginity in their grade, jerked his shorts down during kickball. Making it even worse was that Harold's mom hadn't done the laundry, so he'd gone commando. And there, for all to see on that field in Denver, Colorado, was Harold's pecker on display.

Even to this day, Harold wanted to strangle Jamie Everhorn, wherever he was. He'd love to sic Aroldo on him. Aroldo, who did not tolerate bullies, would see that Jamie got his due.

Halfway through the run, Harold checked his phone to make sure the app was counting his steps, then set off on a jog toward Renzo's apartment. He passed by the entrance several times, hoping that Alice might appear, but he had no such luck.

As he was walking back, sweat dripping from his brow, he noticed the poster for the book club on the bookstore window. Aroldo would go—he *had* to go—because he had moved on from Alice, and he had a life.

After a shower, he stopped himself from turning on the Xbox. Aroldo didn't play video games. His body and mind were temples. He danced the tango and studied new languages. Read poetry and self-help books.

In that spirit, he picked up Bianca's book to read chapter 2, in which Bianca encouraged Peggy Meh to identify the wounds of her younger self, what had possibly led to what she'd confessed in chapter

1. In Peggy's case, she had an overbearing and abusive alcoholic father who'd told her all her life that she was good for nothing.

Though it wasn't funny at all, Harold found himself chuckling as he read, because apparently, he wasn't alone. His father hadn't had a drinking problem, but he'd definitely been an abusive asshole. Few days went by that he didn't hear his father's discouraging words running through his mind. As if Harold needed anyone else to beat him up for his failures.

And what were those? If he wrote them down, the list would go on for ages, but he knew that his biggest failure was not going to college. Because not obtaining a degree defined his future more than any other choice.

Everyone else around him had gone to school, or so it seemed. All anyone was doing during senior year was chatting about all things college: which schools they were applying to, how they were amping up their extracurriculars to beef up their application, how their parents were taking them to tour their top three or four.

Why hadn't Harold even applied? He was still scratching his head over it. He'd had decent enough grades to get in a few places, definitely a state school, but it wasn't like his parents had set up a college fund. He'd have to take out student loans. His guidance counselor had tried and failed to push a few applications into his hand, but he'd always fed her excuses.

It wasn't the fear of being in debt, more the fear of college in general. He hated school. Why endure more of it? He already saw a scenario where he was the geeky lone wolf of his dorm, getting picked on for countless reasons, thrown into a dumpster or whatever else they did to losers. He didn't like leaving his mom either. They were best friends and had learned to survive together. She certainly wasn't pushing him out the door, likely for the same reason. They still needed each other.

Honestly, it was all too much: picking a school, a career, leaving his mom, trying to go it alone. The easier play had been to stay at home, get an hourly job, and buy some time till he felt more enthusiastic about becoming an adult.

What he hadn't planned on was how each month that passed shot him further away from ever going to college and making something better of himself.

In the afternoon, Harold dressed in another new outfit—sharp collars and flashy colors—coming alive as Aroldo, and walked—no, *strutted*—to Renzo's place. He wasn't sure when Alice finished her classes, so he took the same table where he'd sat last time and kept an eye on the entrance while reading Bianca's book and sipping sparkling water. (Aroldo did not drink *acqua naturale*; he drank *acqua frizzante*.)

That Peggy Meh was a mess, even more so than Harold. Today he read about finding the courage to live loudly, to leave burn marks. When he closed the book to take a break, he felt validated. Aroldo was definitely living loudly.

Deciding to stretch his legs, Aroldo dipped into a gallery, and in the spirit of leaving burn marks, spent ten minutes haggling with the owner over a $20,000 painting that he very much liked. "I'll give you ten."

"Eighteen is as low as I can go."

"Twelve."

"Absolutely not."

"Thank you for your time." Aroldo knew about art, and he wouldn't be taken advantage of. The fact of not having even $100 that he could spare for a painting didn't matter to a guy like him.

That night, he sat at an outdoor table of Sorso Sospetto, remembering Alice there with him, his strawberry love stirring her Aperol spritz and gazing into his eyes across the table. If what they had wasn't love, then love didn't exist at all.

He cracked open *Love Lessons*, a collection of translated Alda Merini poems that Moira had insisted he read. Harold resisted giving the words their fair shake, but Aroldo dove in, reading both the Italian and the English versions, saying the words to himself slowly, feeling their rhythm.

The Alice-and-Harold situation was a planet off its axis, a moon out of orbit. And with a cigarette dangling from his mouth, the Merini book resting on his lap, Harold closed his eyes and imagined reaching a hand into the solar system and rearranging the planets and stars so that Alice would come back to him and that all the wrongs would be righted and that the cavernous hole in his soul would once again be filled.

On June 5, he entered the bookstore with more confidence than he'd ever known. Perfectly tailored khakis, an Oxford shirt, and a slight mustache—a Timothée Chalamet sort of thing. He'd purchased a gold watch that was entirely too expensive, but it shone mightily on his wrist.

From behind the cash register, Sandy gave a soft clap, cheering him on. "Look at you."

He ran a hand through his hair and thanked her.

"Have you been practicing your steps?"

He grinned. "Every day. Are we on for tonight?"

She looked pleasantly surprised. "I'll meet you outside at five forty-five."

He tapped on the counter. "I look forward to it." These little gestures, the tapping on the counter, the winks, they amplified Aroldo's confidence.

"Everyone's in the back; they're about to start. I'm sure Moira will be grateful you came."

"How's the turnout?" he asked.

"About fifteen people. Better than I expected."

Aroldo took a breath, holding on to the man he'd become, then strutted under the arch to the main room, where book clubbers mingled around a table of food and bottles of wine.

He knew he looked good, but the shock on Moira's face was enough to rattle even Aroldo. "Oh, my God, is that Harold? You look so handsome." She kissed both his cheeks. "You look dashing."

"Thank you, dear. As do you." He'd noticed she dressed in a lot of black and white, a black skirt, white top today, trying to hide in plain sight. Still, he found her adorable, perhaps even titillating in her attempt at muting herself.

"And I appreciate you coming. Not exactly the turnout I hoped, but . . ." She turned back to look at the people gathered. "It's a start."

"I'm delighted to be here," he said. "And proud of you too. It's something Alice would have done, going out on a limb. I know she'd love to be here. It's her kind of thing."

"Yeah, well, I hope one day she walks in with you."

He thought of seeing Alice kiss Renzo's lips this morning on his way to work. "As do I."

"If not, there's someone even better out there waiting for you." She adjusted her glasses, a ball of nerves. "Okay, I better get this thing started."

Chapter 17

The Inaugural Book Club and Other Disasters

George was busy trying to cut through a block of cheese at the table in the bookstore (*Why couldn't they precut slices in Italy?*), pondering an interaction with Sandy at the cash register a moment ago. A friendship was brewing, and he wondered whether she might have let it become more if he weren't leaving. He could understand. He'd been hurt before. Considering his inevitable departure, why set themselves up for it?

Though she hadn't said much about her own romantic past, she'd glossed over her two ugly marriages. Enough said. As George knew, even one divorce was enough to break you into pieces.

Still, though, he was thrilled to enjoy the spark they so clearly had. He wasn't sure how old she was, early fifties maybe? Still young, but it seemed that finding sparks grew more difficult as the sand ran through the hourglass. He, for one, hadn't experienced a sizzle of attraction like this since his ex-wife.

God, that was a *long* time ago. Motorola had just snagged him fresh out of Arizona State, and he'd jumped into a team refining the Motorola 68000 microprocessor chip, which powered the early Apples and Ataris. And then Faith came along, barreling him over.

He finally maneuvered around the rind and nabbed a couple of cuts of cheese to go with the mortadella he'd piled high. Moira was encouraging everyone to find their seats so that they could get started.

"Can I get you a drink, Dad?" Bianca set a hand on his shoulder, and she couldn't have known how much the gesture meant to him. He'd been nothing but trouble since he'd first arrived, making things worse with every moment. And yet here she was, still trying.

He glanced at her hand on his shoulder, then met her eyes. "Don't suppose they have a beer over there, do they? A Moretti?" Look at that, he was speaking Italian after all.

"Coming right up. Want to grab us seats?"

He found two spots in a circle of chairs that felt more like an AA meeting than a social gathering. Right on time, Moira took the floor. She was so clearly eager to have this club. How many times had she stopped George and Bianca on the street to make sure they would attend? When she began to speak, she skipped whole syllables trying to set words free.

"Welcome to the inaugural meeting of The Only English Book Club in Bologna," she started. "I'm so giddy and nervous all at once. We didn't know what to expect, turnout-wise. I suppose this is a good start. We'll have a meeting the first Tuesday of every month. Please tell your friends. You know, we expats might be a bunch of black sheep, so far away from home because we didn't fit in, but we still need our people. That's what I envision here. A place where we can connect because life's not much without connection."

George took Bianca's hand for a moment. She lobbed a grin back at him.

When Moira continued, she found her groove. "I don't want this to be a formal thing. The way I see it, books bring us together. Which is funny, isn't it? We commit to fifteen or twenty hours, or in the case of Rebecca Yarros or Stephen King, thirty hours alone, immersing ourselves in a book, escaping the world we know. But when we come up for air, we see things differently. We feel more connected because we had the pleasure of slipping into someone else's skin. Our eyes were opened to another world, another experience. We see that even though we're miles or even light-years apart, we're all after the same things: happiness, meaning, love. That's what I find in books, and that's what I want to find here in this room—in this community that I so desperately want to build. This bookstore, it means everything to me. I see her as a living, breathing organism, and she wants this community as much as anyone. Let's give it to her, friends."

She stopped then, and a quiet took over the bookstore. She seemed to shrink some, unsure of her words. But then a clap came from the back, and George turned to see Sandy standing under the arch cheering her sole employee on. George jumped in as well, and within seconds, everyone was lifting Moira up.

Responding to the warm reception, Moira transformed, growing like one of those bath toys that expands when it gets wet. She sure had a way with words. George felt an eagerness to read for the first time in forever.

"Thank you," Moira said, as the clapping died down. "My hope is that we can all share in the decision of which book we choose each month, but today, for the coming month, since this is my party, I'd like to nominate a book written by one of our own, a new neighbor: Bianca Briggs."

She gave Bianca a short introduction, then said, "The first chapter in the book is about being honest with yourself, confessing as if you are both the sinner *and* the priest in the confessional. I've done that a lot lately. If I'm being honest, Peggy Meh, the case study in the book, has nothing on me."

That drew some laughter, especially from Bianca. Perhaps she could see that her book wasn't all for naught. It might not have performed as she'd hoped, but it was being talked about. That was something.

"Mr. Briggs," Moira said, cutting straight to him, "I hate to put you on the spot, but what's your favorite part?"

Wait, what?

Heads twisted, eyes fixed on him. A quiet blanketed the room. He hadn't seen this one coming. Never in a million years. And in the seconds that followed, he made quick moves in his head, trying to figure a way out of it.

He found Bianca's eyes searching his, maybe curious about his answer, or perhaps mortified that he was about to screw things up (which he was). He decided that he couldn't lie. Not that he'd lied before about reading her book. He'd sidestepped the truth, offering compliments, but never had he outright lied and said he'd read it. That wouldn't start today.

"I'm . . . I haven't . . ." Blood rushed to his head.

"What's that?" Moira asked.

George cleared his throat. "I'm ashamed to say I haven't read it." He glanced over at Bianca, who turned her head. He tried to take her hand, but she pulled it away.

"It's complicated, but . . ." Oh, God, what had he done? Was no one else going to say something? They were waiting for further explanation, but they certainly weren't ready for the truth. That he'd been suicidal in the weeks leading up to the book's release? That the only joy he'd felt in his life since retirement was seeing her succeed, seeing her publish a book, but that he hadn't been able to get through her words because they'd cut so fucking deep? Peggy Meh's issues with her miserable excuse for a father had driven a stake through his heart. Bianca could insist all day long that he wasn't the inspiration, but George saw flickers of what he'd done to his daughter, being so absent, making her the product of a divorce, driving her nuts even when he was trying his best.

He had never asked Bianca about it, because he knew it was true: He'd made it into her book in the worst of ways.

"Before I'm put in front of the firing squad, I guess I should say that it's been a long year for me. Not that it's an excuse, but retirement about killed me, and Bianca's book came out at the same time, and I'm afraid . . . I . . . I haven't been in the best shape."

He turned to his daughter, who wouldn't look at him. "Sorry, B."

After that, Moira stepped in and invited everyone to go around the room and introduce themselves. George ate more cheese and mortadella and drank another beer. His daughter didn't make eye contact with him once. Turned out to be the longest hour of his life, and when he left, he left alone, passing by Sandy and offering her a sad smile as he opened the door.

Immediately following the book club, Aroldo and Moira took an outdoor table at Sorso Sospetto and ordered Aperol spritzes. They'd asked Sandy to join, but she'd declined. It looked like it might rain soon, but no one seemed worried about it.

"I can't believe I put George on the spot like that," Moira said. "I feel horrible."

Aroldo crossed one leg over the other and lit a smoke. They were going down easier now. "It's questionable that he didn't read his daughter's book, no? How could you have known?"

"I know, but . . . I can still see the horror on his face."

"Yeah, he's in trouble. Other than that, it was great." He blew out a perfect smoke ring; he'd been practicing.

Moira bit into the orange that came with her drink, then said, "It's like what that person said to Abraham Lincoln's wife in Ford's Theatre. 'Other than the obvious, Mrs. Lincoln, how was the show?'"

Aroldo took a long sip, studying his companion. Who was this woman who hid behind thick glasses and a floppy hat? She was an onion if there ever was one. She'd spoken so eloquently at the event, her love of books infectious. She seemed far wiser than her years. Clearly, she'd distilled down the many books she'd read, and they'd formed who she was and informed her rich and hopeful perspective. Harold might have noticed had he not been up his own ass; Aroldo was far more perceptive.

With genuine curiosity, he asked about her life, what had led her here, what was next. She seemed surprised by his curiosity, that anyone would ever ask, but once she got going, he could see that she so desperately wanted to share, to connect.

"I was married before, and it failed epically. Like in ways I can't even talk about."

"What does that mean, can't talk about?"

She drew a finger across her lips, then adjusted her glasses. "Legally speaking."

He stubbed out his cigarette. "Consider my curiosity piqued. And I guess it will never be quenched. You sure you don't want to elaborate?" He drew a finger across his lips.

"Maybe one day."

"How about music?" he asked, letting her off the hook. "What's your favorite music?"

She listed a few bands and artists. He stopped her when she mentioned P. J. Harvey.

"Wait, what? I grew up listening to all that stuff: P. J., Nick Cave, Beck, Jeff Buckley."

"Get out! Yeah, she's from right where I grew up in Dorset. My mum knew her."

"But I thought you were from Bristol—"

"Dorset but spent most of my time in Bristol. Long story."

"Must be part of your"—he once again drew a finger across his lips—"shady past."

She downed the rest of her drink. "How is your pursuit of the redhead?"

"The subtle change of subject, huh?" He eyed her, wondering what secrets this young woman held, what layers were yet to be peeled back. "The redhead is still clearly in love, last I checked."

"You're checking? How are you checking?"

He laughed quietly. "You think you're the only one with secrets? Actually, I've been like . . . How do I say it without sounding like a stalker? I've walked by their place a few times, watched a little, seen them interact."

Her brow furrowed. "That is actually stalking. You're the definition of it."

Harold looked into his drink, studying the melting ice cubes. Aroldo had clearly dipped into the loo.

"Don't worry. I'm not judging."

"It's not like that, though. I'm . . . We're meant to be."

"I get it. And you're a long way from home and trying to figure out if you can stay."

"Yeah, well, I only have three months, then I have to leave." He raised air quotes with a sly grin. "Legally speaking."

She acknowledged his callback, then: "I bet Sandy would give you a job. She can help you get a visa. Well, I know you have a fancy computer gig and all that, but maybe you could work a few hours a week and find a way to stay."

Light bulbs switched on in his head. "You think she'd do that?"

"What? She loves you. I mean, as much as she loves anyone. Do you think she's ever invited me dancing? No, not once. She mentioned that she kind of felt like your Bolognese mum."

That made him feel all warm and cozy inside. He could suddenly see Sandy—his Bolognese *madre*—on the dance floor, shaking the chandeliers with Tommaso. "She's good, by the way. As good as the teacher."

"That doesn't surprise me. No one knows anything about her. The sales reps always try to get stuff out of her—before she bites their heads off, of course. You might know more than any of us."

"I doubt that. But she's great, seems to care about people in her own way. She's helped me, you know. Find some confidence."

"I do like your transformation. Very handsome."

"Thank you."

A soft rain began to fall. Under the protection of the table umbrella, Moira sat back and took off her glasses and rubbed her eyes. "But I also hope you know that Alice should love you for who you are. I hate to see you trying to be someone else."

"I don't think it's that. I'm just trying to be a better version of myself."

Moira nodded, slipping her glasses back on. "I appreciate that. In Bianca's book, toward the end, which you'll discover if you ever read—"

"I am reading it," Harold interrupted. "I'm about a quarter of the way through, and it's good. Lots of wisdom."

Moira glowed, enough to light their section of Via Giulia. "It's great, right? Deep messages delivered with a comic edge. And I don't want to give anything away, but—"

Harold, with a sprinkling of Aroldo, jumped in. "It's self-development. Not supposed to be a page-turner."

"That's true. Well, long before she transforms to Peggy Megawatt, which I think is hilariously *brilliant*—and *brilliantly* hilarious—she ends up trying to save her marriage and pondering what she might do to make her husband love her again. What she's doing is misconstruing Bianca's message to either change or accept your circumstances. It's sad, really. Because we're lovable as we are, aren't we? We deserve love simply by being the product of the miracle that's life. We, the people who made it this far, to make it to the womb, to develop lungs, and then to breathe air. That's a miracle. And as miracles, we're all worth loving."

The hairs on his arms rose. "That's beautiful. It's in the book?"

A nod.

His arm hairs stood taller.

"What I'm saying is that I see the way you love her, and it's wonderful, but I don't think you need to convince her. Just as Peggy doesn't need to become someone else, neither do you."

Harold felt the war in his mind, the tale of two men, Harold Meh and Aroldo Megawatt, tugging at each other. "It's not that I feel like I need to convince Alice—or be someone else. It's that I need to put my best foot forward."

She gave a "fair enough" nod. "It's none of my business—and there's nothing wrong with that. Just know that I think you're pretty cool as you are."

"Warts and all, right?"

Moira clinked his glass. "Warts and all."

George took a long wander through the city, working his way along the outskirts, visiting some of the gates that had been the entryways to the city for seven centuries. Each one had its own kind of character, ornate stone carvings, rounded turrets, these grand archways that were big enough for the city buses to drive through.

Sometimes, he could see it, the beauty of this place, its old-world magic. It wasn't so bad to visit.

Of course, he wasn't about to move here. Enough with having to hang his laundry on the balcony or staring at the goddamn bidet, wondering what to do with it. Enough with trying to wash dishes without Dawn. How does a country get by without Dawn? And those little cars . . . They couldn't be safe. While he was at it, they had no idea how to do burgers and nachos. They shouldn't even have them on menus. And condiments. You ask for a packet of ketchup and they charge you! Who can eat fries without ketchup?! And they call this city the food capital of the world. He'd put Ruth's Chris in Phoenix up against any of it.

And damn this country for taking his daughter from him. He might not be perfect, and he might be making things worse by the moment, but at least he was geographically closer to her when she lived in Austin. Having an ocean between them was too much. He wished she knew how much he cared for her. He hoped he could show her that before he returned home. Maybe her forgiveness and the promise of another reunion might be enough to keep him from returning to the darkness.

Because yeah, the darkness was only a few handfuls of pills and a light switch away.

George found Bianca sitting on her balcony drinking tea, staring off into space. "May I join you?" he asked, only sitting after she nodded. The sunset hid behind a patch of dark clouds. Church bells marked a new hour. Of course, some of their clothing hung on the line just beyond her; it reminded him to run another load before bed.

"I know you're mad at me," he said.

She didn't respond.

"May I explain myself?"

Nothing.

"Let me try." He paused, feeling like their relationship was a weak thread away from over. So he had better do it right. "You know I'm not much of a reader, but it's more than that. What I've been going through back home since retirement, it's worse than maybe you know. I feel like I'm in the waiting room, waiting for a stroke or a heart attack to rescue me."

He almost said that he'd grown tired of waiting and had considered more than once doing something about it, but no matter how much trouble he was in, no matter how much he was hurting and needed to talk to someone, no matter what, he wouldn't say that.

"I'm depressed, B. The doctor has me on Zoloft, and that seems to be helping, but when I tried to read your book, reading the issues Peggy had with her father, I connected the dots. It ate away at me, how I could have done better, how I wasn't there for you. Every word I read felt like it was directed toward me. Not that I'm blaming you . . . I get it. I failed. But reading it on the pages of your book was a knife twist. I couldn't do it."

Bianca finally turned to him. "I didn't create Peggy's dad based on you."

"Maybe you didn't intentionally—"

"You do realize that all of us are constructs of our upbringing, right? The issues we have, they come from our first interactions with the world, how our parents choose to raise us. Peggy had father issues because everyone has parental issues." Attitude dripped from her tone, reminded him of Faith. "I've been studying this stuff for a decade. This rule is without exception. Yes, you worked too much, but I didn't write the book about you, and I'm sorry you think that."

George half believed her. They both stared out into the night, quietly. The sounds of the city rose up around them.

"Dad, you don't stop, and that's the problem you're having with retirement. You're a racehorse that's suddenly been put out to pasture. Any good psychotherapist would tell you that doing *nothing* is exactly what you need to be doing. But I'm not going to psychoanalyze my own father. And you're not going to change. We both know that."

He didn't argue.

"More to the point, you don't have to read my book. I never asked you to. But you definitely led me to believe you did."

"I never said that I—"

"Do you want to call your lawyers in? I'm not going to argue over semantics. You indicated that you loved it, that you'd read it, that you'd shared copies, telling everyone how much you liked Peggy Meh."

"I do. I love the *idea* of her. And I did share copies. Bought fifty of them and gave them to everybody. I talk about you to everybody I meet." He felt a drop of rain and stuck out his hand to confirm. A few light drops landed. "We should go inside."

Ignoring him, she said, "But you didn't read it. And maybe that's not why I'm mad. It's not the only reason, that's for sure. It's not working, Dad. I thought we could have a good time, but two adults under this roof is too much. I love you and want to be there for you, but I have my own battles right now. You're not the only one who's depressed. I just . . . I hate to say it, but maybe you should go home, find a hotel till they're done with the construction on your place. God knows you don't like it here. And I think you should find someone to talk to."

She turned to him. "I love you so much, and I don't want you to think that I'm kicking you out. It's not that. It's that we're both a mess right now. Why don't we try again in a few months? I don't have anything left for you or anyone else right now. I'm not okay." A tear escaped her eyes.

"Oh, honey." Her pain squeezed down hard on his heart. He wanted to hug her, but he didn't think she wanted that. "You're right. I'll book a ticket home. I didn't mean to bring my mess here."

She wiped her eyes. "It's not that. It has nothing to do with you."

Actually, she'd admitted a moment ago that all issues had seeds in maternal and paternal issues, so it did have to do with him. It certainly wasn't her mother; Faith had given her all to Bianca from day one.

He wasn't going to argue, though.

Trying to keep his chest from caving in and focusing on what mattered, he said, "What can I do for you? I mean, other than get out of your hair. Let's go inside; the rain's picking up."

"I'll be in shortly." Her voice cracked.

After a long minute of silence, he said, "How about a glass of wine? Let's start there." He stood, kissed the top of her head, and went into the kitchen. He felt dead inside, riddled with regret for coming here, for failing her for all those years, for ruining his marriage, for fucking up in a thousand ways. A tear dripped out of his eye, and he felt the warmth of it as it trickled down his cheek. At least he was still alive. That's what a tear felt like, a reminder that he was still breathing.

You can do better, George, he told himself. *Don't let her see you break.*

When he pulled open the cabinet to take out two glasses, he saw small brown pellets on the plastic sheets with which he'd lined the bottom of the cabinets a few days earlier.

Mouse droppings.

Like a soldier called to battle, he gritted his teeth and searched for the enemy. "You have to be kidding me." Before lining the base of all the cabinets, he'd scrubbed every inch with disinfectant. What could they possibly have wanted in here?

Stomping back out to the balcony, he found Bianca still sitting out there in the rain. "B, you won't believe it. You've got a mouse. I'll go down to the store and grab a trap. Is it still open?"

She looked at him with exhausted eyes. "I don't know."

"I'll find something one way or another. Can you believe it? Right after I cleaned every last inch. Mr. Nutz, and now this."

A shrug. She apparently had no problem living in rodent filth. Or sitting in the rain.

"Okay, be back in a few. Get inside before you catch a cold." Half of him realized he was leaving an important conversation, but it would have to wait. It would simply have to fucking wait.

Chapter 18

Eager for the Night

Through a soft rain, a mist really, Harold escorted Moira under her umbrella back to her apartment about ten minutes away, then offered her a hug and headed home. The night had an edge to it, busier than normal for a weekday, despite the rain. There was something magical about how the misty glow of the streetlights lit up all the colorful umbrellas bobbing along the sidewalks.

He was back on Via Giulia, an escape from the madness of the rest of the city, when he heard a door kick open across the street. Bianca's father slipped out onto the sidewalk and opened an umbrella. They exchanged a quick wave, then George swiftly marched the other way, clearly a man on a mission.

Once Harold reached the scaffolding surrounding the bookstore, he heard the opera singer across the street break into song. The man stood in his robe, also uncaring of the falling mist, his hands on the railing, his eyes tilted upward, his voice echoing into the evening.

Harold paused to listen, something he'd never done before. Perhaps Aroldo had an interest in the opera. *What a city,* he thought. So perfect in so many ways. Where else could you happen upon a man giving everything he had to the night, belting out a song in the rain as if he were on a stage.

When the man finished, shaking the city with a long-lasting vibrato, Harold clapped his hands. "Bravo! Bravo!"

The opera singer bowed, causing Harold to smile.

When he lowered his eyes back down, he saw her, his strawberry love, standing under the cover of a bright-yellow umbrella.

"Alice?" he said, taking in this angelic form, this being that he'd been studying from afar, this being that had come back to him . . . *No, don't get ahead of yourself, Harold.*

She wore a khaki jacket that covered all but her legs. The streetlights gave her skin a warmth that was enough to make him shiver. Her strawberry explosion of hair was still a mess, with beads of rain stuck in it, sparkling like gemstones, and she was still as beautiful as ever.

He crossed the street, hoping that this was it, the moment he'd dreamed of. Cobblestones under his feet, he stopped and peered into her eyes. Only then could he see that she'd been crying.

"What's going on?" He was hesitant to hug her, to step closer. "Are you okay? Did he hurt you?" He wiped the rain from his face.

"I'm fine, it's just . . . We got in a fight. I didn't know where else to go."

She needed him and it radiated out from her, that need. He stepped closer, testing the waters, slowly raising his arms. She didn't back away, didn't hesitate. As he inched even closer, she moved into him, and suddenly he was under the protection of the umbrella as well. He wrapped his arms around her, and she wept into his shoulder.

They held each other for a long time, a bubble of dry safety, Harold's heart coming alive for the first time since she'd left. How many nights had he lain awake wondering whether he'd ever touch her again? And here he was, once again with the love of his life, and maybe she knew it now too.

He pulled away and found her eyes. They were close enough to kiss, but even he knew this wasn't a kissing moment. "What did he do?"

"I don't even know how it started, but he raised his voice at me. He'd been drinking."

He touched her cheek, feeling a surge of love run between them. "I'm so sorry."

As they crossed the street, he started to come to his senses and realized he'd completely forgotten about Aroldo, and like Clark Kent dashing into a phone booth, Harold made the switch.

In an instant, he stood taller. His muscles and calves swelled. She hadn't yet noticed his new style but surely would. He felt smarter, wittier, more at ease. One of the chapters in Bianca's book focused on creating reality by visualizing and feeling it. It was true, so true. He felt like a different man, and when he pulled open the large wooden door that led to his—no, *their*—apartment, he set a hand on the small of her back.

"Let's get you dry, dear," Aroldo Megawatt said, the faint yet complex accent suggesting that he'd lived all over the globe, perhaps born in London, then ushered through Copenhagen and Prague in his teens, then his years of study at the Sorbonne before trading commodities in Hong Kong.

Confusion flickered on her face, and he liked what he saw, how the confusion seemed to morph into desire, or something close to it.

Aroldo confidently ushered her up the stairs. He was calculated and caring, whispering that it would be okay. In the foyer, he closed the yellow umbrella and helped her with her jacket. Alice looked him up and down, surely noticing his new waterproof leather boots, and his designer jeans that had cost way too much, and the crisp white shirt that had grown damp in the mist. Not to mention the black-and-white belt that Giovanni had insisted upon.

"Are you cold?" Aroldo asked. "Let's get you a blanket."

She nodded, saying, "You look nice."

"Grazie." He said it casually, like he hadn't been trying at all. This was the man she'd left. Nothing had changed. Only everything.

He moved with intent into the living room and found the blanket. Thank God he'd straightened up. Harold had remained slack about cleaning, but Aroldo always picked up after himself.

"It looks so different in here. All the color. You rearranged."

He wrapped the blanket around her, and she looked like a tulip after a downpour, this wonderful natural perfume rising into his olfactory glands and soothing him, kick-starting his libido, making him miss her more than ever.

And yet, here she was.

"Come sit down," he said, patting the couch. "Tell me what happened."

They sat together, his arm around her. She curled into him, melted into him even, and sighed. He petted her strawberry hair, breathed in his fruity love. "Tell me, tell me."

"Are your shoes new? You seem different."

"Oh, these? Yeah, picked them up from Giovanni's place."

"You know Giovanni?"

"I pop in from time to time."

She seemed to process the news, then melted even farther into him, two warm candles pressed together, her breath on his ear. He stirred below the waist, a month of desperate longing bubbling inside. "You sure you're not hurt?"

"He drinks sometimes, gets angry. For no reason. I was out with some friends last night and didn't tell him, and he got jealous. Snapped at me today when he got home from work."

"I'm so sorry," Aroldo said, knowing that he didn't need to speak much, that what she needed was an ear.

Minutes passed, and he wondered if she'd fallen asleep. He craned his neck and found her eyes open. "What are you thinking about?"

She shook her head, and Aroldo wanted her to say that she was simply feeling the regret of having left him. He had an urge to tell her that he'd been hitting fifteen thousand steps a day, but that was a Harold move. He didn't need to prove he was worthy. All he had to do was be Aroldo. She'd take it from there.

"Can I get you anything? Are you hungry?"

Another headshake. "I want to lie here. With you."

Aroldo pressed his eyes closed and felt utterly and deeply that the earth had rediscovered its axis, that the sun and moon had righted themselves, that God had shown himself. Harold had been praying to Him, begging Him to bring her home, and here she was, the angelic presence that was proof of God and love all in one.

Fishing his phone out of his pocket, he found her favorite artist, Bad Bunny, and let it play. As the beat began, she whispered what sounded like, "I missed you," but Aroldo wasn't sure. Harold wanted to ask her to repeat it, but Aroldo nearly smacked him. *Of course she misses you, whether she said it or not. Have some confidence, turdbucket.*

Alice soon faded and fell into a soft purr of a snore. Aroldo's leg had fallen asleep, but he didn't dare move, didn't dare disturb her. He'd wanted this for far too long to wake from this dream.

He sat through the night, hours stacking up on top of each other, feeling her, feeling their love, pondering the future, considering his next moves. He could enjoy their reunion for a while as is, but he'd soon have to come clean.

If he had any hope of holding on to her, he had to tell her all the things that he'd been keeping back. Now that they had a chance again, they'd have to find a creative way to make it work, because without a visa, he'd soon have to return to Denver.

Perhaps more importantly, he'd run out of money, and his mother had told him she couldn't give him another dime. She was running low because she'd had to buy a new washer. Naturally, he didn't blame her for cutting him off. He felt awful for having borrowed so much of her meager savings. But he'd pay every dime back, that was for sure.

Thank God he still had room on a couple of credit cards.

The sun broke through the clouds of the morning. Bianca sat on the balcony, smelling the city after a rain, that scent of it having been cleansed of its transgressions. If only Bianca felt renewed. She felt more lost than ever before. She'd let her dad down so badly, crushed his soul. And she'd messed up with Corrado. She wondered if this whole journey was a sham, an attempt to run away from herself.

Her dad appeared at the door in shorts and a T-shirt. He'd combed his hair. "Good morning, kiddo."

"I'm sorry." The words took a hundred pounds off her back.

"No, no, you have nothing to apologize for. I'm the one who brought my mess here. It's not fair."

"It has nothing to do with fair, Dad. We're in this together, aren't we? That's what family is. I've been so focused on me and figuring things out and I just . . . I forgot what matters. I don't want you to leave. I didn't mean what I said."

He took a long time answering. "I should have read your book, but I started again last night. It's good."

"You don't have to read my book."

"No, I do. I want to. I was making it about me, but it's not. I get that. You're doing what you do, helping others. I love what you have to say."

"Thanks for that, but seriously, I don't want you to read it. Do me that favor. I didn't write it for you. Apparently, I didn't even write it for me. It was a thing I did because . . . that's what psychotherapists do when they have a full client load but don't feel like they're doing enough. I'm not even that proud of it anymore. It was a stupid idea."

George stepped through the doorway, the light catching his face. "Don't say that. What you did is amazing, just getting something out there."

"At least I got it out of my system." Had she, though? She could still hear Donna Bologna's subtle giggle after Bianca had said, "Trust me, I'm not writing another book."

"Anyway," George said, "you definitely don't owe me an apology. I deserve anything you throw at me."

"What I said, how I give you a hard time. It's because I'm beating you up for leaving Mom, for working so hard. And I have no right to do that."

"You kind of do, B."

"No. I don't. You're trying. That's a whole lot more than a lot of fathers can say. Why don't we try again, huh? Let's be honest, it would be so boring without you. Besides, who would help me with my mouse problem?"

"Speaking of—"

"Nope, don't tell me."

"Just like your mother. Don't worry, I didn't get him. He wouldn't take the cheese. Fresh droppings, though. He walked right around the cheese. I swear to God, this is Mr. Nutz's cousin. He knows I want him, knows I'm after him."

"You're beyond ridiculous."

"Maybe he doesn't like cheddar. I could try peanut but—"

"Not that I'm condoning your hunt, but he's Italian. Where did you even find cheddar?"

"At the store."

"I'm guessing Italian mice like Italian cheese." With that, she slapped a hand to her forehead.

"Make fun all you want, but trust me, you don't want mice multiplying. The authorities will condemn this place."

Her smile came to full form. "Condemn it? It's a tiny little mouse."

"Or ten. We don't know how many. Trust me."

Bianca could see that he was half joking, but he was half serious too. They could apologize all they wanted, but neither of them was going to change, so she had to find a path toward acceptance of exactly who he was.

Aroldo cracked his eyes open, realizing that he'd fallen asleep. Spotify had gone deep, playing similar artists to Bad Bunny. The bass of the music sent vibrations through the couch. Alice was curled into a ball with her bare feet under a pillow, the blanket covering most of her. Her head rested on his thigh. He reached for his phone and turned down the music, then instinctively petted her forehead.

She stirred, pulling her feet away from the pillow, revealing turquoise nails. He thought she might be waking, but she simply snuggled deeper into him. Never had he felt so whole.

He studied her face, drawing imaginary lines from one freckle to another. She had the cutest little nose, a feline nose. Her cheeks had the slightest rosiness to them. He let his eyes drift lower, breathing in her body, the smooth skin of a china doll, the easy curves.

He adjusted himself and then set his mind to wondering what would happen from here. Things had to be different.

If this was his chance, he had to be better than ever before, love her like he never had. He wasn't sure if it was Aroldo or Harold having these thoughts, but it made sense. She was more than her pretty face. He felt for her, the pain she experienced last night. She deserved more.

How dare Renzo treat her like that. How could anyone yell at her?

She deserved so much more, and he'd give her that.

When Alice finally woke, her eyes grew wide.

"Buongiorno, ragazza," Aroldo said, unfazed by her confusion.

"What time is it?"

"Seven."

She rubbed her eyes, the most adorable thing he'd ever seen, a kitty cat pawing at herself. "Did you sleep like that?"

"Yeah, I didn't want to wake you."

She sat up. "Thank you. What a shitty night." She reached for her phone. "Twenty missed calls. Fuck him."

"You picked up a potty mouth since I last saw you."

"Yeah, well, he drives me crazy." She read her messages as she spoke.

Aroldo wondered how he should play it. Then it came to him. "How about I go grab a couple of pastries and some fresh OJ. I'll make you breakfast for old times' sake."

She set her phone down. "Yeah, okay. I need a shower. Did I leave any clothes here?"

He shrugged, pretending like he hadn't once cuddled with the jeans and shirt she'd left in the washer. "You'd have to check. I'm not sure."

Aroldo dressed in casual Aroldo attire, spent longer than Harold might working on his hair, then went out to find breakfast and a flower. Nothing too over the top, simply a tulip to brighten her morning.

By the time she'd finished her shower, he was ready for her. She appeared in his T-shirt, her hair pressed down by lingering water.

"You've been shopping, huh?" she said. "The closet's full."

"Yeah, uh, trying to clean myself up."

He thought she might kiss him, but she slipped into her chair instead, eyeing what he'd done. Pastries, fresh juice, her latte how she liked it. She unfolded the piece of paper he'd left on her plate, then read it out loud, her voice sweeter than any pastry.

"After the fighting, the wars, the pointless battles, with yourself and others; after the storm passes, when the clouds break, when the birds resume their song, you'll still be standing, because that's what we do. We find a way to push through and begin again."

Alice set down the paper. "That's beautiful. Who said that?"

"I got it from this book I'm reading." He pointed to *From Meh to Megawatt* on the other side of the table and told her about the book and Bianca, who now lived on their street.

"Sounds like I've missed a lot," Alice said.

"We definitely have a lot of catching up to do." Not wanting to let her go, he asked, "What are you doing today? Want to sit around and watch movies? Maybe *Say Anything*?"

She took a bite from her pastry. "I guess I could skip school. Did you work last night? How's work going? Still busy?"

He hated to lie, but now was not the time to go into detail. "It's great, actually, but I've cut back my hours. Those late nights were getting to me. I have a team, you know. They can run things. I have to keep everyone on track. And pay them."

"Good. You look good, Harold. Like glowing. Italy's been good for you."

"Thanks. Yeah, it's been a nice run." He wanted to add that he'd missed her, but he still wasn't sure where he fit into this whole thing. Aroldo might have seized the moment and made his move, but Harold resisted, feeling like he was a long way from getting her back.

Chapter 19

Bad Decisions

Still red-faced from an hour and a half of tango, Sandy strolled alongside Harold, elbows hooked, her heels clicking on the sidewalk.

"You're getting better," she said.

"Really? You don't have to say that." Harold was almost unrecognizable compared with the young man she'd first met. Confidence, curiosity. A witty and sometimes dark sense of humor. That silly peach-fuzz beard was gone. Giovanni had certainly done good work. Harold wore skinny jeans and a flashy shirt with a stiff collar. She imagined Alice wouldn't recognize him.

"Alice spent the night two nights ago," he admitted, as if he'd read her mind.

"Hold on, what?" How had he not mentioned this yet?

"Yeah, I guess she and Renzo got in a fight and—"

"You guess? They either did or didn't. This is what we have to work on, Harold. Speak definitively. Words matter. You don't *guess*."

"Okay, sorry."

"And don't apologize."

The little guy seemed to turn into a small deer, whatever they were called. Anyway, Bambi's feelings were hurt, and dammit if it didn't make Sandy feel bad. This kid really meant something to her.

"Sorry, I don't mean to jump on you. I'm just invested, that's all. You're like my . . ." She almost said *son*, but the word didn't feel right as it wound through the neural pathways toward her tongue.

"Anyway," she said, "you were saying . . ."

"She came home. I'd had a drink with Moira, walked her home, then found Alice standing outside. Across the street under a yellow umbrella."

Harold pulled out a pack of Murattis and lit one.

"You smoke now?"

"On occasion."

Sandy held out her hand. "May I?"

He lit her a cigarette and kept talking. "Renzo was being an asshole, and she walked out, came straight to me."

"And? God, you tell a slow story."

"And nothing. She fell asleep in my arms on the couch. I made her breakfast like old times. A flower and a quote, all that. And then we watched a movie, her favorite, *Say Anything*. And then she left."

"She left? Where did she go?"

"To a friend's house. Said she had to figure out what's going on."

"And was that friend Renzo?"

"I don't know. I hope not." He took a deep drag. "He was texting and calling her constantly, all these apologies."

"Ouch."

She enjoyed a puff, the first in months. Not since she'd last had sex with the jazz musician, a postcoital delight.

"Did she say anything about your apartment, your clothes. Your whole vibe? The confidence that you've built up?"

"I guess. Sorry, yes. She complimented me."

"How did she leave it? Are you going to see her again?"

"I don't know."

"Jesus H. Roosevelt Christ. Right back to where we started."

"Yeah, I know. And I'm tired. This whole thing, trying so hard, is exhausting."

Sandy shook her head. "You're not giving up, are you?"

"I don't know." He stopped. "I can't believe I'm telling you this, but I've been referring to myself, well, the new me, as Aroldo."

"Aroldo?" She took a big puff.

"As a way to see myself differently. Kind of like what Bianca writes about in her book, faking it till you make it. Have you read it?"

His strange behavior, the funny accent and different phrasing when he spoke, suddenly made sense. "Um, no. Self-help is something you do when you're in your twenties, maybe thirties. Not in your . . . Well. Forget it. And what does Alice think of Aroldo?"

"I don't know. She seemed impressed."

"And yet you're in the friend zone?"

"Maybe."

She stubbed her cigarette out on a trash can. Enough of that. "Look, it's exhausting to be amazing. I know that more than anyone. You can laugh at that one." Once he did, the fakest laugh ever faked, she continued, "But it's the only way to break through the noise. There's a reason she once loved you. Because you're an extraordinary young man with all kinds of promise. You don't even realize how much passion you have inside of you, but I see it on the dance floor. I see the real you kicking to get out. Whether you call him Harold or Aroldo or whomever."

They continued walking. "Hasn't anyone ever taught you how to play the game?"

"The game?"

"Yeah, you know. Playing hard to get. Making her work for it."

"I'm aware of such a game."

"And are you playing it? It doesn't sound like it to me, letting her fall asleep in your arms, buying her flowers, making her breakfast—"

"What was I supposed to do?"

"She has some work to do. She ran off with another man. Make her *earn* you back."

His voice lifted an octave. "I don't know if she wants me back! And how am I supposed to play hard to get or any other games if I'm not even around her? Here I am, spending all this time playing Aroldo, living this entirely new life to reel her in, and she's barely thinking about me. Then when we're finally back together, I fucking blow it."

She put an arm around him. "You see? This is the passion I'm talking about."

"Stop laughing at me."

"I'm not laughing at you," she said, fully aware of the joy painting her face. "I appreciate you, Harold. Or Aroldo, whatever your name is. There's something so beautiful about the naivete of young lovers."

"I'm seeing nothing beautiful about it."

She let go and found his eyes. "Don't worry. You have me on your side. I'm going to help you get her back. Just don't buy her any more flowers. You see her again, you be cordial, but don't invite her up. Don't cook her breakfast. And definitely don't let her fall asleep in your arms! Got me?"

George stopped by the bookstore. He hadn't seen Sandy since the book club event three days prior but wanted to make good on his offer to help with any handyman needs.

She was behind the counter, tapping away on the keyboard, but she gave a warm smile when he pushed through the door, the bell chiming.

"There he is. How's life in the doghouse? Hold on, what's that in your hand?"

He looked down at the pink toolbox. "It was a gift for Bianca. She didn't even have a hammer."

"What is she, five?"

"I know, I know. I realized it when I brought it up to her apartment. The look she gave me."

Sandy chuckled. "I bet. I'm surprised you didn't get some pink roller skates too."

"That's not a bad idea."

After a shared smile, she asked, "Is she still mad at you?"

"We're moving past it. Trying to find common ground." He noticed a few perusers, as Sandy called them, wandering through the aisles as he approached the counter.

"And have you read her book yet?"

"She made me promise I wouldn't read it."

"What?" Sandy said. "Do you not understand women at all?"

He shook his head. "Not in the slightest."

"Read the book, George. She needs praise from you, of all people."

"What, why?"

"Because you're her father. If she's anything like the rest of the world, a parent's approval is paramount."

"I don't think she cares what I have to say."

"That's not true."

He stepped back and set the toolbox down while she rang up a customer, wondering whether Sandy was right. Probably so. This was exactly why he kept screwing up. He was living life without a compass.

Once the customer had left, he said, "No peruser there."

"No, but she bought last year's Hilderbrand from the discount bin. I made exactly nothing on that. Just as bad as a peruser. At this rate, I'll be out of business by the fall."

"Are you really struggling or just venting?"

She crossed her arms. "I'm doing both."

"Okay, well, at the risk of getting in big trouble, may I offer a few suggestions? It all comes from a guy who spent his *entire* life in the business world and now has nothing to do."

"Should I grab my notepad?"

"If you want to. I can't promise it's going to be any—"

"George. I'm kidding. I'm not getting out my notepad. Feel free to tell me how to run the business I've been in for ten years. But I won't be taking notes."

He looked away.

"Fine, tell me. I'm dying to know."

"Okay. Well, I like everything Moira's doing. You have to build a sense of community. The English speakers here need to have a place to convene. And maybe—"

"Did I hear my name?" Moira came under the arch and said hello.

"You did, actually," George said.

Sandy gripped her throat and pretended to choke herself. He had to give it to her: She was funny without even trying. If he wasn't reading things wrong, she might even be flirting.

"At the risk of being blackballed from the store," George said, "I was adding on to your ideas for drawing in more customers."

"I can't wait to hear!" Moira looked over at Sandy, seeking approval to eavesdrop.

Sandy set both hands on the counter. "That makes two of us. This is a real meeting of the minds here. Moira the Invincible, and George, the newest greatest bookseller on earth, who has been at it for exactly zero days."

"Let's hear him out," Moira said.

"Please don't throw anything at me, but what if . . . what if you included a section of American and British items, things people crave from back home? If they're anything like me, they can't find pancakes anywhere. Or Cheez-Its."

"Cheez-Its," Sandy said with eyes the size of basketballs.

"Yeah. Cheez-Its. I bet even American expats in Venice will come to your store for Cheez-Its. You need more ways to draw them. Slushies would be another good one."

"How about the American version of Coca-Cola with high-fructose corn syrup?" Sandy offered. "Gotta supersize them, though. And don't forget ketchup. We'll need to build extra shelves for all the ketchup."

"Look at funny lady on a roll! And Twinkies. Root beer."

Sandy pressed her hands over her ears, a playful look on her face.

And George fell in love with her. Right then and there.

"How about from England, Moira?" George asked. "What do you miss?"

Moira exploded with glee. "He's got a point, Sandy. There's nothing I miss more than bangers and mash. You can't find good English sausages anywhere. And mushy peas, yum! We'd have to create a refrigerated section."

Sandy pretended to smack her head against the counter. "Please make it stop."

Much more grinning and George's jaw would ache. "Don't worry, I wasn't coming by to push American food products on you, though come to think of it . . . Goldfish, ranch dressing, Kraft Mac & Cheese. I haven't seen any of these yet. And what about peanut butter cups? Do they have them here?" He looked from Sandy to Moira.

Moira appeared to be having the time of her life. Sandy's smile had died.

"Kidding," he said. "I'm kidding. What I did want to offer is my handyman services. I'm happy to stay in my lane." He picked up the pink toolbox. "Besides, you have to let me put these new tools to work. Is there anything I can help with?"

It took a moment for Sandy to gather herself. Apparently, when she'd cut ties with her homeland, she'd said goodbye to the best of America too.

"Actually," she finally said, "I do have some things that need fixing. If you're not busy."

"I'm running out of things to do at Bianca's. Next up, I'll be organizing her shoes, and nobody wants that."

Moira shook her head playfully. "Nope." Even Sandy let loose some. He was having way too much fun with these women. It was nice to find some confidence again. Believe it or not, he'd been accused of being charming over the years.

"I guess I do have a list, if you're really interested."

God, he loved a woman who kept lists. Thankfully, he was able to curb his tongue before he said that out loud. "Let's see it."

"Suit yourself. I'll, of course, pay you. Let me run upstairs and grab it off my computer." He didn't plan on charging her, but he didn't say that either. She returned with some tasks scribbled on a sticky note. "Here you go, my list of broken things."

Taking his glasses out of his pocket, he read through them. "Loose doorknob, wobbly chair in office, broken wheel on Biography shelf, cracked windowpane, flickering overhead light." He read a few more. "All seems pretty basic. Want to walk me through everything? I'll get it done."

George returned every day, the dreaded pink toolbox in hand—a purchase that had backfired beyond belief—and put in a few hours of work. The joy that his pink tools brought to Sandy and Moira made it all worth it, the way they'd snicker at him like two tween girls gossiping at their lockers. He even waltzed in the door one time donning a pink button-down while wielding his pink hammer, and that had sent them both to tears.

The to-do list kept growing, and he hoped that it might be because Sandy was enjoying his company (and the absurdity of all the pink), but it could have simply been that problems requiring a handyman kept presenting themselves.

As far as George was concerned, their conversations in between his tasks gave him a reason to get out of bed. Sometimes when he stopped by, she was so obviously not interested in talking, but other times, she'd quit what she was doing and make time to chat. Weren't women the most confusing species on earth? He always arrived with new ideas to recruit expats, such as BBQ sauce, Saltines, and Hot Pockets, as that seemed like the low-hanging fruit of their relationship. One fine day, he even suggested they sell American-flag Speedos. Sandy laughed so hard she'd had to go hide behind the cookbook shelf.

Other than reading Bianca's book, which he was now doing in secret, drawing a smile out of Sandy became his number one pastime.

Bianca might have held the world record for the number of times she had written a text message to someone and then deleted it. Needless to say, it had been one hell of a week. She could still taste Corrado's gazpacho, among other things, and she wanted to beg for his forgiveness and have him take her in his arms and look into her eyes and make her feel safe and wanted.

It wasn't her body that was the problem. It was all of her that she didn't want him to see. A complete mess.

One night, she told her dad that she was having dinner with friends but actually ate alone at a pizzeria a few blocks away. Two glasses of wine and an on-the-house shot of limoncello successfully removed her inhibitions. On the way back, she snapped a selfie and fired it off to Corrado before she could second-guess herself. She followed it with: I'm sorry. As you can see, I'm a disaster. It has nothing to do with you. I'm a bit lost.

Ten minutes later, she'd never wanted to take back anything more in her life.

George wrapped up his list of tasks at the bookstore around lunchtime on the thirteenth. He felt sad as he set his pink tools back in their fitted places and drew a line through the last item, upgrading a wall plate.

Sandy was crouched on the floor in the main room, creating a new sign for her banned-book section. Looking over her shoulder, he said, "Hey, I didn't know you were an artist."

"There's a lot about me you don't know, George."

"Which is one of the great regrets of my life."

"Oh, please." She cast a look his way. Her eyes were the most beautiful he'd ever seen.

"I'm serious." His heart thumped. Inspired after finishing Bianca's powerful book, he'd decided he was going to ask her out again, but now felt himself turning into a chickenshit. One rejection hurt. Two would kill.

He was well aware of how relationships bloomed. It had to go both ways. He thought he'd done a pretty good job of indicating his feelings for her. But what was she doing? It would be nice if she'd call or text, something to show he occasionally entered her mind.

"I'm all wrapped up here."

She stood and faced him. "Everything on the list?"

He held up the latest of her scribbled sticky notes. "All done."

"I hope you've been tracking your hours."

He shook his head. "No, and I'm not too worried about it. Happy to help."

"Now, that's not fair. You have to let me pay you." She stood and faced him. "And feel free to charge extra for giving me the daily chuckle with your pink toolbox."

"Yeah, yeah. So funny. I've an idea. How about you buy me lunch?" There, he'd done it. "I know I've tried before, but I'm trying again."

She crossed her arms but didn't back away. "You're relentless."

He moved closer, unable to determine his effect on her. "Have lunch with me today?"

Unflinching, she said, "I don't date older men."

"You don't know my age. I could be a decade younger than you."

"I'd hate to hear your guess of my age, then."

"Late thirties, early forties."

"Flattery doesn't work on me."

She was breaking, and he scrambled to figure out how to play it from here. In the end, he decided he'd made himself clear and wasn't going to beg.

"Okay, I tried. And I'll leave it alone now." There was no denying that he felt slightly angry, though. She was ignoring something that was pretty damn magical between them. "Don't worry about paying me. I'm always happy to lend a hand. So long, Sandy."

He headed for the door.

Her heels tapped as she followed him. "You'd regret it. You'd regret going to lunch with me."

He stopped but didn't turn around.

Sandy came up beside him. "Do you hear me?"

Finally, he said, "I'm afraid we're at a crossroads here. I've made it clear where I am in all this. Now it's your turn." He felt a tremendous pride in himself. Enough of being pushed and pulled. She stood staring at him, her thoughts seemingly ablaze.

Finally, she began to soften, her pupils easing up, her stance less rigid. And he knew—sort of—that he had her. He also knew that she liked confidence.

On that note, he stepped to the door and pulled it open, then held it for her. "Do you need to grab your purse?"

Her mouth slowly opened in what he surmised was surprise.

"Chop, chop," he said, his bravado rising.

She bit her bottom lip, starting a nod, which slowly morphed into a headshake. Then she did it, walked by him straight out the door. "I don't need my purse, because you're buying."

Dammit if he didn't smile wider than he had in twenty years.

Chapter 20

Regretti Spaghetti

"Sir Parm?" Sandy said. "You named him?" What was it about the bookstore that made her shut down the way she did? Here at this cozy spot near Porta Saragozza, she was a different person, pulling George deeper under her spell with every moment.

They sat at an outdoor table. The sun hid behind a building, offering some relief from the heat. She'd ordered a Pellegrino and a bottle of Lambrusco. They both glanced at the menus as they spoke and enjoyed their first sips.

"Of course I named him," George said. "He's become a major part of my life. A week in, and I still can't catch him. He won't eat cheap cheese either. So I have to get the good stuff—hence the name. But he has a knack for stealing the piece without triggering the trap, no matter how I place it."

"Bested by a mouse."

"That's right."

"My cat won't eat unless I cover his food with parm."

"The good stuff?"

"This isn't the Olive Garden, George. Yes, the good stuff."

He set down the menu. He was in no rush. "These animals, who do they think they are?"

A smattering of joy rose on her face. *Ah, how sweet you are,* he thought.

At his urging, Sandy told him about her cat, Nicolo, who she'd found during the construction of the bookstore. You would have thought she was talking about her favorite nephew, the way she gushed.

"Can I borrow him?" George asked after a while. "To go after Sir Parm."

Her eyebrows crinkled. "No, you can't borrow him."

"Can I rent him?"

"You couldn't afford him."

"Ah, okay, well, maybe I need to get Bianca a cat. Thought I'd consult her first."

"And there it is, proof you're growing." She shook her head. "I can't believe you named the mouse."

"Of course I did. I know his cousin back in Arizona."

"Sir Parm's cousin? Who is it, King Cheddar?" She took a long sip.

"Close. Mr. Nutz."

Sandy spit out her Lambrusco, blew it into the air in a mist, then slapped her hand over her mouth. "I'm so sorry. Did I get you?"

Far from annoyed, George looked down at the splatter on his shirt.

"I can't believe I did that," she said.

"I'd be the victim of your uncontrolled laughter any day of the week."

She poured sparkling water onto her napkin, then stood and rounded the table to lean down and blot out the wine marks. Her scent was intoxicating, the kind that can't be described. Her dress fell open at the top, and he turned away so as not to do exactly what he wanted to do.

When she finished dabbing at his shirt, she sat back down, a slight grin on her face. He couldn't get enough of her, and he matched her grin, and they both held it for a long while.

"Why Bologna?" George finally asked, his entire body buzzing with something that felt like love. "You haven't told me. Of all the places in the world. I get that you were running away from some tough life stuff. But how did you choose this city?"

She sighed and thought about it awhile, twisting the stem of her glass. "I knew it had to be Italy. I've always been mesmerized by it, since my first visit to Rome when I was a kid. And like Bianca, I studied Italian and lived with a family here my sophomore year at the University of Florida."

"Does she know that?"

"I don't know, but I also wanted to return one day." Then she plowed ahead. "It's a great city, you know. Off the beaten track enough that you don't hear English spoken around every turn. The food speaks for itself. The weather's great."

"Is it?"

"No, the weather isn't great. But when you catch a good day, there's nothing like it."

"Are you here for life?" George asked, thinking that he'd love to drag her back to Arizona. Maybe sell the country club house and return to Phoenix.

"I don't think so. Lisbon's been on my mind lately. I'm ready for a change. New scenery."

"You'd sell the bookstore, the *only* English bookstore?"

"Sell it? I highly doubt anyone wants to buy my failing bookstore."

"They would if you sold pancakes and American-flag Speedos."

Her lips turned up. "Ah, is this when you yet again bestow more of your bookselling wisdom upon me?"

"I was thinking about a franchise. The Only English Bookstore in Rome next. I like your smile. You don't do that enough, you know."

Saying it seemed to kill the mood, and George regretted shining a spotlight on her. "Don't stop."

She fidgeted with the napkin on her lap. Finally, she asked, "Can we go back to Mr. Nutz? I want to hear more."

"I better ask for a smock first." He glanced down at the wine splatter drying on his shirt. He rolled up his left sleeve. "You see these?" He pointed at the healing punctures from where the rake had gotten him. He'd finally been able to remove the bandage for good. "Battle wounds. From fighting Mr. Nutz."

"You have to be kidding me. I remember seeing that bandage around your arm." She reached across the table and ran her fingers over the scabs.

Her touch made it hard to concentrate. He finally said, "We have it out for each other. He's even broken into the house before. Mostly, though, he's after the birdseed, so I'm working on a new design, a Mr.-Nutz-proof feeder."

"I have to give you this, George. You're definitely one of a kind. How did he do that to your arm?"

He told her the whole story, and she laughed harder and harder, as did he, having to wipe tears from his eyes and collect himself every once in a while. He hadn't been this far away from his depression since Intel had axed him.

After their meal, as the server poured the last of the wine into their glasses, George said, "May I ask more about your son?"

She took a while to acknowledge his question. He saw the pain in her eyes as she said, "It's his birthday in two days."

He matched her quiet tone. "Will he call you?"

She shook her head. "I'd love that, but no. He won't be able to." She was fidgeting again, fiddling with something under the table.

"I didn't mean to pry."

"No, it's okay."

Maybe it was, maybe it wasn't, but it took her a while to make eye contact again.

Eventually, though, George dug her out of the mood he'd put her in. All he'd had to do was offer some more advice apropos the bookstore. This time, he suggested she set up a line of televisions under that cathedral ceiling in the main room so Americans could post up and drink beer and follow their favorite teams.

Even George knew that one was funny. There was no way in hell she wouldn't laugh, and dammit if she didn't bust into happy pieces.

Two hours later, they exited the restaurant and started back to Via Giulia. He wondered if she'd had a memorable time or if he was one of a thousand dates, another guy trying to make her laugh.

"I didn't ask," she said. "Did you enjoy your daughter's book?"

He nodded. "It's my daughter through and through. Made me so proud. Thanks for pushing me to read it." He revisited why he'd been so hesitant.

"Don't beat yourself up anymore, George. You're here. Keep trying."

"She's extra resistant to parenting."

"They always are."

"It's just that she's all about taking a big break now, giving up on everything she's built."

"What's wrong with taking a break?"

He shook his head. "Where I come from, that's a recipe for digging your own grave." He almost added *literally* but didn't want to layer on any more darkness. He dreaded his return back home, that place where his lack of purpose waited. Why was it the one woman he'd felt something for since his divorce had to live so damned far away? That was life these days, anything joyful staying far out of reach. What a sad thought that the Zoloft would be the only thing back home keeping him alive.

"Nobody's digging graves here, George. They're enjoying life. It's not a race. Here, it's about treasuring the simple things."

George thought about it. "I like the sentiment."

"I'm a lot of things: a handful, a grump. A porcupine, as I overheard Moira call me the other day. We don't have enough time for me to list my faults. But I've let go of the need to always be doing, to always chase things. That's what Bologna does to you. There's nothing better than a well-pulled espresso at a great café. And it's such a small thing and only lasts a moment, but when you give it all your attention, it makes life worth living. What your daughter's doing is seeking a renewal. She's trying to learn how to capture every second as opposed to racing to the end. Don't discredit it."

"I get your point."

She looked away and started to walk. He took her arm, and she turned back to him.

"It was a nice lunch, wasn't it?" George said.

"Yeah."

Now or never, George.

He moved in and set his lips to hers, letting his eyes fall closed, feeling like a young man again, like love might have resurrected him.

A light gasp escaped her lips, and he knew she felt the same way, too, both of them finding a missing piece. In a flash, he wondered where this was going, and he dreamed of the coming days with her and already felt the pain of saying goodbye, and maybe he would stay and—

Her hands were on his chest, and she pushed him back, and then her hand flew through the air and swatted him on the cheek, full palm, enough to make him dizzy, a slap that would leave a lasting mark.

With his heart kicking, he reached for the pain. "I'm sorry. I read things wrong. Please."

"How dare you," she hissed.

He peered into her eyes, looking for the person he'd had lunch with.

But she wasn't there.

Whoever she was, she turned on her high heels and raced off down the street.

As one does when a man doesn't text back, Bianca decided it would be a good time to check out her latest one-star reviews. Okay, fine, she'd been guilty of not responding to one of his texts before, but that was different. In this case, she'd numbed her prefrontal cortex with wine and limoncello and fired off a selfie. Selfies warranted responses. Demanded them, even. Sending it was the dumbest thing she'd done since deciding to run with the name Peggy Meh.

She was curled up on the couch, computer on her lap, blanket over her legs, ready to inflict punishment upon herself. Because that's what you do when you've lost your flipping mind. Several new reviews had appeared in the last two days. Oh, joy!

Padded. Could have been a list.

Can I give negative star ratings? WTF.

I guess anything can get published these days.

Might be good for young teenagers.

Written for the one percent.

I wouldn't insult my fireplace by tossing it in.

Dear LORD!!!! Peggy Meh! GIVE ME A BREAK.

How could people insult a person so? She'd put everything into the book. Maybe she hadn't executed it as well as she'd hoped. Maybe Peggy Meh was the worst idea to ever be vomited onto the page, but Bianca had tried. She'd pushed through her own self-doubt; she'd written and rewritten it so many times. All so she could be *fried* in public.

Sure, there were positive reviews. But they hardly mattered when drowning in this swamp of disgust.

How could any part of her consider writing another? Answer: Despite all the public vitriol, she craved returning to the blank page, the writing sessions when her fingers started dancing, when the flow took over. Okay, if she wrote another one, she didn't have to put it out there. Like Corrado's friend had done, it could be just for her. She could write it and then burn it, like the Buddha boards you paint on, only to watch the water-based artwork fade away.

The idea soothed her. If only she knew which direction to take.

If Donna Bologna was suggesting that Bianca had missed the mark, then what was the *freaking* mark? What would be worth writing about? What else did she have to say?

Bianca hesitantly opened a new Word document and stared at it for a while, like an alcoholic hiding in the closet with an open bottle of Smirnoff. She put her fingers on the keys, feeling the bumps of the *F* and *J*.

Movement at the door. She slammed shut her laptop. As her father entered, she felt like she'd been busted smoking weed, but then she noticed his distraught face. "What's wrong? How'd the date go?"

He set down the toolbox, then turned and pointed to a red mark on the side of his face.

"She slapped you?"

"Slapped. I guess you could call it that. I'm glad I still have my teeth."

It was not lost on Bianca that there was a lot of rejection going on around here.

She stood and pressed a hand to his face. "What'd you do?"

He shrugged. "I kissed her."

"You kissed her? What did you do, go in with the tongue or something?" She couldn't hide her enjoyment.

"What do I know? We were having a great time, then I kissed her and she slapped me and said, 'How dare you,' and walked away."

"At least you tried, right?"

He sat down and nodded. "Yeah."

"Geez. I don't like seeing you like this. What can I do?"

A headshake. "I need a nap. Two glasses of wine at lunch."

"How long was lunch?"

"Two hours."

"Two hours! What is she even doing hanging out with you? She's leading you on."

"I think she was being friendly, paying me back for helping around the store."

Bianca shifted to protective mode. No one messed with her father. "Whatever it is, screw her. She doesn't deserve you."

He stood slowly, patted her shoulder. "Nap time. It'll be okay. Not the first time I've been rejected in my life."

She touched his hand, feeling so much love for him. It was so easy to put him into some sort of box, to label him. The father figure, the parental unit. A support figure. But that wasn't all he was. Why did she keep treating him this way? He might not show or talk about his emotions, but he had them.

"Get some rest, then we'll do something fun tonight."

He trudged down the hall. Her heart ached as he closed his door.

"You know what ASAP means?" Bianca asked, charging into George's room later.

He turned the volume down on the news. "What's that?"

"Aperol spritz and pasta."

"Yeah. I can do that."

They sat on the balcony. George still couldn't get used to both of their underwear hanging on a line out there. A silly thought passed by. Sandy had mentioned the bookstore had a courtyard out back that she never used. Maybe she could put some dryers out there. Expats could shop for books while they waited for their clothes to dry.

Sandy would have enjoyed that one. Not anymore, though. What a shit show the whole thing was. Love, love, love. What was it anyway? A doorway to pain, really. As if he didn't have enough problems to drown in. There was this . . . this ache in his chest, a longing that could now never be satisfied. He'd almost found a reason to keep going. He'd almost felt young again.

"I want to kill Sandy," Bianca said, pulling him back to the present.

"No, don't do that. You two have a lot in common, as far as having lived here when you were younger, coming back later in life. She's a good person. Afraid of getting hurt, I think."

"When's the last time you kissed a girl?"

"Nineteen fifties," George replied nonchalantly. There'd been a few dates, nothing that had lasted longer than a few months.

"Seriously. It wasn't Mom, was it? You've had girlfriends since . . . No, I don't want to know."

He scratched his arm. "Let me put it this way. I haven't felt like this since your mom. I guess I read the signals wrong."

"Which is understandable, considering Sandy's cuckoo. God, she can be mean."

"But boy, when she lights up, it's something to behold. You get her away from that bookstore, she comes alive. Did you know she's been dancing the tango most her life? And she drives a Vespa. I think maybe not seeing her son enough is what breaks her up. And I can empathize with that."

Bianca's ears perked up when George casually mentioned that he'd read her book a few minutes later. "I know you told me not to, but I did," he said.

Maybe she should have been mad, considering she'd asked him not to, but in this moment, it felt like the sweetest gesture in the world. "I . . . You didn't have to."

"I should have read it a long time ago, and I'm sorry I didn't. I like Peggy Meh, and there's so much wisdom inside. Sometimes you're still my little girl, and to read all the advice you have, all the beautiful wisdom, it gives me shivers, even now."

"Really?"

He showed her the goose pimples on his arms, they read like *love* in braille. "My girl, all grown up. Doing amazing things. I hope you don't stop writing. Not because I want you to work and all that, but because you have a gift. You might not think so, and there might be haters out there, but your book did something to me. Made me see the world differently. Pumped me with some courage." Then he added, "I hope I'm not as bad as Peggy's dad."

She shook her head. "You are not Peggy's dad." At least, she hadn't planned it that way.

"You know what gave me the courage to go down and ask Sandy to lunch today? Peggy Meh."

"Get out."

"'One Life to Live.' That chapter. You know how to hit a guy hard. When Peggy finally considers leaving her husband, and you say the thing about how when it's all said and done and you're looking back on that one life you had to live, the one gifted miracle chance you had, what will be your regrets? I didn't want Sandy to be one of them. So I did it and it didn't work out, but I'll go home knowing I tried. I left my burn mark."

Tears filled Bianca's eyes.

"I was looking at flights. I think I'll head back Monday."

Her chest seized up. As much as she had wanted him to leave, she felt the opposite now. "What? Really? Because of her? Fuck Sandy. Don't leave because of her damage."

"It's time. I need to go face my life, figure it out. And let you figure out yours."

"Queen Bee!" a familiar voice called from down below.

Bianca stood and looked down to the street. Her breath left her when she saw Corrado holding a bouquet of flowers.

"What are you doing here?" she whispered.

"My other job is flower delivery. Someone sent you these." He gave a wink.

George joined her at the railing. "Who's this?"

"Hello, sir. It's Corrado, good to see you again."

"Ciao."

Bianca wanted to hurl herself off the balcony. Well, it was good to see Corrado and even better to see him holding flowers, but having her dad witness it was a bit much.

"May I come up?" Corrado called up to them.

"No, I'll come down."

He shook his head. "I'd like to say hello to your father."

George waved him up before Bianca could stop him.

Sandy sat on her favorite chair with Nicolo on her lap. A cup of chamomile tea steaming beside her, she dialed Jack's number. After his voicemail greeting, she said, "Your birthday's coming up; been thinking about you a lot. All the time. Nicolo says hi too. Don't mind me, I'm running my business into the ground and still being awful to everyone. I keep thinking about Lisbon, a chance to start over. It's been okay, but I'm getting antsy. Might be fun to learn Portuguese, have a new part of the world to explore. I have no idea what I'd do for work. I don't want to do *anything*. I'm definitely over the book business. Someone should have told me that the best way to kill your love of reading is to open a bookstore. Maybe similar to how the best way to hate your country is to let your son go to war . . ."

She set down the phone, her heart breaking.

Lifting it back up, she said, "Sorry, that was a low blow. Dammit, I wish things were different—"

A beep sounded, followed by a message from the operator, asking if she was satisfied with her message.

Sandy hung up and called again. "You wouldn't believe what I did yesterday. Went on what maybe was a date. A nice guy named George. Handsome too. But old, so much older than me. Had a good time, but then he kissed me, and I slapped him. I have your father to thank for that."

Husband #1's face projected on a screen in her mind, the likeness to Jack always haunting her. He was out of jail and apparently living in Tulsa, but that was all she knew about him. They'd not spoken since the day the police had cuffed him in the lobby of the Omni in Atlanta.

She stroked Nicolo. "Love always comes with an ending, honey, as you know, and when it does, it takes a piece of you—of your heart—with it." She let out a brief smile. "I have to protect what little I have left."

The surge of raw life rushing through her was too much, so she quickly changed the subject. "You might also like to know that Moira is at it again. Trying to bring more customers in. We had our first book club, and people actually showed up. We'll see how the next one goes. They're reading Bianca's book; she's the daughter of George. Long story. If you'd ever come visit, I could introduce you. For now, have a wonderful birthday wherever you are and know that your mom always and forever loves you."

While George and Corrado chatted, Bianca uncorked a wine and scrambled to put together a charcuterie board at the counter. She nearly cut her finger off, as she was barely paying attention. Listening to Corrado's voice, she kept wondering what was going on with him, why hadn't he responded to her text, what was he doing here? With flowers?

George was charming and kind as he probed Corrado with questions. "How does one get a Michelin star?" he asked.

"There are certain standards we must meet. The service has to be impeccable, the ambiance exceptional, the food consistent, creative, and extraordinary."

"And who gives the star?"

"An inspector. He's undercover, visits a few times, and the chef's success depends on him. Or her. This is why there can be no mistakes. Ever. Perfection night after night."

"Sounds stressful."

"Naturally. I suppose running a restaurant is a lot like writing a book. The pain is equal to the reward."

Bianca cracked open a jar of olives. "Dad, I'm sorry you won't get to go to the opening. He really is great." She told him about the gazpacho.

Corrado added, "I'm working on a new dish now, a veal cheek braised for twenty-four hours, then served on a fennel root cream sauce; finished with a dehydrated wild mushroom and a sprinkle of rosemary ash."

George's eyes expanded. "I see."

Bianca felt a desperate need to explain. "Dad's more of a meat-and-potatoes kind of guy."

"It's true. I'm more Michelob Ultra than Michelin. But it sounds nice."

"I think you'd like it," Bianca said, ignoring George's awful humor. "You have to open your mind. Food isn't always about eating for sustenance. Corrado's an artist. You should see his Insta page. Pure food porn."

"Food porn?"

"That's what they call it. Pictures of the dishes."

"Well, I wish you well. Sorry I won't get to taste your food." George continued from there, interrogating Corrado, prying deeper than she would have preferred.

Immensely relieved, Bianca sprang to her feet quickly when Corrado suggested that he better go. She followed him down the stairs, and only once they'd reached the street did they speak.

"You didn't realize what you're getting into, did you?" she asked the chef.

"It's great to see him again."

"Right. Because he's so easy, isn't he?"

"He's curious, that's all."

She searched his eyes, so warm and dazzling. "So you don't return my text for days and then show up?"

"Did I not respond?" He dug out his phone. "I texted you back, that lovely picture you sent. Oh, sorry, I never sent the message. I'm a mess with the restaurant opening in two weeks."

He seemed to be telling the truth and took her hand. "What happened, why did you leave me the other day? Did I do something wrong?"

"No, you didn't do anything wrong. I just . . . like I said. I'm a mess, and I was sparing you from it."

"I don't want to be spared, Queen Bee. I like you. I miss you." He ran his hands down her upper arms, then gently pulled her in. "I want you."

She kissed him.

"Come with me," he said, the temperature of the air around them rising. "Come home with me."

She felt the question in all the right places. "I want to, but I can't. My dad . . . it's weird. He's going to freak out about this, worrying that I'm with someone here in Bologna, far away from the States."

Corrado didn't fight her. He gave a simple shrug.

She kissed him again. "I really want to—"

He pressed a finger to her lips. "Say no more. I'm not going anywhere. Take your time."

His words made her want him more. "You've been warned, Corrado. I'm a wreck right now. And you're still here. Why?"

He reached for her shirt, pulling at the fabric. "You're the one who left."

She thought of Sandy, of how the bitch had slapped her father. She didn't want to be like her, mean and alone. And she didn't want to chase becoming Madmiral Megawatt, either, because that was the problem. The entire reason she'd moved to Italy was to escape all things Megawatt, but let's face it, she was treating slowing down and embracing *la dolce vita* with the same aggressive intensity as everything else in her life the last decade.

Why not just be human for a moment?

"Okay," she said, deciding she wanted to be a candle in a sea of light bulbs, like him.

"Okay, what?"

"Take me . . . take me home."

In the morning, they lay naked in the bed. Bianca was on her back, the sheets pulled up above her breasts. He was on his side, an elbow propping up his head.

They'd been chatting, but her focus was on the aftermath of this honeymoon they were on. Sure, the chase was fun. The reunion. She'd never had sex like that in her life. He'd learned some things in Paris. Her legs still quivered from last night and this morning.

But he didn't know the real her. How could he when she didn't even know the real Bianca? Who was she if not a writer and a sought-after therapist? She'd admitted her issues to herself, but she wasn't ready to admit them to others—especially this man lying beside her. He'd made it beyond obvious in so many ways that he wanted more. That he wanted a relationship. But she still wasn't ready. It could be years before she totally sorted herself out and had time to love someone else.

Corrado started to pull back the sheets to expose a nipple, but she batted him away.

The pitch of his voice rose as he pleaded. "What? Do you know how long I've dreamed of being with you again, touching you, staring into these eyes that have haunted me over the years. I've missed you so much." He kissed her cheek and whispered, "You don't know how amazing you are, do you?"

"Stop it."

"Seriously. Why are you hiding from me?" He giggled to himself. "Where are you, Bianca?" He touched her thigh under the sheet, and it made her shiver. "*You* are looking for you; *I'm* looking for you. The whole world is looking for you."

"I'm right here."

"Are you?"

He wouldn't stop looking at her.

"What?"

"Why are you holding back? You ravaged me like a wild animal and now you're hiding again. What's happening?"

She wanted to tell him that it was all downhill from here, but wouldn't dare, so she pulled the sheets up even higher instead and waited for a chance to escape.

Chapter 21

A Shadow on the Pavement

Sandy had never fought in a war, but when the images came to her, they seemed as real as they could get. She'd been up all night, hearing explosions, smelling burning flesh, and seeing young men and women maimed in a far-off land, soldiers fighting for causes that even they couldn't articulate. When she closed her eyes, mortar fire shook her, bullets whizzed by, the screams of the injured echoed.

She reached for Nicolo and dragged him toward her, pulling him in and squeezing him. "You're all I have," she said to him. "My Nicolo."

The images and sounds of war continued to play in her head as she showered and made breakfast. There was nothing more agonizing than the fear of losing a child when you couldn't keep tabs on them, when they were out there fighting wars, surrounded by a thousand ways to die. From the moment Jack had shipped out to Parris Island for recruit training, she'd been a nervous wreck.

But how could she have protested? The marines were his everything.

She drank her coffee by the window, looking out at a clear sky that didn't deserve to be so blue. "What a life I've lived, Nicolo," she said to her stray as he curled up at her feet. "So much pain."

She thought back to how things had been when she'd first moved here, when she hadn't known anyone. A fresh start after a life scarred by two wretched husbands. The promise of Jack one day joining her.

She sighed, remembering how it had always been Sandy and Jack against the world after his dad had been thrown in jail. There was something to be said for being a single mom. The bond was even stronger, because it's two of you, not three. They'd become fighters together, warriors trying to find a way through the world, Sandy parenting alone, Jack hitting puberty without a father to teach him how to shave.

When Jack discovered the ROTC, there was nothing she could do to dissuade him. He'd found himself as a soldier. A soldier, a lover of his country, both a boy and a man who had always been so convinced of right and wrong, no gray area. Looking back, she wished she would have fought even harder to keep him from enlisting.

She dialed his number.

"It's Jack, leave me a message . . . unless you're a telemarketer. Then you can go—*beep*." He'd never changed his message. She must have listened to it a thousand times.

She sang "Happy Birthday" into the phone, then: "Here I am with Nicolo, thinking about you. I do it so much, especially on the big days like today. I was thinking about the bookstore, how it was your idea. Naming it too. That was such a fun visit. I remember feeling like I'd finally escaped all the hell back home, and it was all because of you supporting me. Wouldn't things be different if you'd stayed here, worked with me? I might not even be running the thing into the ground. For the record, though, I did successfully usher the store through the pandemic, so there's that."

Sandy sat up. "The dream's dying now, though, Jack. And I don't even know why. I'm not happy. Well, of course, I'm not happy. All these people want something from me. Can't they see I want to live my life in peace? I've been beat up enough. Lisbon's still on my mind. I have enough money to get settled over there. I'm sure I can get out of the lease. I thought about going back home, too, but the US is falling apart. So much division. Honestly, I feel more Italian now."

When she reached the max limit on his voicemail, which she'd become good at sensing, she said, "Anyway, I'll call again later. Just know that you're always my everything. I love you, Jackie."

Sandy ended the call, then dropped her head and wept.

At work, Sandy avoided everyone, including Moira. It took everything to say good morning to customers. Moira was good at reading her and knew to stay out of Sandy's way and do her job in silence.

When customers entered, Sandy would all but hide behind the counter. Most of the time, she would call out for Moira and then head up the stairs to her office. She was especially fearful of George opening the door. She'd considered that she might owe him an apology, but there was no part of her that was ready to seek him out.

She'd not even thought about Harold in a couple of days when he walked in seeking advice. She eyed him up and down, his new clothes, perhaps a shred more confidence.

"I can't help you today, honey. I'm overwhelmed."

"Are we on for dancing tonight?"

She shook her head, avoiding eye contact. "No, I've had some things come up." It was almost unwarranted how she'd come to care for this kid, but she had nothing to give right now.

"I get it, no big deal. Next time."

Sandy's self-hatred flared up as he'd exited the store. "What am I supposed to do?" she muttered to herself. "Save everybody?"

She couldn't even save herself.

Sandy was lost in thought when she realized Moira was waving a hand at her.

"What are you doing? Jesus. Get your hand out of my face."

Moira stepped back. "Sorry, I was trying to get your attention."

"You have it."

"I was thinking that maybe we could expand the romance section? I've had several customers come in lately and comment on its . . . limited offering."

Sandy's jaw tightened. "That's the point. It's supposed to be small."

"I know, but . . ."

"You know what, Moira, I was thinking we do the opposite." Sandy looked toward the minuscule romance section. "Do me a favor and collect every romance book and move them to the discount table."

"Wait, what? I wasn't trying to cause a—"

"I've wanted to do this for a while now."

"That'll frustrate people."

"Perfect. My job on earth is to frustrate people. In a world where joy is dead, I'm able to dig up the last surviving bits of it by frustrating people. Come on, let's go."

With Moira watching, Sandy started tossing romance books into a box. She was well aware of how absurd she looked, how absurd the whole thing was, but she had exactly zero fucks to give about it.

"Let's go, Moira. We don't have all day. I want every last vestige of romance out of here. And I know you agree with me deep down. You won't tell me about what happened in your past, but I know love has something to do with it. I know, because a victim recognizes a victim."

Moira's eyes widened.

"Don't worry, your secret's safe with me." Sandy took one of the books and threw it toward the discount table. It crashed into a shelf. "Do you know how good that felt? Try it." Sandy handed her a Nora Roberts. "Take all that hate you have toward love and give it a toss." In an eerily Vader-esque voice, she whispered, "Join the dark side, Moira."

Moira slung the book with all the power of a mouse.

Sandy slapped another one in her hand, an Emily Henry this time. "Where is your passion? Tell me you don't make love like that."

Moira tepidly took the book and tried again.

"Nope, not good enough."

She gave her another and another, and by the time she saw George coming through the door, both ladies were laughing madly beside the entirely empty romance section.

"Look who it is," Moira said, but Sandy had already crouched behind the empty shelf. She held a finger up to her mouth, then shimmied to the next shelf, staying low.

Moira looked at her in shock, completely frozen.

"Stop looking at me."

"What?"

"I said *stop looking at me!*" It was her best attempt at a quiet scream.

The mouse finally figured out what was going on and raced under the arch toward the entrance. "Hi, Mr. Briggs. How are you today?"

Sandy peered around the side of the shelves and mapped out her getaway. She had to get past five shelves, then sneak under the arch, and move right to get to the steps to her office.

"I was looking for Sandy," he said.

Sandy got on all fours, removed her heels, and crawled to the next shelf, then the next.

"She's not . . . I don't believe she's here."

Sandy reached the arch. George stood fifteen feet away and was inching closer. Moira was still trying to put together words. "I think she went out . . ."

"Oh, I thought I saw her in the back there. Must be a customer."

"Yeah, we're busy today."

There wasn't a customer in sight. Sandy had to make a run for it.

"Can I interest you in a book? Maybe a cookbook?"

When Sandy heard that, she knew Moira had finally gotten in on the game, because the cookbook section was in the opposite direction. Once George pivoted, she made a mad dash, racing around the arch as quietly as she could, then moving past the cash register and the tower of postcards and—

Her foot caught the postcard stand, and she crashed hard onto the floor.

When Sandy had slapped George, she had not only crushed his confidence, but she'd reminded him of the heartache he'd felt when Bianca's mom told him she was leaving. Their marriage had been suffering for a couple of years, and they both were afraid of what would happen when Bianca left them with an empty nest, but it had hurt nonetheless, because it was the end of the three of them.

After the divorce, George had done everything to keep it together through her teenage years. It was awful sharing his daughter with her mom, having to do those awkward trade-offs, especially when he started noticing another car in the driveway of the home where they'd raised his girl. He remembered feeling so unbearably sick inside. If work hadn't kept him so busy, he would never have survived.

He felt sick inside again now, and yes, it was silly; he knew that. Their *one* lunch might not even be considered a date. So why in the world did he feel like he'd been dumped or served papers?

No longer could he sit in his room thumbing through his iPad or helping Bianca with her place—which was spick and span, thank you very much—or chasing Sir Parm, which was proving to be fodder for Mission Impossible 34. He decided he best apologize. At least he could leave the country with his dignity.

George pulled back the door; the bell chimed. Through the arch in the main room, he thought he saw the top of two heads sticking up over a shelf, but then they disappeared. The bookstore was eerily silent.

As he started toward the arch, Moira intercepted him. That's how it felt, anyway. She literally stood in front of him. When he asked to see Sandy, she started mumbling, then tried to talk him into buying a cookbook called *Pasta Grannies*. George was no idiot. He had a feeling that Sandy was in the back of the store, but he wasn't going to push. As he was about to excuse himself, a loud crash came from behind them, then a scream.

Moira dropped the book and raced toward the cash register. George quickly followed. The tower of postcards had fallen over, and he caught sight of Sandy's bare feet as she raced up the stairs.

One leg crossed over the other, Aroldo sat in the same square near Renzo's apartment, surveilling the entrance. A marble fountain spewed water into the air. The outdoor tables were filled with university students, connecting with friends, studying, killing a minute before class. It was an overcast morning, slightly gray and mystic.

Today was the day. He needed to make his move.

But Harold felt afraid, unsure. Maybe waiting was better. He was also still bothered by Sandy pushing him away, like she'd given up on him. He felt cast away, like the same waste of space he'd always been.

But Aroldo kept telling Harold to zip it. He extracted a cigarette and lit it with his new fancy lighter, then snapped it shut with tremendous confidence. He took a drag, then said as the smoke came out, "I'm in charge now."

He sipped the last of his espresso and looked at the cover of *My Brilliant Friend* by Elena Ferrante, another book that Moira had sent him home with. Harold was barely there now, nothing more than a shadow on the pavement. Aroldo cracked the spine and dove in.

He didn't get far before the door to Renzo's apartment burst open. Right on time. Renzo, the stealer of strawberry lovers, was on his way to work. Though Alice often followed him out, it was only him today, in suit and tie, racing out the door.

Aroldo decided to seize the moment. He sprang from his seat and caught up to Renzo, trying not to be intimidated by the height of the man. "Renzo," he said sharply.

His enemy stopped.

Fearless Aroldo got in his face. "Who do you think you are, treating Alice like that?"

Renzo let his lips curl. "Harold?"

He pointed at Renzo's chest. "I know what you're doing, taking advantage of her. And I won't stand for it. Not anymore."

"Such a little man, aren't you?" His accent was thick. They were so close, Harold could smell his cologne. The guy gave a staccato laugh. "What are you going to do about it? You're not even a memory to her anymore."

Aroldo felt the punch in his gut and said, "That's what you'll be soon. A memory." He wanted to take it back even as he said it. *C'mon, Aroldo, don't let Harold turn you soft!*

"Go home to Denver, little Harold. She wants nothing to do with you."

Aroldo's fist clenched. "I will ruin you."

"Ruin me? Please, I'd like to see you ruin me. In the meantime, I need to go to work so I can hurry home and get back to my lady. *Ciao*, little Harold." He turned and started away.

Aroldo nearly chased after him, wanting to punch the fucker in the back of the head, but he couldn't do it. Dammit, he couldn't do it.

His enemy rounded the corner and escaped while Aroldo shrank back into Harold, the weak imbecile he'd always been. Fuming, he returned to the table and waged war in his mind. Renzo was a terrible man, and he had to be destroyed. And Alice had to be rescued.

Considering biological facts, a physical altercation would not be a good idea. No, he'd best Renzo by stealing back his lover. How could Aroldo do that? The wheels spun. Aroldo was a man to make big statements, gestures worthy of Alice.

Considering her favorite movie was *Say Anything*, he imagined recreating the famous scene near the end with the Peter Gabriel song.

It was a silly idea, but one that might resonate with her. He might have run it by Sandy, but she'd clearly decided to move on. Which was fine. It was time for Aroldo to leave the nest.

Alice appeared at the entryway an hour later. The sound pulled Harold from Ferrante's story, which was rather good. He set down the book and bore witness to all the glory that was the woman who'd captured his heart. A sleeveless top, a casual khaki skirt, legs that sped up his heart rate.

Setting his sights on her made him want to defeat Renzo even more.

When she started his way, he sat back and pretended to be people-watching as he sipped his *acqua frizzante*. He sensed her getting closer, he was sure of it, but he dared not turn yet. This was his moment, and he would not fuck it up.

Then he heard her footsteps, the slight patter of an angel, and he turned in time to find her passing right by him.

"Alice?"

She stopped. "Harold? Is that you?"

He pulled off his designer sunglasses, folding them gracefully and slipping them into the pocket of his shirt. "Indeed," he said with his international accent. "And you, wow. You look wonderful. How are you?"

"I'm fine. Why are you here?"

"What do you mean? I was simply out for a walk, a *long* walk, and thought I'd take an espresso and read." He gestured toward the book.

"Ferrante?" she asked, stepping forward. "That's one of my favorite books."

"It's delightful, isn't it?"

He glanced at her backpack. "On your way to class, yeah?"

She nodded, her hair doing a bounce.

"And how is your Renzo? Are you back with him?"

She slumped some. "Yeah, we're back together, I guess."

I guess. The two sweetest words Aroldo could have ever heard. Finally, a crack.

"As long as you're happy, then I am. But he better be treating you right, love. You deserve only the best."

She lit up at that. "That's kind of you. He's a good guy. A little hot tempered, but nobody's perfect."

Harold might have said that she was the definition of *perfect*, but Aroldo held his cool. "Anyway, I best get back to it. I wanted to get a few chapters in before a hike up to the Portico di San Luca to soak up the view."

She tilted her head. "Really? I didn't think you were much of a walker."

He touched his chest, insulted. "Me? I get in my fifteen to twenty thousand steps a day. No big deal."

She pressed her lips together and widened her eyes. "Who are you, Harold?"

Harold is dead, he said to himself.

"Let's just say that Bologna has been good for me."

"I can see that."

He almost invited her to sit, but that was a Harold move. He simply held her gaze, taking the position of power. Sandy would have been proud. Then: "Enjoy your day, dear."

She adjusted the strap of her backpack. "It's good seeing you, really. Maybe we could have coffee sometime. I enjoyed hanging out with you. Thanks for being there for me, talking me down."

He wanted to say the man she'd encountered that night had been Harold the Weak; he'd been the one to hold her in his arms all night. Had it been Aroldo, she would still be blushing.

"Make sure he's treating you the way you deserve, you understand?"

A quick, insecure nod.

"Alice. I'm serious."

"Thanks, Harold."

Aroldo pushed up from his seat, set a hand on her waist, kissed both her cheeks, then locked eyes with her. "*Ci vediamo, cara.*"

"Listen to you," she chirped.

Aroldo didn't respond. He simply turned and found his seat again, never once looking back.

Once he was sure that she was gone, a smile filled his face as he said to himself, "Well, that was nice. Bravo, Aroldo."

Chapter 22

Running from Yourself

It was midmorning, three days after Bianca had run out on Corrado for a second time, and she was just returning from one of Carol's exhausting Vinyasa Flow classes. During an extended pigeon pose, while Carol had read a passage from *The Untethered Soul*, an idea—a wild and crazy idea—had settled into her, and she was about to present it to her father.

Things had really come to a head in her . . . well . . . in her head. She hated being wishy-washy with Corrado. But she was still pretty damn sure that a relationship with him was a bad idea. Then her father. George; George. *George.* She hadn't done much for him, and he was about to return home. *Bologna* hadn't done much for him, either, except dump heartache on top of his depression. The two of them were having fun—albeit a *mild* fun—but he'd been there so long it felt like they were simply cohabitating now. Not like what it should be: a father visiting his daughter in one of the greatest places on earth. It didn't help that all he wanted to do was execute tasks.

Then there was Bianca and her own . . . whatever it was, an aggro-reset? A supercharged leap abroad? She'd brought her megawatted baggage all the way from Austin, and it was time to take a big freaking step back and truly recapture life's alchemy.

Marching into her apartment, she found George standing at the counter in the kitchen fidgeting with something. No doubt the next task on the list!

He turned and held up a new mousetrap. "Hey, kiddo. I found that other hardware store. Thought I'd try something different."

She resisted the urge to smack her forehead, and instead, leaned into the possibility that her birdbrained idea might just be the perfect solution to throw them both off their hamster wheels.

"I have an idea," she said, only now realizing that there was no way in the world he'd go for it.

"Yeah? Talk to me." He tore open the package and clicked his glasses together to read the instructions.

"Forget going home for now. Let's go on a trip."

Pure focus and determination, he barely stopped reading to say, "I *am* on a trip."

"No, I mean, let's pack a bag and go see more of Italy. A father-daughter thing."

"Yeah, maybe."

"No, I mean now."

He set down the trap and pulled apart his readers. "Now? As in right this second?"

"Or maybe in an hour, after a shower. I want you to see Italy the way I did when I first visited. No agenda; a backpack and a taxi to the train station. We'll decide from there."

He laughed as though she'd told a bad joke.

"Not joking."

"Maybe in a couple of days. I'd like to get Sir Parm out of the house before his babies start showing—"

"Dad, I'm not asking. I need this. I need to go see Italy, hit the road. And I think it'll be good for you too." This was also how she would face the issues she was having with her father. Head-on. They either came back whole or broken, one way or the other.

He rejected the idea a few more times, but Bianca did what her mother always did when he rejected a good idea. Ignored him.

An hour later, she set her backpack and bag down by the door, then went to find her father. He was standing at his bed, scratching his head, and looking down at his bag.

"I don't even know what to bring. Where are we going?"

"Not sure yet. You don't need a jacket or sweater, though. Bring a bathing suit. A nice pair of pants."

"How many days?"

"I have no idea. That's the point."

"Oh, c'mon, I need some kind of reference."

It slightly pleased her that he was going mad with the idea of a trip sans itinerary. No, she *adored* the way he was squirming. It was already so clear how good this would be for him.

"Well," she said, "I have to be back for the next book club. That's in about two weeks."

"Two weeks?"

"I don't know." She held up her hands and repeated herself. "I don't know. We can wash our underwear in the sink or the sea. Maybe find a laundromat."

"Oh, dear God, honey. Are you trying to torture me? What about Sir Parm? That new trap might get him. He'll stink the place up."

Bianca wasn't having it. "Then disengage the trap. I'm sure he'll be waiting when we get back."

He shook his head, the idea preposterous. "He'll be waiting here with a mouse army. I'm telling you, B. I've seen it before. They multiply and will take over a place."

"I'm willing to take the chance."

He shook his head slowly, in the way she knew too well, the way of a man constantly forced to do things he didn't want to under the command of two strong-willed women.

"You know what, though," she said. "This means everything to me. That you'd trust me, that you'd risk leaving your comfort zone. That you're willing to take a leap of faith. Thank you."

That brought a smile out of him, and then his eyes began to glow with determination. "Let's do this."

She couldn't have loved him much more than she did right then.

With summer travelers winding around them, Bianca and George studied the departure board at Bologna Centrale.

An abundance of languages leaped from foreign tongues. Baristas pulled espressos with caffeinated intensity. Muffled announcements crackled out of the overhead speakers. A frantic bodybuilder dragging a bag burst through the crowd in a desperate race to make his train on time.

According to the board, trains left soon for Milan, Florence, Rome, and Venice.

Chills ran up Bianca's spine; this was wonderful. Not only because it made her father squirm, but because she felt young again. Truly, for the first time since setting foot back in Italy, she felt like she was accomplishing what she'd set out to do: find that twenty-two-year-old badass who'd had it all figured out.

Enough worrying about her next move. Enough beating herself up over the book. Time to let Italy wrap her silks around her.

"South or north, Dad?"

"I don't know," he mumbled, his white tennis shoes so bright that they almost gave off a glow.

"We can stop anywhere. Pick one."

"What if we can't find a place to stay?"

"There's always a place. Have you ever been to Venice?"

He shook his head, a shy little boy all over again.

"How about it?"

He shrugged.

"Done. Leaves in nineteen." Before he could disagree, she went to buy tickets.

⁓

They approached the departure board, waiting for the gate announcement. A family next to them dug into a bag of fast food. The smell of french fries spread into the air.

George pulled close the carry-on rolling bag she'd lent him. "How come the gate isn't listed? The train leaves in a few minutes."

The exhilaration of the unknown filled every cell of Bianca's being. "This is how it always works. They let you know about ten minutes out."

He let out a sigh of disgust. "Back in the States, you'd know the gate yesterday."

"Dad, how many trains have you ridden in the States?"

When he didn't answer, she said, "Yeah, exactly. Don't worry, we'll catch it."

For the next five minutes, he watched the departure board like a hungry dog staring at his owner. When the gate was finally announced, George shot in that direction. It was hard not to get edgy around him, but she kept reminding herself to stay patient.

Once they found their seats, Bianca watched George as he studied the others getting on board. What was going on in this man's head?

An older woman in a hijab came racing onto the train at the last minute. She lugged a giant red bag and was trying to figure out where to put it. George was there in an instant, helping her lift it up and cram it into a small open spot in the luggage hold.

"They don't give you enough bag space," he said when he returned.

"That was nice of you."

He shrugged, then looked at his watch.

They were crossing over a bridge to Venice, both of them staring out the window at the passing boats filled with scantily clad Venetians. The train had a nice glide to it, barely a bump, a calming rattle. The excited energy of every traveler filled the car, because Venice demanded a certain reverence and elation when it drew near.

"You ever think that he's hungry?" Bianca asked.

"Who?" George asked, sitting across from her.

"Sir Parm. And Mr. Nutz for that matter. Or what if they're trying to feed their families?"

George wagged a finger at her. "No, don't do that. He's invaded your sanctuary."

That made Bianca smile. "Invaded my sanctuary? He's sneaking into the cabinet for a bite."

George counted on his finger. "Breaking and entering, for one. Leaving diseases, spawning more rats."

"He's not a rat. He's an adorable mouse who's probably a father just like you, simply trying to put food on the table."

He crossed his arms. "We'll agree to disagree here. Soon as we get back, before I head out, I will take him down."

"What are you, some sort of mouse hunter?"

"That's what dads do, honey. We take care of the ugly things behind the scenes."

"The Navy SEAL of the family."

"That's right."

Even *he* couldn't keep from smiling at that one.

"Look at you," Bianca said. "George Briggs is having fun. And we haven't even arrived yet. On top of that, I have yet to see your legal pad. Maybe you didn't even bring it."

He patted the backpack between his legs. "Oh, I brought one."

Bianca sighed dramatically.

"Now, look," he said. "I've agreed to your madcap trip, which by the way is making me incredibly uncomfortable, if you haven't noticed, but you're not taking my legal pad."

"Fair enough." She made a mental note to get rid of it later. "By the way, watch for pickpockets. They'll be worse in Venice."

"Seriously? What have you gotten me into?"

She waved it off. "It's fine, just be vigilant. Maybe we'll get you a murse, you know, a man bag. It'll make things easier."

"A man bag?" He said it like it was a curse word.

"That's right. Don't worry, we'll find something manly. Maybe a Chuck Norris logo on it."

"I'll take my chances."

For the next five hours, as they strolled through Venice, she watched him repeatedly pat his front pocket to make sure he still had his wallet.

Aroldo sat on the balcony in the twilight, sipping on a shot of limoncello, texting back and forth with Alice. Every ding on his phone, each of her responses, worked to restore his heart back to normal. In fact, he'd even started watering her potted plants again, resurrecting them from near death. He and the plants were in this together, metamorphosing from wilted shrivels into their greatest selves.

He wasn't ready to call it a victory, but he was getting somewhere, wedging back into her heart.

Each play had to be exacting.

Several days ago, not an hour after they'd last seen each other, she'd sent the first text of this thread. A simple message: I barely recognized you today!

Aroldo had put so much thought and care into his reply. He'd even made her sweat and not responded till early the next morning with a brief: same ole me.

She'd shot him back a fast one. You're up early.

Off for a run.

Get out.

Training for the Venice Marathon in late October. Looking into a digital nomad visa now.

What was beautiful about becoming Aroldo was that he *had* been running; his body was changing. Was he going to run the marathon? That was yet to be determined.

The texts had continued nonstop, and it had become one of the most enjoyable games of Aroldo's life. He'd become his own avatar and was now playing for real love, the highest of stakes.

He was pretty sure she was enjoying the exchanges as well, as she was the one who started them up in the morning and was always quickest to respond. He couldn't help but believe that she wanted him to come rescue her from Renzo.

That's what he'd decided to do. But he had to do it in a way that would leave burn marks. Yes, he'd finished Bianca's book, and as on the nose as it was, her messages had landed.

Leave burn marks.

It was a hell of a way to live. And with this next play, Alice would feel the sizzle!

The *Say Anything* idea hadn't left him. It was bold, even for Aroldo. And potentially embarrassing. Would he dare stand there with a boom box, playing Peter Gabriel's "In Your Eyes"? And would she come out onto the balcony, witness the depth of his devotion, and fall back in love with him?

Aroldo poured himself another shot of limoncello and, using a few of Bianca's tricks from the book, began to visualize himself as Lloyd Dobler, the character John Cusack plays in the movie. If he were to pull this off, he'd have to dress like Cusack, the jeans and The Clash T-shirt, the long beige, eighties trench coat. And he'd have to somehow find an old boom box like the one Cusack held up outside of Skye's house.

With his eyes closed, Aroldo saw himself standing in the square looking up at the balcony of Renzo's apartment, reenacting the scene. Inside the apartment, Alice lay in bed, perhaps resistance-cuddling with Aroldo's enemy, the evil Renzo. Wasn't that a nice new turn of phrase, resistance-cuddling; this was one of the many fine creations of Aroldo, a man who issued far more poetic ability than Harold.

Upon hearing Peter Gabriel, Alice slips on her nightgown and sneaks out onto the balcony, where she—

Hold on, had it been reenacted before, the *Say Anything* scene?

With an imploded chest, Aroldo inquired with ChatGPT, and the news jabbed him in the eye. At least thirty to forty times, including on *The Simpsons*, *Family Guy*, *South Park*, and *How I Met Your Mother*.

"Great job, Harold, you schmuck," Aroldo said. "Way to be original. Next time, let me handle it." He nearly cast his phone off the balcony. That fast, he'd been knocked down—better yet, *demoted*—back to Harold.

A weaker version of himself looked at the limoncello. He didn't even like lemons. He didn't even drink alcohol back home.

Then, a song broke through the air.

The opera singer was at it again.

The man stood with his hand on the railing, several balconies up, looking out over the city, belting out a song.

Aroldo let the aria pierce his soul.

When it ended, Aroldo gave the man a standing ovation. He wasn't the only one. People from other balconies and on the street did the same.

"Bravo," Aroldo cheered. "Bravo!"

The opera man bowed and retreated inside.

As the man's vibrato still lingered in his ears, Aroldo suddenly knew how to make his next play all the more powerful. And far more original.

Sandy arrived early to work, but Moira had still beaten her there. The guppy sat on the stool behind the counter, staring at the computer through her windshields for glasses. *"Buongiorno."*

Sandy growled at her.

"Can I get your approval on some things?"

"What things?"

Windshield Face started going as if she'd been wound up. "I'm working on another newsletter, and some flyers. See?" She twisted the screen Sandy's way.

The flyers were impressive, but she refused to offer praise, or even approval. "Okay," Sandy said in short.

Moira's enthusiasm shrank. "I wanted to see if you could give me more of a budget."

"I didn't know you had one."

"Yeah, that's kind of it. I was hoping for five hundred euros, so I can run some ads on the social media sites, maybe put something in the English paper. Print out a stack of flyers. Our printer's the worst. I want to do color. Get them out all over the city. What do you think?"

"I think I need more coffee." Sandy started toward the steps to her office.

"Yeah, I understand," Moira called out to her. "If you're wanting to stay frugal, I could cover the cost?"

Sandy pivoted and took a big step toward Moira. Why did Moira care so much? "Yes, frugal is right. And no, I don't have five hundred euros that you can waste printing *color* copies of your silly flyers. Let me save you the time, as I thought I'd done before. Don't bother. There is no supercharging this dinosaur of a store. No one reads books anymore; therefore, no one needs a store of them; therefore, no one wants a book club. Besides, George says Bianca hates her own book, so even the author doesn't want to attend."

Now that felt like a victory, a mighty general climbing back on her horse after defeating the enemy. But Moira's silence ruined everything, penetrating through the steel walls around Sandy's ticker.

In a move that even surprised Sandy, she let the posture of the general inside her slacken, and said, "Sorry, I wasn't supposed to say that." Ugh, she hated apologizing.

"I know she was frustrated about some of the reviews, but why does she hate the book?"

Sandy looked up to the ceiling, wishing it would fall on her. "I don't know. Yes, the reviews. And it hasn't sold like she'd hoped. I think she regrets trying to be a writer."

Concern, a classic mark of weakness, reared its ugly head behind Moira's windshields. "That's so sad. It's such a good book."

Sandy gestured toward the books no one was buying. "They're all good books. That's why they get published. But books, along with book clubs, are dead, Moira. And that's why I'm moving to Lisbon." She couldn't help herself.

"What?" Moira covered her mouth.

"You might as well know. I'm selling the bookstore. Or shutting it down. You wanna buy it? I'll give it to you for cheap."

"You're not serious. I know you." Again, *why* did Moira care?

Sandy couldn't help but keep going. "You don't think I'm serious? Do you know me as someone who jokes around?"

Moira shook her head, and the pitiful look on her face kicked at the fading embers of Sandy's dying heart. "I'm sorry," Sandy said. "I didn't want to tell you yet, but you're just . . . You won't let up with the Megawatter crap and all your efforts to promote the book club. I shouldn't have let you start it in the first place."

"How long do I have?" The guppy sure could throw a pity party.

"I don't know. I haven't looked into it yet. I just decided."

Moira nodded and closed out the screen with her flyer. "Okay, I guess I'll cancel. I didn't realize Bianca hated her book. I was just trying to help."

"And now you see what helping does, right?"

Moira shook her head, and a tear fell from her eye.

"Nope," Sandy said, "we're not doing this again. I've already seen enough tears out of you to last till I come back to haunt you from my grave." Sandy thought herself funny, but Moira ignored her.

"Do you mind if I take a sick day?"

Sandy wondered if stabbing herself in the jugular with a pen would do the trick. They had nice pens with "The Only English Bookstore in Bologna" printed on them. No one ever bought them, so maybe they could be repurposed. Good news was that there would be an opening for another clueless romantic who might think an English-only bookstore in Bologna was a good idea. Even bookstores in Madrid offered other languages. But Sandy couldn't do that because she'd clung to a name that had seemed clever at the time. It would be an abomination to suddenly offer a Spanish section in the corner.

Moira was still waiting for an answer.

"You've never taken a sick day."

"Which means I'm entitled to one."

"Of course." Sandy wasn't about to start begging or offering more apologies. It was probably best for Moira to learn that the world wasn't a pretty place. Certainly nothing like the settings of the soulless books she liked to get lost in.

Moira quickly gathered her things, pressed her floppy hat to her head, and started to the door. "See you tomorrow," she muttered.

Sandy didn't like how she felt inside, so purely for selfish reasons, she said, "Now, c'mon, Moira, settle down."

It was too late. Her sole employee was out the door and gone. It had already been so damned quiet after George left. And now she'd run Moira off.

Sandy hated herself even more than she normally did. She took her phone and texted, Okay, I'm sorry for being a bitch. Don't cancel the book club. You've put too much work into it already.

Then she called Jack.

Chapter 23

A Father Out of Water

"May I have some cheese?" George asked, sitting at a table outside of a restaurant on the Campo Santa Margherita square in Venice. Despite the punishing heat of the early afternoon and a mob of tourists bumping into each other while all trying to take the same pictures, this city had an impenetrable charm.

They'd secured an outdoor table draped in a white tablecloth, resting under an awning and roped off from the crowds spilling gelato all over themselves. Italy had a smell to it, a combination of pasta cooking in a pot, coffee, a hint of cigarettes, fresh flowers, and maybe chocolate.

The handsome server, dressed in black, shook his head. *"Non capisco."* I don't understand.

"Queso, I mean. Or . . ." George looked at Bianca, who was immersed in her bowl of squid ink pasta—totally black pasta—quite possibly the most disgusting dish he could ever imagine. "How do you say cheese, B?"

She looked up, oblivious to the conversation he was trying to have with the server. *"Formaggio."*

Back to the server, George asked, "Can I get some *formaggio, per favore*?" How was it possible that these Italian men were all so good looking? No wonder Bianca wanted to live here.

Suddenly paying attention, Bianca mocked him. "Can I get some *formaggio*? Dad, please never say that again. It's: *potrei avere del formaggio?* Try it."

George mangled it but did his best.

The server shook his head. "No." Then he said something in Italian. George looked at Bianca for a translation.

"He's asking why."

"Why? Because I need cheese."

"For what?"

Growing slightly frustrated at how difficult this seemingly simple request had become, he gestured toward his shrimp pasta. Or *gamberetti,* whatever. It was getting cold, that was for sure.

"For my pasta. Why else would I need cheese?"

The server shook his head and spoke more Italian to Bianca. They were sharing a "moment" that George didn't appreciate for a host of reasons.

"What's he saying?"

Bianca broke into an infuriating laugh. "You can't put cheese on seafood pasta. It's a sin. Like dipping fries in soy sauce. You don't do it."

He unfurled his hands. "It's my pasta. I want cheese." *Was this a fucking* Seinfeld *bit?*

"He won't give it to you."

A standoff followed. Dead quiet. George looked at Bianca, then the server. He wasn't sure whether they were pulling his leg. "Are you messing with me?"

"No," Bianca said through a giggle. "The Italians take their food seriously. He won't give it to you."

"Okay, fine. *Gracias,*" he said to the server.

"It's *grazie*!"

"Grazie," George corrected. "And keep your eyes off my daughter."

When the server left, George took a sip of his water. "I don't know how you do it. These people are nuts."

"Because they don't like cheese on pasta?"

"Because I can't put cheese on my pasta. I'm not putting it on his pasta."

"Still, it's an insult to the chef."

"He should try it. I think he'd be surprised." George looked at his plate. Six shrimp still in the shell. "And they couldn't even take the heads off. I should get a discount for having to do it myself. Do I have to go back and wash the dishes afterward?"

Bianca motioned to a table of people who were gawking at them.

"What?" he said, not appreciating how she was making him out to be the bad guy.

"Dad, you're ridiculous. Please stop embarrassing yourself and go with the flow. This is what travel is, learning other cultures. Seeing that things are done differently."

George sighed. She was right. "Okay, okay." He took a bite. "It is good, though. I'll give them that."

"Darn right, it's good. We're in Venice. Some of the best food in the entire world." She twirled up a bite of her black pasta with shellfish. "Taste it."

"Um, no thank you. I prefer my pasta without black toxic goo. And so sue me, I like it with cheese." He shook his head, then looked up at Bianca. God bless her, she was giving him some slack and grinning, accepting him for who he was. Even *George* had a hard time accepting George.

And her patience for him, layered with the obvious and infectious love, did something to him deep down, rattled his cage.

He laughed at himself and at this whole absurd ride called life. "All right, okay. Let me try again. I don't mean to be obnoxious."

"Look at you," she said. "I think you're having fun. Even without cheese on your shrimp pasta." She offered him a bite of her black sludge noodles again.

He backed away. "Muffin, not even Sir Parm would eat that vile concoction."

Bianca wasn't having it, and he knew that look in her eye, because her mother often had the same one. She wanted something and wouldn't let up until she got it.

"Want me to do the airplane?" While making a motor noise with her mouth, she turned her fork into an airplane and tried to land it in his mouth.

"Okay, okay." She was hard to say no to. "What the hell."

He let her land the sludge plane and then chewed the bite, trying not to think about it being squid ink.

"Oh, wow," he said after a few chews, feeling his eyes widen. He felt lighter inside, not only because of the pasta but maybe because he was letting go.

"I told you." She leaned forward and said, "And Dad, don't you see? There's nothing wrong with you. You simply need to find more moments like this, whatever it takes."

In a flash, the light feeling died. He stuck a fork back in his own pasta, wondering if this was okay, him talking to his daughter about his stuff. She'd been working on him for the last two days, prying out of him the difficulties of retirement. He'd opened up, though he'd certainly not told her of his suicidal ideations.

"Don't do that; don't get in your head," she said.

"I don't like talking about it. It doesn't matter that you're a shrink. I'm your dad."

She poured them both more Pellegrino. "That's what your generation does, hides it all. What are you afraid of? You know what I'd tell you if you were on my couch? That you don't need another job. You don't need to beg Intel for another chance. Nor do you need consulting work. You don't even need to hunt Sir Parm as if he were Bin Laden. You need to find another purpose, a real one, not hunting mice and squirrels."

It'd be funny if it weren't true, he thought.

"Let's look at it another way," she said. "I agree, you're not a golfer. You don't need to get into baking sourdough boules or playing the flute."

He set his fork down with a clang. "The flute? If I were to play an instrument, it wouldn't be the flute."

"What's wrong with the flute?"

He shrugged. "I'm more a trumpet guy."

"Okay, trumpet then, Louis Armstrong. What I'm saying is you have to find purpose in the present moment. And I'm the pot calling the kettle black. I'm working on this too. But what if we both simply gave each moment the reverence it deserved? It's not about choosing a hobby. It's about choosing *life*. What's that thing Alan Watts said about how you should measure your days by the degree of presence, not productivity?"

"Yeah, but I still have to do something. I can't sit around waiting to die, present or not."

"That's a matter of perspective: waiting to die versus enjoying each precious breath."

Bianca plowed ahead. "Even the simplest moments, like being rejected when trying to get cheese for your seafood pasta, are all one needs to find purpose. No matter your religion, I can't think of a better way to give back for being gifted life than to be fully engaged in the now."

She took a moment to enjoy a bite, then: "It's difficult to put into practice because we all have our fears. Our doubts. Our insecurities. Why do you and I both work so hard? Why do we have to-do lists? Why can't we sit still? Why are my career goals moving targets? Why have I spent the last ten years going nonstop, trying to become someone?"

George reached for a slice of bread from the basket and swiped it across the oily sauce on his plate. "Because you have gifts that you want to share with the world."

"Thanks for that, but no." She counted on her hands. "Two reasons: One, I have a desperate need to prove myself. Why? I don't know. But also because staying busy keeps me from having to sit in my own mess. Retirement may be the best thing that ever happened to you, because you're being forced to sit with yourself, to get to know yourself. You've been stripped of your biggest excuse for not being present. Sure, find something new to do. But don't find it from a place of desperation. That's all I'm saying."

George grunted and mulled over what she'd said. Part of him resisted her advice, maybe because she was so much younger, and even more to the point, *he* was the one who was supposed to give her advice. But a bigger part of him knew that she'd hit the bull's-eye.

He rested his elbows on the table and waited for her to look at him, then: "You have it figured out, don't you?"

"Far from it."

He stared into the eyes of this woman that he and Faith had created. "Thank you. You give me hope."

Two days after his latest scheme took hold, Aroldo prepared to approach the opera singer. He'd gotten pretty good at stakeouts and knew the man left his house at exactly two every day, likely going to lunch. He was methodical about it.

Aroldo had gone by the bookstore to run his idea by Sandy, but once again, she hadn't been in a talkative mood. She wasn't exactly mean, but he could tell she had other things on her mind. He *had* spoken to Moira, though, and she loved the idea, said it was the sweetest thing she'd ever heard.

So here Aroldo was, standing under the portico, watching the clock. Precisely at two, the opera man exited his building, glanced up to the cloudy sky, then started to stroll, his hands clasped behind his back. He had a Super Mario quality about him: a pudgy body with short legs, a honker of a nose, big blue eyes, and a mustache and eyebrows that could use a trim.

Aroldo padded across the street and called out, *"Mi scusi, posso parlarle?"*

Take that, Duo.

"Si," Super Mario said, pausing his waddle.

Aroldo had translated and printed out his request. As he reached for the folded sheet of paper from his pocket, he said, "I don't suppose you speak English . . ."

"I speak a little English. What can I help with?" His voice was as rich and vibrative as his singing.

Aroldo gave him the sheet of paper—several paragraphs explaining his plight. He let Super Mario read for a while, then said, "It's a strange request, but it would mean everything to me."

Super Mario folded the sheet and handed it back. "It would be an honor."

On their last day in Venice, Bianca and George sat in the back of a gondola navigating the Venetian waterways with a gondolier named Luca, who wore the classic red-and-white-striped shirt. There was no way they weren't going to give it a go, despite the brutal sun and absurd price tag.

As far as Bianca was concerned, you couldn't put a cost on how much fun they were having, how much fun George in particular was having. They'd meandered to Piazza San Marco, stopping for an *arancino* along the way, and even toured the Doge's Palace, and her father hadn't shown any signs of rushing. He'd moved slowly, soaking it all in. It seemed to her that he was *trying* hard, and trying was a whole lot like loving.

Here he was now, donning a new wide-brimmed hat and leather man bag, his eyes scanning the views, seemingly immersed. He put his arm around her, and she loved the feeling. It had been a long time since she'd seen him so relaxed.

"You know what you remind me of?" she said. "A wild stallion who's finally been broken."

He chuckled. "Oh yeah? Who's wrangling me?"

"Italy, of course. Seriously, look at you. I haven't seen you like this in a long time. Maybe you should move here."

He straightened his hat. "Don't push it." He was handsome when he tried. Sophisticated, sharp. All they had to do was get rid of those shiny tennis shoes.

The gondolier ducked under magnificent brick bridges as he silently steered them through tight canals, maybe fifteen feet wide. On either side, stunning buildings aging like golden-era movie stars and painted in lovely pastels rose up out of the water. Lush vines cascaded down from balconies that offered glimpses through windows into the lives of everyday Venetians: a woman knitting as she watched television, a father speaking sternly to his son, a little girl twirling for her mother.

A green shutter swung open, and a man dipped his head out of the window, checking the weather. Bianca and George exchanged waves with him.

"Where to next?" Bianca asked, feeling incredibly light and enthused. Her joy seemed to parallel her father's. Of all the things, it was this spontaneous trip that seemed to have jarred them both loose. It wasn't that they were running away. Maybe more that their unplanned movements were keeping them on their feet, forcing them to let go of control, to let life steer.

He removed his hand and wiped the sweat from his brow. "You tell me."

"Really? You have no opinion?"

"You've done well so far." He gestured toward the canal weaving through San Polo. "Look at this. I don't know if I've ever seen a more beautiful place in my sixty-plus years."

Bianca could have thrown her arms around him. It was a heck of a sensation to be proud of your father. "And you're okay continuing on to another city?"

He set his hat back on and said snidely, "Oh, that's right. I do have to get back to work. Wait . . . nope. I have nothing to do."

Bianca had been considering options all day. "Did you know Shakespeare set *Romeo and Juliet* in Verona, which isn't too far away? That could be fun. And we could go see Lake Garda. I never have. Would be nice to have a car, though."

"Then let's get a car."

"Can you drive stick? I can't."

Her father's chest expanded. "Naturally. I could teach you."

"Um, yeah, okay."

He patted her leg. "Maybe I do have a thing or two left to show you."

"Maybe you do."

The next day, they spent the morning strolling through Verona, of course visiting Casa di Giulietta. Then they rented a car at the airport, headed north, and found an empty parking lot where George could teach Bianca to drive stick. No surprise, she picked it up quickly, and more importantly, he had a blast teaching her.

It felt good to be needed. If only he could hold on to this optimism when he returned to the States. The only problem was that he'd go back to being all alone, back to a world where not a soul needed him.

He drove them to a town called Salò on the western shore of Lake Garda, and along with that feeling of being useful came a strange sense of youthfulness. She'd certainly prescribed the right medicine by suggesting this adventure. And maybe he'd even admit that the Italians were far better drivers than Arizonans.

"I was thinking about what you said yesterday," George began, moving into fifth gear to pass a car, "about working hard to prove yourself. I want you to know, I'm proud of you for all the things you've done. The degrees, the practice. Of course, your book. But you know what? Despite me always pushing you, I'd be the same level of proud even if you'd never done a thing."

"Thank you, Dad." A canned response.

"No, I'm serious. Don't thank me and move on. I was never good at showing it, but I've always been proud to be your dad."

"Will you stop beating yourself up? You being here with me makes up for anything you did or didn't do years ago. And I mean it."

He almost had to pull over, her words hit him so hard. "I don't deserve that."

She leaned over and kissed his cheek. "I love you, Dad, and I'm proud of you for stepping out of your comfort zone. I had no idea how this would work, us going on a trip, but I'm glad I trusted my instincts."

"Me too. Believe me. For a million reasons." He didn't say it out loud, but this trip had squashed some of the pain of Sandy's rejection, too, which had kept him up for far more hours in the night than he wanted to admit.

"I feel like I did back in the old days," Bianca said. "Flying by the seat of my pants. The hostel."

"Honey, that was the only hard part about Venice. And I mean that literally. Worst bed I've ever slept in."

"And that's why we're in an Airbnb tonight. The reviews promised two great beds."

"Thank God."

They had the windows down, and an hour later, George could tell when they got close to the lake. There was a cool and humid bite to the breeze, blowing their hair back.

He turned down the Italian radio station. "You haven't mentioned Corrado much. You two still chatting?" He'd avoided the subject, partly because he could never get used to her dating men. And even more so, because he was afraid what would happen if she fell in love while she was in Italy.

She shook her head. "Not really."

"Something happen?"

"He wants more, but I'm not ready."

That was a relief.

She put her feet up on the dashboard, something Faith had done, too, a practice that wasn't altogether safe. Still, he bit his tongue.

"But I want to be," she said. "Add relationship issues to my list of problems I have to work out before I entertain a relationship. I'm the worst kind of girlfriend, which I've already shown him twice."

"How so?"

"It's not important."

"He'd be the luckiest guy in the world to have you." George meant it.

"You know what stinks? I think I love him."

Huh.

It was all fine and dandy till she'd brought up *that* word. "You love him? You barely know him."

"I've known him forever. We basically lived together when I was last in Bologna."

Get. Out. Of. Here. This was news. He knew they'd spent time together, but he'd had no clue she'd been spending the night with him. "How do you know you might love him?"

"How did you know you loved Mom?"

He laughed and cast a quick look at her before returning his eyes to the road. "I knew it in my bones, but I wouldn't hold your mom and me up as the standard."

"When you two were happy, it was really good. I have great memories."

"I wish it was the same for me. It's hard to see past some of the things I did." He shook his head, remembering the early mornings and late nights at Motorola and Intel. He didn't know how else to live. His only mission was to keep the lights on.

"Corrado's a good man, Dad. *I'd* be the lucky one."

"Very much a good man. But a chef. Opening up his own place. You know how many restaurants go out of business in their first year?"

"His won't."

"You don't know that."

"I do."

"And think about his hours. You going to raise a kid with a chef? In a city? I appreciate that you have feelings for him, but be careful. You don't want to get involved with a chef long term. Trust me."

"Because you have so much experience?"

He looked over and could see she'd checked out, watching the container truck they were passing.

"Sorry, I crossed a line," he said. "It's none of my business."

Her head swiveled his way, and he braced himself. George had done it again. "And maybe you could trust me. I'm not an idiot."

"I don't think you're an idiot." So much for being a good parent.

"I might not be perfect," she said, "but I can definitely read people. I would be the luckiest girl in the world to be with Corrado, but he deserves better. That's the simple truth."

"Don't ever say that."

"Just being honest."

More silence.

He thought what he might say to earn back the trust he'd gained recently. "Can we pretend like I didn't say anything? Please let me start over."

No response.

"I'm like a big ship, Muffin. I know I have to make a turn, but it takes time. I hear you. Everything you're saying and have said the past few days, and I do trust you. You have it more figured out than me." He tapped her leg. "Just let me keep trying."

She let out a long exhale.

Chapter 24

I'll Never Be Here Again

There are days that define a man. Days when he must step onto the battlefield, axe raised, and fight for his life. Fight for love.

Today was that day for Aroldo Gibler.

Harold was now dead, and in his place stood a man who knew exactly what he wanted, a man who'd broken through the walls that had been holding him back.

He'd dressed exactly as John Cusack, which had taken more effort than he'd thought. The dark gray sweatpants, The Clash T-shirt, *and* the trench coat had come from Amazon. The white high-tops, he'd found at a vintage clothing shop. And he'd settled for a JBL Bluetooth speaker that was far too modern for a scene reenactment, but it would have to do. At least, it could get super loud.

To his left walked the opera singer, otherwise known as Vittorio Spina. The man had appeared dressed in a black tux with a white bow tie, à la Pavarotti. What was left of Harold thought it was a bit much, but Aroldo had seen the brilliance in the formality and had eagerly clapped, saying, *"Bravo, signore!"*

Spina had bowed. Actually bowed, right there on the cobblestones of Via Giulia.

They'd not rehearsed, as the mission wasn't exactly complicated, but they'd worked it out as they walked to Renzo's apartment. The earlier clouds had cleared, and the sun shot harshly down over the city. Thank God for the porticoes.

"Can I ask you something?" Aroldo said. "Who do you have lunch with every day? I see you leave at the exact time. I'm just curious."

"My wife," Spina said in his resonant tone.

"I didn't realize you were married." Only then did he glance over at the gold ring resting on a chubby finger. "I've never seen her."

A long quiet.

As they crossed the street, Vittorio said, "She passed two years ago, but I still take a table at our favorite place and pour a glass of wine for her."

A wave of chills ran over Aroldo. "I'm so sorry. I can't imagine."

Vittorio touched his heart. "This is why you must love with all of yourself, *ragazzo*. I like this that you're doing. I'm happy to be a part."

"Thank you," Aroldo said. "I hope it will—no—I *know* it will work."

In an admittedly stalker fashion, he'd figured out Alice's new schedule and knew that she'd be home any minute. And Renzo typically didn't show up till six, which gave him a perfect window of forty-five minutes to resurrect his dying love from the ashes of unrighted wrongs.

When they reached the square and saw the people gathered at tables and around the fountain who would soon bear witness, Aroldo started to shake. Or was it Harold?

He quietly invited Harold to take a hike, then glanced up at the balcony and pointed. "That's theirs."

A fresh wave of chills hit him again. Every hope of living a full life rested on this moment. "Leave burn marks," he said to himself. *"Leave burn marks."*

Shaking the last of Harold away, Aroldo glanced around again, then nodded at the sharply dressed Spina, who looked like he was ready to take the stage at Carnegie Hall.

Aroldo fished the phone from his pocket, connected it to the speaker, and pressed play. Out came the beginnings of Peter Gabriel's song, "In Your Eyes," first the synthesizer, then the silky drum rhythm. It wasn't loud enough, so he turned it up. And he turned it up again.

People started turning their heads.

Hey Duo, how about this for burn marks?

Aroldo cranked the volume and then raised the JBL boom box over his head. Timing it with Peter Gabriel, Spina stepped forward, opened his mouth, and let loose an extraordinary vocal, perfectly capturing Gabriel's lyrics, his voice easily topping the volume of the speaker.

Within seconds, people had pulled out phones and were snapping shots and capturing videos. Aroldo stood tall and proud, a man—no, a warrior—here to reclaim love.

Spina sang louder, rattling light posts, shaking the bloody walls of the city around him with his vibrato, pumping Aroldo's chest with so much voracious ferocity that he thought he might soon levitate off the ground.

Beside him, the opera singer gave everything he had, like he was calling upon the eternal love of his deceased wife.

Aroldo watched the balcony and windows, hoping for movement. Tiny, puny little Harold crept back in, and he heard his dad's voice in his head. *You unoriginal dipshit, Harold. Do you know how many times people have recreated this stupid scene? Hell, you're probably not the first buffoon to pull it on Alice! She's probably not even in the building!*

"Stop it," Aroldo whispered. Or maybe shouted.

Mid-note, Vittorio stopped and looked over.

"No, not you," Arold said, dismissing his interruption with a wave of the hand. "I'm sorry. Please continue."

Vittorio jumped right back in, and Aroldo raised the volume on the boom box even louder, praying to his God and all gods that his strawberry love would appear and realize that she was nothing without him.

A shadow, movement.

The balcony door cracked open. Out into the warm air, four floors above the square, came his destiny, a T-shirt and shorts and a red mess of hair.

Her mouth fell open, and Aroldo's heart swelled with love.

There was no place for Harold here.

Aroldo, this is yours.

Your win.

The sight of her gave Spina extra steam, and he wrang every bit of soul from the song. Aroldo simply stared up with loving eyes, stretching his arms higher, the speaker a lightning rod that would guide them back together.

She came to the railing and watched, her mouth still open.

And he thought he saw a smile, a flicker of one. He said to himself, "She'll be mine by nightfall."

Harold, no, Aroldo let the song play through, knowing his love was filling every one of her cells, reconstructing her.

After the last note, she called down to him, "Harold, I can't believe you."

He stepped forward and opened his arms like a gladiator in the Colosseum ready to accept his prize from the empress. "I love you, Alice. With all of me. And I don't want to be friends. I want all of you, and I want to marry you and spend the rest of my life with you."

Aroldo had forgotten about the crowd till he heard an audible gasp. He looked around and discovered at least fifty people staring at him, watching the scene. Cameras out. Some women holding their hearts. He'd be all over the socials.

Alice held up a finger. "I'll be right down."

Yes.

Yes, fucking yes! He'd done it. Here she came. Aroldo wrapped his arms around Spina and gave him a tight squeeze.

"What a victory, *amici miei. Grazie*!"

Spina put his hands on Aroldo's cheeks. "Love her like it's your last day. Every day."

"Si, signore. Lo farò." I will.

When she appeared down below, everyone clapped, and Aroldo rose to the occasion, waved as if he were one of the royals, and took a grand bow. When he came back up, he watched his love come to him, the angel of his life floating his way.

What a hell of an idea it had been.

Leave fucking burn marks! That was the way!

God bless Ione Skye and John Cusack and the whole idea. Forget that it had been overdone. Never once had it been reenacted with an opera man.

That's when he saw it, the flash on her finger.

A blade found its mark in his stomach. He had to fight not to fold over as he searched her face for an explanation.

"Harold," she said, shuffling over in slippers, "I'm so sorry I gave you the wrong impression, but I love Renzo. We're getting married."

The fifty spectators let out gasps. Cameras clicked louder.

She looked up toward her balcony. Renzo stood there in boxer briefs, nothing else. He wore a shit-eating smirk and raised his middle finger.

And there, in the square, Aroldo died.

During their stay in Salò, Bianca and George hiked up to take in a mesmerizing view of the massive Lake Garda, which had been carved out by glaciers during the last Ice Age and was hugged by the Alps on the northern side. On the way back down to their place in town, they chatted with a couple from Germany who were on a three-month tour of Europe. They'd just come from an island off the coast of Naples called Ischia. Bianca had never been.

As the couple professed their love for the island, Bianca and George both said almost simultaneously, "I guess we're going there next."

After a two-day train ride, including a stop in Florence for a night, they'd taken a taxi to a ferry and were now standing on a bus that circumnavigated Ischia. They were headed to Sant'Angelo, a place supposedly a bit quieter. You always knew you found something special when people gave the recommendation, followed by, "Just don't tell anyone." They'd heard that a few times since leaving Lake Garda.

They'd been gone almost a week now, and aside from a few bumps, they were both in good spirits. Bianca was still in shock, actually. Italy was speaking to her father, waking him up and giving him a renewed sense of life, and she was experiencing the same herself. How strange that they'd gone through it together.

But how beautiful too.

Though she was absolutely blown away by the beauty of the island so far, palm trees mixing with vineyards and olive groves, all climbing up mountains that rose from a turquoise sea, the current situation was difficult.

She'd always been victim to motion sickness, but this bout was the worst she'd ever known. Clearly, George was going through the same thing. They'd boarded the crowded bus at the port; not a single seat was available so they'd both stood, *trying* to hold on to their luggage with one hand and their life with the other. The streets couldn't have been any tighter. Motorcyclists and scooters snuck through tiny gaps in the flow of traffic, as the bus traversed hills with constant jolts and hesitantly descended into small towns packed with jaywalkers.

It was all Bianca could do not to vomit, and by the time they stepped off the bus near their hotel, they were desperate for fresh air. But then they looked at the view: sparkling blue water surrounding a whitewashed, picturesque town nestled up against a giant rock mountain jutting out of the Mediterranean, and she knew it had all been worth it.

Travel was a lot like life, wasn't it? Ups and downs, learning to find the most graceful way through the downs.

What had started as a seed in Bologna grew more by the day, the idea that she belonged here in Italy, that she'd come home to her ancestors and there was no going back.

They checked into their rooms and met in the lobby. The journey south had worn him out, but George was being a trooper and had agreed to hop in the water before they took a siesta.

Passing houses that were cut into the mountain, they found a steep set of steps that descended to a tiny beach with a restaurant carved into the cliff. People were diving off the larger rocks; others splashed in the shallows. There were a few swimmers a long way out, near several sailboats anchored for the day.

Bianca wasn't sure whether she'd ever seen a place more beautiful.

Her Italian was improving, and she haggled with a guy and acquired an umbrella and two chairs for €10. Within moments, they had stripped down to their swimsuits and stepped into the water. Despite it being late June and incredibly hot out, the chilly water took her breath away.

"Greatest idea you've ever had, this trip," George said, beaming with youthful delight. He dove forward and came up a few feet away with a shout.

Bianca did the same, feeling the chill press her full into the present moment. "This is exactly what life's about."

They swam for a while, watching boats pass and more people jumping from rocks. Then they took a table for a quick bite, sharing *calamari fritti* and a plate of *pasta con le vongole*, spaghetti with clams.

"I noticed you didn't ask for cheese. You don't want to give it a shot?"

"I've learned my lesson, Muffin."

They returned to their loungers, and both snoozed for a while.

An hour later, they were back in the water, floating and chatting. Bianca could have done it all day, all month, all summer.

"I was wondering something," George said, wiping seawater from his face. "You mentioned the idea of sitting in your own mess, getting comfortable with it. I'd love to talk more about that."

Bianca lit up. Was her father directly asking for advice? She might not be the poster girl for perfect right now, but she had a few answers. They'd invented the phrase "Do as I say, not as I do" just for her.

"If we haven't built up our emotional stamina, then we often can't handle confronting how we feel. Which is why we reach for our phones or *legal pads* or a glass of wine. Anything to grab a dopamine hit and avoid sitting with what's going on inside."

She drew in a breath and let the sun warm her face. "It's like an itch. An annoying one. You can distract yourself from it, but have you ever felt into it? Completely given all your attention to it?"

He shook his head.

"With practice you can get to a place where you can tolerate the itch or pain, where you can handle the present, even when it's uncomfortable or even agonizing. Let's give it a whirl." She lifted up a handful of water and let it fall from her fingers. "Let your thoughts pass through. Feel your body, your head to your toes. Accept that your brain isn't you and let it take some time off. Use your senses. Simply be."

He instinctually turned toward the horizon. Bianca did the same, again admitting to herself that, even here in Italy, she was still guilty of so much megawatting, attempting to force a new book and a new career decision, racing to figure out what went wrong all in a day. Only during this trip had she been able to break away.

She let thoughts fade and sank into the water.

A long time passed.

As she felt again this complete immersion into the present moment, a thought swam by.

I'll never be here again.

I'll never be here again, so soak it up. Stop living in the past or the future. The only thing that matters is here. And you'll never be here again in this moment. It's all one long goodbye.

It was so easy to see what was wrong with others, and even with herself. But why was it so hard to do anything about it?

She looked over at George, who was about ten feet away, still lost in the horizon. She couldn't know what he was thinking—if at all—but she was pretty sure he was feeling it, too, the miracle of totally letting go.

In the morning, they enjoyed a delightful breakfast in the dining room at a table overlooking the Med. The crumbs of homemade pastries and the broken shells of hard-boiled eggs littered their plates. They were both on their second cup of coffee, neither of them wanting to let go of this view, of this moment.

George had surprised himself, the way he'd finally found a groove here in this foreign land. He was watching a fishing boat on the horizon when Bianca threw a question at him.

"Why don't you ever talk about your past, Dad? You always gloss over it. Is it that you're ashamed?"

He stuck his finger in the handle of his mug and slowly guided it toward him. "Yeah, I guess I am ashamed, Muffin. It was a hard life." He chewed on her question. "But I wasn't in a bad place back then. All these low, down feelings are new. Not for a second in my whole life was I depressed. Sure, I've been sad, but I've never fallen into a hole like I did this year, not even after the divorce from your mom. Not until a few days after Intel let me go. It was like waking up as someone else."

She leaned in. "You always had a purpose till then. You were a big sports guy growing up. Football, baseball. That was your life. And taking care of your little sister. Taking care of your mom, even."

George nodded. He didn't have to be reminded. He often thought of those days.

"And then it was college, where you got straight A's. Who had time to be depressed? Then Motorola snatched you up, and you were off to the races. I don't know, maybe there was always a sadness inside of you that you managed to keep buried."

"Fair enough."

For a moment, he thought he might tell her what was really going on, how he'd considered ending his life. It had been such a relief to tell Faith. In a way, sharing it had distanced himself from it. But telling Bianca now wouldn't do any good. She was already giving him her best advice. Knowing the truth would only scare her.

Especially since he wasn't sure what to expect once he returned home.

Chapter 25

What's the Point, Duo?

A notification dinged on Harold's watch. He hoped that it was Alice, despite it having been several agonizing days without a peep from her.

Hey, it's Duo. Let's get a new streak going.

Lying on the couch in his tighty-whities, surrounded by empty pizza boxes and drained cans of Coke, Harold stared at his phone, wondering how someone, or *something*—he wasn't even sure of Duo's gender, or maybe it was a robot—could be so invasive.

"Do you see what I'm going through, Duo?" Harold asked out loud.

Even worse, Duo's only purpose, only mission, was to get him to start a new streak and keep learning Italian, which was absolutely fucking pointless now. The programmers at Duolingo had found every possible way to nag a man until he felt broken and riddled with shame.

"What's the point, Duo? Soon as I can get the freaking landlord to respond to my emails, I'm going home. Of course, he doesn't speak English, and you're a terrible teacher, so my Italian is nonexistent."

Another notification popped up. Hey, it's Duo. You still there?

"Oh, I'm here, Duo. Where else would I be? Have I told you how much I hate you? My feelings of fury toward you bubble up from the deepest corridors of my being. It's you and Hitler and Pol Pot and maybe Genghis Khan, the worst entities to have ever come to being. How's it feel to be grouped with them?"

Deciding he'd had enough, Harold opened his phone and navigated to the Duolingo Support section, scrolling through the FAQs. At the bottom, he found *Send Feedback*. It finally gave him a text box to express himself, and that he did, starting with: I have no idea how Apple lets you infest my life with your antics, but it stops today. Sure, I can delete the app, but we're way past that. I'm coming after you, do you understand? Full legal battle. I will take this company down if it's the last thing I do.

A ding on his watch and phone.

A desperate hope that it might be Alice.

Nope, it was Moira. How'd it go? I still haven't heard from you.

He set down the phone and fell back onto the couch. Everything had fallen apart. Aroldo lay dead in the square outside of Renzo's apartment. And here was Harold, the pointless piece of shit he'd always been. His dad had been right all along.

Oh, give up the pity party, Harold, he told himself.

But what was there to go back to now? His awful job? His awful life? He couldn't keep living this lie, that's for sure.

No college degree. That was the biggest issue. Why couldn't he have been brave and made something of himself?

Moira again. If you need someone to talk to, I'm here.

He shook his head. Oh, he needed someone to talk to, all right. He needed major help.

Glancing back at his watch, the watch he'd bought for *her*, he accepted that no number of steps could have out-thwarted Renzo. Even Aroldo was no match for that man.

All he could hope for now was to one day celebrate their inevitable divorce, because that bastard didn't love her, and she certainly didn't love him. No, she was a victim of Stockholm syndrome, and in fact, love didn't exist at all.

Love was dead.

He looked at his step count for the day. Thirty-five and it was almost noon.

Thirty-five.

That summed up Harold: a fake, a sham. Even if she had come back to him, he'd have had to eventually tell her the truth, and she would have run out on him all over again.

Standing, he went out onto the balcony, noticing that it was gloomy out, and rightly so. If love was dead, then the sun had no right to shine.

Harold unstrapped the watch and slung it into the air, sending it four floors down to its death. "That's what I think about your step-counting and your Duolingo."

He even considered hurling himself off the balcony but then heard a "Hey!"

He approached the railing and timidly glanced down. Sandy stood below, looking up at him with piercing eyes. "Was that you?"

"Me, what?" It was a quiet morning, only a few others passing by—a woman pushing a cart of groceries, another wrapped in a scarf, chatting away on her phone.

"You hit me with your watch!" She held it up in the air.

"Oh, my God, I'm so sorry. I'll be right there."

Harold shot down the steps and came onto Via Giulia. Sandy waited for him on the cobblestones.

He rushed toward her. "Are you okay? I'm so sorry." He looked for signs of blood, but all he saw were signs that she wanted to stab him with the closest dull object.

"I'm fine, settle down, but what's wrong with you, throwing a watch off the balcony? And you look like hell."

He turned away, highly aware of the passing pedestrians staring at him. Even the freaking construction workers were gawking at him.

Sandy sighed. "Are you okay, Harold?"

As he turned to answer, he realized what he was wearing. His freaking underwear.

"Oh, my God." He covered himself, now knowing exactly why everyone had been staring at him. "Gotta go."

He raced to the door, jammed in the code, then rushed back upstairs. He put on sweatpants and a T-shirt, then went back onto the balcony. He slowly peeked over the railing and saw that she was still standing there.

Sandy held up the watch again. "Forget something?" She snapped and pointed at the ground. "Get your ass down here."

She didn't have to ask twice. He hurried back down, forgetting his shoes again, so he crept carefully over the cobblestones.

"Spill it, Harold. What's going on with you? What did Alice do?" In an instant, he felt like he was speaking with his mother, and a flash of anger flared.

"Where have you been?" he snapped. "I needed you."

"What do you mean, where have I been? Working. And working. Right underneath you."

He hated how weak he sounded. "I went to the tango place; you weren't there. I tried to talk to you."

Her eyes softened. "It's been busy."

Sandy almost hugged him before remembering she wasn't a hugger. "What happened? Out with it." For God's sakes, why did people come to her for advice? If that wasn't a sign for the end of the world . . .

"It's over," Harold said.

"You and Alice?"

A nod. His cheeks quivered. He definitely needed a hug, but Sandy had to be in the right state of mind to touch people.

"Out with it, Harold. I can't read your mind."

His eyes reddened. Tears rose up.

Dear God, what am I doing? she asked herself.

"I made a play, tried to get her back. Told her I loved her."

"Hold on, didn't we talk about playing hard to get?"

"Yeah, but we also talked about you helping me. And then you disappeared. I had to do it on my own. Surprise, surprise, it didn't go well."

Her hackles went up. "This is my fault?"

He shook his head as a tear fell.

"Oh, hell, come here." Sandy pulled him in and wrapped her arms around him, and he broke into a full-on cry on her shoulder.

She, who assumed she didn't have a heart anymore, felt it pump, and her own tears crept up and threatened to spill. "I warned you, didn't I? Love isn't something you mess with. It'll get you every time."

He cried harder.

Not caring that they'd caused a scene, Sandy held him tighter and closed her eyes, feeling his pain. "I've been there, baby. Lord knows I've been there."

His shoulders heaved, and it brought back all the pain she'd known when transfixed by love. And then she thought of Jack. It'd been so long since she'd seen him, and it hurt more than ever, but something about holding this scrawny kid made her feel like a mom again.

He eventually let her go, and she was surprised to find that she didn't want him to. "Tell me what happened," she said. "Wanna take a walk?"

He wiped his eyes, then joined her as she started down Via Giulia away from the bookstore. He told her of his absolutely ludicrous plan to get Alice back, reenacting the *Say Anything* scene with Spina, the opera singer.

Sandy couldn't ignore the humor of it. "Harold, I have to give you this. That's a big gesture. A beautiful one. You are amazing. I would have never guessed it, but you're full of surprises." She rubbed his head. "You know what, Alice is an idiot. That's all there is to it. Time to let her go. There's someone else out there waiting to break your heart, trust me."

"Thank you for the bleak input," he said in a tepid whisper as he slumped over.

"What? You want me to lie to you now? The one thing you get from me is the truth. Trust me, I thought I'd escaped after my two marriages and a bunch of flings with Italian men, but then comes this George character, wedging his way in."

"Bianca's dad?"

"That's right. The guy with the awful white tennis shoes."

"You like him?"

Not having him in the bookstore checking off tasks on her to-do list hurt as much today as it had yesterday and the day before. Where was he, anyway? She hadn't even seen him out on the street in a week.

"I'm not answering that," she finally said. "I don't even want to say it out loud. What I know is that I've had one too many heartaches to ever give a relationship another try. You, my little wiry and clever friend, probably have more in you. Takes more than one hard lesson to learn. Who knows, maybe you'll get it right down the road. What is it, one in fifty relationships works out?"

"Is it that bad?"

"I was being optimistic. But what I *can* say is that this thing you were trying to do, becoming Aroldo, you don't need to do that. Sure, you should dress well and get your act together. Shave and get that mangy hair in order. But you still need to be yourself. Because I've seen you, truly seen who you are, the one and only Harold Gibler, and there's a woman out there who will fall desperately for you, young man. You're one of a kind, and you love harder than any man I've ever met. You hear me?"

He inclined his shoulders a hair, then let them fall.

She stopped and made him face her. "Do you hear me, Harold? You're a good man, and there's someone out there who's lonely and sad and about to give up, too, and one day, you're going to walk into her life, and the whole world will light on fire. Got me?"

"Yeah."

She pulled him in for one more hug, and she felt so grateful to have him in her life.

Deciding to stay in Rome a couple of nights, Bianca and George found an Airbnb in the Trastevere neighborhood and were able to grab a last-minute table at Rimessa Roscioli for one of the best meals of their life, including a *cacio e pepe* pasta that came close to giving Bianca a new religion. Such a simple pasta—black pepper, pecorino Romano, maybe some Parmigiano-Reggiano, butter, olive oil, and noodles—but a dish that took generations to master. What better captured Italy?

Cones of gelato now in hand, still high off their meal, they strolled to the Colosseum to see it lit up at night. To be here with her dad meant everything to her. She even wished that Faith were here, too, not to bring her parents back together in a romantic sense, but just for old times' sake.

The good times really had been good.

The next morning, they both woke complaining about the firmness of the beds. Bianca had made the giant mistake of not reading the reviews beforehand. Unfortunately, the day they'd planned was not the best to tackle on limited sleep.

They went at it hard, starting with a hefty walk to the other side of the city to experience the National Gallery of Modern and Contemporary Art. Some of the exhibits were a bit much for George, but he found a few that apparently captured him. Mistiming the day, they had to skip lunch to connect with a group for a walking tour that an ambitious Bianca, who hadn't yet known how bad the beds would be, had committed to.

All was well until it wasn't.

By the time they wrapped up near the Spanish Steps, George was complaining about the new shoes she'd talked him into buying (they didn't have the cushy soles), and Bianca was hangry. Maybe the tour wouldn't have lasted so long if George hadn't asked so many questions. What type of stone is this? Where exactly did they source it? How did they transport it? Apparently, walking tours were his jam—and he didn't even know it till now.

It was after three when they started looking for a restaurant for lunch, but with it being the last few days of June, the city was overly crowded, making for limited dining options. George's meat-and-potatoes mindset made it even more so.

Deciding they might have better luck in Trastevere, they flagged down a cab, both sighing as they climbed in. It went without saying that they'd both be happy never walking again.

Bianca rested her head on the back seat and closed her eyes. She just wanted to grab a slice of pizza and crawl onto the couch.

But George had to open his big fat mouth.

"Can I say one thing, B? Before we get back?"

"What's that?"

"I have a feeling about that guy. Corrado. Forgive me for saying so, but I do. You're right, you're all grown up, but I can still have my say, and the last thing I want is to watch you go through a divorce like me."

Pressure swelled up around her eyes. *Was he really doing this right now?* "You're talking about a guy that I'm not even dating," she said through clenched teeth, then drew in a slow breath, held it for a count of five.

"Yeah, but I can see it. I see how this whole country is."

"So this whole country is to blame? Oh, c'mon." Another breath.

"It's like anything new. It's exciting, invigorating, inspiring even, but then you settle in and realize you might have been swept away for the wrong reasons."

Fuck the slow breathing. She couldn't believe he'd chosen this moment to attack Corrado, and Italy. Catch her on any other day and she might have been able to bite her tongue.

"I love that you're suddenly an expert on life. He who is in his sixties but still can't figure out how to be happy." She didn't give a shit if she'd hurt him. "What?" she said. "You fired the first shot. Did we not learn anything on our trip? What happened to the George from yesterday?"

He shrugged.

"I'm serious. Don't you see . . . what you've felt since Venice. It's not a romantic illusion. It's the real thing, a way of life."

He was silent for a while, then: "Look, forgive me. I shouldn't have said anything."

Hopefully the cab driver didn't speak English. Either way, Bianca didn't care enough in the moment to let that stop her.

Her words came in an avalanche. "You're damn right you shouldn't have said anything! And this isn't even about Corrado. This is about your war on Italy. And about me abandoning you *and* your vision of what makes life worth living. Honestly, *you're* the reason I'm here . . . this misery of needing to overwork, to never stop. You know what you learn when you study psychology? It's your father who's supposed to give you confidence. Guess what? You weren't there, so I missed that bit. So I very often hate myself."

He reached for her hand, opened his mouth to speak.

It was too late. She'd flipped her lid.

Swatting him away, she said, "And you know what I hate most about myself?" She paused, to let the next bit seep in. "That part of me that's you!"

Her words seemed to freeze time, and despite her bubbling rage, she wanted to pull them back.

Her dad let his head fall and gave a nod. "Yeah, I understand."

Her whole body shook. "Stop the car," she said to the driver in Italian. Once the taxi rolled to a stop, she climbed out. "I'll see you back at the place later." Not even an apology was possible right now.

As he tried to say something, she slammed the door and let out a frustrated yell that echoed across Rome.

Bianca didn't return to the apartment until well after six. She found George perched in a chair in the living room watching BBC. Sunlight cut through the lone window and painted a yellow line across the scratched wooden floors.

George pointed the remote at the television and switched it off.

"I'm sorry," she said, knowing it wasn't nearly enough. How could she ever forgive herself for saying such a thing to a man who'd dedicated so much of his life to making sure she'd be okay?

Setting the remote by the lamp, he stood and wordlessly held out his arms. When she went to him, she didn't let go till she'd bathed his neck in tears.

Chapter 26

Taking Chances

It was the last day of June. He was having a bowl of granola for dinner when a knock punctured the quiet of his apartment.

"It's Moira," spoke the voice on the other side of the door. "I came to say hi."

"One second," Harold replied. He dropped his bowl in the sink, scrambled to get dressed, and made a quick effort to clean up, then returned to let her in.

She wore a black top over white pants. The hat she often wore was rolled up and poking out of her purse. Her glasses rested on her nose at a slight angle. A sweet smile lifted her lips. "Sandy said things didn't go well with Alice; I thought I'd check on you."

Harold put a hand against the doorframe. "Yeah, sorry I didn't text you back. I've been pretty upset."

"I can imagine." She held up a bottle of Lambrusco. "Want to bury your sorrows in bubbles?"

It wasn't so bad of an idea.

They sat on the balcony and drank a glass as he told her what had happened. As July approached, each day was hotter than the last, but the evening still cooled into something wonderful. Had he the bandwidth, he might have enjoyed the tangerine sun dropping in the west, its rays sneaking around the buildings and painting a hazy glow over Via Giulia.

They talked about the bookstore for a while but eventually got back to Alice. "Still," Moira said, "even if it didn't work, I think it's wonderful. You gave it everything. You're a rock star, Harold."

"Yeah, I wish that were true. You're right, though. The wine does help." He took another sip, feeling the burn of the bubbles. Aroldo was the kind of man who might have studied wine and food, understood the origins, but Harold had no clue. Still, it tasted good going down.

"So what now? Are you leaving?"

"Yeah, I need to book my flight. The landlord won't give me any money back, so I have another week here before the lease runs out."

"You should stay longer."

"I wish I could." He wished a lot of things. But he was broke and in debt. His mother would kill him if she knew he'd maxed out his credit cards. He'd made sure that he was receiving paperless statements so she wouldn't get that surprise in the mail. As far as wishing he could stay, he wasn't sure. Being heartbroken here probably wasn't any better than it'd be in Denver.

"At least you have another week; you better start cramming it all in."

"I've barely left the apartment since . . . since all that happened."

"Oh, dear."

"Yeah."

A long silence came over them, and Harold found himself slipping back to the same thoughts he'd had for more than a week. What was next? Was there any point? Not even Bianca Briggs could help him now. Peggy Meh had nothing on him. He'd royally botched his one chance to save himself, and now he'd have to go right back to a life that was barely a life at all.

"You wanna see something neat?" Moira asked, twisting to him.

"What's that?"

"Come with me." She stood and grabbed her glass and the rest of the bottle.

"You mean, outside?"

"Yes, outside. You can't keep hiding, Harold." She took his hand and pulled him back through the house. He put on his tennis shoes, and they were out the door. Downstairs, she guided him through the scaffolding to the bookstore.

"We're going to your work?"

"Just wait."

She lifted up the corrugated metal door that secured the entrance at night, then stuck the key in the doorknob and twisted. He followed her inside as she switched on a few lights, the sconces coming alive and giving the air a golden coat. Though he didn't say it, there was something dazzling being in a bookstore after hours. Especially this one. He'd never seen one so stunning.

"Did Sandy tell you what happened? That I hit her with my watch?"

Moira shook her head. "Why'd you do a thing like that?"

"Because I'm at war with Duolingo and the step counter on my watch, and I lost my cool," he elaborated as they entered the main room, where a series of accent lights brought the cathedral ceilings and its frescoes to life.

Her echoing laugh made him feel like he wanted to laugh too.

"It does sound dumb. And you should have seen me trying to fake steps, sitting on the couch, flapping my arms in the air." He mimicked himself, flip-flopping his wrist, and she laughed so hard she had to bend over and gasp for air.

It was absurd, wasn't it? He finally fell into giggles, too, and it was a relief, because even an hour ago, he thought he might never feel anything that resembled joy ever again.

When she finally got a hold of herself, she said, "Seriously, Harold, you shouldn't have to try that hard. Come on."

The problem was that he hadn't tried hard enough. Too much Harold had snuck into his Aroldo.

Going through a door that read EMPLOYEES ONLY, they came into a musty storage room filled with boxes of books and other supplies. In the back, she cracked open another door that led outside into a lush patio hidden by tall stone walls covered in ivy. A table and two chairs rested on uneven bricks.

He walked into a quiet that Harold hadn't known since he'd landed in Bologna, a total escape from the city.

She flipped a switch, and a strand of lights came alive, revealing rows of well-cared-for potted plants and flowers. Several weathered statues of women looked back at them, as if protecting the place.

He lifted his gaze, counting up to the fourth floor and seeing his bedroom window. And beyond the building, the brightest of the stars had started to show in the graying sky as the last of the sun fell away.

"It's beautiful out here."

"It's a favorite spot of mine."

"I can see why."

They both sat, and Moira refilled their glasses.

"What's next?" she asked. "Once you get back to Denver."

"I don't know." He squirmed as the memory of life before Alice came to him. "I didn't leave much behind." He shook his head. He had no answers.

"Honestly," he finally said, becoming less filtered due to the second glass of wine, "I'm not who she thinks I am. I'm not who anyone here thinks I am."

She cracked a grin. "I bet I have you beat."

"No offense, but you don't, trust me." He thought of how one lie builds onto the next, and then you get to the point where you don't even know the truth.

"Okay, suit yourself." She lifted her glass and stared at the bubbles in the light.

"Fine, please. Tell me how you have me beat."

"I can't."

"Why not?"

She set her glass back down, sat back, and crossed her legs. "I shouldn't have teased you. Besides, you wouldn't even believe me if I did tell you."

"Now you *have* to."

"No way."

Something had always seemed off when she'd talked about her past. That time she said legal reasons kept her quiet, and the whole P. J. Harvey thing when she'd stumbled over saying she was from Dorset. "C'mon, you can't leave me hanging."

"Not a chance," she said, a pretty smile filling her face. "Believe me, I'd love to share, but I can't."

"At least tell me what you did for a living. Did you work in a bookstore in Bristol or Dorset?"

"Let's just say I was indeed in the book world."

"In Dorset?"

"Somewhere on planet Earth."

"Dear God, you're an enigma." His curiosity was starting to bother him. "What if I told you my secret, then would you share?"

"I doubt it. Sorry. Can't we be okay with having our secrets?"

"That's a good question. Can friends be friends if there are secrets between them?"

"Are we friends?" she asked.

He thought about it. "I think so."

"And what if we were more than friends?"

"What?"

"I shouldn't say this, but I'm going to, and who cares? You're leaving anyway. I was always jealous of Alice."

"Jealous of Alice?" The idea was beyond preposterous. The tone of his voice said so.

"Yeah, the way you love her, Harold. No one has ever loved me like that. And maybe it was more than that. Maybe because it's you."

"What do you mean?" His foggy brain was spinning. Was she making a move?

Her eyebrows squinched together as she seemed to lose herself in thought. Then she removed her glasses and rubbed her eyes. Returning them to her face, she set her green eyes on him. "I sometimes wonder what it would be like to kiss you."

"To kiss me?"

"You say it like it's a bad thing. Yes, Harold. To kiss you. You know, you go on worrying about Alice, and you don't even see something that's right in front of you. I've had a crush on you since the first day we met, and yes, I wonder what it would be like to kiss you. So fucking sue me."

Harold reached for an itch at the back of his neck. "Um, I don't . . . I didn't—"

"Of course you didn't. I'm no Alice."

"That's not what I'm—"

"Oh, screw it." She sprang up from her chair and swooped down and grabbed his head and kissed him, holding her lips against his long enough for him to realize what was happening.

He hadn't seen any of this coming.

"Hold on," he finally said into her lips.

"What?" she said, stopping.

"I'm sorry. I can't. I didn't know what this was."

She stood tall over him, the stars coming to life over her head. "What *this* was."

Not that it wasn't nice to kiss her, to be wanted. "I'm so sorry, I'm still in love with Alice. I didn't mean to . . . I think you're amazing and—"

She backed away like he'd hit her. "Don't even go there."

"Look, don't be offended." He held up a hand. "You're so awesome; it's . . . you know . . ."

"I get it, all right." She swept up the bottle and stemware. "Let's go. I need to lock up."

"Moira, please."

"Get up, Harold. I need to go home."

He looked at her, puzzled. How could she think that he had room in his heart for anyone other than Alice?

George and Bianca had been back in Bologna a few days. It was now the first of July. He had fittingly locked in an early flight on Independence Day and had mixed feelings about it. Of course, it was time to get out of her hair and figure out what life might look like back home, but he wished they were parting on better terms.

She'd apologized a thousand times for Rome, as had he, but what she'd said, the thing about hating the part of her that was him, still divided them like the glass partition that separates inmates from their visitors at a prison. No matter what either of them said, they couldn't get past it. He didn't want to leave like this, but if he stayed, it could get worse.

As far as his return to Arizona, he'd been searching online for volunteer opportunities. There was an Adopt-a-Senior program available. The Scottsdale Fire Department was looking for "older adults" to educate the public on various programs, such as fire prevention and hiker safety. The Scottsdale Historical Museum was looking for a docent to welcome and orient visitors.

Though nothing had seized him yet, he liked the idea of helping people. What better purpose could there be?

That's what was on his mind as he wandered around the old town, looking for a gift for his housekeeper. A piece of jewelry? A bottle of balsamic vinegar? A box of artisanal chocolate? Beyond lost in this grid-less city, he started to fish out his phone to consult the GPS when he heard his name.

"*Signor* Briggs."

George twisted toward the voice. "Hi, Corrado."

It took him a moment to process the encounter. He'd spent entirely too much time thinking about how the man could cause a disaster in Bianca's life. Now, he stood there before him.

The two of them, man-to-man.

There were indeed such things as coincidences, but there were also moments in life that came together due to more than chance.

"How's your visit going?" Corrado's English carried a British air to it. He wore clogs, black pants, and a white chef's jacket with his name and the name of the restaurant embroidered on the chest. His short brown hair was slicked back.

"We had a nice visit around the country." George gave an extremely brief overview of their trip, then asked, "You ready for the big night?"

"I hope so. And I hope you'll be joining us. I haven't heard from Bianca."

"She hasn't said anything about it lately. Besides, I have an early flight back home the next morning."

A nod. "Well, I hope you had a nice stay."

George let out a grunt. "Very nice."

This felt like an opportunity, his only chance to say a few things to the guy who had his teeth into Bianca. Corrado was the main reason she might not ever come home, and though he knew he was exposing himself to more trouble, he couldn't *not* seize the moment.

He took a long breath, came up empty when he tried to second-guess himself, then said, "She's special, Corrado. One of a kind."

Corrado furrowed his brow. "I know."

George held up a finger. If there was an alpha male here, it was him—a father who'd do anything for his daughter, even risk further fury. "But she's also fragile. Especially right now. It's clear that she has feelings for you, but I think she's confused. While I have you, I can't help but ask that you not lead her down the wrong path. Sure, you two might have something going, but you need to consider what's best for her. I'm worried she'll stay for you, and frankly, I think it could be the biggest mistake she ever makes."

Corrado pinched his chin, clearly agitated but trying to keep his composure.

George kept on. "She's going to realize that she abandoned the life she worked so hard for, and it'll be next to impossible to get it back if she doesn't return home within a year. You understand?"

Corrado dropped his hand from his face. "How would she feel about you telling me this? Warning me off?"

"You and I both know the answer to that. Naturally, I'm hoping you won't tell her what I've just said. I know I can't force you not to see her. I'm just trying to help guide her along the right path and asking for your help. Man-to-man."

"The right path," he mused. "I suppose that's an objective consideration."

"I've got sixty-five years of experience. Trust me, I know what I'm talking about."

Corrado nodded a few times, then cut George a look. "I need to get to work."

"Good luck with things," George said as he turned to leave.

A half hour later, George walked into the bookstore. The last time he'd come close to a Sandy encounter was when she'd hidden from him. He'd hoped that she might have found her way to giving the two of them a chance, but his hopes were cinders in a dying fire now.

She sat at the computer behind the counter, glasses on, her hair scraped into a ponytail. When she looked up, she visibly sighed, which wasn't a good start.

"Are we back from our travels?" she asked.

"Word gets around, doesn't it?"

"A friend of Bianca's was in a couple of days ago, mentioned it."

George approached hesitantly. An instant longing came over him. So many questions that all centered around *Could there have ever been a world where you and I worked?*

They held eye contact for a while. He felt his cheeks swell into an uncomfortable smile, but she wasn't budging.

Were he not so infatuated with her, in love with her, captivated by her—some damn thing—then he would have walked away and let it die.

Something kept him there, though.

He crossed his arms. "I'm leaving in a few days and . . . and I didn't want my last memory of you to be you running from me."

"I don't know what that means."

"Technically, you ran from me twice. First after a heck of a slap. Then when I came here to find you a few days later."

She set down her glasses and massaged her temples.

"Hey, I get it. I'm not here to convince you. I totally understand if you're not interested, but I want to be friends." The words sounded dumb as they left his mouth. What the hell, though. He meant it.

"What does that mean, George? What are we going to get out of being friends?"

"Well, you might have a stock of friends, but I don't. There aren't too many people I want to spend time with, get to know, but you're one of them." He held her gaze. "I'd like to call or email you from the US. There's a good chance my daughter's not going anywhere, so I might even be back before too long. Would it be so bad if we kept in touch?"

She looked left past the postcards.

"Anyway, I'm not here to harass you. It's just that meeting someone like you doesn't happen to me every day, and you can bet I'm going to fight to get to know you, to be your friend."

She shook her head in disbelief. "You realize that people call me The Porcupine behind my back. Why in the world would you want to get to know me? Trust me, George, it gets worse the closer you get."

George touched his chest. "I'm not looking for perfect. I'm far from it." A pause to collect himself. "You come across just a few people in life that . . . that you connect with. You're one of those for me. And if all we're meant to be is friends, then so be it."

She shook her head at him. "You're a real problem, George Briggs. You know that, right?"

"Isn't that the truth."

They looked at each other for a while, then she asked, "How's it going with Bianca?"

"We had a great trip—mostly. You would have been proud of me. Venice, Verona, Lake Garda, then down to Florence, Naples, and Ischia. Finished in Rome. Got new shoes."

She leaned over the counter to check them out. Gave a thumbs-up.

"But I continue to screw things up every once in a while. I guess that's what dads do." He couldn't help but think about Corrado. If only he hadn't run into him.

"I'm sure she knows you're trying," Sandy said.

"It's true, I am trying. A long way to go, though."

"A work in progress."

"That's right."

"Aren't we all?" she said. "Look, George, in another life, we maybe would have had something. But I'm in no shape to ever be in another relationship, not a serious one."

He raised a hand like he was swearing an oath. "Yeah, I understand."

"I hope so. You're a good man, and I enjoyed spending time with you. I hope you can figure out retirement."

"Yeah, me too."

"And I'm sorry I hit you. That was uncalled for."

He touched his cheek, then waited, wanting her to say more.

She shook her head for a while. "I've left a wake of bad relationships behind me. Ones that have hurt too much. Even the idea of another is too much to stomach."

"I get it. I'm not happy about it, but I get it." She glanced at the door, his signal to leave.

How extraordinary that this woman could break his heart when they hadn't even been together.

"Okay, well, glad we got this far," he said, starting to go.

"I *would* like to be friends, though," Sandy called out.

"Okay, then friends it is. Maybe I'll see you before I take off." He left before she could see how much her rejection had cost him. He'd be okay with friends, but the whole thing felt a bit one-sided.

Chapter 27

From Hot Mess to High Voltage

On the day of the book club, Bianca woke determined to reach out to Corrado, but an email from New York derailed her morning. The gist was that her agent was letting Bianca go.

After all the work it had taken to land an agent, the countless query letters, the rejection. The *celebration* when something like the eightieth letter had drawn interest from a hard hitter at the Mark Russell Agency in Manhattan, who'd been impressed with both the concept of *From Meh to Megawatt* and Bianca's established platform.

Pop!

Bianca could still hear the cork bursting from the champagne bottle that night, when her friends had taken her out to Hestia in Austin to celebrate.

She'd never been fired for anything in her life, and the swell of rejection was enough to drown her. What a *wonderful* day to have her book be the focus of today's book club. All she wanted to do was lie in bed and cry, but instead, she had to wax poetic about her piece of literary dung to a few disinterested expats whom Moira had likely convinced by force to attend.

The only good that came out of her agent throwing her to the sharks was that she was running out of fucks to give, rejection being her new currency, so after a few necessary tears, she fired off a text to Corrado, the man who kept ambushing her thoughts.

I know you're busy, but could I see you for a few minutes?

Mess or not, she had to explore whatever feelings there were between them. And yes, George's stance against the relationship made her want it even more.

She knew she was acting five years old. George was acting four, though. How could they have such a great time and make such headway but end up right back where they started? You're goddamned right she'd crossed a line by saying what she'd said, but he'd backed her into a corner. There was no question she wished that conversation hadn't happened, that she'd kept her composure and not ruined any positive momentum they'd built together, but she wasn't the only one to blame. George had crossed lines too. Her love life was exactly *none* of his business.

She breathed a sigh of relief when Corrado texted right back. Sono a casa mia. Vieni. I'm at my house. Come over.

Corrado lived near Piazza Santo Stefano on the third floor of a building that faced the square. She'd caught him with bedhead. He wore athletic shorts and a sleeveless white shirt, showing off the butcher knife tattoo.

"Ciao," he said, kissing her cheeks and letting her in. His breath smelled of mint. "I thought I might never see you again."

"Yeah, I'm sorry. I know I'm sending mixed signals."

He laughed. "That's a good way to put it. Can I offer you coffee? I'm just waking. Late night at the restaurant."

An L-shaped couch and a chair faced a large television. A stocked wet bar rested against a wall. The kitchen was chef worthy, an oversize island with various gadgets crammed in the shelves underneath. A single candle burned on the counter, giving off a citrusy scent.

He invited her to take a seat at the kitchen table while he ground beans and made two cappuccinos. "Kenyan beans," he said, sliding a short mug her way. "An organic farm. Very intense flavors. So what's going on?"

She took a sip. "That's . . . incredible."

He smiled into his own mug as he took a sip. "It is nice, isn't it?"

Bianca tried not to think about what it would be like to wake up to a cup of his coffee every morning, but that's exactly what she thought about. Waking up to him, to his coffee, to his . . .

She better get on with it. "Look, I'm sorry, okay? I'm not good at this kind of thing, relationships."

The air grew thin.

He slipped into the chair opposite her at the table, moved a potted plant out of the way, and waited for more.

"Are you going to make me say it?"

He grinned. "Say what? I've no idea what's on your mind."

Her pulse pounded in her wrists.

"Can we try again? That's what I'm trying to say." His silence forced more words to tumble out. "A real try, where I don't run out on you." She set all five finger pads onto the table. "But I do feel like I need to come with a disclaimer. I can't promise that I'll be perfect. There's so much going on in my head right now. I mean, I'm getting better. Being here has been so good for me, but I have a long way to go. Still, you seem to want something, so let's go. Let's give it a shot."

Silence.

"Fucking say something, I can't handle this . . . this whatever it is you're doing."

Corrado cupped his mug with his hands. He stopped and started a few times, then finally let it out. "We all have a long way to go, Bianca, but you seem to be waiting till you get there to live. Your book taught me so much about you . . ."

"Oh, God, please don't bring up the book." The reminder of her agent dumping her cut fresh wounds into her psyche.

"Why can't I bring up the book? It's important to what I'm trying to say. You said Peggy Meh was a placeholder, right? It's funny, because that's sort of how she lives her life till the end. And I think that's how you're living too. You've put a placeholder in your life, while you go searching for yourself, while you're trying to realize yourself. You have to live now, you know, *while* you're searching."

"I *am* living now. That's the reason I'm here. In Bologna. To get back to who I used to be."

"I appreciate that. And I've asked you this before. Do you realize that your book is truly autobiographical?"

"Um, it's definitely not autobiographical. Peggy's an insane conglomeration of all the clients I've worked with over the years."

He nodded with a cocky air that said that he was right, that he didn't need to keep arguing. Which pissed her off.

"Fine, please elaborate, Corrado." These days everyone had a fucking psych degree. Rather dramatically, she held out both hands and motioned for him to bring it on.

"Back to the placeholder reference, you're refusing to start living, start *loving*, until you've become your supercharged self. When will that be, Bianca?"

She shook her head, not ready to be psychoanalyzed today. "Look, Corrado, I didn't come here for a fifty-minute session."

He put his hands in prayer position. "I'm saying this, Bianca, because I care about you. But I can't *be* with you. I don't want to dwell in this waiting room where life is put on hold. To be honest, I like Bianca Meh more than I do Bianca Megawatt. At least she's real."

Wasn't it funny that things that seemed so obvious could elude you if you were too deep into it? His placeholder point was well taken. The question hitting her now was: Did anyone on planet Earth want to become so fully charged? Wasn't chasing such an idea exactly what had led to her breakdown?

Wait, was that what Donna Bologna meant by getting something wrong? How had she not seen it before? The problem wasn't her writing; it was that she'd made turning into Bianca Megawatt her goal. No one needed supercharging!

Hold on.

The placeholder thing. Donna Bologna had said that if you let bread rise too long, it collapses. It was time to stick herself into the oven of life. Is this what she was talking about? That tricky little witch.

Bianca tried to swallow with a dry mouth.

Corrado brought her back. "I've wanted to say this since we were at the restaurant. I wondered why you ran out, and then it all made sense."

She nodded slowly, taking it all in. So much for the follow-up that she'd been kicking around: *From Hot Mess to High Voltage*.

Ultimately, no matter what she realized in this moment, he was still dumping her.

Without finishing her cappuccino, she stood and said, "I'm going to go."

"Okay, and I'm sorry. I'm not trying to push you out of my—"

"That's pretty much what I'm hearing."

"No, I still want to be your friend; I'm pulling for you."

"Oh, thanks. That's my pity prize. I appreciate that. Maybe we could have coffee on Tuesdays, talk about the *fucking* weather."

"Don't do that."

She started to the door. "You're right, okay. I'm a mess and trying to figure it out. Have a nice life."

He raised his voice. "It's not the mess that's the problem. It's that you won't give yourself a break. Be happy where you are—with *who* you are. Your book is brilliant, Queen Bee. So many thoughtful insights, but it didn't need to be so long. I liked Peggy in the middle more than I liked the robot she became."

It was all too much. "Take care, Corrado."

He raised his hands and dropped them on his lap in frustration.

She wanted to congratulate him on the grand opening of his restaurant, but what was the point? Better to just get out of there.

Walking home, Bianca dialed her mother. "How are things going?" Faith asked. "It's been a while."

"How are things going?" Bianca repeated. "Let's see. I've totally messed up with Dad, my agent broke up with me, and the only man I've ever loved tore me a new one and told me it was over. So that's my life. No, wait, I get to go talk about the book I hate at this book club here in a little while."

"Oh, my," her mom replied. "Why don't you come to Palm Springs after? Take a breather."

"Um, no," Bianca said, "I don't want to come to Palm Springs. I need a break. From everyone. From me too. I want to go to sleep for a year and then wake up and see if it's better."

"What happened with George?"

Bianca was plowing through tourists on her march back home. "We were having a great time, but then he caught me at the wrong moment and started going off about how I need to stay away from Corrado. He doesn't even know him. And then I lost it, said a bunch of things I regret." Bianca told Faith exactly what she'd said.

"Ouch, B."

"Yeah, I know."

"You know why he meddles, right?" Faith asked.

"Oh, yeah. It's why he screws up everything. Because he thinks he knows what's best."

"Yeah, well . . . maybe cut him some slack. When's he leaving?"

"In two days. And we're getting along, mostly, but it's just weird. I'm so mad at him—and not only for trying to manage my love life. I feel like it's all coming up, how he wasn't there for me when I was younger, and even when he was, our time together was another item on his to-do list."

Faith tried to jump in, but Bianca already knew what she was going to say. "Yeah, yeah, he was focused on making sure we had a comfortable life, but I wanted a dad." Then it occurred to her. "Maybe that's why I try so hard to be somebody. Because I want his attention. How have I not seen that?"

Crossing Piazza Maggiore, Bianca thrust her hands in the air. "It was right in front of my face!" She didn't care that people were staring; she had every reason in the world to be animated right now.

"You *do* have his attention," her mom was saying when Bianca put the phone back to her ear, "and you know he loves you."

"Do I?"

A text came in from Corrado. I'm still holding you a table. Just let me know how many people. I need you there. Missing what her mom was saying, she stabbed out a quick reply. Mixed messages much?

A hint of anger appeared in her mother's voice as she said, "You know, Bianca, sometimes you make things about yourself and forget about everyone else."

"Oh, great, thanks. Please kick me while I'm down."

"I'm going to tell you something, but you have to promise me you won't let on that you know. It's important, though. You have two days left with him, and I want you to make them count."

Her heart skidded to a stop. A note of fear had sounded with her mother's words.

Bianca stood hopeless in the middle of the square, waiting for Faith to continue. Tourists gathered around their walking guides. A busker was exchanging tunes for coins. A juggler smoked a cigarette in between performances. And the whole damned world was carrying on like everything was A-fucking-okay.

"Don't tell me he's sick. Jesus, Mom."

"No, he's not sick. Like cancer sick. But he's depressed."

"Well, holy shit, didn't know that one. For God's sakes, Mom, I am a therapist."

"It's worse. He's been . . ."

A pause.

Bianca started to put it together, before her mom said more.

"He came close to killing himself."

Dead quiet. A thousand people milling about the square, but Bianca was sucked into a vacuum of silence.

"He almost bought a gun, honey. But then settled on pills."

The words knocked the wind out of her. She trudged toward the Basilica di San Petronio that dominated the square and sat on one of its stone steps.

"Why didn't you tell me?" Bianca asked.

"Um, because that's not something you go around telling people. He didn't want you to know."

Bianca grew dizzy and had to prop herself up. "I can't believe I'm only hearing this now. Mom, I freaking screamed at him. Told him I hated that he was a part of me." Suddenly, she felt scared. "I have to go. I need to go find him."

"Honey, you can't tell him I told you."

Bianca hung up and started running back. She'd not seen him yet today. She'd assumed he was sleeping in.

"I met with a financial adviser today," Sandy said into the phone. "Trying to figure out if I could potentially sell. I can discount everything, get some publishers to take back stock." A flush of sadness came over her. "I wish you were here, Jackie. It would be so much easier. I'm falling apart. I wish you'd bust through these doors and give me a hug and tell me everything's going to be okay. Because it's not okay, Jackie. None of it's okay."

Tears rolled down her cheeks. "Goddammit, I don't cry and here I am crying."

After hanging up and removing all evidence of her breakdown, she descended the stairs into the bookstore. Moira was just coming in. She'd had yesterday off.

"So you get a day off, and now you're coming in ten minutes late?"

"Sorry," Moira whispered, removing her hideous black hat.

"Oh, God. I can't handle it. Please. Tell me what's wrong with you today. Because I need it to get worse. I want the sky to fall."

Moira shook her head and crammed her purse behind the counter.

"Nervous about today's turnout?" Sandy asked, showing a molecule of humanity.

Nothing.

"Hello?" Sandy knocked on the air between them. "Anyone home? Today's the big day, right?"

"Yep."

"I don't like short responses from you. Go ahead, let it out, what's your problem? Couldn't touch the shitty week I'm having, but let's hear it anyway."

Apparently, Sandy hit a nerve because Moira whipped around with the fury of a demon. "You know what my problem is?" she started. "Well, one of the thousands. It's that you don't even try, and yet people are *still* attracted to you. You do everything you can to chase people off, but somehow, everyone wants to break through your icy walls and be your friend and seek your advice. And you appreciate no one. Me. George. Harold. Who knows who else. Do you know how lucky you are to have people like that? Especially considering how much of an epic *bitch* you can be."

Sandy smiled, but it wasn't a happy one. "Look at you, Moira. Mousy Moira standing up for herself. How impressive."

"Wipe that grin off your face. I'm not being funny." Moira, who wasn't a mouse today, stepped forward, a big bold step directly toward her boss. "Fuck you, Sandy. Fuck you for giving up on life. Fuck you for pushing all of us away. And a giant, triple *fuck you* for giving up on this bookstore, which is the best thing I have in my life."

Sandy's smile fell away.

Moira let out a gasp and headed out the door, slamming it shut so hard the bell came crashing down.

"You better get your ass back here," Sandy called out. "You're not going to leave me to deal with your stupid book club."

But Moira was already gone.

Chapter 28

I've Never Told Anyone

Bianca hadn't run like that in a long time. Bursting through the door, she kept going down the hall.

"Dad? Dad?" she spat out as she gasped for air. No response. Louder. "Dad!"

She tore into his room, unsure what she might find, her heart breaking, guilt washing over her.

He lay on the bed.

Feet crossed.

A closed iPad resting on his chest.

Eyes closed.

His chest unmoving.

Her heart sank, the world crashing as she rushed to him, unsure what was wrong, not knowing how to . . .

He opened his eyes. "Hi."

"Are you okay?" she asked, setting a hand on his leg.

"Yeah, yeah, taking a nap. What's going on?"

Bianca put her hands up to her face. "I thought something had happened to—" She stopped as she remembered her mom had begged her not to say anything. "I'm sorry, Dad. For everything. I keep beating you up, and it's not fair."

He took a minute to sit up. "What's gotten into you?"

"I demand so much from you, forcing you to earn your way back in, punishing you over and over. I know you're just trying to help."

She imagined what life would be without him, imagined how badly he must be hurting inside, and she couldn't hold back. "Mom told me about . . ." She couldn't finish the sentence.

He turned rigid.

". . . about you wanting to hurt yourself. She told me not to tell you I knew, but I do."

His shame was tangible.

"You should have told me. This is what I do, help people. There's nothing to be ashamed of."

"It's not a conversation a father has with his daughter."

"What else is family for? Is it better hidden? I don't think so."

She threw her arms around him, squeezing him and meaning it, feeling the years of anger she'd had toward him melt away.

Bianca and George sat next to each other on the couch. Wasn't that a beautiful metaphor, both of them on the couch, both of them patients of life, flawed humans trying to figure it out. What in hell had she been thinking, trying to preach to her dad, teach him her wisdom? God, she'd proved her lack of it by spewing out her bird's-eye-view advice, the great Austin therapist bestowing her vast knowledge upon her broken father.

Give me a break.

George might have been struggling lately, but he was a good and wise man who'd lived a full life. Maybe it wasn't what Bianca would have chosen, but that wasn't the point. This was a man who'd always given to others. The way he helped from the moment he arrived. How he'd cleaned the courtyard, actively giving the gift to her neighbors, who were mere strangers. The way he'd assisted the woman on the train with her bag. How he went out shopping for a gift for his housekeeper.

The way he'd helped out at the bookstore—for free. How he'd dedicated his life, sacrificed it even, to make sure that Bianca and Faith never knew poverty.

If anything, George belonged in the therapist's chair facing her on the couch. He was the wise one, the selfless one. And she'd not seen it. She'd been too angry that he hadn't been at her beck and call throughout her childhood. She'd been so up in her own head that she hadn't made room in her heart for sympathy.

She saw it now, all of it. The absolute beauty of this man. She thought back to his Intel coworkers, the ones she'd met over the years. She'd always resented him when they'd told her how great her father was. They were the ones getting all of his love. But no, everyone in his life was a beneficiary, even those like the woman with the red bag on the train, the neighbors. And Sandy. She had no idea how lucky she was to even be in his orbit.

He crossed a leg over the other and threw his arm up over the back of the couch, facing her. "Don't worry, kid, I've come out of it. Your mom coming to my rescue helped. The Zoloft, it took a few weeks, but things started to ease. *You* helped. Welcoming me here, making up for lost time, seeing this country with you."

"I can't believe I've been such an asshole."

"Oh, stop it."

"No, seriously." She peered into his eyes. "I want you to know that your commitment to serve people is extraordinary. I'm not even sure that I became a therapist to help others. I did it for the glory." She laughed at herself. "If that makes any sense. I did it—and even wrote my book—because I liked the idea of being a healer, of being an authority. I'm not sure I'm even selfless enough to truly want to help people. I mean, I know I'm good at it, that I can see into people. Ugh, forget it. What I'm saying is . . . you're an inspiration, Dad."

"An inspiration until lately."

"Yeah, well, nobody's perfect. You're allowed to crash sometimes."

He nodded and looked toward the kitchen.

"Can I ask about the suicidal ideations? I don't want to dig up bones, but I want to know. When's the last time you had them?"

He sighed. "I was pretty close in March. That's when I called your mom." Then he added, "You know what saved me? When I was . . . when I was really close. My daughter. You." He faced her again. "I'd taken some pills, was about to take more . . . and . . . you sure you want to hear this?"

"Yeah."

"A message from you saved me. Saved my life. You were reaching out to say you were sending an advance reader copy, said that even after all these years, you still wanted your dad to be proud of you." A tear dropped down his cheek. "I *am* proud of you, kiddo," he said, his words broken. "More than you could ever imagine."

She slipped into his arms, feeling his tears wet her neck. "I know that, Dad. I know."

"What if you'd never written your book? What if you hadn't reached out in that moment because you had this great book you wanted to share with me?"

She let go of him. "I would have reached out anyway."

"Yeah, but . . ." He brushed away his tears.

"You should have told me about what you were really going through."

"Maybe so, but it's over now. I have what it takes to get through. And half of it is just knowing the truth, how dangerous a lack of purpose can be." He patted her knee. "I'm going to find something else to do, but in the meantime, I'm going to learn to be okay without anything going on. Next time I visit, I might not even clean your fridge."

"Let's not get carried away." She looked around. "You've put a sparkle into this place, made it feel like home. Made me feel loved. Every time I see that pink toolbox, when I open my cabinet and find the Tupperware organized to perfection, when I go into my closet and see the fresh coat of paint, the way you added extra hooks and made a special place for the vacuum cleaner and broom and . . . Every time I walk through that courtyard, I'll be reminded of who you really are."

"An obsessive clean freak?"

"No. Someone who serves others, who puts others first. The best kind of someone, really. My dad, George Briggs. The greatest man I know."

This time, it was her tears that fell.

While George started packing, Bianca sat there for a long while, rebuilding her love for her father, seeing him in an entirely new light. It was she who'd stomped on their relationship lately, and now, it was time for her to put in the effort. Not only by inviting him back to Italy, but by getting on a damn plane, turbulence or not, and going to see him. After all, she did kind of want to meet this squirrel who was giving him such a hard time.

A while later, she flipped through her phone. Corrado had texted again. I'm holding you a table. If you decide not to come, I'll replace you with a life-size cutout.

She hammered out: Again, mixed messages much?

A minute later, he sent: Still four of you?

Bianca: You're ignoring me.

I will not accept a world where we are not friends.

Friends. What was she supposed to do with that? How could they possibly be *friends* now? Because he would always have the upper hand. She wanted more and he'd drawn the line. There would always be a divide between them.

She dialed Carol. "Hey, about tomorrow night."

"Oh, my God, B. I'm so sick and totally forgot about it. We can't go."

Relief settled in. "Yeah, that's okay. I'd prefer not to go either. Corrado and I decided that—actually—*he* decided that we're not compatible, so I'm bailing too."

"I don't believe it," Carol said. "He's obsessed with you."

Bianca explained everything that had happened but only skated the surface of how he'd basically ripped her apart with his psychological assessment.

"He's kind of right, right?"

"Not you too."

"Hey, it's none of my business, but this is exactly what you told me when we first met, that you'd been chasing this moving target, trying to prove yourself."

"Yeah, yeah, yeah. I know. And I know he's right, and that's the problem."

"You should still go. Don't shut him out of your life for calling you out."

"I don't like being called out. And I hate being wrong."

A chuckle from Carol.

Though Bianca hadn't planned it this way, hadn't even truly seen it till he'd shoved it in her face, she supposed the book had captured pieces of her life. She was always striving, always had been. It was always about the goal, reaching for something, trying to reach that pinnacle that would finally be enough.

"Okay, *amici*," Bianca said. "I hope you feel better. We'll catch up soon."

After the call, Bianca continued to chew on what her two friends had said today. It seemed that in a matter of weeks, she'd gone from a flawless go-getter to a troubled, broken woman splayed upon her own couch.

It wasn't comfortable being the one on the couch. That's why she'd gone to grad school, so that she could be the one in the chair with a notepad and a long list of solutions.

And yet, she knew she may find some peace in surrendering to her own vulnerability. If she were on her own couch, she'd tell herself that she should listen to her friends, that she's lucky enough to have ones that were willing to say it like it was.

Her dad returned to the living room. "Trying to decide which shoes to wear, my tennis shoes or the new ones."

"Dad, those tennis shoes should be burned."

What was far more important than her discomfort was the fact that she could have lost her dad. Her mother was right. She had such an awful tendency to cut people off and put all her focus on herself, consumed by her own troubles. All the while trying to hide them from the world.

Meanwhile, everyone else had their troubles too.

Enough cutting people off, she thought. *That ends today.*

"Carol and her husband can't go to the dinner," Bianca said, "so it's you and me. Unless you want to bring Sandy?"

He gave a false laugh. "I don't know."

"Oh, c'mon. What are you afraid of now?"

"Rejection?" George suggested. "Continuous heartache? The agony of being friends with someone you might love?"

"Don't even get me started, Dad. Hey, you're the one who said you wanted to keep her in your life. It's dinner; you're not sleeping together. *Eww*, I can't believe I said that."

"Fine, I'll ask her today."

She texted Corrado. Please hold my table. Just three of us, but we'll be there. I'm excited for you.

Two hours later, Bianca opened the door to the bookstore, noticing that the bell that typically chimed was missing. The far bigger news: There was already a crowd of people there.

In normal cases, Bianca would have been thrilled. Today, she decided the only thing worse than people not showing up was people actually showing up. If Corrado was correct, which he was, then Bianca figured that she and her book had unintentionally been building an army of aggro-humans who wouldn't stop till they'd supercharged the world. Okay, she'd picked that possibility up through some of the horrid reviews, but today was the day she'd finally accepted it.

Corrado had said he preferred Peggy in the middle. What a kick in the stomach.

Her poor former clients back home; she wanted to apologize to all of them, tell them to erase everything she'd told them.

As she walked under the arch, Sandy approached and gave a distracted hello. "Don't suppose you've talked to Moira, have you?"

Bianca shook her head.

Sandy pressed her lips together. "She was here earlier, ran out angry, long story. She's not answering my calls. I figured she'd be back by now. Hi, George."

"Hi."

Bianca watched them hold eye contact for a little too long before Sandy broke away and looked back at the crowd gathered around a table, munching on food and sipping wine.

"Huge favor, Bianca," Sandy said. "Could you start this thing while I go track Moira down? I'll try to be back by the time it starts, but if not, maybe do a reading or something. I don't know." Then she looked at George. "Would you mind pulling out more chairs from the back? Apparently, we're going to have a crowd, which is boggling my mind."

"Happy to." It was comical to watch George light up at being given a job. Either that, or he was madly and desperately in love.

Maybe both.

Poor guy.

Rushing out, Sandy wasn't angry. It felt strange not bubbling over with fury, especially when her one overpaid mouse of an employee had abandoned her. She wasn't mad at Jack, who should be living in Bologna right now. She wasn't even angry with George for darkening the door of her bookstore with his bothersome interest in her. Not even at the idiot tourist who she nearly plowed into while speeding on her Vespa through the old town toward Moira's place near Porta San Stefano.

All she felt was guilt at how terribly she'd treated Moira. The sweet girl had put up with Sandy for so long, and maybe she was finally over it all. Who could blame her? Sandy had pretty much abused her for a year.

Ten minutes later, she rang 2B at an apartment building tucked between a dry cleaner and a formaggeria.

"Yes," came a broken voice through the intercom.

"It's Sandy."

A long pause.

"Can I come up?"

Nothing.

"Hello?"

After what felt like forty-five minutes, the main door clicked.

Sandy pulled it back and raced up the steps in her heels to the second floor. Moira cracked open her door. "What are you doing here?" She was in her pajamas, a horrid matching set in yellow. Were those? No. Dear God, they were sheep reading books.

Sandy chose not to comment on the outfit and went straight for the guts of the matter. "Um, did you forget you were hosting a book club?" Sandy looked at her Cartier. "In five minutes?"

"I'm not going back." She still had her head poking out the door, keeping it barely cracked.

Sandy's first urge was to scold her. *What do you mean, you're not going back? You made a commitment. You need to follow through.* But she didn't do that.

Enough was enough.

She wanted to offer an apology, but she hadn't had much practice in a long time. There were rocks in her mouth.

Moira waited, glancing about the hall.

Sandy finally said, "I'm sorry, okay. I'm awful. Dreadful. And I made you the butt of it. All year. Can we *please* move on, and you come back and host your darn book club? By the way, there were already like forty people there when I left. Your whole thing worked out. Do you hear me? You proved me wrong. Surely, that's worth a smile."

Nothing.

Sandy reached deeper because she knew Moira deserved it. "Okay, fine. You want more? You're my best friend, Moira. Believe it or not, I don't have anyone else. And you not showing up today, the idea of you quitting, that's not an option. I can't handle it. Actually, I can't handle the idea of not seeing you. Who else is going to laugh at my stupid jokes?"

Still, nothing.

"Jesus H. Roosevelt Christ." She stretched out her arms. "I'm sorry, my friend. I want you to come back. I'm not selling the store. I was being stupid. And I want a second chance to prove to you that I'm not the Wicked Witch of Bologna."

Moira looked more surprised than anything.

"My arms are getting tired."

Moira finally let out a sigh and pulled open the door. "You know, you really are a handful."

"Oh, I do. You ought to live in this skin."

"I can't imagine."

"Right? By the way, those pajamas are absolutely abysmal."

"I think they're adorable."

Moira finally let Sandy wrap her arms around her, and when she did, she kissed Moira's neck, then squeezed hard, never wanting to feel as lonely as she had this morning again.

"Now, might you get dressed and we go deal with this mess you've made?"

She felt a nod on her shoulder, then: "Are you reading *Outlander*?"

Sandy pulled back. "What's that supposed to mean?"

"Jesus H. Roosevelt Christ. That's what Claire says. Is Sandy Cooke reading a love story?"

Sandy started to deny it but halfway surrendered. "I'm just skimming through it. A bookseller needs to know what she's selling."

"Uh-huh."

"Oh, wipe that smile off your face. Yes, it's good. The series is good. And we can talk about it later. For now, we have somewhere we need to be."

Moira snickered as she disappeared into the back, and Sandy looked around the apartment. There were far too many books, random stacks of them. A video game was frozen on the television screen. A worn copy of Bianca's book with sticky notes protruding from the pages rested on a glass table. Above a velvet couch hung a collection of twelve small modern paintings, all in bright and bold colors, all by the same artist.

"You have great taste," Sandy said. "Not in pajamas, but I like the art."

Moira appeared, tugging on a white shirt. "Forty people?"

"And maybe more by now. A horde of perusers. All sitting there waiting. I left Bianca in charge." She looked back at her Cartier. "Time's a tickin'."

After Sandy left, Bianca inched her way into the crowd and made small talk till someone recognized her and realized she was the reason they'd all gotten together. Suddenly, everyone was circling around her, prodding her with questions. She answered kindly, trying not to beat herself up for writing a book that had missed the mark.

Simply put, there were bigger problems out there in the world. She didn't have much to complain about, when here she was doing a stint in Italy while trying to figure out her next moves. She had money, a degree, a client base that would likely take her back.

So what if she wasn't the next Brené Brown.

A few minutes after the event was supposed to start, Bianca clinked her wineglass and motioned everyone to their seats. There were more people than chairs, so some were forced to stand in the back.

"I want to thank everyone for coming." She felt strangely nervous and shaky, despite typically having no problems speaking in public. "While we wait on Sandy and Moira, I thought I'd introduce myself and see if you had any questions or wanted to throw tomatoes at me. I'm the author of the book, and I moved down the street a couple of months ago."

A few hands shot up.

The first woman, midsixties, wearing a string of pearls, said in a strong British accent, "I'm so glad you're here. It's a great book."

Bianca waited for the *but*.

None came.

"Where did the idea for Peggy Meh come from?"

"Isn't that a question. Right to the heart of it." She was about to give them more of an answer than they bargained for when Sandy and Moira came rushing in.

"There they are! Our lovely hosts."

Both were out of breath as they joined the circle. Moira sat down next to Bianca and took the floor. "I'm so sorry, everyone. I was held up, but welcome! I can't believe the turnout. What a thrill. I don't even want to interrupt. I suppose you've met our guest of honor."

"I was starting to answer some questions."

"Wonderful. Please don't let me get in the way."

All eyes went back to Bianca. It was now or never.

Bianca had never been one to open up about herself. *Never let them see you sweat.* Today felt different, though.

Who in the flipping world cared whether she was perfect? Perhaps it was better to be honest and open, to pour out her heart. If she were to ever write another book, that's what she'd do differently. She wouldn't hide behind a fake name. She'd own her damage. Strut it, even!

Bianca rubbed her hands together, ready to start a fire, ready to leave some serious burn marks—the right kind. "Someone asked where Peggy Meh came from. Let me tell you." She set the stage for those who hadn't read the book yet, then spoke about the name being a placeholder. "I was going to search and replace it with a proper name once I found one, but then my agent, who fired me today, decided it was catchy. According to the reviews so far, I wouldn't say 'catchy' is what readers are saying." Damn right she finger-quoted *catchy*.

"The reviews aren't good?" a woman asked, this one part of a trio of fortysomethings.

"Um, no," Bianca said. "I've been shredded to pieces, actually. But that's okay. I could have done better."

"I loved it," Moira said. "And you know what, screw the reviews. People have no idea what they're talking about these days."

"That's sweet of you to say."

Others chimed in, saying similarly nice things.

"Thanks to all of you, but if I could do it again, I'd do things differently. Firstly, I'd search and replace Peggy's name with my own, because what I've realized is I wrote this book for me. Or about me. Maybe both." Saying it soothed her soul.

She raised her hand high. "I am Bianca Meh . . . trying to become Bianca Megawatt. That's who I've always been, on a desperate path to supercharge myself. And I've refused to let anyone see the real me till I became that supercharged person. But thanks to a few friends lately, and my dad, and thanks to Italy, too, I've realized that I've gotten this whole thing wrong. I built a practice back in Austin based on what I thought would make a person matter, the importance of becoming supercharged, of leaving burn marks, but that's not what life's about."

Bianca looked over at the stack of her books featured on an endcap of the self-development section. "Forgive me, Moira. I'm so grateful for your help in promoting this book, but I need to do something that I've wanted to do all day."

She stood and took one of the copies of the book and held up the cover, then she pointed to the middle figure in the evolution of Peggy Meh, who grew taller and skinnier and stronger with each transformation.

"This is where the book should have stopped. No one needs to be a Megawatt. In fact, I'm officially disbanding the Megawatters right now. What I've laid out is an unachievable path to perfection. Yeah, there are good ideas here, but I went too far. What about Peggy in the Middle? What about Bianca in the Middle? A slightly damaged human trying to better herself without beating herself up. Without being ashamed."

Bianca smiled, feeling everyone staring at her but not worried about it. This was the best she'd felt since swimming in the sea in Ischia.

You will never be here again, Bianca. Own this moment with your entire self.

"My readers always ask if I'm working on anything new. What I want to do is rewrite this book. No, not even rewrite it. Just tear it in half." She opened the book, guesstimated the middle, then started to tear.

"Okay, this was a lot easier in my head."

Everyone laughed.

She dug in with all she had, eventually finding a way to separate the pages and tear apart the spine.

Two halves in her hands, she tossed the last half over her shoulder and let it drop dramatically. "That part, that's what we don't need. No one ever needs to achieve megawatt-dom. All we have to do is our best, right? And leaving burn marks? What was I thinking?"

Bianca turned to find Moira shrinking, and she recalled the tattoo on her arm. "I mean, it's a fine sentiment." No, she wasn't going to back off. "Look, Moira, and all of you, I'm sorry, but I feel like I misled everyone, and I can't hold it back another moment."

To Moira directly, she said, "I'll pay for it to be removed if you want. I know this is horrible to say, especially since you were so kind to have me, but I messed up with this book, and I don't want anyone to leave burn marks. I want people to own who they are at any given moment and to love their entire selves."

"I don't think you messed up," Moira finally said. "I mean, okay, point made. No one needs to live to the extremes, but your book changed my life. And I'm proud of the tattoo. I still love the idea of leaving burn marks. I'm not here to float through life. I'm here to disrupt. To be irreverent. To break free. Maybe what the book means to you has changed, but once you put a book out into the world, once anyone puts art into the world, it becomes the possession of the reader or the one experiencing it. You didn't mislead me. You led me to me. The reason we're all here is this book actually. The reason that I'm becoming stronger and finding a reason to keep going, despite my terrible past, is because of you. So no, you can't take away this book, and you can't even tell me what's right and wrong in it."

Bianca had no words.

Moira glanced at Harold. "I even tried to kiss a man yesterday, which was the first time since my divorce. It didn't work out but that's okay. I tried, and that's what living is. That is what leaving burn marks is. Taking chances. Seizing every moment."

"Fair enough," Bianca said. "My God, sister, you're the one that needs to write a book."

A clap, then another, then the whole room.

Moira sat back and crossed her arms.

"May I say something?" It was Sandy.

The rest of the room quieted and let her speak.

Holding her phone out, she said to Bianca, "I want to read some of the reviews to you. Sure, I see a few bad ones, but art is subjective, isn't it? I don't like anything that Moira reads, but does that make her wrong? Well, okay, in that case, I'm righter than her, but that's beside the point."

Sandy held her hand high to shush the laughter. "Let me read some of these."

Bianca braced herself.

"This book saved my life." Sandy removed her glasses and looked at Bianca. "You could stop right there, couldn't you? I have never saved anyone's life. How many in this room have? You've saved a life, Bianca. That's on top of giving your all to make a book and then putting yourself out there."

Sandy went back for more. "Another five-star. *I'm leaving my husband because of this book. I won't let him walk over me anymore.* There you go. I haven't read your book, but if it would have given me the courage to walk out on my first husband sooner, then what you did is enough. So tear your book in half, beat yourself up. Whatever you need to do. But then get back to writing because the world needs authors. Especially authors like you who care so much about what they're doing. And I can see that."

Bianca felt eyes on her again; her hands trembled. "You're going to make me cry; thank you." Then she did it, darn tears gushing out.

Moira put a hand on her. "Let it out, girl."

Someone in the audience whispered, "Best. Book club. Ever."

The whole room, Bianca included, exploded with teary-eyed laughter.

Chapter 29

Awakening 101

Harold sat in the last row, swallowed up by the crowd standing behind him. His face was still red from being called out by Moira, but now he was considering jumping into the fray of discussion.

What he wanted to say was that yeah, Bianca's book had perhaps misled him. Or maybe he'd misled himself. He'd gone from Harold Meh to Aroldo Megawatt, and now here he was back to the beginning. A fucking boomerang. What she'd said about the middle? It made sense. The whole thing made sense, and hearing her talk, hearing Bianca be so honest with herself and with others resonated in a profound way.

He wanted to be a part of her awakening, and before he knew it, his hand went up and Bianca pointed in his direction.

"May I chime in, as someone who enjoyed your book? I'm sort of where you are. I tried to become someone I wasn't, and it wasn't achievable. Or sustainable." He glanced over at Sandy because he felt her looking at him.

"I'm trying to start over and figure out what's next," Harold admitted.

"What is next?" Bianca asked, the tone of a woman who cared deeply. "You're Harold, right? What's your story? Can we do a deep dive?"

"You've hit gold if you want to do that."

"I do. If you're up for it. I won't even charge."

A snicker from everyone.

Harold felt nervous but also inspired. Here was a woman who'd torn her book in half and then cried in public. "Yeah, okay, where do I start?" The birth of Aroldo seemed like as good a place as any, but then something made him think back further. "You want the truth, like the real truth?"

"That's the best kind. Don't worry. We're all family."

What did he have to lose? Alice? No. His dignity? Maybe.

"I'm a . . . well . . . I was a barista living with my mom a few months ago, working at a coffee shop in Denver, when a redhead appeared and altered my universe, as if my destiny had walked through the door. I was coming from the back with two jugs of whole milk when I set eyes on her. She ordered, took a seat at a table by the window, and started looking at her phone. I'm not sure what came over me—love, or lust—but I had this desperate urge to talk to her, but I didn't have the confidence. Or a chance in hell. So I created this new person in my head."

Harold's heart pounded but he kept going. "I took off my apron, fell into an alternate persona, like an avatar, and took a seat next to her. No longer was I the hopeless barista living with his mom, too chicken to apply to colleges. I'd become a different Harold, and somehow, I was able to improvise as we spoke. I introduced myself and said that I was an entrepreneur who liked to occasionally work in the coffee shop. Alice was visiting friends but living here in Bologna, a student at the university. She was younger, which made the whole thing easier. For some crazy reason, she took to me, and we were laughing within minutes. And that fed this person I'd become and gave him confidence. Before I was busted by my manager, I suggested that she and I go for a walk."

He shook his head, remembering that out-of-body feeling as they strolled the street chatting. For once in his life, someone had shown interest in him.

"Go on," Bianca said.

"And then we had lunch and spent the afternoon together. Had dinner. Kissed that night. I couldn't believe what was happening. Of course, my manager was texting me nonstop. By the end of the weekend, there was no turning back. She had a flight out, and as we were saying goodbye, I suggested I could take my work with me and come visit for a while. That's how I got here."

Everyone in the bookstore listened intently, and it was only then that he remembered that he had a tremendous fear of public speaking. What was happening?

Bianca said softy, "I'm so glad that you're sharing, Harold. How brave of you."

"And it only gets worse from there." Settling in, he told them about pretending to have clients, but they were actually his gamer friends back home. He shared everything about Aroldo, admitting how he could barely remember the transformation. "I wouldn't blame it on your book per se, but I was certainly on a journey to supercharge myself. Really, the reason I'm sharing is because I'm tired of hiding and you've inspired me."

He looked over at Moira, wondering how she fit in. He wasn't even sure who *he* was, so how could he know what she meant to him?

Bianca took over. "Harold, your courage and the love you're capable of is who you are. And there's absolutely *nothing* wrong with who you were in the first place. It's one thing to better ourselves, another to change into someone else. You and I were both guilty of it, but we still have time. We always have time. Why not go find your Harold in the Middle."

"Yeah. I guess so."

"Seriously. Even us at our worst is enough. Can you imagine all the things since the beginning of time that had to align to lead to you entering the world and taking your first breath? There's nothing more beautiful. We're all miracles. By simply breathing, we're enough."

Shivers of hope ran up his spine. "But how do we believe that and live that?"

"Great question." Bianca sat up, and he could see she was truly thinking about it. "Because the same force that made rivers flow and flowers bloom made you. It wasn't an accident. You're part of the design."

Harold spun her answer around in his head. "Yeah, but that just means I happened to make the cut. My dad's sperm swam fast. Actually, he told me one time he wished he'd worn a condom. How do I really believe that I'm enough as I am?"

"I suppose that's where faith comes in, Harold. Something far greater than me and you said *yes* to us. We got the green light. Okay, you might not have realized your purpose yet. We're born miracles, and then we have to find out how to shine our light the brightest. How to give thanks for this miracle of life. But even when we're not shining the brightest, when we're still trying to find our way, we're enough."

"You're still not answering the question, though. Give me proof that we're enough. That I'm enough."

Bianca sat up straighter, pure light on her face. "I get you, Harold. I see you. And I'm going to throw something back at you. Why don't you believe it? Where is your faith?"

"I've never had any."

"Why?"

"Because of life. Because I had a father who wasn't really a father. A mom who was just trying to survive. I've been kicked around all my life, failed at everything except this one thing I did, this finding Alice and chasing her here. And that might have been my biggest failure so far . . ."

"Well, if you're trying to figure out your next moves, don't sleep on going to law school—if you've ever considered it. You have a natural talent for argument."

Everyone laughed, but in a warm way. In a way Harold wasn't used to.

Bianca continued. "Okay, fine, maybe we can't ever know for sure if we're enough as we are. No grand authority in the sky is going to come down from on high and deem you worthy of your life. You have to believe it. Every day. Not because you may or may not be a wealthy entrepreneur, or because you have great style, or because you've landed a stunning redhead. Or because you've written a book that's set the world on fire. You're worth it because you decide to be. No one can take that from you, Harold."

"Yes!" someone shouted.

"Hear, hear," said another.

What she'd said took his breath away. Maybe it was that easy.

Bianca stood and went to him. When she got close, she reached out a hand and pulled him up, then hugged him. Everyone else rose and started clapping, and when Bianca let him go, the next person was there to hug him and then the next, then the next.

For the first time in his life, Harold felt truly whole.

After everyone had dispersed, George found Sandy ringing up a last customer. "What an event," he said.

"Yeah, not what I expected." She gave the customer their change, then faced him. "You must be proud of her. That was special."

He looked through the window at his daughter, standing outside chatting with some of the other guests. "I'm endlessly proud of her." Back to Sandy, he said, "I wanted to see if you might be interested in joining us for dinner tomorrow night. It's my last night." He told her the details of Corrado's restaurant, then drew a line through the air. "Just as friends."

"I see. Who else is joining?"

"It was going to be a couple of Bianca's friends, but they had to cancel. So the three of us, if that's okay."

"Could you make it five?" She looked over at Moira stacking chairs. "I'd love to invite Moira and Harold. I have some making up I have to do with them. I'll pay for—"

"Sure, they can come," George blurted out. Anything to spend one last night with her. Even if it was just as friends.

As he waited for Bianca to finish up with her new fans, George wandered around his mind, putting together the pieces of what Bianca had said today. And how Harold had experienced such a breakthrough by simply being honest with himself and everyone else.

George concluded that he had to tell Bianca what he'd said to Corrado.

But how, and when?

Harold found Moira putting away chairs. Most of the guests had left. "May I help?"

"Yeah, sure."

He picked one up and folded it, searching for what he should say. Then it seemed obvious. "I'm sorry. For lying to you. For leading you on. For not seeing how you felt."

"We don't choose who we like, Harold. You have nothing to apologize for."

He helped her for a few minutes, unsure of what else he could do. It felt like a stupid move to tell her that he did like her, now that his blinders were off. He didn't want to make her feel like second place.

Not that she was.

"What are you doing later?" he finally asked.

She shook her head.

"Wanna hang out?"

"Harold, I don't need pity."

"This isn't pity. What if I told you you're the only friend I have?"

She laughed. "I'd tell you that you're the second person who's told me that today."

"Okay, wasn't expecting that. Maybe that's what you do to people, make them feel like they matter." He took her hand and pulled her toward him. "I'd like to get to know you. You're the only friend I have and maybe more."

"Maybe more." She pulled back her hand. "Don't do this."

"I'm asking if you want to hang out tonight. I have to go home in the next few days, and I refuse to leave until we're back to normal."

"What's normal?"

"You know what I mean. Gosh, stop giving me such a hard time. I can understand if you don't ever want to see me again because I'm a fraud and a liar, but if you can look past it, then maybe we could start again. I could show you who I am. And if that person, the real me, is still someone you want to kiss, then you should probably be certified legally insane—but nevertheless, I'd welcome it with all of me."

He found her eyes and took her hand again. "You were the first one to ever tell me that I didn't need to be somebody else. I'm sorry for not listening. Will you forgive me?"

"I might be able to look past it." She gave him a wink that sent flutters into his heart.

If he was looking for proof of a greater design, he'd found it in her eyes then.

"Hey, you two bozos," Sandy said, appearing out of nowhere. "Wanna go to dinner tomorrow night? Fancy Michelin place with Bianca and George? It's his last night. And don't worry, I'm paying. I'll buy my way back into your hearts with good food and wine."

And if Moira's eyes weren't proof of miracles and a greater design, then Sandy asking them both to dinner surely was.

Sandy surprised Harold even more by lightly taking him by the arm. "Can I talk to you for one moment?"

Guiding him to a spot between the Mystery and Sci-Fi shelves, she crossed her arms and struggled to get it out—whatever it was on her mind. But when the words finally left her tongue, they seemed to escape easily.

"You're not the only one to blame for the whole Aroldo thing. I'm afraid I pushed you into becoming him. I see so much of my son in you, wanted so badly to help you to get Alice back, that I got carried away. You're spectacular just as you are." She took a long breath. "As you can imagine, I'm not one to sling words around like that often. So when I offer a compliment, consider it gold. If you're struggling right now to accept that you matter, let my assurance do the heavy lifting until you get there."

She'd joggled something loose in Harold, and a warmth ran up his spine. If Moira's eyes and Sandy's invitation weren't enough to prove the existence of a higher power, Sandy saying this to him certainly was.

Breathing back tears, he replied, "You have nothing to apologize for, my friend. Even little ole Harold can put some effort into his clothes, into his appearance. And maybe even little ole me deserves a spot on the dance floor."

"Isn't that the truth?" Sandy reached up and touched his chin. "You're a gem, Harold. Like a son to me."

He matched her shockingly sweet gaze. "You can be my Bolognese *madre* any day."

Chapter 30

The Warmth of Blank Pages

George eased out of bed, not wanting to tell Bianca what he'd done, but he knew he had to. He'd put it off last night because she'd been on such a high. She'd made spaghetti Bolognese, and they'd laughed about the book club and their journey around Italy and to-do lists and a million other things.

He couldn't take that day away from her.

But now, he couldn't put off his confession any longer, because he couldn't be the father she deserved if he didn't come clean. He marched down the hall, ready to tear off the Band-Aid.

She sat on the balcony, her feet up on the table. "Morning, Dad."

"Mornin'. What are you working on?"

A smirk appeared as she said, "A book."

"What?" Last he'd heard, she was done writing books.

"I was on Substack this morning, sending out a post that I might regret, when I saw a quote by a guy I know. Kevin Kermes. It was about Van Gogh moving to Arles, a small town in Southern France. He was escaping the rat race of Paris to create in a more powerful way. Not for anyone else, only for him. Anyway, the quote was, 'When you stop performing for applause, you start creating for eternity.' How good is that?"

He chewed on the quote as best he could, despite his mind being elsewhere. "That's powerful."

"Yeah, an uppercut to my chin. I knew this but forgot it. I have a freaking degree in how to deal with human angst, and maybe I'm pretty good at dealing with others' but not mine. I'm the slippery one."

"You are good at what you do," George said. "I won't soon forget yesterday. What a powerful couple of hours. I suspect everyone is rethinking their lives now."

"Maybe."

How could he tell her that he'd betrayed her when she was sitting here so happy? And finally writing again!

"What are you creating for eternity, then?" George asked.

"I don't even know that it matters. I'm just writing, working out a bunch of revelations. No agenda, like our trip, you know? Just faith. That's my future."

He'd never seen her so inspired, and no, he couldn't tell her. Not now.

"I can't believe you leave tomorrow." She set down her laptop. "What does life look like for you going forward? You gonna be okay?"

He thought about it, imagining that bottle of pills waiting for him, the ones he'd immediately dispose of when he got home. "You know what's funny? I actually miss Mr. Nutz. He and I need to work some things out."

"Oh, God, here we go."

George took a seat. "No, I'm serious. I came up with something while you were talking yesterday. I've spent so long fighting against retirement—fighting against everything—but what if I leaned into it? I started designing a squirrel feeder in my head. You ever seen one of those?"

She shook her head, her bright smile growing wider.

"Me either. I could be onto something. Maybe if I make him his own feeder, then he'll leave the birds alone. It's an idea."

"I like it."

"And then there's the elusive and slippery Sir Parm. Guess what I did late last night? Got out of bed to do it. I removed the trap."

"Get out. You conceded to Sir Parm?"

"I suppose so." He held up a finger. "But I did something I'm proud of. I left a big hunk of the older Parm, the expensive stuff. Honestly, he should be rewarded for his ability to beat me. He and Mr. Nutz are true talents at what they do."

Bianca was beaming. There was no way he could admit that he'd cornered Corrado right now.

He shook his head. "As much as I miss being home, it's going to hurt to leave. I like seeing you every day."

"Me too, Dad."

"And I'm dreading the turbulence."

"Yeah, I hate it too. Hopefully, it's a smooth flight. You want some medicine? I have Xanax for exactly that reason."

George shook his head. "No, thank you."

"You sure? With the meds, I can be in a full-on nosedive and not be worried about it."

"That's a visual that'll keep me up tonight."

"Sorry. And I shouldn't be talking about pills anyway."

He cut a hand through the air. "You have nothing to worry about."

She patted her chest. "I believe that."

Taking a Nespresso back to his room, George started to empty his drawers. Was he eager to get back to the life he'd left behind? The life he'd been pushed into? Though he certainly wasn't going to pick up golf again or start baking classes, he'd take with him what Bianca had said on their trip.

Treat every moment with the reverence it deserves. Because you'll never be back there again.

He'd have to come clean to B before he left, and she'd lose it on him, and he'd return to Scottsdale with his tail between his legs. But he would *not* go back and swallow those pills. He'd try again at life. Maybe he'd return to Bologna in the fall—if she'd let him. He'd at least send her messages and try living the life she'd advised. Whatever he chose to do, build a squirrel feeder or maybe even start dating, he'd give every moment the reverence it deserved. He might even take a break from to-do lists for a while. There wasn't much to put on them anymore anyway.

Maybe he'd get around to that, though. Find something to put on them. Something that mattered. Maybe he did have another purpose waiting for him. In the meantime, he'd give each moment its due and feel gratitude that his little girl had grown up to be a superstar and that he'd lived long enough to see it.

Bianca was probably right, that he better get his head straight without jumping into something that would distract him from facing his demons. From that renewed place, he might just find that the best years were yet to come! What came after the golden years? A decline in health and functional capacity?

No. Not by a long shot.

It was the platinum years that came next.

"You know what it is, Dad. For both of us," Bianca said, storming into his room thirty minutes later, while he was folding his pants. She plopped into the chair by the window and kicked up her feet on the ottoman. "Actually, let's back up. The turbulence thing."

"Oh, yes, let's bring that back up, please." George set his troubles aside, feeling how much he was going to miss her. Especially the way she could light up a room.

"I've never admitted this," she said, "but I have to use apps when I fly. I track the plane, follow the weather, and measure G-forces. If the turbulence is bad, I close my eyes and wait to die. It's the freaking worst. People with turbulence anxiety, maybe even people who suffer any kind of motion sickness from riding in cars, boats, planes, they all have something in common. Control issues. I've had plenty of clients who suffer from it, and like a lot of things, I diagnose and help them while quietly sweeping my similar issues under the rug."

George sat on the edge of the bed, enjoying seeing his daughter getting wound up. He'd love to take that thirst for life back to Arizona. Of course, before he left for the airport, he planned to tell her about his run-in with Corrado. But an idea had started to surface. He could pull Corrado aside tonight and ask forgiveness, tell the kid he didn't mean anything by it. *Please don't tell Bianca. Forget I said those things.* It wasn't the prettiest solution, but maybe this was one of those rare times when you don't have to totally come clean.

"Point is," she said, "I have control issues, as do you. What does that mean, you might ask. For me, it means that I don't want anyone to know that I'm not perfect, so I keep up a facade. I don't like relationships because they obviously require a huge surrender of control. You have to deal with someone being all up in your space, leaving dishes in the sink, deciding what you watch on television, asking for things, *needing* things. I stay on top of life because I want to be in control of every piece of it, leaving nothing to chance. Even the act of sitting and doing nothing is so hard exactly because it's the opposite of being in control."

George could barely keep up.

"And even my issues with my weight. I have a hard time controlling it, like this writhing beast inside of me that I can't tame, despite diets and all the other shit, which naturally means I've created an unhealthy relationship around my body shape . . ."

That broke George's heart. "Honey, you're perfect the way you are."

"No, I'm not perfect. But that's okay. No one is. Trying to be perfect is controlling. Chasing an impossible standard is controlling. Trying to be Peggy Megawatt is controlling. Living and dying by a to-do list is *controlling*."

"Dammit, I'm going to miss you, B."

She sighed, having gotten it out. "You know where to find me."

"Yeah, I know. Trust me, if you can tolerate me, I'll be back. I need this—your wise words—for my soul. I never thought I'd say it, but I may miss Italy too."

"What's that?"

"You heard me."

"By the way, please don't eat. Text Sandy and tell her not to eat either. Nine courses tonight. No one better show up full."

"Nine courses?"

"That's right."

Bianca felt like she was running wide open. Okay, many of the things she was thinking about would take work. Accepting her body for what it was. Accepting that she'd written a book that had misled people. Accepting that her life was a mess and might always be a mess. She had no idea what she was going to do going forward. But that was okay.

It was all okay.

What she wanted to do now was write. She grabbed her laptop, assumed her position in the shade of the clothes drying on the clothesline, and cracked open a blank document. She'd been making notes and writing deadly honest Substacks, but this was her first true venture into what might be a new book.

The empty page eyed her, and in a flash, she saw the negative reviews since the release of *From Meh to Megawatt* and felt all the ways she'd fucked up, how she'd wasted ten years living and working in a trance, and she saw the blank page of her life and how she'd thrown away her practice and given up on her life back in Texas. She had NO IDEA where she was going or what she was doing from here.

But she didn't have to know.

She could be here now.

Living in freaking Italy with a blank page inviting her in. Not demanding that she write anything in particular, but waving her over and saying, "Come in. The water's warm."

One word, one sentence at a time.

She hovered her fingers over the keys, then took a breath and started to hammer away.

This one's for me. But you're welcome to peek over my shoulder if you want, because we're likely going through the same stuff. And it all starts here, where the blank page beckons.

"Mom, guess what, I'm coming home," Harold announced. "I found a cheap flight that arrives on Friday night. Can you pick me up?"

"Can I pick you up?" his mom asked sarcastically. It was 6:00 a.m. over there. "I was about to catch a flight to Italy and come drag your little ass back."

"And guess what? I've been invited to the opening of a fancy new restaurant. Nine courses! Can you believe that? Don't worry; Sandy, the bookstore owner I told you about, is paying."

"Nine courses? How are you going to eat all that, Harold. Last time I saw you, you were as skinny as a pole."

"I know. Sandy just texted, saying that I shouldn't eat beforehand so I can make room."

"I want pictures. We're doing a whole slideshow when you get home. And please tell me you aren't going anywhere else for a while. It's gotten lonely here."

"No, Mom. I'm not going anywhere. Actually, I was thinking about trying to get into CCD—after I pay you back for this trip." He'd spent the morning checking out the Community College of Denver, looking through the degrees. It wasn't Harvard, but it sure beat sitting around waiting for a break.

"You know I support you, Harold. I think it's a nice idea." He heard her strike a match and light a cigarette.

"I *do* know that, Mom. You've always been there for me."

"Always will!"

After they'd hung up, Harold texted his group of gamer friends. He'd never met them in person, but for years, he'd been playing role-play games like *Project Zomboid*, a slow-burn survival sim, and *VRChat*, where you hang out as avatars in virtual worlds.

Hey, guys, would you mind if I invited my friend Moira to play? She's one of us.

While he waited for a response, he accepted that in becoming Aroldo he'd taken his role-playing too far. It was best to leave it in the virtual world.

A burst of energy struck him, and he said out loud, "I matter because I choose to matter. Take that, Dad, and Duo, and all you other doubters out there."

Charging up to a stand, he said again, "I matter because I choose to matter. Just the way I am."

He couldn't remember feeling better in his life. With a renewed sense of purpose, he beat on his chest, like an ape in the jungle signaling his dominance, like a once lost man who has finally found his way.

He pounded on his chest harder and harder, shouting, "Harold Gibler matters!"

Sandy hid in her office, about to dial Jack. Moira was on the sales floor, basking in the fucking glow of hosting a successful book club. If Sandy weren't so proud of her, she'd be upset. Sandy hated being proven wrong.

At least she used to.

She liked being wrong in this case. Moira had been correct: People really are looking for connection. They'd had a banner day yesterday, selling more books than the entire week before. That's what you get when you turn the bookstore into a Jerry Springer event.

"Jackie," she whispered into the phone. "What a summer, and it's not even over yet. Moira somehow pulled off the book club event, the one I told you about, if you ever listen to the messages all the way through. It turned into a Jerry Springer or Oprah thing, long story, but we had a banner day of sales. We're back to the usual now, though, a bunch of perusers. Had a woman today who brought seven books to the register. I rang her up, ran the card, and then she changed her mind. Returned six of them. I can't with these people."

Moira's voice rose up the stairs. "Sandy, you have to get down here."

Sandy stormed halfway down the circular steps. "Dear God, I'm in the middle of something."

"You have to see this!"

Sandy put the phone back to her ear. "I have to go, Jack. Apparently, there's something I *have* to see."

Moira stood at the bottom of the stairs, gleaming in orgiastic splendor.

"What is it?" Sandy asked. "Did Taylor Jenkins Reid have a cover reveal? Emily Henry announce a new one? Harold take you to tongue town last night?"

"Sandy Cooke. I can't believe you said that."

"I can't believe you can't believe it. Since when do I have a filter? So did Harold take you upstairs last night or what?"

"We had spritzes, that's it."

"Uh-huh," Sandy said, a smile ambushing her. "Maybe tonight's your lucky night."

"Okay, noted. Now can I tell you why I called you out from your lair?"

"My lair?"

"That's what I call it now." She clasped her hand to her mouth playfully. "Oops, should I have filtered that?"

"Oh, dear God. Is this still part of the gloating for being right? I can't handle it."

Moira laughed. Like really laughed. Not a mousy laugh, the real McCoy. Then, she said, "They're taking the scaffolding down."

"What?"

Moira pointed toward the entrance.

Sandy marched that way, immediately noticing that more daylight crept in than usual. She pushed through the doors and found, to her surprise and perhaps delight, that five men looked to be taking down the scaffolding. Okay, two of them were leaning against the columns of the porticoes, smoking cigarettes and chatting.

"Hai finalmente finito?" she asked the more handsome of the two.

He said through a smoke cloud, *"Si, abbiamo finito."*

Sandy lifted her arms to the sky. "*Meno male.* Thank God."

She turned back to Moira, who'd followed her out. "I guess this means I can't move to Lisbon."

"You were never moving to Lisbon."

"Don't test me, Moira. I'm not sure I love this new version of you."

"It's not a version of me. It's the real me."

"Poor Harold."

"Harold and I aren't a couple."

"It's a matter of time. You wait and see. I've an eye for these kinds of things."

"Is that right? She who doesn't even allow a romance section in her bookstore is now an expert of all things romance?"

Sandy cackled and said over her shoulder as she led them back inside, "Oh, no. I'm still not a romance gal. There will be no romance section in this bookstore as long as I live, but I know when I see two people who still haven't learned the hard way. Future victims, as I call them."

"For your information, we decided to be friends. He's going back to the States, anyway."

"Friends," Sandy said, rather snidely. "Famous last words."

Twilight fell over the Piazza Maggiore, painting the sky a caramel hue. The church bells of the Basilica di San Petronio pounded out the hour. The smoky scent of coffee wafted out of a café just as busy in the evening as during the day. A young blond busker sang the daylights out of a Coldplay song. Tourists and locals alike wandered into the evening, perhaps seeking an Aperol spritz or their first sip of Lambrusco, some of them surely reconnecting with long-lost friends and nearly forgotten lovers.

Bianca stood below Michelangelo's eagle, the stone carving perched on a wall near the statue of Neptune. Its wings were spread, ready to take flight.

Feeling her own renewed trajectory, her wings eager to flutter, she set her hand on the stone wall and let her eyes fall closed.

The sounds around her dissipated. The concerns of who she might one day become, what she might do, where she might go, fell away.

Only the whispers of her ancestors remained.

Chapter 31

The Big Circus—er, Night

In the entryway to Il Minerva, Bianca kissed Corrado's cheeks. "The big night."

"That's right." He couldn't have been any more handsome in his chef uniform and black clogs. His sleeves were rolled up, revealing his tattoo and muscular forearms.

She hoped he didn't notice her nerves. She'd thought about him far too much lately, wondering whether he'd ever give her another chance, and now that she stood facing him, her heart was vibrating.

"You seem very calm," she said.

"Inside, I'm screaming." He looked at the others: George, Sandy, Harold, and Moira. Bianca had texted to see if she could up the number in the reservation, and he'd welcomed it. "Please, please, welcome. Alfonso will take you to your table."

Alfonso, dressed impeccably, opened a door, and a burst of jazz and conversation came rushing in from the dining room. As the others entered, Bianca hung behind.

"You do look even keeled," Bianca said to him. "That's how you know you're doing what you're supposed to be doing."

"Maybe wait till after you try the food." He clasped his hands together. "I must get back to the kitchen, but please know how happy I am that you're here."

"Si, si," she replied. *"Felice di essere qui."* We're happy to be here.

Perhaps she was hoping for more. Maybe something like, "I missed you."

He clearly had his focus elsewhere, so she found his eyes and said, *"Buona fortuna."*

"Grazie." Joy filled his face, then he was gone.

Alfonso appeared again and led her in.

It was 9:00 p.m., rather early for Italians, but most of the tables were occupied. Along the back wall, close to the huge painting of the woman with the flock of birds forming a V between her thighs, a sommelier scaled a ladder in the glass wine cellar to retrieve a bottle. Each marble-topped table hosted a small abstract sculpture and a table lamp and was neatly set with modern and elegant stemware and silverware.

George handed Bianca a menu. "Can you believe it? Nine choices of water. Look at that last one."

She scanned the menu. Each water had a place of origin, along with a description and price. The last was a steep fifty euros, melted glacier water from the Arctic Circle. "I'm up for it."

"Dear God, no," George said. "I'm fine with tap."

A server appeared in a white shirt and black vest, carrying a bottle of wine. "Good evening, I'm assuming English is preferred." A few nods. "Very well. Corrado would like you to start off with a Col Fondo from Bele Casel, which is an older-style Prosecco from the Asolo DOCG." He smoothly and quietly opened the bottle and poured the cloudy wine into each glass. "Unlike normal Proseccos, this wine experiences secondary fermentation in the bottle. *Col Fondo* means 'with the bottom,' meaning including the sediment or lees. You'll find the result slightly funky, and even sour, but ultimately, transporting."

Once the server vanished, Bianca held up her glass to the others. "I'm so glad to have everyone join tonight, for what is my father's last in the city. I'm going to miss you, Dad. *Cin, cin.*"

"Hold up," Harold said thirty minutes and several dishes and glasses of wine later. "You got those scars fighting a squirrel?"

"Don't make him feel like a hero," Bianca said, laughing. Her nerves had fallen away after that first glass of Prosecco, and she'd been laughing ever since. What an exquisite evening, and it was even more marvelous that she'd started writing a new book today and that her dad was doing better than she'd ever seen him. What a perfect way to send him off.

Her mom wouldn't believe it.

George rolled back down his sleeve. "Mr. Nutz is no squirrel. If I know him, he's in my jacuzzi bath right now, sipping on a martini in my finest crystal."

A burst of laughter.

"And the squirrel feeder idea," Harold said, "it's brilliant. I'd fund that if I had any money, but I don't." The Prosecco and the other four or five glasses of wine had clearly gotten to Harold, but he wasn't alone. They'd all not eaten all day, so they were easy victims to alcohol.

In an instant, five servers appeared with the next dish. Before each person, they set down a series of small clay cylinders of various heights, each topped with a different delicacy from the sea.

The lead server pointed to each of Bianca's selections with his pinkie, saying, "This is a Hokkaido scallop laid back in its shell, topped with a blue shrimp caviar from Quebec. Then we have a tentacle tip of Italian octopus grilled over charcoal from our local forests and finished with a brush of black garlic–infused olive oil. And here, we have a sea urchin steamed custard, made with dashi and cream, drizzled with a warm saffron licorice butter. Lastly, a single shucked *Ostriche di San*

Teodoro from Sardinia, the finest oyster in Italy, presented inside a half shell resting on crushed ice, studded with edible flowers. It's topped with a black pearl sphere, which is a frozen orb of squid ink and sake that will melt into the brine after you pierce it with your teeth." He gave a chef's kiss.

There was barely a blink between the diners.

Another server handed him an opened bottle of wine. "And to pair, we've included from Emilia-Romagna an Albana, which is a white wine dressed in a red body, quite muscular and taut, very nice with the seafood. Please enjoy."

After pouring each a half glass, the server and his colleagues disappeared, leaving Bianca and the others to gawk at Corrado's mastery.

"Out of this world," Sandy said, lifting her fork.

"No can do on the octopus," Moira said, clearly buzzed. "They're smarter than me. I can't eat the tip of a tentacle. Not after I read *Remarkably Bright Creatures*."

"I'm the same," Harold agreed. "Did anyone else see *My Octopus Teacher*? No way."

"How about squid?" George asked. "Are they equally as smart?"

"It's their ink, though," Bianca said. "You have to at least try it."

"Oh, I will," George said. "I'll try every single thing, trust me. This promises to be the best meal of my entire life. It's not the same as the food back in Scottsdale, but the Italians definitely know how to cook."

"Um, yeah," Bianca said.

George raised a glass of the Albana. "This is a heck of a night, guys. Thank you for having me." After a sip, he said, "I must admit, Italy used to drive me crazy. Traveling used to drive me crazy. But I can see why you're here."

"So you'll be back soon?" Sandy asked, and Bianca thought she heard a twinge of hope in her voice.

"I'll certainly be back. You know, it's not every day you find community. What I've seen since I've been here, what I had the pleasure of witnessing yesterday. You don't find that everywhere. Maybe it's not Italy. I think it's that bookstore."

"That's what I keep telling Sandy," Moira said.

"Speaking of yesterday," Harold said, slightly mumbling his words, "Bianca and I came clean. Maybe this is a good time for everyone else too. Anyone else have secrets?" He slid his eyes to Moira, who shook her head.

"Bad idea," Sandy said.

Harold took another sip of wine. "Oh, c'mon, we're all friends here."

Silence.

Then a hand went up.

It was George, and all eyes went to him. "Actually, I have to get something off my chest, if you'd allow."

Oh, God, Bianca thought, *don't do it.* He was about to confess his love to Sandy.

The wine had gotten to George. He wasn't quite swimming, but he'd had enough to care very little about what might leave his mouth. Besides, he'd scrapped his plan to pull Corrado aside and had recommitted to telling Bianca the truth.

Might as well be now.

George cleared his throat and loaded the chamber. "I'm going to get in trouble, but I can't go home without coming clean." He stopped himself from having another drink and put his attention on Bianca. "Shortly after we came back from our trip, our father-daughter adventure, I . . ."

A sobering freeze hit him. "Shit, I shouldn't be doing this," he said.

"Of course you should," Harold slurred. He'd clearly taken Bianca's orders to heart not to eat all day. Poor kid probably weighed only one thirty.

George turned back to Bianca, feeling like the most epic of failures. "I ran into Corrado on the street. Told him that the two of you weren't a good fit, that he was acting selfishly if he continued any relationship with you."

"What?" His daughter's eyebrows crinkled. "You're kidding me."

"I'm so sorry. It's none of my business, and I screwed up, and I . . . I don't seem to learn, but believe me, I'm trying. And this is me trying to make it right. I have no right to get in the way of your life. You have things figured out *far* more than me." His throat tightened. "I was trying to get you back home. You're all I've got left, B." He stopped there, unsure what else to say.

Bianca felt everyone watching her, waiting for her to snap at her dad. Their lovely night had possibly reached its conclusion. Her mind spun. When and how and why? Well, not why. She knew why.

Her father wouldn't learn.

"When was this?" Her words were arrows dipped in poison.

"The day we got back from Florence."

Bianca nodded. She'd gone to see Corrado a day after that. Was that why he'd rejected her?

"And you think getting in the way of my love life, or my life here, will make things better between us? You think that's what will bring me home?"

No one else at the table moved.

"Old habits, honey. That's all. That wasn't the man I want to be. That wasn't the man I am. It was like this leftover remnant of the me who came here, that shell of a man who nearly took his own life."

Sandy gasped, worry painting her face. Harold and Moira stared down at the table. Bianca hated hearing Geore say it out loud, but there was strength in admission.

"It wasn't the man I am, the one you helped me rediscover on our trip." George glanced at Sandy, then back to Bianca. "I'm sorry. I didn't want to tell you, but that wasn't the way for me to leave, hiding behind a lie. I totally get that you're angry and you can't wait till I'm on that plane, and . . ."

His words trailed off.

Bianca could see through all of him, knew him so well. He'd been exhibiting the same patterns all her life. Breaking and fixing things, over and over.

Had anything changed?

She didn't know. But she thought of her father back home a few months ago, kicked to the curb by the company he'd dedicated his life to, faced with a lifetime full of regret and empty of purpose.

An image of him holding a pill bottle emerged.

But just as quickly it turned to smoke.

In the last couple of weeks, she'd seen flickers of light and hope that could be signs of change. He *was* trying. She could see that. He couldn't have been more graceful and loving when he'd taken her into his arms after she'd said such unforgivable things to him in Rome.

And how could she let him return home in even worse condition than he was upon arrival? If she cut him loose now, how long till he held those pills in his hand again? Or considered buying a gun?

He'd just admitted to this group that he'd been suicidal! That level of awareness, the ability to admit your weaknesses, spoke to a man who was ready to change.

And who the hell did she think she was, riding in on her magic carpet of perfection? No, no, *no.* If anyone was flawed here, it was her. But, dammit, life was hard, and everybody needed a break sometimes.

She tucked a stray strand of hair around her ear, glanced at everyone, then went back to thinking. They could all sit and fucking wait if they had to, because she had things to figure out.

A choice had to be made. Shut him down and tell him to get out of the restaurant and her life. Or she could connect with him, forgive him. If she thought that he was going to do a sudden one-eighty and have it all figured out, then she was nothing more than a hopeless romantic.

It was okay to be damaged and to have screwed up and to have missed chances, because we're all human. But we have the potential to resurrect, to forgive.

To love.

"Dad, I forgive you."

The surprise on his face was an image she'd hold on to forever, because it marked a change in her relationship with herself and with him and with everything around her.

"You don't have to say that."

"Of course I don't." The stage was hers. The table was dead silent. "I don't want perfection, Dad. I want *trying*, and I know you're doing that. Trying equals love. You admitting this to me, in front of friends, is what matters. We're all damaged, Dad. I have all the room in the world in my heart for damaged people who are trying to get better every day. People like you. People like me and everyone else at this table. For the first time in my life, I'm willing to start living despite being damaged."

She sighed. "I guess what I'm saying is, I'm here for you even when you mess up. And maybe you'd say the same to me."

"You're damn right, I would. There is no world, no possible reason, where I'm not there for you."

"That's enough to keep me going right there."

"You and me both," George whispered.

Bianca reached for his hand, knowing she'd never loved her father more than in this moment.

Shortly after, Sandy made one of the hardest decisions of her life.

"Okay, okay, I'll jump in. I don't like being left behind." For one, she wanted to spare George from more of the spotlight. The sweet man had put it out there. And what a man for doing so. It just about killed her to know he'd been suicidal; he'd never once hinted at it. Thank God he was doing better. And she couldn't remember seeing a dad care so much for his daughter. What a man, indeed.

"For the record, George," Sandy said, "I know you do what you do out of love. Bianca knows that too. You're both very lucky to have each other, and that's why . . . why I want to—no—need to say this."

Their ears perked up like Dobermans. Nobody touched their food.

"My son. Jack." She felt for the coral in her purse. Sandy sighed, the weight of the world pulling her down. "He's not coming back."

"He's mad at you?" Harold slurred.

A sharp pain hit her chest. Sandy could still see the two men who'd been waiting outside her apartment after work eight years ago. It was a chilly December day, drawing near to Christmas. Strings of lights illuminated Via Giulia. Wreaths adorned many of the doors. And an embassy staffer and a marine in dress blues, younger than Jack, stood with their hands behind their backs.

Sandy had folded, her heart shattering.

Upstairs a few minutes later, as she brushed tears from her cheeks, the marine had said, "The Commandant of the Marine Corps has asked me to express his deepest regret that your son, Lance Corporal Jack Cooke, died last week during an enemy action in Syria."

That was the day Sandy had died inside. She'd never told a soul in Bologna.

Till now.

"No," Sandy said, finally able to get her tongue to work. "He was taken from us."

"What?" Harold said. "I thought he was in the Middle East."

She couldn't believe she'd said it out loud. "Not anymore. I still call him, leave messages. I've kept his cell phone account active, just so I can keep hearing his voicemail, talk to him like he's still here."

Moira reached for Sandy's hand. "I can't imagine."

Sandy dropped the piece of coral and collapsed her head onto her arms on the table, spilling out tears around her untouched course.

The other four swarmed her, patting her neck and back and assuring her it would be okay, and that they loved her and understood. So much of Sandy wanted to either rise up and start swinging or slip down low and crawl out of there, but the rest of her felt their love and acceptance, and she let that part win.

Harold had never had a night like this in his life. Not even Aroldo had had a night like this. They made a strange crew, but it felt like his crew nonetheless, and he felt as sad as ever to leave Bologna.

They were all returning to their chairs after comforting Sandy when Moira suddenly said, "May I admit something?"

Everyone laughed, because if it was a joke, it was a pretty good one.

"We already know all your secrets," Sandy said, her old self poking through. "What now? Did you read the last chapter of *Where the Crawdads Sing* before you started? Or did you have gelato for breakfast yesterday?" A smile surfaced, because she was joking this time, teasing. And that probably had to stop too.

Moira said with surprising attitude, "Do you want to keep going?"

Sandy whispered a sorry and said, "I'm done. And I'll try harder, Moira. I'll do better."

"You don't have to quit being you, Sandy. You're funny when you're not being mean. As I was saying . . ." She leaned forward and whispered, "This is maybe the stupidest thing I've done since marrying my ex, but I want to share something because I'm tired of hiding. I'm tired of no one knowing the real me."

Silence.

"And maybe by sharing you'll see what you people mean to me. I know it sounds silly, but you're the only family I have left in my life . . . and I . . . I want you to know who I am. And I suppose it goes without saying that you can't tell anyone else. Because it would put me in danger, and I'd likely get moved to another city, another country."

"Um, maybe you shouldn't say anything else," Harold suggested.

Moira drew in the last breath of a woman protecting a secret, then let it out. "I'm in the UK Protected Persons Service, the British version of the witness protection program."

Eye rolls ran round the room.

Moira didn't flinch.

The table sat silently, waiting for her to laugh or admit she was kidding. In the seconds that passed, what felt like a full minute, Harold started to think that maybe she was telling the truth. He knew she'd been protecting her past.

"You're serious, aren't you?" he asked.

"Deadly."

A fist slammed down to the table, knocking the tentacle tips off their towers. "I knew it!" Sandy yelled. "You and your made-up story about your aunt. I knew there was something fishy going on."

"Wait, what?" Bianca said.

"Details, please," Harold said. "I mean, if you're really confessing."

"For what it's worth, I didn't do anything wrong, other than marry the wrong man."

Bianca asked, "Your family back home doesn't even know?"

Moira gestured behind her with her hand. "Mum and Dad both died a few years back. Had to start over here."

Harold set his hands on his head. "Is Moira even your name?"

She shook her head.

"Well, don't tell us," Bianca said. "Don't get yourself in trouble."

"I'm not. I can't. Last thing I want is all of you googling me."

"It's a thing?" Harold asked. "You were in the papers?"

Her lack of response indicated a resounding *yes*.

Harold couldn't deny that her sexiness factor had shot up by millions. His friends had no idea who he was bringing into their gaming club.

The silence forced Moira to keep going. "He was messing around with some baddies. I suppose he was a baddie himself."

"I like that word—*baddie*," Harold said.

George shushed him. "Let her speak."

Moira shook her head. "I can't believe I've said it out loud. I have to admit, it feels so . . . liberating." She continued, "I was a harmless librarian who fell in love with a—"

"A librarian?" Sandy said. "That explains it."

Moira nodded. "Anyway, I saw something I shouldn't have—something his business partner had done—and told him we had to call the police. He lost it and threatened to kill me if I opened my mouth. Apparently he'd been part of it, a criminal enterprise of sorts. I had *no* idea. And I didn't heed his warning. Snuck out a window, climbed down a fire escape, and ran to the police station. Left my whole life behind. I've been hiding ever since." She shrugged. "Other than when I attended the trial. He and a few other men were sentenced to twenty-plus years. And I'm in Bologna unless they find me. Then I'll be thrown into a Grisham novel, running for my life."

"That's right," Sandy said. "One of Grisham's books was set here; the protagonist was hiding."

Moira gave a nod.

"You're a badass," Harold declared.

Sandy was shaking her head. "And there I was, calling you a mouse, you lion you."

Moira shrugged. "Can't judge a book by its cover."

"Oh, God," Sandy said. "Please don't end this spectacular revelation with a cliché."

“Sorry. But seriously, please, let’s not talk about this ever again. If my protection officer even got suspicious, she’d send me packing. I’d lose my job, the bookstore. You guys.”

Harold raised his wine to toast Moira. “Your secret is safe here.”

Everyone agreed and clinked glasses.

As Harold brought the glass to his lips, he saw Alice enter the room. Leading the way, guiding her diamond-studded hand, was Renzo, the thief of strawberry lovers.

Chapter 32

THE ARCHNEMESIS

It wasn't the diamond that shone. It was Alice. The girl could still command a room, be it a coffee shop or a fancy restaurant, by simply walking into it. Renzo admittedly had a way about him, too, so smooth and effortless, a model right out of *GQ*.

Harold was minorly relieved when the host guided Alice and her evil guardian to a table on the other side of the restaurant.

"What's wrong?" Bianca asked him, then followed his gaze. "Ah. Is that the redhead you talked about yesterday?"

A nod.

As Renzo helped Alice into her chair, he happened to glance up and see the table of gawkers staring at him. A second later, he locked eyes with Harold. The man confidently extended his middle finger.

"Ouch," Bianca said.

"Asshole, right?" Harold said, incredulous. This wasn't even about Alice. Not now. If anything, this was more about Renzo and Harold than Alice and Harold.

"I can't believe they're here," Moira said. "What are the chances?"

Harold was trying not to look, but he noticed Alice pull her napkin onto her lap, then say something to the server. He hoped she was ordering that fancy Arctic water. The least she could do was waste Renzo's money.

Harold had gotten over her. Aroldo would want her back, but only for the game of it. And it didn't matter because Aroldo was dead. Alice had never really known Harold and certainly had never loved him. And now he wasn't even sure he'd ever loved her. Only in the last day or so had he felt like himself, and she hadn't held much weight in his mind.

"This must hurt," Sandy said. Everyone at the table was silent, picking at tentacles and oysters, sitting in the discomfort of this unfortunate coincidence.

"Oh, c'mon, guys," Harold said. "We're having so much fun. Anyone else have another secret worth sharing? I wish I could say something like I was undercover right now, busting bookstores that didn't have romance sections. But I have nothing else. A few days and I'll be back in my mom's house and trying to figure out how to pay her and the credit card companies back for financing my trip. Then maybe I can take out some loans for college."

Sandy seized that nugget. "And what will you do with a degree, dear Harold? I'm proud of you, by the way. We're going to miss you here. Who else will I tango with?"

Harold dipped a spoon into the sea urchin. After a bite that was somewhere between delicious and bizarre, he said, "That's very sweet of you, and you know what, I did have a fleeting thought, that despite my clumsy sensibilities, I might find a dance class back in Denver. The tango resonated with me."

"Let me tell you something. And I promise I'm not sugarcoating. You have an innate talent on the dance floor. I so hope you'll keep dancing."

"Thanks, Sandy. I appreciate everything you've done for me."

Two courses later, Chef Corrado appeared at the table. "How's everyone enjoying the meal?"

George gave a thumbs-up and swooned over the slow-cooked scorpion fish ragù. It was the most normal and delicious course so far. Sandy and Bianca golf-clapped and professed their love of everything.

Harold had to ask, "Just curious. See that couple over there? How'd they get into your special night? Friends of yours?"

Corrado looked over, then: "Yes, Renzo. He built the hotel, so he receives good treatment. Do you know him?"

"Barely." *He only tried to ruin my life and is now taunting me.*

Corrado left with, "If I can do anything for you, let me know. The best is yet to come."

The five of them returned to their remaining courses. A duck liver pâté, a roasted pigeon breast scattered with cocoa nibs. Foods that Harold had never even heard of before, but he tried them with an open mind.

"What do you think about all this?" Moira asked Harold on the seventh course. The others had fallen into their own conversation.

"I think I'm drunk and can't eat another bite."

"I'm a wee bit tipsy too," she whispered. "I can't believe we have two more courses to go."

"That's almost as shocking as you dropping the biggest nuclear bomb of a secret in the history of secrets."

"I know, I know. Regret is currently nipping at my heels."

Harold rubbed his belly. "Would it be strange if I stuck my finger down my throat in the bathroom? Just so I can keep going."

"No, I think it's a great idea. You could even start all over." She chuckled. "No, Harold. No fingers down your throat. It's not even funny."

"It kind of was, though, right?" Harold said. "Don't get all prim and proper now. Your dark sense of humor is one of your most appealing qualities."

"That right?"

"And now I know where you get it from. Married to the English mob. Is it called the Mob in England? Or Mafia? Or is that only Italian?" He leaned closer. "You have to tell me more. I mean, don't tell me your name. Or his name. Unless you want to."

"I can't. You'd have a proper shock reading about it. We were all over the place back in . . . Well, anyway. And no, I wouldn't call it the Mafia, but it's similar. How about organized crime?"

"Look at you, the wife of a—"

"Ex-wife."

"Ex-wife of an organized crime boss. A librarian, no less, who took down an entire organization? Sent men to prison. And here I am, departing after a few months playing a digital nomad on a stage without an audience. A residency, if you like, and now I'm heading back to my mom's basement, where we will watch Bob Ross and eat microwave dinners. I don't even have a right to sit next to you."

"That's not true," she said quietly, their exhilarating conversation shrouded in secrecy. "Will you stop it? Didn't you learn anything from Bianca yesterday?"

"I did. And I get it. No more Aroldo if that's what you mean. Still, in the competition for most interesting at this table, you're lengths ahead. I'm dying to know what your real name is. Can we play the name game? Because I think a person's name typically captures them well. You might be a Ruth? Or a Dolly? No, something more British? Jane or Elizabeth? If I were a British librarian, I might be a . . . Francis? Or a Sarah?"

Smirking, she pushed the plate with the pigeon away and set her fork down. "I don't think you want to know."

"I kind of do if we're going to be friends forever. Am I supposed to keep calling you Moira? Who came up with Moira, anyway? Your handler?"

"She's not a handler; she's a case manager."

"Not as glamorous. But I do like that she's a *she*." A conversation they'd had earlier in the summer came back to him. "Sidebar," he said. "Remember that night when we were at the wine bar. You'd said you were from Bristol, but then all of a sudden you were from Dorset."

A flash of knowing came over her. "You were onto something."

"Ah, I should have been paying more attention." He leaned in closer. "Don't worry, I am taking this seriously. I won't ever utter a word to anyone."

Interrupting, the collection of servers brought them each a plate with a small square on it, something that looked like dessert.

"This is a towel to clean your hands; please don't eat it," the lead server said, then lifted up a kettle and poured hot water over Harold's square. It expanded like one of those bath toy sponges that grow into dinosaurs.

Moira sat back so the server could transform her square into a towel next. "You know what? When you're being yourself, you're curious, incredibly funny, and handsome too. I love how your brain works, the way you're onto one thing, and then onto another before you finish. You're such a bright guy, Harold. And I think whatever it is you do, you'll be great at it."

"You have me confused with someone else," Harold said, reaching for the warm towel and unraveling it.

"Stop it." Moira gestured across the dining room at Alice, who was stabbing at something on her plate. "Trust me, one day, after their divorce, she'll be craving someone who actually loved her."

Harold cleaned his hands and then patted his lips with the towel. "I don't know if I loved her. I really don't. I look over there now, and I see a stranger. It doesn't matter what she thinks, anyway. I've moved on."

Moira took her towel off the plate. "Just like that?"

"Believe me, I have no feelings at all toward her. Nada."

"That's Spanish. Try *niente.*"

"Niente," Harold said, perhaps too loudly. Everyone at their table, and the surrounding tables glanced over.

Brave and drunk Harold said again, "*Niente!*" Then he pointed at Renzo, sitting there guzzling wine, and repeated, *"Niente!"*

As if only to draw a reaction from Harold, Renzo reached for Alice's hand and started to pet it. The large diamond shone under the light. Then he looked back at Harold and winked.

A fucking wink.

Next thing Harold saw was a piece of focaccia crossing in a grand arc over three tables, spinning like a ninja star and striking Renzo in the side of the head. It then tumbled onto the table.

Renzo whipped around, his forehead so tight the skin might tear.

"What a jerk, taunting you," Moira said, a sinister grin lighting her face. She'd done it, thrown the focaccia. This girl was full of surprises. If she wasn't careful, Harold was going to fall in love—the real kind.

Then Alice called out, "Harold?"

He raised a drunken wave, still dumbfounded by the fact that Moira had just slung a piece of bread across the dining room of the fanciest restaurant Harold could ever have imagined. All for him!

Bianca, George, and Sandy were now involved, wondering what was going on.

"I better go say something," Harold said, the wine giving him ample courage.

He rose and planted a surprise kiss on Moira's mouth; she gasped. Even Aroldo didn't have that in him. "Thank you for defending me," he said. "Be right back." He crossed the restaurant to the rhythm of the silky bossa nova track that played in the background.

Reaching their table, he said to Alice, *"Buonasera."*

She lifted her hands, palms up. "What are you doing here? And did you really just throw bread at us?"

He glanced over at his partner-in-crime, the former librarian who'd risked her life to testify against her husband, a superhero fighting for justice. The girl who'd just now stood up for Harold. The girl he'd just kissed! Even he hadn't seen that one coming.

She and the rest of his table were watching him.

"That was my friend. Sorry about that. We're a little rowdy over there." The hurled slice of focaccia rested innocently on the white tablecloth. "And how are you?"

"Fine! Yeah, fine."

"And goodbye, Aroldo," Renzo chimed in. "You'll be walking away now."

Harold had nearly forgotten he was there. He swiveled his head and inspected him, slowly taking him in. The guy wasn't as intimidating as he once was, despite the fury running through him. Which maybe he wasn't to blame for. He had been the victim of a bread assault.

Harold pointed to a patch of whiskers above Renzo's upper lip. "You missed a spot shaving, just so you know."

"You need to walk away."

Harold held his gaze long enough for Renzo to see that he wasn't afraid of him, then twisted back to Alice. "You can do better than him. I hope you know that."

Renzo forced a laugh.

Harold pointed at him, still looking into Alice's green eyes. "This isn't me trying to get you back. I've moved on. But I still want the best for you. And this guy, he's not the best for you." He let his eyes slide to the ring on her finger.

Renzo pushed away from the table and stepped toward Harold. He was a good six inches taller and probably had fifty more pounds of muscle. "You don't know me."

Other patrons were watching now.

"Don't get in my face," Harold said, feeling no fear.

"Is there a problem?" Renzo poked Harold in the chest. "You need to go back to your friends before you regret it."

Harold inspected the impression the Italian Stallion's index finger had left on his shirt. *What to do?* he wondered. The guy needed to be taught a lesson.

Then Renzo pushed him, two hands on Harold's ribs.

That was it, the answer Harold had needed. Before he second-guessed himself, he struck Renzo in the stomach, and then popped him again, right in the cheek, two hard and fast jabs.

Harold and Alice both watched in shock as Renzo dropped to the ground, his head smacking the tile.

He was out cold.

Embarrassed.

Mortified.

Ashamed.

Gutted.

Words couldn't capture Bianca's inner turmoil as she watched the scene unfold. Moira chucking bread across the restaurant, Harold throwing a punch, the man going down. An enraged Corrado racing from the kitchen and seizing Harold by the arm and escorting him out of the restaurant. An army of servers tending to the assaulted man on the floor and offering apologies to the redhead and the other nearby diners.

Once Bianca regained some clarity, she looked at her table compatriots. "We better go. Right now. I'll take care of the bill." Quiet nods rounded the table. The four of them stood and wordlessly moved toward the exit.

Corrado was just returning from the hotel lobby. He shot sharp looks at the retreaters.

Bianca stopped him in the reception area. "I'm so sorry. I don't even know what to say. That was freaking awful."

His jaw tight, he gave a sharp nod.

She dug into her purse and found her wallet. "Let me give you my card. We didn't get a chance to pay the server. I just wanted us out of there."

He stopped her with his hand. "Don't worry about it."

"No way, Corrado. I'm paying."

"Please," he said with grating patience, "just take your friends a long way from here. I have to deal with this."

Fighting him on it now would only make things worse. Deciding she'd pay him later, she stuffed her wallet back in her purse. "I really am sorry."

He gave another nod and raced back into the dining room.

Sandy was the first to reach Harold outside on the sidewalk that ran along Via dell'Indipendenza. "Are you okay?" Pedestrians weaved around them. Cars whizzed by.

He was pacing in circles. "I don't know what came over me."

Sandy held up his hand to inspect his raw knuckles. "You'll need to take care of that when you get home. Wash and put some Vaseline or something on, then Band-Aids."

"Don't worry about me. God, I feel like such a fucking idiot. I just hate that guy."

"Didn't I warn you about love?" Sandy asked. He made no comment.

George and Moira joined, and Harold made the first of a dozen apologies. When Bianca exited the hotel, he said to her, "I am so sorry, Bianca. He was such an asshole to me, and it happened so fast and—"

She stopped him. "It's okay."

"Seriously. I'm mortified. I had too much to drink, and he was taunting me, then pushed me . . . I'll pay the bill."

"Corrado covered it."

Harold dropped his head, defeated, cursing himself. Sandy's heart broke for him. He'd been beat up enough in this life. At least he'd stood up for himself. There was that.

Moira slipped an arm around his waist. "Why don't we get you home?"

He nodded, offered another apology, and the two of them disappeared into the night. Sandy saw it for the first time, that Harold and Moira had a chance at love if they had the nerve to give it a try. You couldn't find two better people, that was for sure.

"I guess this is it," George said, appearing next to Sandy. She giggled to herself. She, on the other hand, did not have the nerve.

Sandy crossed her arms, knowing she was leaving something on the table here. As if she had a choice. "I can't believe you're going back."

"What a way to go out, huh?"

"A night to remember. I feel so bad for Bianca. I know she's devastated."

"And Corrado," George added. "On opening night."

"Yeah, I know." A silence cut through them. Sandy couldn't handle it and asked, "How long till we see you again?"

George glanced at his daughter, who'd backed away to let them talk. "Whenever she's ready."

"You better start working on your Italian again. I get the sense she's not coming home any time soon."

"Yeah, me too."

More silence. Sandy couldn't deny that this was hard, saying goodbye, shutting the door on could-have-beens. Men like him didn't come around too often.

She straightened the collar of his shirt, then said, "Make sure to leave things in a good place between you two. Because you never know when you're saying goodbye for the last time. Know what I mean?"

He lifted a corner of his lips. "I do."

Their eyes held each other in limbo for a long time, the world spinning around them, the night carrying on.

"Was nice to meet you," George said, and she could tell he was frustrated. And he had every right to be. She'd screwed it all up and let her wretched past win. What was she to do? It was too late now.

"I'm sorry, George. You're such a good man. Make sure to look me up when you get back."

"You know I will. Bye, Sandy."

She feared he might stick out his hand for a shake, so she leaned in, kissed his cheek, and pulled him in tight, wishing things could be different, wishing he'd been the first man with whom she'd ever fallen in love.

Chapter 33

Leather in the Rain

Sandy went walking. She wandered for a good two hours before finally reaching her apartment.

So much on her mind, so much regret.

Pushing open the door, she kicked off her heels. Nicolo came rushing down the hall and weaved between her legs. *"Che notte."* What a night.

She poured herself a glass of wine and sat at the dining room table. Her stray curled up below, his head on her foot. After a while, she dialed Jack's phone, listened to his greeting, then said, "Guess the cat's out of the bag now. Does it change anything? I don't know."

The hole in her heart swelled.

She fell silent. Only when the phone beeped did she realize she was still leaving a message.

She hung up and dialed again. "Sorry, I was drifting off. So here I am, Jack. I don't know what to do. You're gone and not coming back. What do I do without you? I don't like being alone. I don't. Like. Being. Alone."

A sigh escaped her. She ended the call and let her head fall. As she collapsed onto the table, all the loneliness she'd ever known pecked at her, making it worse than ever.

She withdrew the coral from her pocket and ran her thumb over it. Despite a difficult childhood, Jack had always loved Florida and had carried this piece of coral in his pocket during deployments to remind him of what he was fighting for. After his death, the army had shipped her an envelope holding his wallet, his dog tags, and the coral. She'd kept it near ever since.

Though the coral often brought her comfort, tonight it only made things worse. What a terror to be human, to want connection so desperately but to be so vulnerable because of it. It wasn't that she'd lost Jack eight years ago; she lost him every second of every day, over and over again.

Was it any wonder she didn't want to endure more loss?

Nicolo stared up at her, and she said, "I know you're enough. It's that I . . . Maybe you're not. I don't know. Maybe you're not enough. Sorry, close your ears."

Leaving the coral on the place mat, she retreated to her bedroom to fade away. After a sleepless hour of stewing in a cauldron of loneliness, she took a shower, then tried to sleep again.

Nothing. Eyes wide open, her mind on fire.

Nicolo kept his distance, clearly insulted by what she'd said earlier.

Not even a book—not even Diana Gabaldon—could take her away from the emptiness inside. Who the hell wanted to read about love that they themselves would never experience? As far as Sandy was concerned, the only banned books should be romance! That's the dumb shit you think about when you're exhausted.

In fact, another sleepless hour and she was going to host a book burning right outside the store. She'd burn every love story left in the store—even if it was a side plot—but she'd start with the one that'd caused all the trouble in the first place, the book that had instilled hopeless romantic dreams for more than two centuries: *Pride and Prejudice*. How sweet it would be to watch those pages burn. Enjoying the end of all hope for Mr. Darcy and for love itself.

Sandy went to the window and looked down on the street, and as stupid as it was, she wondered whether George was up. Knowing him, he'd have already left for the airport to be three hours early. She let go of the blinds and returned to bed.

Eventually she grabbed her phone, put on her readers, and googled his name, George Briggs. There he was on LinkedIn.

He was too old, too organized. And he lived in Arizona. She wasn't going back to the States. "No offense, US," she whispered out loud. "You're fine and all, but you've got nothing on Bologna."

Still, she couldn't let him leave without a proper goodbye. He'd been good to her. The least she could do was show up for him and say that it had been nice, them talking and getting to know each other. He was funny. Terrible shoes, but he was one of the few on earth who could make her laugh. Great hair too.

While she was at it, she had to admit that his love for his daughter, though clumsy at times, was the same kind of love she'd always felt for Jack, even now, eight years after her son had left this earth.

Sandy dressed and descended the steps. She decided she wasn't going to do some stupid Nick Hornby–novel thing, where she chased George to the airport. He'd either be there or he wouldn't. Note to self: Burn all the Nick Hornbys tomorrow!

Via Giulia was dead quiet at 3:15 a.m. Even the Italians had closed down their celebrations for the night. A street cat dashed into an alley. A mourning dove was perched on a wire waiting for the sun to peek through the buildings.

A lone taxi passed by, stopping in front of Bianca's place a block down.

Sandy's heart felt strange, the way it seemed to come to life. Then she saw him, dragging a bag over the hump of the doorway.

"George," she called out.

He didn't hear her.

Damn him, he was going to make her run, and that's what she did.

If that wasn't a sign for something.

Sandy was not one to run. Not even if she was caught in suede in the rain.

Sandy Cooke ran for no one.

But she was running for George and calling out his name as the taxi driver popped the trunk and climbed out.

George was slinging his bag into the back when he finally heard her. "Sandy? What are you doing?"

"I've no idea," she said, their proximity driving her mad. "Couldn't sleep. Nice cool night too." She had to say more. She wasn't here to comment about the stupid weather. She kept approaching, and she wasn't sure whether she could tolerate another handshake or cheeky hug.

Sandy stopped three feet from him, this man who'd invaded her heart. What was she to do now? She looked at the taxi driver and said, *"Potestri aspettare in macchina, per favore? Ho una queastione in sospeso con quest'uomo."* Will you please wait in the car? I have some unfinished business with this man.

He gave a nod and retreated to his seat, shutting the door.

Back to George, she said, "You kept me up all night."

"Why's that?"

She looked into his eyes. "Dammit, why are you doing this to me?"

Poor George looked at her like he'd done something wrong. "Doing what?"

Ripping the words from her throat, she said, "For some God-knows-what reason, I don't want you to leave, and I think I'm sad about it."

He gave his handsome laugh. "Ah."

It wasn't only his laugh. Something she'd said seemed to wake him, his face gathering color, his eyes widening.

Sandy moved closer, wanting to take his hand but terrified. "I don't want you to go. There. I said it. And it's your fault, all of it. I tried to stay out of the way, but I'm sad about you leaving. And yesterday. Last night when we said goodbye. All I could think about was how I couldn't lose you. There was no way I could lose you, not see you again. Not see those stupid white tennis shoes and even stupider pink tools and your great hair. I hate the idea of you not being around to make your silly jokes, always trying to make me smile."

George ran a hand through his hair, probably frustrated with her—or soaking up her "great hair" flattery.

She wasn't done. "Okay, fine, I surrender. I want more from you than just being friends, and I have no idea how it would ever work, but I'd like to try. I *want* to try." Something else occurred to her. "I'm sorry I lied about my son, by the way. I won't lie to you again; it was this thing I kept doing, pretending, holding back the pain, burying it away."

He nodded. "I understand."

She raised a finger. "For the record, I've tried to spare you from me, but it seems you're dumber than you look and maybe I am, too, and . . . Ugh, I've never talked so much in my life. Do you hear what I'm trying to—"

The taxi driver reached a hand out the window. *"Andiamo!"*

"Are you kidding me? *Puoi aspettare.*" You can wait. She said a few less ladylike words too.

"I do have a plane to catch," George said sheepishly.

Her mouth fell open, wide enough to fit the whole damn collection from the Library of Congress. "I spill my guts and that's all you have to say?"

"What do you want, Sandy? I tried. You can't throw all this at me in the final hour."

"The final hour? What are you, dying? Don't be so dramatic. There are always more planes. Every day there are planes."

Doing something that Sandy Cooke didn't do, she reached for his hand and said, "I like you, George. And I don't want you to leave."

"I live in Arizona."

"Which is dumb. You don't belong there."

"What else do you want me to do?"

"What do you think? Move to Italy."

"Are you kidding? I can't move to Italy."

"What else do you have to do?"

He shook his head. "Sorry."

"Okay, fine. Then how about you come upstairs? Don't look at me like that. It's not a brothel. I'm saying come up to my place so we can talk about it. Get a flight tomorrow. Or the next day. But give me a morning to work through whatever the hell has brought us to this moment."

He laughed. "You're a mess."

"Got that right. But you do something to me, George, and I don't want you to stop doing it. You hear me?" She squeezed his hand tighter. "You've broken through and now I'm all yours. I want to give us a shot, and I don't give a shit if you're living on a golf course in a state with such high temperatures that it cooks people in the summer, while I'm over here in paradise. We'll figure that out. For now, let the taxi go, and let's drink a cup of coffee, because I'm tired and you don't look too perky yourself."

George glanced back at the door to Bianca's apartment, then at the cab and Sandy.

"That's all I got, George. I wouldn't blame you if you climb into that taxi and run from all that's me, but what I hope you do is close the trunk and come upstairs for a coffee. I don't do Nespresso. I make the real thing. You'll never have another one like it."

George held eye contact for a while and then turned back to the car. He lifted his bag out of the trunk. Sandy's heart grew wings. That's what she got for opening herself back up to love.

George set his bag down, slipped his arm around her.

"Good choice," she whispered, moving closer to him, inches away.

"It better be great coffee," he whispered, their eyes drawing each other in.

She pressed a grin into his lips. "The best you've ever had." They kissed warmly, deeply, without any holding back.

The driver yelled through the window, *"Andiamo!"*

"Lui sta con me!" He's staying here with me!

In the elevator, she said, "No one's been up here, other than the plumber and electrician, since Jack."

George was still tasting that kiss, thinking about how long he'd wanted it. Now he couldn't stop thinking about how there was promise of many more of those. Maybe he had done something right along the way.

"Nicolo will probably try to kill you," she said, as she jiggled the keys in the lock.

"Nicolo? You have some sort of Russian bodyguard up here?"

"He's my cat, remember?"

"Oh, that's right."

She led him in, and the cat came running.

"Hey, Nicolo," George said. He'd never been much of an animal person but ran his fingers through his fur and made short conversation. The cat kept swerving around and coming back for more.

"How about that?" Sandy said.

"He's got good taste in men," he said.

She took his hand to show him around. The place was as classy as she was. Remarkably clean. Wonderful art. Sharp furniture. A stack of jazz records in vinyl next to a pair of large speakers in the living room.

They stood on the rug, and she folded into him. "About that coffee."

George tasted her again, wondering where any of this was going to go. The morning. The day. Tomorrow. The next.

"Sugar and cream," he said, feeling his nether regions come alive.

"You drink it black here."

"Fair enough."

He ran his fingers up her sides, then went in for another kiss, and maybe it was him, but the lights flickered and the walls shook.

An hour later, someone rang the bell.

"Si?" Sandy said into the intercom.

"It's Bianca. Can I please come up?"

Sandy looked back down the hall. George was in the shower. "Um, yeah, okay." Somehow his daughter knew where he'd ended up. Had he texted her?

Sandy opened the door to find Bianca standing in a near fighter's stance. "Can I say something to you?" she asked Sandy.

"Yeah."

"You just let a great man leave this city without you. You let a great man walk out when you know damn well he loved you. When you know you'll never find another like him."

Sandy started to reply, but Bianca didn't let her.

"You're a cliché, a classic wall builder, who lets the good things pass you by because you're too afraid to open yourself up to them. And I'm sorry about your son. I can't imagine, but the idea that you refuse to let love into your heart ever again, it's moronic. You push Moira around like she's nothing. Same with everyone in your life. And yet people still try with you. George *tried*, and he would have been the best thing that ever happened to you."

Sandy attempted to interrupt, but—

"He might not be perfect, but who is? What I can tell you is that he's loyal and sweet and loves harder than he can handle; that's why he messes up sometimes. But let's be honest, there's nothing perfect about you. I guess I'm here to say that you messed up, and you better know it. He's such a good man, a great father, a—"

"B?" came George's voice from over Sandy's shoulder.

The two women turned to find George standing in a towel, his hair soaking wet.

"Dad?" Bianca looked to him, then to Sandy.

"I was trying to say," Sandy started. "I didn't let him leave."

Bianca pointed at her dad, then Sandy, then back. "Wait? You two?"

"She was pretty convincing," George said.

"What about your flight?"

"There'll be more planes. Sandy's asked me to hang around a few days. Figure us out."

Bianca turned to Sandy again. "Well, this is awkward. Can I take back everything I said? Actually, not everything. As a textbook wall builder—and it takes one to know one—you better get to work deconstructing."

"Fair enough. May I say that I very much appreciate a gal who looks out for her dad?"

"Yeah, well, he's a good one."

Sandy reached out to him, and George joined her. "Yes, he is," she said.

Epilogue

Snapshots of Afterward

Five days later

The elevator door cracked open, and Bianca looked left and right. There was no one in the hallway, no one stirring, not even a mouse. Without second-guessing herself, she tore off her top and dropped her skirt, then removed her undergarments, leaving it all in a pile at her feet.

He was home, as he'd just buzzed her in.

She wore nothing but heels and a pair of earrings as she approached his door. A small voice told her that she better stop these shenanigans, but a bigger voice told her that this was who she was and that's who she was going to be.

Bianca knocked on the door, then hid out of sight so he couldn't get a sneak peek through the peephole.

Thank God no one else on his floor appeared.

This *was* her, all of her. Bianca Briggs. Fully living in this moment. Not waiting till she weighed less or until she had it all mapped out.

Was she leaving burn marks? Yeah, perhaps. What was wrong with that? Maybe her book did have a few good pieces.

The door finally cracked open. She took a breath, closed her eyes, then stepped forward and held open her arms. "I am officially giving you all of me."

With her eyes still closed, she waited for him to seize her. Because she definitely didn't look *that* bad, and let's be honest, he'd never shown anything other than a mad desire for her. The only thing in their way had been her mind.

Corrado did not seize her as she'd hoped.

Instead, she heard a harrumph that sounded distinctly female, then a few Italian words spoken so quickly that Bianca couldn't catch the meaning.

She opened her eyes to find a woman twice her age staring at her.

It was Corrado's mother.

"Oh, my God!" Bianca said. She'd only met her a few times ten years ago. She raced for her clothes.

Once she'd covered herself, she turned to find Corrado walking out the door to join her in the hallway.

"This is a surprise," he said.

"I am beyond mortified. Oh, my God. I'm leaving." Her shoes in her hand, she frantically pressed the down button on the elevator.

He came up behind her and tugged her to him. "Where do you think you're going?"

"Off to find a hole to hide in." She pressed the down button again, and then again and again, mashing the damn thing.

He started laughing. "I'm sorry I wasn't the one to answer the door."

"I bet. Your poor *madre*."

He took her arm and turned her toward him. "What if she hadn't been here? What was your plan?"

She had to work hard to lift her eyes to him. This required a full admission. "What do you think the plan was, you dummy? To show you that I'm done running. That I want to try again if you'll give me one more chance. I was scared and you seem to like me just the way

I am. But now your mom has seen me naked, and that might change everything."

He laughed again.

"Also, I'm sorry about the other night. How things have gone since then. I guess that's what this was going to be. A naked apology is the best kind when you've messed up royally. I'm sorry."

"As you are not naked now, I cannot accept your apology."

She looked at the door. Thank God his mom had left them to it. "Okay, how about another time when your mom's not here?"

"I'll tell her to leave. Be right back."

She grabbed his arm. "Can I ask one thing? Did you turn me away because of my father talking to you?"

"I bet you can answer that."

"I can't, that's why I'm asking."

He took both her hands. "No, Queen Bee. I turned you away because I was waiting for you to show up naked and commit."

"Here I am, then."

He stepped forward and kissed her, then whispered into her ear, "I turned you away because I didn't believe you. Now I do. So let me go tell my mother that she and I will have to catch up another time."

"Wait, I can't see her again. Not now."

"Then go take a walk, come back in ten, and let's try this again. The whole show. And this time, I'll forgive you."

She kissed him. "Deal. See you in ten."

Seven days later

Moira rode in the taxi with Harold to the airport. She climbed out to say goodbye, and as they hugged, he said, "I'm going to come back and find you, okay? Soon as I get out of debt and figure out what I'm doing. Soon as I have a degree."

He let go of her and thought they might kiss, but they didn't. Cars rolled in behind them; travelers raced out with their bags.

"I did want to say something, though," she said. "It's strange to live in a world where no one knows your real name. I want you to know it. Just you, okay?"

"You sure? I won't be able to not ChatGPT you."

"I don't care. I want someone to know the real me."

He mulled that over.

"My real name's—"

He put a finger to her lips. "No, don't. I know the real you. Your name has nothing to do with it. How about you tell me next time we see each other? I know you can't come to Denver, but I'll be back."

"You promise?"

"Yeah, I promise."

She surprised both of them by kissing him.

"But we also promised we wouldn't kiss each other," he said. They'd hung out the day after the dinner debacle at Corrado's restaurant. And the day after that. And all the days since. But the one rule they'd made was that they couldn't let a romance grow between them. No kissing. Because saying goodbye would hurt so much worse.

Moira kissed him again. "Yeah, some promises are worth keeping. Others are just dumb."

Three months later

George walked out into his backyard in Scottsdale. He couldn't have imagined it, but he felt emotional saying goodbye to Mr. Nutz.

He filled his old bird feeder for the last time, saying, "I know you're watching me. Come on out, you tree rat."

When the feeder was full, he poured the rest of the seeds onto the rocks. A whole bag. "There you go. Have at it. I've got no fight left. This is my surrender."

No sign of Mr. Nutz.

With a strange longing in his heart, he backed away and started to go. One day he might return with his squirrel feeder invention, but he'd put it on the back burner due to some major incoming life changes.

When he opened the door, he glanced back one more time. Mr. Nutz had shown his smug face and was now creeping toward the pile of feed.

"There you are." George watched him eat for a while, then raised a hand. "*Ciao*, Mr. Nutz. I'll say hi to your cousin in Bologna."

Fourteen months later

With the help of her friends, Sandy had fallen back in love with The Only English Bookstore in Bologna. And thanks to Moira and her relentless pursuit of dominating the bookstore world, they were having their best year yet. The store had been featured in some of the latest travel blogs and had recently garnered all sorts of press for the event today, the European launch party for Bianca's new release.

Book events were still kind of the worst, but it felt good to have a line around the block, and Sandy was proud of Bianca, who'd penned a new effort certainly worthy of celebration. Bianca stood next to the devastatingly handsome Corrado under the cathedral ceiling, both of them smiling brightly as they chatted with a group of Megawatters, or whatever it was her groupies were called now.

The couple had a lot to be happy about. As of a week ago, Corrado was the newest chef in Italy to have earned a Michelin star. And *The*

Megawatt Detox: Recipes for a Slow Life had just hit the *New York Times* bestseller list. The publisher had rushed the release because Bianca's uninhibited rants on Substack and Instagram had turned her into a superstar. What a life they were stepping into.

From her position behind the cash register, Sandy watched George working the crowd, pushing his daughter's book like his life depended on it. Okay, Moira didn't deserve all the credit for their upward sales trend. George was no doubt one of the best booksellers to have ever lived. Maybe it was the green apron. Ever since taking the job, he'd started wearing one, for no other reason than he thought booksellers should don green aprons.

Even watching him work made her happy, and she felt so grateful that it had all worked out.

Once he'd shocked everyone by moving here in the spring, securing an apartment right around the corner, he'd started niggling Sandy about a job. She'd refused to hire him a hundred times but had eventually caved and even let him open up an "American items" section. The Doritos and Cheez-Its may or may not have had a little something to do with the uptick in sales. Sandy would never admit it, though. Nope, not ever.

Sandy would, however, admit that having George around was wonderful. No man had ever lifted her up so. Along with spending hundreds of hours on the phone with him, Sandy had visited him twice in Arizona while he'd been packing up, selling the house, and working on a visa, and now that he was here, they were officially a couple.

She looked at her green-aproned boyfriend. What a strange word, *boyfriend*. They were too old for such a word. How about *lover, partner, significant other*? He was also the inventor of a squirrel feeder, the designs of which he was now shopping to manufacturers. Who knew if there was a company out there crazy enough to bite? And who knows, maybe she'd be crazy enough to give marriage another go if he ever asked her. He spent most nights at her place anyway, and she adored waking up to him.

George must have sensed her watching him. He pressed Bianca's book into a potential customer's hand, then beelined it through the swarm of Megawatters for Sandy.

Winding around the counter, he said, "I think we might have to cut people off. Fire code issues."

Sandy's jaw dropped so low not even George R. R. Martin could have filled her mouth with words. "You know how long I've wanted this many people in my store? You can cut my arm off before you cut off that line."

Sandy looked across the room at the two new sets of shelves they'd built. "If the romance section wasn't so damned big," she said, "we'd have more standing room for these perusers. This is what I get for letting you and Moira run the show."

He cracked a charming grin. Drawing closer to her, he whispered, "Dammit, I love you, woman."

She let him kiss her, then said, "I'll believe it when you can say it to me in Italian. Or . . . if you ever get the guts to pull on one of those American-flag mankinis you insisted on me bringing in here."

They both looked toward George's "American items" shelf tucked into a corner near the stairs to her office. There were Pop-Tarts, Cheez-Its, Oreo cookies, marshmallows, jars of maple syrup, and Jif peanut butter. And on a rack at the end hung several pairs of American-flag Speedos.

Okay, she'd admit it. His efforts had drummed up some new customers. Whatever it took to keep the lights on.

George straightened his apron. "Did I ever mention my idea of turning the back room into a laundromat? They *still* don't have dryers in this city. You can shop for books while you dry your clothes."

"Oh, dear Lord, here we go," Sandy said.

"And while I have you, I'm still on the lookout for a slushy machine."

"A slushy machine?" It's a good thing Sandy wasn't in the middle of drinking Lambrusco, because she would have spit it all over him.

Out of nowhere came Moira in her own green apron. "Did I hear *slushy machine*?"

"Oh, yeah," George said enthusiastically, winking at Sandy. Boy, did he have her number. "Sandy was hoping we could get a cherry blue-raspberry flavor."

Moira's eyes grew to the size of watermelons. She'd been extra giddy lately because Harold was coming for a visit during his new school's fall break. "Perfect," she said. "And oh, how pretty the bright slushy colors would be. Right at the entrance." Then she leaped into an American accent that Sandy had never heard before, a not-so-bad Scarlett O'Hara. "You know what I think would bring them in droves? Good ole American apple pie. Fresh baked, flaky crust, smell of cinnamon filling the store. I bet Sandy makes a mean apple pie, coming from the South."

George offered a wretched yet adorable accent that evoked Atticus Finch. "I bet she does, Moira. It'll be the only American apple pie in Bologna."

Moira let out a cackle that likely shattered every window on Via Giulia. Cracking up herself, Sandy playfully began to massage her temples. The two of them loved razzing her. And you know what, Sandy deserved every bit of it.

Wiping away happy tears, she held out her arms. "Come here, you two buffoons. Give me a big hug."

Lo and behold, the last of her icy walls did melt as Sandy squeezed tight two people who'd showed her that life wasn't over yet; it would keep rolling out in front of her in true choose-your-own-adventure fashion. Well, she was tired of crawling the cracked sidewalk to Lonelytown. It was far better to be surrounded by those you loved—and books, of course, *heaps* of books—as you strolled the Yellow Brick Road toward the great unknown.

Acknowledgments

In June 2025, from an Airbnb in Estepona, Spain, I called my agent, Danielle Marshall, in a pure state of panic. "This book is kicking my arse! I've hit the midpoint and have no clue if it's working. Some of the characters don't even have external goals. Many of the scenes I'm writing make me belly laugh, but I don't know if anyone else on earth will find them funny. It might be too absurd! And the ending, it's straying massively from what I'd planned. These characters are monsters, taking over my story, holding back information from the reader, doing whatever they please."

Calm as she could be, Danielle said, "Send it over. Give me a day to read it."

Now that's an agent who believes in you. To drop everything. Boy, did she come back with some good thoughts. Among a list of wonderful ideas, she pointed out Bianca's excessive interiority, to which I immediately deleted eight thousand words. She suggested that I start the book with Sandy, that I needed to establish the bookstore as the anchor of the novel. And she gave some wonderful encouragement, which I desperately needed.

I remember hanging up and feeling like I was walking out of a halftime pep talk with Vince Lombardi. It was go-time, victory in sight. Thanks, Danielle, for never letting me doubt myself, even when maybe I should. Let's go do big things together.

This book got me, folks. At times, it wrote itself; others, I wasn't sure I'd make it through. But every moment, I had lovely people around lifting me up, giving me green lights, and guiding me.

Once I found my way to the end, I had the great fortune of having Jodi Warshaw, the editor with the mostest, waiting for me in the wings. Let me tell you something. Authors don't take books to the next level without a wonderful developmental editor. When you have one who sees eye-to-eye with you, you're plain lucky. Like last time Jodi and I worked together, I agreed with 99.9999 percent of her suggestions. And when we get on the phone for a discussion, it's magic. We live on different coasts, but I know exactly what she's saying before she's halfway through saying it. We basically finish each other's sentences. It was extra special to learn *after* I'd turned the book in to her that she'd coincidentally visited Bologna earlier in the year. Now that's meant to be!

I'm so grateful to Nancy Holmes at Lake Union Publishing, who took me over as an author and has given me nothing but support since day one. I'd sold to Lake Union a different story idea two years prior, but I wasn't feeling it anymore, so I suggested another idea instead. "I love it, Boo. Go, go, go!" That's blind faith right there, amigos.

Thank you to the whole Lake Union team. You're world class and I'm nowhere without you. What's this? Our eighth book together? Last I checked, we just hit 1.4 million books. What a ride we're having!

Linda and Nico, a.k.a. Lindsey Records and Nicolas Hummer of San Rafael, California, what is there to say? That we were always destined to crash into one another? That we certainly knew each other in past lives? I can't think of Europe without you guys popping into my mind. What a time we had running around Valencia as expats. I hope some of this story takes you back to those glorious memories, all starting with our first meal together: Nico trying to find parking while we drank wine and bombarded him with texts saying: Hello? Here we are approaching a decade later, still saying, "Hello?" You teach me how to be a great friend, and we're so lucky to have you in our lives.

As always, I give a nod to my favorite writing group, the Tiki Bar Pals, who regularly linger on WhatsApp to distract me from hitting my word count. The Honorable James Blatch, the only Brit in the crew, you're in Cypress right now, likely cycling the island before enjoying a tasty beer overlooking the sea. You're one of the coolest cats I know. Cecelia Mecca, I'm not sure I've ever met someone with a more rabid thirst for life. You're such a badass. Lucy Score, don't change a thing. You're simply the best, that big heart of yours, your constant pursuit of bettering yourself.

And Nathan, dear Nathan Van Coops, the airplane maestro, time traveler, and brilliant novelist. You get your own paragraph because I don't thank you enough for what you do for me and my work. I'd be lost without you. You understand the mechanics of story like few others, and you're never too busy to pick up the phone while you're taking apart an airplane to diagnose the issues with my work-in-progress. Thank you, brother! You're one of a kind.

You know who deserves far more than they ever get? My beta readers. One billion carats of diamonds and a thousand hugs to y'all for selflessly dedicating so much time to my stories. Along with catching the bajillion mistakes that sneak from my fingers *and* pointing out ways to elevate the story, you help me understand what's working and what's not. It's gold to have a team that can do that. Forgive me if I miss someone, but I want to name each of you. Thank you, Stefanie, Lauren, Michele, Ruth, Candace, Tanya, Christine, Bill, Beth, Michele, Julie, Shari, Lynn, Donna, Kathleen, Kim, Catherine, Marcia, Kristie, Jan, Marta, Alicia, Gina, and Pat.

Lauren Cormier, my secret weapon, my beta reader, my friend. I'm so honored to have you in my life. As you know, you're often my first line of defense, the brave soul who reads before anyone else. I value your opinions so much and cherish our relationship. Much love to you!!!

Sara Lane, my walking guide through Bologna, I hope you enjoyed the final product. Thank you for two absolutely wonderful days showing me your magical city, one bite and glass at a time.

A truckload of gold bars to my parents and brother, who continue to put up with me and care for me no matter what. Your love for Mikella, Riggs, and me is a warm blanket on our souls. We feel it all the way from North Carolina.

Patty and Bert, the greatest in-laws to ever have in-lawed, thank you for being in our lives, for giving up yours in Florida to be here in Maine, for always offering a loving ear and a hug. I'll joyfully help you with your printer problems any day. Also, who else could I keep inviting to take us to dinner!?

Jack and Gerri, our dear friends on Peaks Island, you mean so much to us. Thank you for showing us how to love, how to serve, how to be good friends. I'm not sure there's anyone on Peaks Island who you haven't supplied with one of my books. Who does that? Only the best. I haven't come across many people like you two in all my life, and it's a shame, because I wish the whole world were filled with your kind.

Ruth Chiles, my guru, you're always there, always in my ear and heart, guiding me. What a most memorable meal in Málaga. It's one of the great honors of my life to know you. Thanks for everything.

To all my friends and family, thank you for continuing to let me steal stuff from your lives and for reading my books and spreading the word, ever cheering me on. I'm a lucky guy. Seriously.

To my son, Riggs. Keep chasing your dreams. That's what I want you to take with you when you walk out the door every day. Your heart and soul are almost too big for this world, and I know you'll one day light it on fire. In a good way, of course. Mostly, don't grow up too fast. Keep snuggling with me and holding my hand and letting me tuck you in at night, because I can't bear the end of that.

Mikella Walker, you are the muse of all muses. The Queen Muse. An international treasure if there ever was one. Sorry you had to end up with a runt like me, but I'm going to keep trying every day to live up to the man you make me believe I am. Your presence and love give me hope even on the darkest of days.

Lastly, there's a big chunk of you out there who make this whole thing possible. You, the readers. You, the booksellers. You, the bloggers and journalists. You allow me the great pleasure of playing make-believe for a living. How could I not wake every morning with gratitude in my heart? Thank you for understanding me, reading my stories, and spreading the word. If it weren't for you right now, I'd likely be on my initial trajectory of becoming an astronaut. Wait, no, that's not true. I'm terrible at math and science, have a wretched fear of heights, and can't stand dehydrated space food. Honestly, I don't know what I'd do if you guys weren't out there supporting me, so thank you, thank you, *thank you*!

Book Club Questions

1. Were you able to find empathy or sympathy with Sandy from the outset?
2. When did you suspect or realize Sandy's truth?
3. Do you know anyone like George who took a nosedive after retirement? How did they come out of it? Discuss the need for purpose in life. Can it be found both internally and externally?
4. Harold doesn't believe in himself and thinks the only way to gain anything positive in his life is to become someone else. Have you ever pretended to be someone you're not? Why?
5. Have you ever loved someone for the wrong reasons?
6. Bianca put a placeholder in her life, deciding she wasn't ready to truly live until she'd reached a better version of herself. Can you relate?
7. Who was your favorite character? Did that change as each of them grew? Discuss.
8. Boo's novel *Red Mountain* also weaves together the lives of four characters living within close proximity. How would you compare the two books?
9. Have you traveled or lived abroad? Share your favorite memories. What were the biggest challenges?
10. When Boo travels, he reads a book set in that locale. Have you ever done the same? Do you enjoy reading novels set in faraway places? What's your favorite?

About the Author

Photo © 2018 Brandi Morris

Boo Walker is the bestselling author of *Before We Say Goodbye*, *The Secrets of Good People*, *An Echo in Time*, *The Stars Don't Lie*, *A Spanish Sunrise*, *The Singing Trees*, *An Unfinished Story*, and the Red Mountain Chronicles, among other novels. Boo tapped his creative muse as a songwriter and banjoist in Nashville before working his way west to Washington state, where he bought a gentleman's farm on the Yakima River. It was there, among the grapevines and wine barrels, that he fell in love with telling high-impact stories that now resonate with book clubs around the world. Rich with colorful characters and boundless soul, his novels will leave you with an open heart and a lifted spirit. Always a wanderer, Boo currently lives in Cape Elizabeth, Maine, with his wife and son. He also writes thrillers under the pen name Benjamin Blackmore. For more information, visit www.boowalker.com.